LOVE COOLS

ALSO BY W. EDWARD BLAIN

Passion Play

LOVE COOLS

W. Edward Blain

G. P. PUTNAM'S SONS   NEW YORK

G. P. Putnam's Sons
Publishers Since 1838
200 Madison Avenue
New York, NY 10016

Library of Congress Cataloging-in-Publication Data

Blain, W. Edward.
Love cools / W. Edward Blain.—1st American ed.

p. cm.
ISBN 0-399-13779-3
I. Title.
PS3552.L3448L68   1992   92-15704 CIP
813′.54—dc20

Printed in the United States of America
1 2 3 4 5 6 7 8 9 10

This book is printed on acid-free paper.

ACKNOWLEDGMENTS

For information about fires and burn victims I am indebted to Scott Haas of the Orange County (Va.) Sheriff's Office; for a glimpse at the world of banking and of fraud schemes, I thank my sister, Virginia Kuertz, and my friend Eric Chafin, both of whom are impeccably honest but are aware of ways people cheat; for a chance to sit in on rehearsals of the Four County Players in Barboursville, Virginia, I thank Brent Cirves and Sara Smith; for their editorial suggestions, I thank my manuscript readers, Nat Jobe and Johanna Smethurst; for information about Virginia law, I thank my brother, Stuart; and to the numerous friends at the Mill Mountain Theatre in Roanoke, who allowed me to tour the backstage facilities and watch a rehearsal, I offer my gratitude and and my congratulations for their consistently fine work. Particularly I must cite Ernest Zulia and Tom Mason for their interest in my writing and their bestowing of numerous favors. Kay and Dusty Maynard kindly provided a quiet house at Myrtle Beach, where much of this writing occurred. Frann Hockman surrendered her computer printer and her typewriter when I needed to move the words from the disk to the page. I could never have finished this project without the encouragement of my family and friends in Roanoke and at Woodberry Forest School, the two places I call home. And to Nancy and Stacy, for your patience and your advice and your encouragement, I am mightily beholden.

W. E. B.

FOR NIGEL TRANTER

*Love cools, friendship falls off, brothers divide.
In cities, mutinies; in countries, discord; in palaces, treason;
and the bond cracked 'twixt son and father.*

—the Earl of Gloucester, *King Lear*

PART I

Hamlet

IN late May, six weeks after Sarah Davidson died in the fire but a month before the other deaths, Richard Blackburn was dismissed from school. On the Sunday of his departure Richard sat on the bench outside the headmaster's office and felt nothing—no remorse, no anger, no shame, no glee, no pride. He was empty of every emotion but the urge to get even. He leaned back on the gloomy bench and watched late spring try to invade the shady administration building of the Montpelier School for Boys. Through the open door across from his seat, sunlight glowed on the Oriental rug of the empty Faculty Reading Room. He could glimpse blue sky through the shiny green leaves of the dogwood outside the window. But it was cool and dark in the hall where he sat. He'd never been in this part of the building on Sunday morning before. Tomorrow the ambience would change when secretaries in floral dresses clicked past in their heels on the checkered tile floor, but today he had the place to himself—except for the occasional faculty member, wearing seersucker or poplin, no more winter tweeds even among the older men by now, who would enter or depart the office through the closed door to his left. Sometimes they'd speak to him. More often they'd give him one of those polite, bracing little serve-them-all-my-days smiles, the kind of look intended to say *buck up, old chap,* or *it's always darkest before the dawn* or *this too will pass,* as if he were some British schoolboy at the turn of the last century instead of an American soon-to-be-ex-schoolboy in the 1990s. The old farts on the faculty had seen so many damn miniseries on PBS that they'd actually started to act them out, wearing bow ties and shit and inviting students over for weekly teas. Having seen *Dead Poets Society* about thirty million times, the young dicks on the faculty now tried to be like the film's Robin Williams character, this cool teacher who really understood his students and wanted to liberate them and be their pal. Right.

It was 10:15 on Sunday morning. May 21. Exams started next week, but not for Richard, not unless his father had managed through some bribe to buy him another chance. There was nobody in the office now except Lane himself. What the hell was taking so long? Richard was out. It was automatic. If they didn't kick him out, then he'd buy some fucking gasoline and burn down the Homestead and the gym and Stringfellow Hall itself. He didn't want to be here anymore. If they weren't going to believe him, he didn't want to be at the school.

Ralph Musgrove, who looked like Lurch the Butler posing as a high school sophomore dressed for chapel, came around the corner from the lobby, saw Richard, and stopped.

"Hello," said Richard, in a voice that was too loud and too cheerful.

Ralph turned around and left without saying anything. That was the way it was with the students nowadays; they acted as though Richard were either invisible or contagious. If they didn't look straight through him, they ducked.

Then Ralph surprised him by coming back. "I'm going to my uncle's for the day," said Ralph. "After chapel. I'll be gone till supper."

"Fine," said Richard. "I'll be gone for good." He avoided Ralph's gaze.

"Maybe I'll see you around someday," said Ralph.

That was typical of Ralph. Richard found himself wanting to smile and be friendly. He resisted the urge.

"Yeah," said Richard. He wouldn't meet Ralph's eye. He knew this was the place where they were supposed to shake hands, but he wouldn't do it. Eventually Ralph walked back around the corner and disappeared. For the next few minutes it was quiet in the hall. Then, with a shudder and a bang like a rifle shot, the door to the headmaster's office opened. At last, Dr. Lane himself, the old gray pompadour, the old gray suit, the old gray mare, stood with his hand on the knob and told Richard to come in.

It was not the first time Richard had been in this office. But it was the first time he'd been in to be dismissed. He took the chair he always took, the brown leather one, the chair closest to Lane's gleaming wooden desk. The shiny brass lamp looked as though it had just been polished. So did the surface of the wooden desk. Richard leaned forward and planted his fingertips on the smooth wood. His prints weren't even visible when he pulled his hand away. That irked him. Then he reminded himself that it was just another confirmation of his status as a loser. He was a nothing, a zero, a ghost. In just a few minutes they would get rid of him, and then everybody here could forget that he'd ever existed.

Eldridge Lane, the headmaster, sat on the other side of the desk and kept his arms rigidly on the green blotter in front of him.

"Richard," he said, "this has been a difficult year for all of us."

Come on, get it over with, Richard thought. There was no way they were going to come up with another probation for him. He'd had enough last chances already.

"We've lost several students," said Lane. "Departures are always a sad time for us, but particularly this year, when the circumstances were so unpleasant."

Richard had planned not to say anything if he could help it, but he had to chuckle over that one. "Unpleasant." Son of a bitch could really lay on the understatement. "Yeah," said Richard. "This year has sucked." He worried that Lane might be having second thoughts about booting him because the enrollment was down. That would be a hell of an irony: The greatest punishment they give you is to make you stay in the school. He hated it here and wanted to leave, but he also hated the fact that he was leaving under duress. He'd always wanted his departure to be in the grand manner of the stage. In typical Blackburn fashion. Richard was the King of the Pranksters, but the King was about to be deposed.

"I'd hoped," said Lane, "that now, with just a couple of days left before the year was over, we could avoid any more departures. But it seems to me that you do not want to remain here."

Good boy, thought Richard.

"A cheating incident is always very disturbing to me, Richard," said Lane.

The bastard was going to run through his whole spiel.

"I'm furthermore disturbed by your failure to admit your error," said Lane.

"There was no error," said Richard.

Lane let that one rest on the desktop for a moment before he brushed it aside. "So you say," he said. He never took his eyes off Richard. "Richard, it would be much, much worse for you to leave this school under the cloud of a lie than for any of these other infractions."

"I'm not lying," said Richard. He'd said it enough times now that it had lost all punch.

"All right," said Lane.

"I'm telling the truth," said Richard.

"That's very difficult for me to accept," said Lane. "It has also been difficult for the students on the honor council to accept. They have voted to find you guilty of plagiarism."

"I didn't do it," said Richard. "But I'll go. I'll do anything to get out of here. You are kicking me out, aren't you?"

You had to admire the way Lane kept his temper. It was hard to rattle the old prick.

"Richard," he said, "I am officially informing you that your name has been withdrawn from the rolls of the school."

Thank you thank you thank you.

Lane tried to soften the impact. "It's one of the most extraordinary cases I've ever encountered, I must say."

"You should be getting rid of Davidson, not me," said Richard.

Lane gave no reaction to Richard's suggestion. "I want you to know," said Lane, "that we will retain our interest in your welfare. All of us at the school wish you well, Richard. This kind of event is unfortunate, but it often allows a boy to start over in a new environment and to enjoy a kind of success that he'd never experienced before. I've been on the telephone with your father in Rockbridge, and I have recommended that you enroll in a good day school. For some boys, boarding school is just not a good match." He went on talking about how concerned he was about Richard's attitude, yackety yackety yak, blah blah blah. Richard didn't need to listen anymore. He had his freedom. Then he tuned back in when Lane brought up transportation.

"We need to get you off the campus. Are you packed?"

"When's my dad coming?" Richard asked.

"He's not," said Lane. "Your brother is coming. He left Rockbridge an hour ago. He should be here in ninety minutes or so."

"Dad couldn't make it," said Richard. "What a surprise."

"He said he had an unavoidable conflict."

"He's big on work," said Richard. "Of course, so's Tucker. They must have fought over who had to come."

Lane said he'd never met Richard's brother.

"He couldn't get in here," said Richard. "He wasn't a big enough asshole.'' It wasn't fair to Tucker, but it felt so great to be able to talk this way in front of Lane and know that the guy couldn't do anything about it. Getting kicked out was not all bad.

"Your brother is a student at the university?"

"Yeah," said Richard. "He takes a few courses. But mostly he just fucks around."

He still couldn't get Lane to flinch. "They finished the session at Virginia two weeks ago, didn't they?"

"Tucker gets extensions," said Richard. "He's in a special program. Everything about Tucker is very special. Special, special guy.'' He knew he should shut up.

"Richard," said Lane, "you need to pack."

"I packed last night."

"Then perhaps there are some people here to whom you'd like to say good-bye," said Lane.

"No."

"You've already spoken to your friends?"

"I haven't got any friends," said Richard. He could tell that statement bothered Lane more than anything else he'd said so far.

"Maybe you'd want to speak to your adviser."

"No."

"Or write a note to Mr. Davidson? He's had a bad time since his wife's death.''

"No."

"Mr. Davidson will be living in Rockbridge, Richard. You're likely to see him again."

"I hope so," said Richard.

"Mr. Davidson is not angry, Richard," said Lane. "He understands that you're upset.''

"Nobody understands shit about me," said Richard. "Can we at least get that one thing straight, Dr. Lane?"

They didn't talk much longer. In the end, Lane tried to shake hands with him. Richard stood with his hands at his sides. They stepped into the hall.

"Get something to read," said Lane. "It's nearly time for chapel. You may wait on the front porch until your brother gets here."

"You don't trust me, Dr. Lane?"

"It's standard policy, Richard."

"Well, I'm not exactly your standard kind of guy, am I?" said Richard.

Eldridge Lane looked at Richard as though he'd known him forever. "You're not nearly as bad as you think," he said. He put a hand on Richard's shoulder, and for the first time all morning, Richard lost his temper. He shook Lane's hand away and stepped back.

"Don't touch me," said Richard. "I think there's something weird about older men who want to touch me."

Lane still wouldn't be rattled. "I wish you the best of luck," he said. Lane stepped back into his office, and Richard was alone again in the hall. He wanted to break something. He wanted to hurt himself. He walked down the hall to the men's room and went inside, then ran cold water over his hands until they stopped shaking. He glanced at himself in the mirror, flicked water all over the image. He looked like such a geek, the round glasses, the stringy hair, the skinny neck. He splashed more water onto the mirror and then smeared it over his reflection. But when he stopped, there he was again, blurred and dripping, so he squirted out a handful of liquid soap and spread it over the glass until he could see nothing. And then he washed his hands until they were sore.

❈

At 11:30 on Sunday morning Ellen Spencer, at last able to spend some time with her husband and their four-year-old son, was watching a videotape of yesterday's NBA playoff game when the phone rang. She hoped it was a wrong number. But it wasn't.

"Some guy from Charlottesville," said Matthew, her husband. He handed her the cellular phone.

"I'll take it in the kitchen," she said. "Stop the tape, would you? I don't want to miss anything."

Sunday was supposed to be her day off. She was tempted just to let the telephone sit on the table until Monday, let the Charlottesville cops pay the toll. Here in Rockbridge, in the Shenandoah Valley, she was two hours away by car, but with this damn telephone in her house she might as well live at Monticello. She sat in one of the wicker chairs and held the phone to her ear. She was thirty-two years old and had been a detective with the Rockbridge City Police Force for six years.

Two stray hairs fell across her face, one red and one gray. She brushed
them both back.

"Okay," she said.

"It's Casey," said the man on the line. "Casey O'Shea. Remember
me?"

"The man with the fire," she said. "It's been a while."

"A month," he said. "Remember Oscar Davidson?"

"Barely," she said. "His wife is the one who died." These guys
from Charlottesville must not have much to do. She'd been up until
three in the morning with a shooting in Rosalind and didn't feel like
being civil. Especially since she remembered the case so well. A month
and a half ago. Big house in Charlottesville, Victorian style. Huge fire,
with a fatality in the upstairs bedroom. A dead lady college professor.
They'd been sniffing for arson. "Did you find something?"

"Yes," he said. "We got the lab work in Friday. Six weeks. An all-
time speed record. No liquid accelerants, no booby traps, no timers."
She waited impatiently for him to get to the point. "But there were
tool marks, like maybe from a wrench, on the coupling from the gas
line into the stove of the basement apartment. An indication that the
coupling was loosened."

"So it wasn't an accident." The fire had started when an electric
space heater in the basement had ignited a poster and some papers
nearby. But the house had been destroyed through the help of a leaky
coupling in the gas line.

"That's the tricky part. You can't tell when tool marks were made.
The gas company had been in the week before to check on a supposed
leak. So the marks might have come from that."

"Any oxidation?"

"None. But the basement's dry. We can't date the marks for
certain."

"What did the autopsy show? Any CO_2 in the blood?"

"Yes."

"So she was alive when the fire started," said Ellen. "Any signs of
blunt trauma?"

Casey O'Shea said the victim had a fractured skull.

"That's not unusual in a fire death," said Ellen. "Any hematoma?"
If the victim had been struck before death, there would be bruising
under the skull.

"Yes," said O'Shea. For a moment Ellen thought they had a lead, but then his next words changed her mind. "The problem is that a brick wall collapsed on the victim during the fire. We just can't tell if she was struck by anything other than a brick."

"Any snitches?"

"Nobody's heard anything on the street."

"So what the hell are you calling me for?" she said. "You've got nothing."

"I wanted you to know that Oscar Davidson has just notified us that he'll be moving to Rockbridge for the summer." He paused. "You know, the husband."

She could feel her impatience increase. "He just notified you? This morning?"

"Actually, it was last week."

"And let me guess," said Ellen. "You weren't working, but you're on today, so you thought you'd call me while you were logging time anyway. Right?"

Casey O'Shea pleaded guilty. "But it's a legitimate call. Oscar Davidson is moving to Rockbridge."

"So?"

"So maybe he'll elope with his sister-in-law," said O'Shea. "Or rob a library. Just listen for his name to come up. His wife was killed, if not by him, then by somebody he hired. I just don't know why."

"You said that to me last month," said Ellen. "Word for word. I wasted a lot of time because you were so positive." She'd been asked to check on Oscar Davidson in Rockbridge. He and his wife kept an apartment here and came down during the summers to teach at the Arts School, where Sarah Davidson's sister was principal. The Rockbridge investigators, like those in Charlottesville, had wondered about the fire—an electrical space heater in April? While the husband was conveniently gone?—but there had been absolutely no discernible motive for Oscar Davidson to kill his wife. He was the one with all the money. The late Sarah had earned a decent living from her chair at the university and her other writing, but Oscar's annual interest income alone was seven times her entire total earnings. He was not tied to his wife with any unfavorable prenuptial agreement. He was not having any apparent affairs, his relationship with his sister-in-law being, from all accounts, strictly platonic. He'd published a book himself, so there was no reason to suspect professional jealousy. And there had been an earlier complaint about leaking gas from the tenant downstairs. The fire was apparently a fluke. "Let me ask you something, O'Shea," she said. "How long have you been an arson investigator? Two months?"

"Three now."

She should have read him off in April. "So in other words," said Ellen, "you're on a witch hunt. Time to mark this one inactive or closed. Stay around long enough, you learn you won't always get an answer to every question."

He wouldn't quit. "Will you at least look at the files if I send you copies?"

"For what?"

"These people are relocating," said O'Shea. Even his voice sounded green. "That graduate student who lived in the Davidsons' basement? Chris Nivens? He's in Rockbridge for the summer too. He's working at the Arts School with Oscar Davidson. He was hired by Anne Lindsey, the dead woman's sister."

So what was she supposed to do with that? Rush out and arrest them all? "Isn't that understandable?" she said. "The kid's home got destroyed. Davidson and the sister want to give him a break. There's nothing here. I looked last month, remember?"

"It seems awfully cozy, though. All three of them there together."

"Send me the files," she said. "And don't call me back." She pushed the button to hang up the phone as hard as she could and returned to the television room. Blue plastic blocks lay scattered across the plaid rug. Matthew and their son, Paul, were spreading newspaper across the sides of the coffee table to make a fort.

"I'm glad I've already read that newspaper," said Ellen.

Matthew reacted to her tone. "Hey," he said. "It's yesterday's." She sat down beside him and tried to concentrate on the television set. He reached over and rubbed her neck. "What did that guy want?" he said.

"Nothing," she said. "Absolutely nothing. Nothing at all." She kept her composure. But they both knew why she was so annoyed. Today was her day off, and the phone call had given her something to think about. Despite her advice to Casey O'Shea a few minutes earlier about not expecting an answer to every question, she didn't like to leave puzzles unsolved herself. What made this one so difficult was that she first had to figure out what was puzzling about it.

Chapel began and ended while Richard sat in elevated isolation on the front steps of Stringfellow Hall. At noon, after the service, students came and went without speaking to him. Even before this business with the honor council, he had lost most of his friends—everybody but Ralph Musgrove, his roommate, who was as loyal as a dog. The King of the Pranksters was in exile. He'd come back from spring break in March angry and bitter. His parents had made him go on a special program with Outward Bound, and he had hated it, had despised his father for making him go, had despised himself for his reaction to it. He hated outdoorsy activities and camping and hiking and that personal esteem crap. You were supposed to get to know yourself with Outward Bound, and Richard's problem was that he had.

Tucker did not arrive until almost 12:30. Richard saw the white Corolla pull onto the campus drive in the distance and waited to hear the rattles. What a piece of shit. It was garbage when Tucker bought it two years ago, and he'd managed to keep it garbage ever since. Tucker had no respect for machinery at all. Twenty years old, and he couldn't even keep up with changing the oil. He washed the car maybe never, except after that one time Richard was mad at him and poured honey all over the windshield so that ants would gather. It was weird, such a blind spot in a guy so eager to please everybody. They'd had to buy a new lawn mower just last summer because Tucker never bothered with basic maintenance like lubrication and cleaning the blades. It was the lawn mower that had finally caught up with Tucker. It was the lawn mower that had brought about his accident.

Tucker parked under an oak tree thirty feet from where Richard sat surrounded by his luggage. He got out of the car and hurriedly limped over to the stairs. Look ma, no crutches. He'd had the cast removed five days ago. Even from the distance of the porch, Richard could see the white scars like glycerine running down his leg. In this glare Richard could understand why Tucker wore sunglasses, and since the guy was a student at Virginia, he could accept the orange T-shirt in a school color. But why tennis shorts? The shorts made Richard angry, as though his brother wanted to advertise the scars that ran down his right leg and crisscrossed like plastic gladiator thongs. Richard fought the affection that struggled to surface as Tucker approached. Wouldn't it be nice if he and Tucker could be friends, like usual? But Richard no longer deserved to have a friend like Tucker. And Tucker seemed to recognize that today.

"Let's go," he said. Tucker had an actor's voice. "I'm killing my whole day."

"So what the hell were you so late for?" said Richard.

"I ran out of gas, Richard." So typical. His fuel tank gauge was broken. But neglecting his gasoline supply was the only thing typical about Tucker today. He stood below Richard on the asphalt and looked up at him ready to fight. Tucker was not usually the belligerent sort.

It was hot in the bright sunshine. Richard tossed down a laundry bag full of dirty clothes and then a suitcase that bounced on the asphalt but didn't break open. Tucker picked up the laundry bag. He hadn't combed his hair or shaved today. He carried the bag to the car and then returned for the suitcase, which he wrenched upward, grunting at its weight. Richard carried a tote bag with his notebooks and tapes and favorite CDs inside. He had his stereo in a couple of boxes that took them a while to squeeze into the car. He didn't care about his easy chair. It was still in the dorm with his bookshelves. Let it rot there.

They loaded everything into the trunk of the car except for the stereo boxes, which went into the backseat, and Richard's tote bag, which he put under his legs in the front so that his tapes would stay out of the heat. Judging by his car's interior, Tucker's life consisted of Big Macs, tennis balls, newspapers, and old mail. Richard reached into the car and tossed as much of the trash as he could find into the parking lot. He tried to spread it around. Even magazines, letters, everything he could throw. It was fun until Tucker yanked him back from the car.

"Put it all back," he said.

"They'll clean it up," said Richard.

"Put it back," said Tucker. He slugged Richard hard in the upper arm. It was real. He and Tucker had grown up on fake stage punches and kicks and slaps. They used to fool people who came to visit, Tucker slapping Richard in the face, Richard fake-kicking Tucker in the shin. But they'd grown into the real thing. Richard gave him a shove. Tucker's bad leg bumped up against the side of the car. For a minute Tucker breathed unsteadily with the pain. But he did not give Richard the satisfaction of a retaliation. Richard really hoped that his brother, who'd been such a superjock before the accident, would pound him into oblivion. But Tucker had decided to restrain himself. "Just get into the car, Richard. I'm sore from driving up here."

After Richard cleaned up the trash, he picked up a couple of pieces of gravel from the parking lot and threw them into the car with the rest of his belongings. Then, as though he'd won some victory, he got into the passenger seat and slammed the door.

Tucker still didn't start the engine. "Do you have anything besides this stuff, or . . . ?"

Richard knew he'd never get to the end of the sentence. It was part of his dyslexia, this inability to articulate words when he needed them. "Or what?" said Richard. "Or did I bring a piano? Or should we wait for a bus?"

It was one of the ways he could get at Tucker, showing him how quick he could be. But Tucker still would not hit him again. It was as though the one were his quota for the day.

"Hell, Richard," said Tucker.

"What? What's the matter? Am I supposed to thank you for coming? Because Dad was too busy?"

"Don't start in on Dad again."

"I didn't ask you to come," said Richard. But he was so glad that Tucker had. He wanted to say so. He fought the urge. He was a very good actor. "I suppose you're here to remind me of what a fine education I've thrown away."

"Shut up." Tucker started to drive before he said more. "I've never been the greatest student in the world," he said. "But I've never been a cheater."

So that was the way it was going to be. Fine. Part of Richard wanted to shout over the unfairness of it all. Another part said he deserved it.

"Let's get out of here," said Richard. "Drive home. You don't want to be late for your date with Moonie."

"You're behind in the news, Richard. As of yesterday, Moonie is dating somebody else."

Somebody who can read, Richard thought, but he didn't say it. That would have approached the unforgivable, and the unforgivable was a realm he did not wish to explore with his brother. At least he understood that Tucker's rage was not entirely directed at Richard's honor offense.

It was a beautiful day for a drive. Their home in Rockbridge was just under three hours to the southwest. Dogwoods bloomed along the campus driveway, and Richard could see several Montpelier boys playing softball on one of the lush green fields. Nobody waved to him as he left. Tucker drove in silence. Richard leaned his head back and let the warm air blow into his face. The King of the Pranksters had never known a lower point. But he would not surrender his throne without a fight. He would get his revenge. He was isolated from everybody he knew, and he wanted to get even somehow with all of them—with his father and mother, with Dr. Lane, with the honor council. And especially with Oscar Davidson, the teacher who had run him out of the school. There was no rush. He had the whole summer, he had the rest of his life if necessary, to find some way to work out his purposes. Before he died, he would make Oscar Davidson scream.

❄

Ellen and Matthew Spencer talked about the Davidson case as they ate hot pastrami sandwiches. The taped game still played on the television in front of them, but Ellen had lost her enthusiasm for watching. The phone call from Casey O'Shea had wrenched her attention back to work. Besides, she'd already seen the score in the morning paper.

"It's a big house in Charlottesville," said Ellen. "Four floors, if you count the basement and the attic. The wife is in her bedroom upstairs, the fire starts in the basement, the wife never gets out of the house. O'Shea is convinced that it was planned. He's sure that the husband killed her."

"So maybe it was planned, but not by the husband," said Matthew. He wore tennis shorts and the long-sleeved yellow dress shirt he'd had on in church this morning, minus the tie. He was thirty-four years old and nearly bald, and she loved him for never complaining about his hair loss. He checked the score of the game. "What about the guy living in their basement? The graduate student?"

"Chris Nivens," said Ellen. "O'Shea made a big deal about how they were all leaving Charlottesville and converging on us in Rockbridge. But it makes perfect sense for Nivens to work at the Arts School. Davidson and Anne Lindsey want to give him some support."

"Or keep an eye on him," said Matthew. She hadn't considered that. Matthew was good at asking the right questions. "Didn't the cops in Charlottesville talk to this graduate student? Chris Nivens. Where was he on the night of this fire?"

"Nivens was there earlier in the day," she said. "Davidson had his Montpelier students down for a cookout at five o'clock. Nivens was definitely around while that was going on. But he left to go to the university library and the gym."

"On Saturday night?"

"He's apparently very much into impressing the English department. There was some doubt as to whether or not he'd be allowed to stay on to work for his doctorate. So apparently the guy is studying or researching or writing all the time."

"So the tenant was gone before the fire started," said Matthew.

"Yes," she said. "But that afternoon he saw one of the kids in the basement and overheard a big fight between Sarah Davidson and Patricia Montgomery."

"The actress?" Now Matthew perked up. Paul tugged on their feet from his hiding place under the coffee table. "I was just reading about her in the paper." He began to look through the newspaper sections on the sofa beside him. Patricia Montgomery played Tru Lovinguth on *Adam's Garden* (weekdays on CBS at 1:30). "Didn't she just lose her job?"

"Right," said Ellen. She'd seen the article this morning, too, and hoped he'd find it. She began to consider a new possibility. "Her son was one of Davidson's students. She was there to pick him up for a dinner of their own before Davidson drove him back to Montpelier."

"So did the cops in Charlottesville talk to her?"

"They talked to everybody. Montgomery and her son were gone from the house by five-thirty and back at seven-forty-five. Davidson drove the van of kids to Montpelier at eight o'clock and didn't get back until just before ten o'clock."

"And the fire started—"

"Around nine P.M."

"So the husband couldn't have done it," said Matthew. "He was driving a group of students to a place how far—?"

"Forty-five, fifty minutes."

"—forty-five minutes away from Charlottesville. He couldn't have set any fires."

"Except," said Ellen, "he doesn't drive straight from the house to the school. He stops at the little yogurt shop down the street, and he says okay, boys, get out of the van and get yourselves some yogurt. I've got to go back to the house for the cupcakes I forgot to give you for dessert."

"Oh, crap," said Matthew. "That's too obvious."

"Plus," said Ellen, "all the students say it's completely uncharacteristic of Davidson to be so nice. He's usually a jerk. So he could have planned the whole excursion to give himself an alibi."

"Except that he doesn't have a motive," said Matthew. "He has everything to lose and nothing to gain."

Ellen Spencer said that she could not agree with him more. Casey O'Shea was pursuing a personal vendetta.

"Why the husband?" Matthew said. "You mentioned a fight between Sarah Davidson and Patricia Montgomery—"

"Which wasn't really a fight," said Ellen. "The actress was mad because Davidson had written her out of the soap opera."

"That's right," said Matthew. "I just read about that. Where the hell is that article?" In Rockbridge everyone had been surprised to learn after her death that Sarah Davidson was a contributing writer to *Adam's Garden*. Such credentials were much more impressive than her career as a Shakespeare scholar. "Here." He found the entertainment section and handed it to her. Ellen looked at the elegant picture of Patricia Montgomery in the newspaper. It was a publicity still from a few years ago, emphasizing all her intelligence as well as beauty. "There's a motive for you," said Matthew. "Writer destroys actress's career, actress seeks revenge. Why don't you arrest Patricia Montgomery?"

"Because it doesn't work," said Ellen. "Sarah Davidson was alive when Patricia Montgomery went back to the house to drop off her son."

"Of course she was alive," said Matthew. "She died in the fire."

"She died upstairs lying on her bed," said Ellen. "Let's say this Patricia Montgomery gets herself down into the basement to flick on the electric heater in the office down there. Let's say she even pulls down a poster and spreads some loose papers around to help the flames along. We'll even say that she walks into the basement apartment— which is fortunately empty now, because Nivens has gone to the library and the gym—and she uncouples a gas line. How's she going to know that Sarah Davidson won't leave the house? Or go downstairs to work in her office? Or that she'll be reading with headphones on so that she can't hear the smoke alarm? The wife has to be incapacitated before the fire starts."

"Maybe Montgomery just turned on the heater for spite and got lucky. Actresses are temperamental, aren't they?"

"Maybe," she said. She had considered the same possibility herself. "Though it's not like we're talking about a great theatrical role she was robbed of here."

"Go back a minute," said Matthew. With one foot he nudged Paul, who laughed invisibly beneath them. "The professor had on headphones? She was a music lover?"

"She didn't care for music at all. She wore headphones to read. She was dyslexic. She listened to recordings of books while she read along with them."

Matthew rubbed his forehead. "It sounds to me like you've got plenty of suspects other than the husband. This Nivens guy, the student. He's got the best access to the basement. He lives there. He's a stranger."

"He lived there for two years," said Ellen. "He liked the woman. He worked with her as a grader and a research assistant. She spoke up for him last year when the rest of the department wanted to bump him from the program. The kid admits things were a little tense toward the end when she told him she wouldn't be his thesis adviser, but that's all."

"So he kills her for not being his thesis adviser," said Matthew. On the television set the crowd was screaming. They watched the instant replay.

"Nivens got another adviser," said Ellen, "before she died. He was planning to keep on living in their basement next year. All his belongings got burned up."

"So did the husband's."

"The husband owns a place here in Rockbridge, a house at the beach, and another house in western North Carolina."

"Servants?"

"You mean in Charlottesville? They had a cook and a maid, both of whom left the house by seven-thirty on Saturday night. Neither lived in. Both had worked for the Davidson family since before Oscar was born."

"And what about the sister?" said Matthew. "Anne Lindsey. The one that lives here in Rockbridge."

"That's exactly where she was on the night of the fire," said Ellen Spencer. "Here. In Rockbridge."

"But would she have a motive for wanting her sister dead?" said Matthew.

"None. She and her sister were very close." Ellen went through the entire history. Eight years ago, when Anne Lindsey was teaching high school and trying to publish a small literary journal, Sarah used to send her money. After Sarah married Oscar Davidson, Oscar bought a house in Canterbury Hills for his new sister-in-law and his niece. "Anne edited Sarah's manuscripts for free, Sarah and Oscar worked in the Arts School for token salaries, everybody got along with everybody else."

"So in other words," said Matthew, "you've got no case."

"Nothing," she said.

"So why are we discussing this?" he said.

"I keep coming back to where we started," she said. "O'Shea sees something strange with the husband, the tenant, and the victim's sister all ending up in the same town this summer."

"But you just said that it was understandable," said Matthew. "They live here, they're looking after the poor graduate student."

"Yes," she said. "But then you reminded me that Patricia Montgomery is no longer living in New York. She's coming back to Rockbridge, too. The newspaper says she's flying in today. Spending the whole summer. And the kid will be here, too. That gives us another two people—four in all—who were in the Davidson home on the night of the fire. The husband, the tenant, the actress, the student. Plus Anne Lindsey, the sister. What would O'Shea say about that?"

Matthew stared at the newspaper. "On television they'd call it your basically weird coincidence," he said.

The information appeared in print under the photograph. Patricia Montgomery would be in Rockbridge for the summer to work at the Stone Mountain Theater. She planned to perform in Shakespeare's *A Midsummer Night's Dream,* which would be directed by her husband, Milton Blackburn. And she was quoted as saying she hoped "to spend quality time" with their sons, Tucker and Richard. Richard Blackburn. Ellen remembered him well. He was one of the boys who had been in

the Davidson home—had been there to meet with his mother, in fact—
on the night Sarah Davidson died.

❊

Patricia Montgomery had never hesitated to keep her maiden name
when she married Milton. Not only was "Patricia Montgomery" the
tag by which her audience knew her professionally, but it was her
anchor. Because her vocation was to play roles, she needed to have
one core identity that was not a pretense. Had she changed her name
and become "Patricia Blackburn," she would have felt like someone
inhabiting a character, like someone wearing a label only temporarily.
By contrast, if she entered into marriage as Patricia Montgomery, then
she would not be leaving at the end of the run. She was signed on
forever. Or at least till death did them part, though her career had served
to do quite a bit of separating. She was coming home unenthusiasti-
cally, and she did not like that. She should be thrilled to be back on
the stage, thrilled to be back with her family. But life in Rockbridge
was not merely the slow lane. It was the shoulder.

Even sitting here, motionless in a queue of planes at LaGuardia waiting for an open runway, she regarded joblessness in New York more
exciting than employment in Rockbridge for the summer. Life in Rockbridge was set, static, frozen. But Rockbridge was also her home, the
home of her children, the home of her husband. Till death did them
part. She supposed that a relationship could suffer a kind of death. Love
could expire. Or at least its initial heat could cool. Love could go on
a vacation and simply take longer and longer to return. She did still
love Milton. When she saw him, she'd be excited. But there was something about returning to that beautiful but dreadfully serene section of
Virginia which made her almost resent Milton for wanting to do regional theater. Almost. But that had been their decision together. Partners. Till death. And the irony was not lost on her that she and her
family would be reunited because of a death, the death of Tru Lovinguth, her character on *Adam's Garden*. She felt faintly guilty for missing Tru so much. It wasn't as though she wanted the part forever. And
it wasn't as though she didn't have plenty else to feel guilty about.

There were relatively few people on the plane, just over half the
capacity. She would have preferred sitting in first class, but the days

of luxury were over. It seemed impossible that she and Milton could be so broke. At least she had a seat to herself so that she could be free from chatterers or, even worse, fans. But she wondered if this meant yet another airline would decrease its routes in and out of Rockbridge. The railroad had packed up and gone to Atlanta. The G.E. plant was cutting six hundred jobs. The attempt by the Arts Council to bolster the tourist industry had stalled, but she'd heard that Ramsey Paxton had taken over as chairman. Perhaps Ramsey could do something to liven up the valley tourist trade again. Just as long as she didn't have to listen to any pontification about bottom lines or balance sheets. She had deliberately avoided flying home yesterday so that she could miss the awful brunch that Ramsey and Harriet would be throwing for themselves. Yet now her son Richard had managed to get himself tossed out of Montpelier. It was a family crisis of sorts. They'd had their share of those this year. So here she came.

She'd worn her dark glasses onto the plane and had hidden her honey-colored hair under a plain gray scarf. Anyone who had recognized her had kindly avoided asking her for an autograph or gushing over a performance. Or offering condolences over the demise of Tru Lovinguth. Tru had stepped through a hole in the floor of a skyscraper under construction and plunged eight stories to her death. They'd wanted to film her lying splattered on top of a cement mixer, but Patricia had refused. What could they do? Fire her? They'd finally used a stand-in.

The plane lurched and rolled for twenty yards on the runway before it stopped again. This plane was still probably eighth or ninth in line to take off and was already delayed half an hour. She gave up on the magazine she'd been holding in her lap and allowed the guilt to absorb her full attention. Throughout the past year guilt had followed her like a persistent odor. There was so much of it. Guilt over leaving Milton alone in Rockbridge. Guilt over how she'd handled the aftermath of Tucker's accident. She'd given the bulk of her attention to Tucker, as was perfectly natural, but it was Richard who seemed to need the most help. Tucker limped; Richard seemed disabled. And now he'd been dismissed from school. She felt guilty for agreeing that he go to boarding school in the first place, guilty for taking a job that made it necessary for him to go, guilty for not being more of a nurturer. But being a mother was not a role that she played especially well. No awards committee handed her any nominations on Mother's Day. She'd been happy to leave Richard to his father so that she could catch up with the career she'd put into limbo while she'd waited to have him. Richard had always been something of an inconvenience to her. She loved him, of course, this product of her flesh, this creation that she'd carried for nine months. But having Richard after having Tucker had been like re-creating an old performance with an inferior cast. The novelty had worn off. She'd given Richard all the affection she could spare, and that wasn't much. She blamed herself for Richard's obsessive need for attention, but this latest business at Montpelier represented a troubling deterioration in his behavior. Until this year his prankishness had always been harmless—putting salt into the sugar bowl, taping cellophane under the toilet seats. Now his moods had turned darker. He actually picked fights with Tucker and shouted at Milton. Within a few months he'd turned into a mean, angry child, and yet the one member of the family who escaped his wrath was the one who, in her own eyes, most deserved it.

And she felt guilty about that, too.

But the part that bothered her most was the manuscript. The notorious missing manuscript of Sarah Davidson's last Shakespearean criticism. Sarah had given her that manuscript in good faith on the afternoon of the fire. On her last afternoon alive. Sarah had expected her to deliver it to Milton or to Ramsey or to somebody on the Arts Council, but instead Patricia had concealed its existence. Everyone thought it had burned in the fire, and she had allowed their misconceptions to stand. She wondered if Richard had known what was inside that brown envelope, the envelope that Sarah had handed her because they had supposedly settled their differences. For all her intelligence, Sarah could be so naive about human psychology sometimes. Patricia had been livid over the loss of her job on *Adam's Garden,* and yet she'd managed to convince Sarah Davidson that her initial rage had passed and that all was forgiven. It had been a magnificent performance. But now circumstances demanded an encore. Inside her bag in the rack overhead she had the manuscript, still in its brown mailing envelope. The whole text was only what, twelve or fifteen pages long, and yet it seemed so terribly heavy for her to carry. The one benefit she could see from her return to Rockbridge was the chance to rid herself of this presence, this reminder of Sarah Davidson, this property that had never been Patricia's to keep. No matter what else went wrong today, at least she would get rid of the manuscript. At least she'd perform one decent act before she proceeded with the rest of her plans.

❖

On Sunday morning Oscar Davidson slept in. But he rose in time to print out his essay and to call Montpelier to hear the verdict on the Blackburn business. Guilty and dismissed. He felt a cold thrill of satisfaction at the news. He had won. He had won again.

He dressed in a blue suit at 12:30 P.M. and drove himself to the home of his sister-in-law, Anne Lindsey. His suit was new and uncomfortable. All his weight seemed to be gathering at his waist, though he thought of himself as more soft than fat. At thirty-six years old, he could not govern his body. His face sagged. His dark hair, which he'd recently started to part in the center, drooped across his forehead. Even the famous Davidson nose, thin and long and elegant, had begun to display a tiny network of capillaries at the base of the nostrils. He resented his loss of control.

He pulled on sunglasses as he steered his green Mercedes down Madison Street to the stoplight at Jefferson Parkway. The former furniture store to his left was about to become condominiums. It was amazing to him that a city like Rockbridge, with a population of under two hundred thousand people and a dwindling tax base, could keep its downtown so attractive and so healthy, even with a thriving tourist industry. This was Sarah's hometown, and for him it was the most bearable city in the Shenandoah Valley, despite the inevitable summer humidity. It was only a few minutes' drive to Anne's house in Canterbury Hills. He saw that the wide lawn had been cut so recently that blades of grass still littered the brick sidewalk. The large white house he had purchased for her sat like a monument in the shade of its oak trees. He pulled into the driveway, drove up the hill to the porte cochere, and parked beneath. He left his manuscript under his seat.

Inside the house, her blond hair clipped short and impeccably like the lawn (he knew that she would leave no stray hairs in the bathroom sink), Anne waved him inside. She had on a white apron over her yellow silk dress and pearls, and she held a pot holder in each hand exactly the way Sarah used to—with the square pad folded once and palmed like a floppy pincer. Today was one of the days when Oscar could see a lot of Sarah in her—the thin mouth, the pale blue eyes, the short hair, even though Sarah's hair had been darker.

"Is this a potluck party?" he said.

"Moonie's birthday," she said. "You forgot?"

"Today?"

"Tomorrow, Oscar. She'll be nineteen."

He said that Sarah had always remembered the birthdays. Then he noticed the magazine on the counter. An issue of *The Shenandoah Review* from eight years ago, its worn gray cardboard cover serving as table of contents for the stories inside.

"What's this doing out?" he said.

"Now that Sarah's dead, I was thinking about reviving it," Anne said. She had founded and edited the *Review* a decade earlier, when she was still working as an English teacher in the public schools. It had survived for fifty-six months, five issues' worth, with a peak circulation of 750. Virtually everyone had admired it. Virtually no one had read it, a magazine specializing in fiction about southwestern Virginia.

"Are you crazy?" he said. "The last thing we need is to remind anybody of *The Shenandoah Review*."

"I wasn't expecting you to fund it," she said. "I was hoping maybe the Arts Council would."

Oscar told her he would buy her the rights to *The Saturday Evening Post* if she'd drop the idea of resurrecting the *Review*.

"Stop being so self-centered," she said. "It probably won't happen anyway. Ramsey's already told me that the Arts Council doesn't back losers." She removed from the oven two round layers of cake, the smell of which reminded him of how hungry he was. She did not offer him anything to eat, but left the cake on top of the stove to cool.

He was still rattled by the sight of the magazine. "So Ramsey won?"

She said yes. "I fought his election at the meeting. But no chance. He's going to be head of the whole Arts Council as of June first."

"Ten days," said Oscar.

"I can read a calendar, Oscar."

"Ramsey's star is ascendant," said Oscar. "A new position. A new wife." Today's brunch celebrated the marriage of Ramsey Paxton to Harriet Mason last week. It was a second marriage for both.

"It was just so hard to campaign against him without making it seem personal," she said.

"It was personal."

"I know," she said, "but I didn't want it to seem that way."

"I should have written your lines for you," said Oscar Davidson. "You protested too much."

Anne Lindsey came as close as she ever did to laughing.

"You?" she said. "Write my lines?"

"I am a writer, after all," he said.

"Oscar," said Anne Lindsey, "I'm not one of your students. You don't have to try to sell me anything."

"I do write," he said. "I spent most of the past four weeks writing."

"Four weeks," she said.

"I am a professional writer. I have written a novel, Anne."

"Yes," she said. "I know all about your novel. And frankly, I think it's time for other people to know about it, too."

Oscar Davidson couldn't read her tone. "Are you threatening me?" he said.

She reached across the counter, picked up the gray-covered copy of *The Shenandoah Review,* and fanned the pages at him.

He took the old journal from her and placed it under the telephone directory at the end of the counter. "You're so juvenile," he said. "Why don't you go to the brunch with Alex?"

"Alex is tiresome," she said. "And he's not invited."

"I wouldn't expect him to be," he said. "But I wouldn't expect you to date him, either."

"Alex was good for my ego," she said. "Being genuinely adored wasn't at all bad." She took off her apron and folded it neatly. Then she looked at him hard. "Why don't you try playing the kindly old Mr. Chips for once, instead of the punctilious ogre? What if your students ever learned the truth about you?"

"Don't needle me," he said. He tried to smile. "I could kill you."

"You do kill me, Oscar," said Anne Lindsey. "You killed Sarah, too."

❧

When Alex Mason heard the telephone ring, he sat upright in bed and checked the digital clock beside him. Half past noon. Somehow he knew it would be Anne Lindsey calling. It would be Anne, calling to say that she didn't want to attend the brunch either, and could she come over and apologize for the way she'd treated him lately. That was the fantasy that briefly entertained him before he picked up the receiver and recognized Milton Blackburn's voice.

"Alex," said Blackburn, "I need two favors."

"Yes?" he said. "Hello? What is it?" He'd been sleeping in the pajama bottoms Harriet had given him for their honeymoon. The honeymoon had ended two years ago. The marriage had ended in October, half a year ago. The pajamas weren't in especially good condition either.

"Patricia's flying in today," said Blackburn. "She asked if you could pick her up."

Wake up. It's Milton. He's talking to you. It has nothing to do with the Stone Mountain Consultants account. He wants you to pick up his wife at the airport.

"Sure," said Alex. He had something to tell Milton, too. He couldn't remember. "What time is the flight?"

"One-fifty," said Milton. "Can you do that?"

"Yeah," said Alex. One-fifty. An hour before he had to leave. "Why me?"

"Because she figured you wouldn't be going to the brunch today," said Milton Blackburn.

"Correct," said Alex. It was his ex-wife Harriet who had married Ramsey Paxton.

"And she insisted that I go. For appearances. For politics."

"Right," said Alex. "I got you." He rubbed his head briskly in the hope that the friction would get some circulation going in his brain. Alex had a blond crewcut. His beard was gray, so he shaved his face twice a day. Nobody who met him could believe he was forty-two years old.

Milton Blackburn heard the drowsiness. "Are you all right, Alex?"

"Sure. Yes."

"Then why are you still in bed on Sunday afternoon?"

"Because I'm depressed and suicidal," said Alex. "My ex-wife has married the biggest jerk in town. Is that what you're thinking?" He and Blackburn were professional friends. Alex ran the drama program at the Rockbridge Arts School and occasionally hired Blackburn to do consulting. Blackburn occasionally hired him for tech work at the Stone Mountain Theater. And now Alex remembered what he wanted to tell

Blackburn. "We're going to do *Hamlet* this summer at the Lyceum," he said.

"In high school?" said Milton. "Isn't that a little ambitious?"

"You do *A Midsummer Night's Dream;* we do *Hamlet,*" said Alex. "Let the critics decide which is better."

"Alex," said Blackburn, "I'm in a hurry." He had the kind of deep, growly voice you would have expected Hemingway to have, only Hemingway's was higher. But Blackburn's voice suited the rest of him, a tall man's voice, a voice of authority. And what he said next finally woke Alex up. "Richard's been dismissed from school."

Blackburn told him about the honor violation at Montpelier. "It must have been a joke," said Alex. He had known Richard for eight years, ever since Milton Blackburn had founded the Stone Mountain Theater Company and Alex had worked in a show. He liked the boy. He did not especially like Oscar Davidson, whom he knew from the Arts School. "Richard was pulling a stunt on him. Where's the man's sense of humor?"

"This wasn't a joke," said Milton. "Alex. Listen. Richard doesn't need for you to be telling him that what he did was okay."

"Yeah," said Alex.

"He needs to grow up, Alex."

"I understand," said Alex. He and Richard had always been pranksters together. It was Alex who had taught Richard how to tie a rope around two or more doorknobs so that nobody inside could open the doors. Alex had shown him the little disk in the telephone speaker that you could remove so that nobody could talk on a phone. He'd taught him how to use a rubber band to hold the sprayer hose at the kitchen sink open, so that the next person who turned on the water would get soaked. He had never taught Richard anything about plagiarism, though. It was terrifying to think that a prank could lead to such serious consequences. He thought again of the Stone Mountain Consultants. "When does he get home?"

"Tucker's picking him up right now. That's why Patricia's coming in early."

"Does she think Richard's going to open up to her?" said Alex. He was better friends with Richard than Patricia was.

"For appearances, Alex," said Milton. "At least she can make the gesture."

Alex could appreciate that impulse. Appearances were important.

The costume was essential. Right now, for example, he looked like a prisoner in a concentration camp. "What can I do?" he said. "Do you want me to come over?"

Milton was concerned mainly about summer school. "I'm not sending Richard away again," he said. "He needs to be home. What about the Arts School? I imagine the enrollment is closed by now."

"I don't know about enrollment," said Alex. "You know that Anne and I are no longer what they call an item."

"You still work for her," said Milton. "Of course, I'll probably see her myself at the brunch." His voice sounded muffled.

"Are you putting on a tie?" Milton hardly ever wore one.

"It's my wedding party costume, Alex. Patricia gets in at one-fifty. You'll be there?"

When he hung up the telephone, Alex dialed Anne Lindsey's home number.

"Hello?" A young version of Anne's voice, not as curt, still warm. It was Moonie, her daughter. Alex said nothing. Sometimes Anne would pick up the extension downstairs. But she must have already left for the brunch.

"Hello?" Moonie again. A pretty voice, a pretty girl. Then he heard a male voice, indistinct, in the background. Moonie replaced the receiver and left Alex listening to silence. He did not yet hang up. The silence clicked into a dial tone, and then the dial tone to a recorded operator's voice telling him to hang up his phone. Still he waited, and then it came—a loud, harsh beeping noise that hurt his ears and punished him for being so bad.

Oscar Davidson waited until they were on the road before he showed Anne Lindsey his manuscript. Reaching under his seat, he extracted the twelve sheets of laser-printed paper and handed them to her. "What would you think of giving Sarah's lost essay to Ramsey as a wedding present?" he asked.

They were on the Jefferson Parkway, ten minutes from the Rockbridge Country Club. The glare from the chrome on the car ahead irritated Oscar Davidson, and he changed lanes. Anne Lindsey riffled through the pages. "What is this?" she said.

"It's Sarah's last manuscript," said Oscar. He motioned for her to read. "The one we supposedly lost in the fire."

She read one paragraph and looked up. "Where did you get this?" she said.

"You want the official version?" he said. "I found it on one of the disks she left in our apartment here in Rockbridge."

"Save that for your fiction class," she said. "I edited Sarah's last manuscript two months ago. The only thing this has in common with it is the topic. Where did you get it?"

"I wrote it."

"Hogwash," she said. "You've stolen some graduate student's work."

"I wrote it," said Oscar. "I've spent a long time on it."

Anne Lindsey read a little more. "You actually wrote this?" she said. "You're writing again?"

"So now we announce that a miracle has occurred," said Oscar Davidson. "The monograph Ramsey commissioned for the Stone Mountain playbill has turned up after all. Just when we despaired that all copies had disappeared in the fire, we find one on a disk in Rockbridge. Happiness all around."

Anne skimmed over the rest of the essay. It took her five minutes. When she finished, she left the pages on the car seat between them.

"What's the point?" she said. "If you wrote it, why try to pass it off as Sarah's?"

"I asked Ramsey three weeks ago if he'd like for me to write something for the playbill," said Oscar Davidson. "He said I was known only as a pop novelist, not as an expert on Shakespeare." It had been two years since the publication of *Sally Galloway: A Romance* by O. H. Davidson. He still was uncertain of how to sort out his emotions whenever he saw a copy in a bookstore or on a library shelf. Just as he was uncertain of how to sort out his emotions after the fire. He changed lanes again. "You know Ramsey," he said. "You know what a snob he is."

"It won't work," she said. "Forget it, Oscar."

"I will not forget it," he said. "I've spent a long time on this. It's good. It's original. Even if Ramsey doesn't go for it, I'm going to submit it to *Feminist Renaissance*."

"You're joking," she said.

"They love Sarah's stuff."

"Same question again," she said. "Why use Sarah's name? Why not your own?"

"Because it would look suspicious," he said. "Ramsey's right. I'm known as a pop novelist. My dead wife was known as a Shakespeare scholar. A monograph appears, and suddenly I claim to be the author. No. Everyone will think that I stole one of Sarah's unfinished pieces."

"No one will think that," said Anne, "because it's not good enough. This is not professional scholarship."

"Then let me try it," said Oscar. "I'll bet you they'll print it because of the name at the top of the page."

"No. Sarah was brilliant. This is beneath her."

"It will mean extra income for you. You've got the rights."

"I'm not a whore, Oscar."

"Not for a couple of hundred dollars, you mean."

She glared at him. "No one would fall for such a fraud."

"Ramsey Paxton would," said Oscar.

Anne Lindsey played with her pearls. "What would you get out of all this?" she said.

"Satisfaction," he said. "I wrote it. I'd like to see it published."

"And what would I get out of it?" she said.

"Revenge," he said. "You wouldn't want Ramsey to use one of Sarah's real monographs anyway, would you?"

"No," she said. "But I hate to see you exploit my sister's reputation."

"Think of it as a nom de plume," said Oscar. "You and Sarah had no problems with using pen names." Sarah had published under several pseudonyms before she had married Oscar, and she continued to use them afterward.

"You have no malicious intent?" Anne said. "For example, with Milton Blackburn?"

"What does Milton have to do with it?"

"It's his theater," she said. "And his son just got dismissed for plagiarism in your class." She nudged the manuscript on the car seat. "You see no connection?"

"He was convicted of submitting somebody else's work as his own. I'm submitting my own as somebody else's. There's a decided difference."

She lowered the sun visor and used the mirror to check her face. "Tell me which is more corrupt," she said. "To see your own work published by using somebody else's name, or to get the author's credit when another person did the writing."

"Your sister Sarah was never this nasty, Anne." They were almost at the country club.

"You're going to see Milton today at the brunch, Oscar. What are you going to say to him?"

"I'm going to tell him it's a shame that his son made a mistake," he said. "And it is."

"Oscar," she said, "you wouldn't be using this boy as some red herring, would you?"

He tried to stare her down, but she would not blink.

○○

By the time they reached the highway, Tucker had lost most of his anger. That was typical. Tucker could never stay very mad at anybody for long. He didn't say anything, but Richard could tell by his posture that he'd relaxed since they'd started back for Rockbridge. That he was trying to think of something to say to relieve the tension. Richard debated about whether to help him out or not.

In all the old stories, the blond, blue-eyed guy was always the hero, and the brooding, dark-featured guy was always the villain. You weren't supposed to have stories like that anymore because they reflected ethnic biases, but the old tales still existed. Richard was convinced that his parents had read those stories over and over again before they'd decided to have children. Then they'd gone to some witch doctor or genetic engineer or satanic church and had arranged for their first son to be born fair and good, and their second son to be born dark and evil. Richard was the dark, evil one, and he was frankly tired of playing the part. But it was the part he was born for. Tucker was popular and athletic and hard-working and respectful. Richard lived on the fringe.

Tucker was also very popular with girls. Richard was a virgin, and it ate him up, because he knew everybody else knew it. They had to. He'd never had a girlfriend, and he was already a year and a half older than Tucker had been when that nineteen-year-old actress had lured him into the woods behind the amphitheater. Tucker hadn't even bragged about it. The only reason Richard had known was that their mother had caught them a couple of weeks later in the storage shed for the lumber. The actress had gotten fired. Tucker had gotten talked to. His parents always forgave Tucker. They always understood with Tucker. It was never Tucker's fault, poor Tucker, good Tucker, Tucker who could serve the hell out of a tennis ball but couldn't read until he was nine years old.

It was really weird to be in the car with Tucker on Sunday afternoon, as though they were on some vacation. Richard kept thinking that he ought to be exhilarated. The sky was a perfect blue with those stage-set billowy clouds, the landscape green, the mountains purple in the distance, the road silver, and the air-conditioning cool. But Richard could not shake the gloom. Ahead loomed the terrible prospect of home.

"Have you ever wanted revenge?" said Richard.

"Come on, Richard," said Tucker. "All you have to do is admit your mistake, and it's all over."

That's not so easy, Richard thought. "And what if I didn't make a mistake?" he said. "How would you feel, if nobody in your family and none of your friends believed you?"

"Let me ask you this," said Tucker. "If you were in my position, would you believe the story you're telling? You're saying a teacher has deliberately lied to get you thrown out of school."

"He did," said Richard.

"Why?"

"Because," said Richard. Should he give him the long version or the short version? "Because he doesn't like me." The short version.

"So he fooled the headmaster and everyone on the faculty and the entire honor council. He typed up a short story out of a book and put your name at the top and tore up the story you gave him and handed in this one instead. Your signature was on the cover sheet, Richard."

"He saved my original cover sheet," said Richard. "He threw away everything else."

"And he got your roommate to testify that you hadn't even started on your short story the day before they were due."

"I never start early," said Richard. "You know that."

"And in your name he checked out a library book containing the same story you turned in," said Tucker.

"He told us all to check out short story collections," said Richard. "It was homework for his class."

"And he put a dead bird under his car seat to embarrass himself," said Tucker.

"I did that."

"And he submitted a cartoon of himself to the school newspaper."

"I did that, too," said Richard.

"And he was constantly looking for ways to humiliate himself," said Tucker. "I've got to hand it to you, Richard. You came up with a really original trick. It would have humiliated the hell out of him if he hadn't recognized the story. But it backfired. You got nailed. You were stupid. You ought to admit it."

Richard wanted to say that when he did something wrong, he admitted it. But that was not true. He kept silent. Two summers ago the theater troupe had done *Twelfth Night*. There was this one character, Malvolio, whom nobody else could stand. He was an outsider, always unpopular, always out of the party. He was the character Richard identified with the most. And at the end of the play, he had a great line, one that Richard had never forgotten. "I'll be revenged on the whole pack of you," he'd said. Richard wondered what the sequel would be like. *Malvolio's Revenge.*

After two hours Richard could see Stone Mountain looming in front of him, the houses along the base, the tree line guarding the upper ridge. Along the top, even at this distance, he could see the green clearing for the park, the white speck that would be the amphitheater, and the yellow box that would be the Pinnacle Inn itself. He even imagined that he could trace the thin scar of the path down the side of the mountain through the trees to home, to his parents' house, to where he was going. He did not want to go there. There was nowhere else to go.

"I'd like to live on the mountain," said Richard.

"Ask Dad," said Tucker. "I'm living there."

"I don't mean at the Inn," said Richard. "I mean out in the woods."

"You can't run away from everything, Richard," said Tucker. "Take control. Take charge. Set some goals. You don't like your life, change it."

Richard turned away and looked out the window. Farmlands had given way to warehouses and motels. They were almost in Rockbridge.

Tucker could be so out of it sometimes. Richard had goals, but they were all impossible. He wanted to win a physical competition—a wrestling match, a footrace, a tennis match, anything. He wanted to get laid. And he wanted somehow to be the good guy, the hero.

"So what's this about Moonie?" he said. "You broke up?"

"She doesn't like to be called Moonie anymore," said Tucker. "She's now Ramona."

"Ramona?" said Richard. The name sounded awkward to him.

"She's going out with this other guy," said Tucker. "Chris Nivens. You know him?"

"No."

"He used to live in the Davidsons' basement in Charlottesville," said Tucker. "Moonie's mom got him a job at the Arts School for the summer."

That guy. Richard knew who he was. He'd walked into his apartment by mistake that day at the Davidsons' house. The guy had books open all over the place and was working at his computer when Richard walked in. Tucker had some competition there. The guy was older, maybe twenty-four, and looked pretty cool; he was dark-haired and athletic. But he'd sure given Richard a dirty look through those round glasses.

"Did this happen recently?" said Richard. "With Moonie? Ramona?"

"Two days ago."

"She still working at the theater this summer?" said Richard.

"Yeah," said Tucker. "But she's not living there."

Richard took a perverse satisfaction in thinking that maybe Tucker would spend the summer as horny as he was. Then Tucker mentioned that he already had a prospect for a date with a woman he met at physical therapy.

"So how's your leg?" said Richard. He hadn't meant to make it sound so harsh.

"It's sore," said Tucker. "They might want to do more surgery next summer."

Richard had not been there for the accident, of course. He'd been off with that stupid Outward Bound program and hadn't even found out about it until a week after it was over. The wheel on the lawn mower had come off when Tucker was on a hillside. He'd overbalanced and fallen, the mower tumbling on top of him, the blade mangling his leg. Richard quivered just to think of it, to imagine the pain. So why couldn't he tell him how sorry he was?

They turned right at the hospital, past the main branch of the public library and the gray stone of the Episcopal church, and then past the apartment and office buildings, until the larger structures gave way to gas stations and 7-Elevens and then finally to houses. The road sloped gradually upward. Left on Canterbury Lane, up, around the big curve by the Butlers' house, then the next curve by the Paxtons', the oak trees overhead dappling the street with the bright sunshine, and then right into the familiar driveway, the dark red brick, the Tudor beams, the gables, the two chimneys, the flagstones, the boxwoods, the rich green grass. Home.

Richard helped unload his luggage into the driveway, then stood on the pavement and watched Tucker lug his laundry bag to the house. Richard did not enter the house himself. He rested his tote bag on the rock wall that kept their lawn from spilling into the driveway. When he was certain that Tucker was inside the house, he walked up to the open door of the garage and found the lawn mower, a new riding mower, different from the one that had tilted on Tucker. He rolled it out of the garage onto the flat part of the driveway, just below Tucker's basketball hoop. He unscrewed the cap to the gasoline tank and saw that it was nearly empty. In the garage was a red plastic canister of gasoline. He could get it and slosh it all over the machine. Gasoline would turn the asphalt of the driveway darker and drip from the blue metal of the mower. The smell would be very strong. Then, if he only had a match, if he only had a flame, he could send the entire machine up in a whoosh. But he simply rolled the machine back into the garage and retrieved his suitcase and tote bag. He was going to be here for a long time. There was plenty of time for damage. He felt utterly, entirely without ambition or energy. It was all he could do to lift his suitcase from the driveway. And he knew why. He had the longest trip of his life ahead of him: up the sidewalk and inside, where, sooner or later, he'd have to speak to his father.

※

Inside the cool of the house Richard listened for the sounds of his parents. He could hear only Tucker upstairs clumping around. Richard climbed the staircase and entered his bedroom, where Tucker rested by leaning one hand against the wall.

"They're not here," said Tucker. "Mom's plane arrived an hour and a half ago, supposedly."

Richard dropped his suitcase and looked at his room. He hated it suddenly, this place he'd spent so much time in when he wasn't in school. The matching twin beds with the cowboys on the bedspreads. So childish. The posters of Megadeth and Johnny K and the Brigsters and NWA on the walls. With Tucker there in the room he pulled everything off the walls except his poster of *The Phantom of the Opera* and crammed everything into the small wastebasket. He pulled off the bedspreads, too, and stuffed them into the bottom drawer of his dresser. Now his beds looked like hospital beds. He could put beach towels or something over them. Anything.

"What are you doing?" said Tucker.

"I don't like it anymore," said Richard. "It looks like a kid's room."

Tucker sat down on one bed, stretched his leg out on the sheets, and supported himself on one elbow. It was the position he always took when he came into Richard's room. It made Richard feel good to see it. "This is much better," Tucker said. "Like a shelter for the homeless. Almost as nice as the rooms up at the Inn."

Richard wanted to talk to him so badly. "I want a change this summer," he said.

"No more King of the Pranksters?"

"I'd like to expand my territory," said Richard. "Being the King of the Pranksters has gotten old."

"So you want to join the Young Republicans? Or the Boy Scouts?" That was pretty good for Tucker. "I want to get into shape."

"You can go swimming with me at the Y," said Tucker.

"I hate to swim," said Richard.

"So do I," said Tucker. There was an awkward beat of silence. They both knew what he'd left unsaid: that swimming was Tucker's only alternative for now.

"Do you miss tennis?" said Richard.

"I'll play again," said Tucker. He absently scratched his chin against one shoulder. "You want tennis lessons?"

"I don't know what I want," said Richard. "I just want to be different." He appreciated the way Tucker did not ask him why.

"Why don't you jog?" said Tucker. "That's easy as hell. You can wear your Walkman. Listen to tapes. It's not bad."

Richard said he'd consider jogging.

"And weights," said Tucker. "You could lift weights at the Y."

"Not at the Y," said Richard. "Not with all the superjocks."

"Here at home, then."

"No way," said Richard. "If Mom thought I was interested in weight lifting, she'd buy a couple of Nautilus machines for the living room and make me work out three times a day. I just want to get in shape in private."

"We could rig you up a weight room at the Inn," said Tucker.

Richard thought that was a stupid idea. "Where?" he said. "In the scene shop? With everybody working?"

"In the attic," said Tucker. "It's unfinished and unused. Sealed off, as a matter of fact." He motioned to the one remaining poster on the wall. "You could be the phantom of the opera."

Richard's stereo was still down in the car. Neither was in any hurry to retrieve it. They were remembering how to enjoy each other.

"Tuck," said Richard. "I'm sorry if I've embarrassed you." He was determined to make Tucker proud of him before the summer was over.

"Getting rid of that Megadeth poster would never embarrass me," said Tucker.

The atmosphere was clearly improving. He didn't deserve to be friends with Tucker. But he'd take the friendship anyway.

"I'm going to get my hair cut short," said Richard. "I'm going to be a stud."

"Me, too," said Tucker.

"You're one already," said Richard.

"Not good enough," said Tucker. "You know what this guy Nivens did with Moonie? Her mother invites him over to dinner on his first night in Rockbridge, right? And he reads poetry to her. She ate it up."

Richard didn't know what to say. He couldn't teach Tucker to read any faster.

Tucker kept talking. "I mean, I can't really worry about it," he said. "Everybody likes to be good at something. I was always good at sports. And then when I stopped being good at sports, it was like Moonie suddenly had time to get to know me. And she just didn't find anything there."

"Why don't you memorize some poetry and recite it to her?" said

Richard. Tucker had the most amazing memory you'd ever seen. He could always remember every line from every show of the summer.

"It's not poetry," said Tucker. "It's not like poetry is some magical charm that hypnotizes her. It's . . . me. If I can't get my body back into shape, then there's not much brain to compensate. I'm a guy who can't particularly do anything well."

"You could act," said Richard.

"No," said Tucker.

"If you've already got a date lined up," said Richard, "you must do something right."

"Well," said Tucker. He grinned. "Yeah. Okay. But you can only go so far in taking pride in your glands."

"Why don't you call up Spandex Lady? Now's your chance."

"I don't even know her name," said Tucker. "She was just for looking." Spandex Lady was a legend between them, a student Tucker had seen at the university who rode her bicycle to class and always wore those tight spandex shorts. Just the idea of spandex as a clothing material was enough to get Richard a little hot. He kept thinking he'd get down to Charlottesville for a weekend to see the Spandex Lady in person.

But Tucker was not in the mood for digression. "See, I'm not saying Moonie left me because of my leg. I'm saying my leg got Moonie to look at the rest of me. And the rest of me wasn't that interesting. For me it's the physique, or it's nothing. So I can't jog up the mountain with you yet, but I hope I'll be doing it before the summer is over. And maybe we can pump some paint cans together."

Richard felt as if he had really come home. He walked over to Tucker and gave him a fake stage punch in the stomach. They wrestled around for a minute. Then Tucker banged his leg against the leg of the bed.

"It's okay," he said. But it hurt. "Oh, Spandex Lady, come and give me a massage." He stood up slowly. "Let's get the rest of your stuff." Richard stayed on the floor. He wasn't ready for this reunion to end. Tucker walked to the door. "You want to tell me now?" he said.

"Tell you what?" said Richard.

"Why?" said Tucker. "Why'd you have to cheat?"

"I didn't," said Richard. "The teacher framed me." They were im-

mediately back in the land of the chill. But Richard saw with some
tiny satisfaction that Tucker reacted not with impatience or anger, but
with doubt. At least his brother had started to wonder whether what
Richard told him was true.

❖

Nancy Gale Nofsinger hated the sticky feeling of traveling all day.
Maybe she should stop at a motel to take a shower before pulling into
Rockbridge and introducing herself to the Blackburns. She drove the
maroon Saab her father had given her for Christmas so that she'd be
able to travel safely from Atlanta to Charlottesville and back again.
Already she had 9,000 miles on it; that was a lot for five months. But
Nancy Gale liked cars, liked to ride around in them, liked to go out
and buy pizzas and ice cream and beer and whatever, liked to burn off
nervous energy by just getting into the car and going. It was a habit
she'd picked up back in the days when she was fat, which she was no
longer.

   Her bicycle was strapped to a carrier on the back. She didn't know
whether Rockbridge would be good for riding or not, but she'd ride
anyway for the exercise. In the trunk and the backseat she'd neatly
packed everything essential for the summer—clothes, books, stereo,
compact disks, posters, hot plate, bedspread. She was always awed by
the beauty of Virginia, no matter how many times she made the drive
between home and school. The Blue Ridge Mountains really were blue.
Along I-81 the graying barns, the checkerboard farmlands, the white
houses, and the old abandoned stone railroad bridges over clear streams
reminded her of her trip to the English lake district when she was
thirteen. The landscape was much cleaner than Nancy Gale. She kept
a washcloth in a little plastic sandwich bag beside her on the passenger
seat, but the cloth was hot and sour by now. Still, she felt as though
her body had been rubbed with cheddar—she wriggled at the thought—
and she looked forward to a bath. She also looked forward with what
she could only classify as a sexual stirring to the prospect of living and
working as an administrative assistant at the Stone Mountain Theater
this summer. Ever since Patricia Montgomery had hired her last month,
she'd felt absolutely liberated, emancipated from servitude to her
parents.

The issue was control. Nancy Gale Nofsinger wanted control of her own life. She was twenty-one years old and ought to be able to live where she wanted to live. She did not want to live in Atlanta, Georgia, for the summer. She had first wanted to live in New York. She thought she'd get herself a little place in the East Fifties and hang out at the Shakespeare festival in Central Park, maybe audition for parts down in the Village and get a job as an usher in a Broadway theater where she'd get to know producers and actresses and make connections and find out what a big cattle call was like and fall in and out of love and sit in the sunshine in the sculpture garden at the Museum of Modern Art and meet guys and eat great food and have close calls on the subway but never anything too dangerous.

But her parents had said New York City was absolutely out of the question.

"You don't know anybody in New York City," her mother had said over the telephone.

Nancy Gale reminded her of Rachel, her ex-roommate, in White Plains.

"White Plains is a million miles from New York City," said her mother.

"What if I just go?" said Nancy Gale. "What if I just up and go?"

"We won't pay for it," said her mother.

So then she'd tried for Washington, D.C. She could get a little place in Georgetown and hang out at Arena Stage and do mime for the tourists waiting in line for the Washington Monument and fall in love and meet congressmen and Shakespearean scholars at the Folger and get a job as a waitress in some trendy restaurant and eat good food and jog past the White House and have close calls with crime on the sidewalks but never anything too dangerous.

"We want you in Atlanta this summer," said her mother. Where they could control her, of course. Where they could watch what she ate and when she got up and whom she went out with and how often she went to the bathroom. There was some good theater in Atlanta, but it was in Atlanta. There was no adventure about Atlanta. Nancy Gale knew Atlanta, knew all about it, even though she'd gone off to college three years ago and had stayed away from home as often as possible. Now she was on the verge of becoming an actress. And she had the looks for it, she knew she had the looks, she was thin now, and she was going to stay thin as long as she could stay away from home for the summer.

"Momma," said Nancy Gale, "I promise you I will vomit every day if you make me spend the summer at home."

That got her mother quiet until the next argument.

"Tell me about this theater again," Momma said.

"It's Stone Mountain," Nancy Gale said.

"Nancy Gale, Stone Mountain is right here in Georgia."

It had taken Nancy Gale eight minutes to explain that this was a different Stone Mountain, a smaller one in the Shenandoah Valley of Virginia. With a theater on top. "It's famous," Nancy Gale said. "Haven't you ever seen *Adam's Garden* on television? Tru Lovinguth? Her husband runs Stone Mountain."

"How big a city is Rockbridge?"

"It's just the perfect size, Momma." She'd explained how it was smaller than Atlanta but big enough to have museums and symphonies and a regional arts school and a nice airport with direct daily flights to Atlanta. She wasn't sure about the air schedules, but so what. If you got into an airplane in the South, you ended up eventually in Atlanta.

"We'll see," Momma had said.

And, of course, that had meant yes.

Nancy Gale had left the house in Buckhead at 11:30 this morning. It was now 3:00 in the afternoon, and she estimated another four hours to Rockbridge. It would have taken less time, but Nancy Gale liked to stop a lot. She wore her pink Polo shirt that matched the pink frames on her sunglasses and the miniature pink pompons on the backs of her footie socks. Nancy Gale was five feet, eight inches tall, and she weighed a hundred and twenty-five pounds. In high school she had weighed a hundred and seventy. She was proud of the weight she had lost. She had a lot of dates now. She got good parts in the shows. Not leading roles. She wasn't that good an actress. But parts that weren't just for the ugly fat girl.

On the seat beside her was a box of doughnuts she'd bought half an hour ago somewhere before the Virginia state line. There was now only one doughnut remaining. As soon as she passed the blue sign announcing a rest stop in one mile, she brushed her sand-colored hair out of the way with one hand and then picked up the last doughnut delicately with two fingers—she hated to get the glaze all over her hands. The doughnut tasted marvelous, as had the previous eleven. As she pulled into the rest stop she used one free hand to fold the box neatly for the little plastic trash can she kept on the hump between her bucket seats. Then she parked, emptied her waste basket in a trash receptacle, locked it back inside the car, and walked to the brick rest room. She ran the water and washed the doughnut glaze from her fingers, then shut herself into one of the stalls. Standing in front of the open toilet in a ritual she had perfected by now, she raised her clean right middle finger, still wet from its brief immersion under the faucet, and stuck it down her throat to that magic spot. She had to rid herself of all those doughnuts. Too fattening. Far, far too fattening for somebody as svelte as Nancy Gale.

It seemed to Alex Mason that Patricia Montgomery had forgotten the reason for his trip to the airport. He had driven out to pick her up. He had driven out to do her a favor. He had waited for an hour when her flight was delayed en route. So why the hell was she bitching him out as soon as she got into the car?

"I disagree completely about the Arts School for Richard," she said. "Milton and I have not discussed that. I do not think it's the right place for him."

Alex paid for the parking (with his own money! Was she blind, or what?) and then drove toward the ramp for the highway before he answered her. "You want to ship him off again?"

"He's at a bad age," she said. Alex was just thinking the same thing about her. Her looks were still good, no doubt about that, but she was far too old for the ingenue. And not old enough for the matriarch. No wonder she hated losing Tru Lovinguth. It was one of the few things she could play. Other than her permanent roles, the ones she played every day, on stage or off: Lady Macbeth, Medea, and Regina Giddens in *The Little Foxes*.

"Plus," said Patricia, "I'm not at all sure that it's healthy for Richard to spend so much time with you."

He had known her for eight years, and he was aware that she spoke this bluntly only to very good friends. Conversing with casual acquaintances, she was quietly, laconically polite—almost cryptic. But he still did not regard what she'd said as a compliment. "If I'd realized how much fun this trip was going to be," he said, "I'd have driven up to New York to get you yesterday. Saved you the plane fare."

"I'm right," she said. "It's the way Richard responds to you. You bring out the worst in each other. You're not a good match."

"Examples?"

"The poison ivy in Feste's costume two summers ago."

"That guy was a jerk."

"And last Christmas, down at the Lyceum?"

Alex had directed *Annie* at the Arts School. Richard, home for Christmas break, had helped him spell "Tru Sux" in red ornaments on the Christmas tree that appeared during the final scene of the show. "We thought you'd appreciate the attention," said Alex.

"And last March?"

"I didn't think he should have to do Outward Bound if he didn't want to," said Alex. "I just stated my opinion."

"You're not his parent," she said.

"True," he said. She glared at him, thinking that he'd made a joke out of her late character's name. "Correct. Right. I agree."

They passed a car and went the next three miles in silence.

"You know," said Patricia, "I'm looking for something different this summer. If I'm going to be in Rockbridge, I need to be busy."

He knew her well. It was the closest she would ever come to apologizing: she'd changed the subject. "Aren't you doing Hippolyta in *Dream*?" he said.

"Boring," she said. "No challenge."

He was not going to invite her to do Gertrude in his *Hamlet*. No way. He was not even going to mention *Hamlet* to her.

"I've been thinking about the Stone Mountain Consultants," she said. "That might be a way of making the summer more interesting."

Now what the hell was that supposed to mean? "How?" he said. "I thought you'd lost interest."

"When I was in New York," she said. "But in Rockbridge, it's different. What if I did the Consultants by myself? Independent of Milton?"

"Very bad idea," said Alex. It was a horrible idea. What was she bringing this up for? First Ramsey Paxton gets elected head of the Arts Council, and now Patricia has decided that she needs to moonlight. "There won't be any consulting available for *Hamlet* this summer."

"You're doing *Hamlet* at the Lyceum?"

Now there he went. He'd told her. But she was not going to be involved.

"Have you finished casting?" she said.

"No, no," he said. "It's going to be an all-student production. I'll have to wait until we start summer school before we audition."

"I might be available for Gertrude," she said.

"I don't think we can work the rehearsal schedules out," he said. "And we couldn't pay you."

"We could arrange something with Equity," she said. "Keep me in mind."

"Absolutely," he said, but he was thinking, *Never. Never.*

They rode another thirty seconds in silence. "Alex," she said, "can you keep a secret from Milton? From everybody?"

"Probably not," he said. They were almost at the exit ramp. What was she up to now?

"I'm serious," she said. She reached into her shoulder bag and pulled out a brown mailing envelope from the Arts School. "Did you hear about Sarah Davidson's lost manuscript?"

"The one that burned up in the fire? Of course."

"It wasn't lost," said Patricia Montgomery. She pulled a set of typed pages out of the envelope. He glanced at them. He could see Anne Lindsey's writing in pencil in the margins. "She gave it to me. Before the fire. I was supposed to deliver it to Milton. Or to Ramsey. Or to Anne. To anybody connected with the Arts Council."

"For what?"

"For use in the Stone Mountain playbill," she said. "Ramsey wanted something by a prominent Shakespeare scholar for the grand opening of the Inn. And Sarah knew I'd be seeing Milton after my trip to Charlottesville."

"So why'd you hide it? Didn't you hear how upset everyone was after she died?"

"I was angry that she'd written me out of the show," said Patricia. "I didn't want anything connected with Sarah Davidson to be a part of the Stone Mountain season."

"And now you've changed your mind? Why?"

She wasn't sure. "Richard, I guess," she said. "He was dismissed for cheating in Oscar's class. I—I don't want it to look as though my family is carrying on a vendetta against the Davidsons. Enough is enough."

"Why didn't you just destroy the manuscript? Why do you still have it?"

She tried to explain what she had wondered for so many weeks herself. "I don't know," she said. "I just couldn't. It was the only existing copy of her last essay, the only one in the whole world, and I just couldn't do it. So I kept it. And here it is."

She folded it and placed it into his glove compartment.

"And this is why you requested me as your chauffeur today?" said Alex.

"You and Anne are close," she said. "I thought maybe you could stick it back into those files she has at home."

"The archives?" he said. "You don't visit the Lindsey archives without a papal dispensation."

They exited the highway and passed the country club on the left.

"You see her every day," said Patricia Montgomery. "Can't you return the manuscript without letting her know where it came from?"

"Slide it under her pillow or something?" he said. "I think you have the wrong idea. Anne called it off. We're not dating."

"I never understood how you and Anne could ever match up," said Patricia. "It was like Peter Pan going out with Jocasta."

Should he pull off now and throw her out of the car? Or maybe he should just offer to let her run him over a few times. "Anne is terrific," he said. "She said I was the first man to make her laugh since she was eighteen years old."

"All right," she said. "I didn't mean to offend."

"Anne kept me going when Harriet moved out. I missed two straight weeks of work. I didn't leave my house, and she saved my job and brought me food and got me out of my funk. Okay? Don't say anything bad about Anne to me."

"I understand, Alex."

"Someday I'm going to take her to Paris. She's never been to Paris."

They did not speak for a full minute.

"You're wondering why she broke it off," said Alex.

"No," said Patricia.

"She told me we were stagnant," said Alex. "But we were good for each other. She had problems, too. I still think we've got a chemistry."

"Then won't she be grateful if you produce her sister's long-lost essay?'' said Patricia. "I just don't want the thing with me anymore.''

He would love to find some way to show Anne Lindsey how much she mattered to him. Maybe he could tell her that the manuscript had appeared in the bottom drawer of his desk, and she would say, Alex, it's a miracle, you found it. I love you. No, she wouldn't. But he'd try anyway.

"I'll take it,'' he said. "You can forget about it.''

"I'm trusting you, Alex.''

"But you won't trust me with Richard?'' he said. "We'll be a good team at the Arts School.''

"Oscar Davidson will be there, too,'' she said. "Is that healthy for either one of them?''

Alex told her he'd never heard of anybody who regretted getting a second chance.

She let another half minute go by. "If Richard does enroll there,'' she said, "do you think I could still play Gertrude?''

Now she had herself already cast in the part. "I'm sure there's plenty for you to do with Stone Mountain this summer,'' he said.

"It's the usual bunch of college kids,'' she said. "They take care of everything. If I don't take Gertrude, what can I do? Hippolyta is nearly invisible.''

"You could direct,'' said Alex. It was out before he'd thought.

"Direct,'' she said. She considered it. "Yes, I think I could.''

Milton would be furious with him for giving her the idea. But Alex could not have Patricia at the Lyceum while he was putting together a play. And he could not have her searching for ways to occupy her time that might call attention to the Stone Mountain Consultants. That, he knew, could lead to a real-life tragedy.

⋈

Chris Nivens was a little drunk after all the Bloody Marys and champagne he'd guzzled at that deplorable brunch at that tasteless country club, but he was not too drunk to go after what he wanted. It was 5:00 on Sunday afternoon, and he was alone in the Lindsey home with Ramona. He refused to call her Moonie. It was a child's name. Or a pet's. He had told her that it was demeaning, and she had agreed with him. It was not the proper name for this effervescent young woman whose mother happened to be Sarah Davidson's sister and literary executor. He'd loosened his tie and removed his jacket as soon as he'd entered the house, and now he sat on a stool in the white kitchen of the Lindsey home as a ceiling fan turned slowly overhead. Ramona had changed into casual clothes, a lavender shirt that matched her eyes and a pair of black shorts that matched her hair. She was so petite, so cute, so fetching, with her short little needles of hair soft as a pelt, her flawless teeth, her exquisite proportions. And she had what he wanted. He watched her stir an avocado and lemon juice and salsa into guacamole, and he felt tempted to go for it, but he restrained himself. He took a sip of Perrier—both of them had cotton mouth after that dreary party—and told himself to be patient.

"Mother was pleased that we went to the brunch," said Ramona. Moonie. What a terrible nickname, implying bare bottoms and Korean cults and calf-like stupidity. Completely inappropriate for such a bright woman. Girl. Whatever. She would be nineteen years old tomorrow. "It's always good to keep Ramsey happy. He'll take over the Arts Council in ten days, and that means he'll have a big say in the budgets for next year."

"The world is too much with you," said Chris Nivens. He took another sip of Perrier. "Let's skip the business arrangement between the Arts Council and the Arts School, if you don't mind."

Ramona grinned at him and tasted the green dip with a nacho chip. "Sorry," she said. "All we ever talk about in this house is money. Aunt Sarah was the only one who could ever get Mom to talk about literature."

Chris Nivens observed that such a phenomenon was strange, considering that her mother was the head of a school devoted to the arts.

"She used to edit a literary magazine, too," said Ramona. She pulled out the copy of *The Shenandoah Review* from where her uncle had stuck it under the telephone directory. "But even then, all she would talk about was how she needed more money."

Chris Nivens riffled through the pages and was not impressed: short stories and poetry by people of whom he'd never heard. "Why didn't she go into banking?"

"She loves art," said Ramona. "Painting, poetry, drama, dance, music. Photography, architecture, sculpture. She loves every bit of it. It's hard to explain. She loves the sense of knowing that she's made it possible to have art in Rockbridge. She likes to think of herself as a patroness. Like one of the Medicis.''

"Please." Ramona liked his tone. That was good. It might be easier to get inside than he'd figured. "She hired me anyway," he said. "That shows some discernment in taste."

"Don't start bragging yet," said Ramona. "She hasn't got the greatest taste in men." She told him about her father, who left when Ramona was five, and about the various suitors who'd come and gone over the years. "Then there was Alex Mason. Harriet Paxton's ex."

"Today's bride? Your mother dated her former husband?"

"Alex does the plays at the Arts School. You'll meet him. He's fun for a while. If you're ten years old."

This sort of small-town gossip was of no interest to Chris Nivens, but he played along. "She dumped him for your Uncle Oscar?"

"As I said, she doesn't have the greatest taste in males."

So Ramona didn't like Oscar Davidson. Mildly interesting, and another thing they had in common. "What do you have against Oscar?" he said.

"Nothing much," she said. "Except the way he's always reminding us of how much money he's got. As you know."

Nivens had told her of his encounter with Oscar in front of the house on the night of the fire. Nivens had driven back from the library about 10:30 P.M., maybe 11:00, in time to witness the end of the nightmare— the smoke, the steam, the flames, the lights, the noises, the lightning, and the cool cascading rain that did nothing but add to the damage. Oscar had met him on the sidewalk. "We had that leaky gas line checked," he'd said. "I am not liable." As though Nivens had cared about suing him. Money was irrelevant to Nivens. What mattered was his work, and except for the disks that he'd kept in his car, virtually no work of his own had survived. One of those remaining disks was, of course, his *A Midsummer Night's Dream* file, his most precious possession, a copy of which he'd carried with him in the car, another copy of which had vaporized in what was now the shell of a basement. He had worked so hard to fill that disk, to produce his essay, to do that research for Sarah, to help with her own analysis, and even if all copies of his essay had burned, he could still have remembered his argument and could have reconstructed his paper if he'd had to. He could not, however, reconstruct Sarah's.

The guacamole was good. "Your mother will be home soon, won't she?" said Nivens.

"Hard to tell with Anne," said Ramona. "She spends a lot of time at the school."

He left the literary journal on the counter, reached across, and rubbed the top of her hand with his fingertips. "How about what we came for?" he said.

She silently took his hand and held it as she walked around the counter to his side. Then she led him out of the room, down a carpeted hallway to a closed door. His heart began to pound. He couldn't help it. The anticipation was unbearable. In two years as a monastically serious graduate student, Nivens had learned not to act out, as the psychologists put it, not to put his impulses into actions. He was mostly successful, but occasionally he simply succumbed to whatever urge took him. On the night of the fire, for example, when they had told him that Sarah Davidson was dead, he had kicked the outside mirror off his car. Sarah Davidson had been more than his landlady. She had been like his parent.

Moonie opened the door at the end of the hall and led him to the gray filing cabinet behind the sturdy wooden desk in front of the window. She pulled out her key ring and produced a small key that released the locking mechanism in the filing cabinet.

"Here it is," she said. "Here are the archives. Everything Aunt Sarah ever wrote. Mom proofread it and then saved the manuscripts."

He gently pulled open the top drawer, felt it submit to his touch, and gasped with pleasure at the sight of the lovely files revealed inside. He ran his fingers lightly along the creamy tops of the folders, caressed the divider pages, clutched at the boxes of stationery in the back of the drawer. Four drawers, all of them full. It was better than treasure for an impoverished graduate student. The complete works of Sarah Davidson, all her secret pseudonyms, all her manuscripts. His fingers moved across the file tops with greater urgency. Nothing, nothing there, nothing here, nothing behind the divider labeled for this year.

And then Ramona cut him off by slamming the drawer closed. "You said you just wanted to look," she said. "Mom doesn't let anybody go through the archives."

He was ready to plead with her, just a little more, just a few more minutes, I was almost there. But she looked at him with such wry amusement that he could not speak. He was so frustrated that he was ready to push her out of the way and open the drawer anyway. Then she looped a finger through one of his belt loops and pulled him closer. She was almost a head shorter than he, and much lighter. Nivens was strong and fit and powerful. With her free hand she reached up and clutched the wavy dark hair at the back of his head.

"Come on," she said. "Can't you think of anything more fun to do till my mother comes home?"

"As a matter of fact," he said, "no." And he laughed along with her.

Chris Nivens drove back to his apartment on Madison Street at 5:30 P.M. still feeling a bit hung over. He was ashamed of himself for drinking so much at the wedding reception. Every sip of alcohol, delicious as it was, washed away a small clod from the continent that was his brain. Drinking to excess by a scholar made as much sense as a pianist taking a hammer to his fingers. And Chris Nivens was a scholar. He was. He'd gotten himself accepted to the graduate program at Virginia, and he'd kept his fellowship. He'd made friends with Sarah Davidson and had withstood the assault from those members of the faculty who had wanted to release him after a year, who had wanted to send him away with what they called a "terminal" master's degree, who had threatened to take away his funding. What Chris Nivens wanted more than anything else, what he had always wanted, what he had promised himself he would attain ever since his father had told him he was stupid for the thousandth time, was a professorship at a college. He had not seen his father for four years now, not since the fatal car crash that occurred during Chris's junior year at George Mason. When he'd received the phone call, when he'd learned that the car had flipped over and burst into flames, had heard that the body was charred almost beyond recognition, he had left school and had gone to the morgue to see it. And the last words he'd spoken to the shriveled black mass of gristle in that drawer were his promise to earn a Ph.D. He would do it for spite. He had said good-bye to his father that day, but he had not forgotten his promise.

Yet there were so many obstacles for him. When his work the first two semesters had been soft, when the committee had informed him that they could no longer renew his funding, when he'd heard that he would not receive permission to proceed in his studies toward the doctorate, he had gone to his landlady. His landlady and friend, his protectress, his fairy godmother. Sarah Davidson had spoken up for him, had told the others that he had promise, had taken him into her Shakespeare seminar, had requested him to work for her as a research assistant. He had received the department's endorsement to proceed. That Sarah, too, had turned on him in the end, that she, too, had decided that his work was not up to professional standards, had only renewed his determination all over again. He'd found another thesis adviser. He believed this was the year in which he had produced his best work, had finished his own monograph on *A Midsummer Night's Dream,* a study of the very play that Sarah had asked him to research for her. He was not bitter toward her for her betrayal. He never would have made it this far without her. She was, in a sense, still with him, considering that he was working for her sister, working with her husband, dating her niece.

And he was also looking for her lost manuscript.

Nivens had nearly defecated in his undershorts today when Oscar had announced at the party that he'd found it. Nivens had been certain that all copies of Sarah's last monograph had been destroyed in the fire. In the days after the blaze, he had searched her office at school himself—as a grader, he had a key—and had found no copies of her essay. He had not even considered the apartment here in Rockbridge, where Sarah rarely came during the academic year. She hadn't been out of Charlottesville since they'd started working on *A Midsummer Night's Dream,* with Nivens doing the research for both of them—for both his monograph and her own. As a result of that research, he'd always considered Sarah's essay to be partly his as well as hers. He'd been negotiating with her, in fact, for a partial credit in the byline. But before he dredged up all this old business, he wanted to study the essay that Oscar had found. It might be nothing but a draft of something she'd published years ago. There was no need to get himself worked up yet.

Still, there was something disturbingly bizarre about the manuscript that Oscar had been waving around at the wedding brunch this afternoon. Nivens had only glimpsed it, but from just a cursory reading of the opening paragraph, he was certain that it was not the essay Sarah had completed just before her death. It didn't sound at all like anything she had been working on all year. Anne Lindsey, however, had happily confirmed to the world that this was indeed the lost manuscript, the monograph she had proofread for her late sister back in early April, the analysis supposedly destroyed by the fire. Why would Anne Lindsey lie? He had hoped for a clue with his peek into the Lindsey archives granted this afternoon by Ramona, but those archives, whatever jewels they might contain, did not appear to hold a copy of Sarah's most recent monograph on *Dream*.

And now Ramsey Paxton, that hulking philistine soon to be head of the local Arts Council, wanted to publish this "lost essay" in the souvenir playbill for the Stone Mountain Theater. Such publication might be to Chris Nivens's advantage. But before that happened, Nivens wanted to see the text. He had done the research for Sarah's last essay; he had a pressing interest in what became of it. If the circumstances were right, he might even wangle a coauthorship credit without any risk to his own career. That career had to be paramount. And what bothered Nivens especially was the news that Oscar would submit this newly discovered essay to *Feminist Renaissance* for posthumous publication. Of all the hundreds of possibilities, why did Oscar have to choose that periodical? That was where Nivens had already made his own submission: "Love as Metaphor in *A Midsummer Night's Dream*," by Christopher Nivens. He had not yet heard from the editors, did not know whether they would accept his writing or not, and he did not want Oscar to foil him by sending a competing essay about the same play.

Nivens wanted that publication credit desperately as a résumé-builder for his career. It was apparently crucial to Professor Vita that he publish as well. He had met with Professor Vita only three days before the fire. He could remember the time (4:54 P.M.), the place (Wilson Hall at the university), and the atmosphere (paranoid and stressful). Vita, who was round and kindly and courtly and something of a pariah among the rest of the faculty because he liked to teach rather than to publish, had escorted out of his office another graduate student, a woman, while Chris Nivens had sat on the cold tile floor and waited for them to finish their meeting. The student leaving his office had hair straight down her back and red-rimmed, bulging eyes, and damned if Nivens hadn't seen a teardrop at the end of her nose. She'd been crying. *O spare me the fits of melancholia,* he'd screamed at her silently. Graduate school could drive anyone crazy. It was tough and unfair and pressure-packed and brutal. But the snivelers got no sympathy from Chris Nivens. Things were tough all over, toots.

Nivens had stood up and dusted off the seat of his jeans. Typical of nearly everything he'd worn in those pre-fire days, they were shabby but comfortable. The young woman clomped her way down the tile floor in some floppy clogs, and Vita, smiling like Santa Claus, motioned him into the office. Like the rest of Wilson Hall, it was claustrophobic and sterile. Books were everywhere, piled on the desk, on the floor, occupying the cold metal bookshelves against the walls. But the room was so modern, so devoid of personality, that it looked not so much like a professor's workroom as it did a temporary storage area for the library. Vita sat down behind the desk and pulled on his half-glasses. Then he searched for and found a typed manuscript of approximately fifteen pages. He laid it flat on the green island of blotter that held off the icebergs of books on all sides of his desk.

"I've read this," he said, "and the answer is yes. It's quite brilliant."

Brilliant. Not stupid. Brilliant. Suddenly Chris Nivens felt as though he'd been addressed by the angel Gabriel.

"You liked it," he said.

"I liked it very much," Vita said. "Frankly, I wasn't prepared to. Professor McMillan told me yesterday that everything of yours he'd read had been a hash."

That was typical of the graduate faculty, the way they could compliment you by insulting you at the same time.

"I didn't think you participated in departmental gossip," Nivens said. Vita was notorious for going his own way. "I didn't think you'd care if you weren't my first choice for adviser."

"I don't," said Vita. He was all business now. "I'd consider supporting a dissertation based on this premise. It's quite original. I'm surprised Sarah did not go for it."

He accepted the praise quietly. "We've agreed that it might be healthier for me to work with somebody else for a while."

"She's too busy to take you on," Vita said. "Is that it? She's got herself involved in too many projects."

"Not exactly," Chris Nivens said. "She claimed not to like it. I had to wonder if she was jealous of what I'd discovered."

The fire had occurred three days later. Two days after the fire he had been back in Vita's office, this time in stiff new clothes purchased with Oscar Davidson's money. Vita had called him in not only to offer condolences, but also strategy.

"Submit it immediately," Vita said. "If it's accepted by a significant periodical, it will make a great impression on the committee." He handed Nivens the monograph across his desk. Nivens placed it into his new briefcase, which was otherwise empty. Until the end of the term he lived in a motel.

"I'll need a couple of days," said Nivens. He had so much to consider.

Vita was sympathetic but insistent. He suggested *Feminist Renaissance* as a starting point. "Take a couple of days for recovery, then send it off to Chicago," he said. "You won't hear for months anyway. This strikes me as exactly right for them. It's clear that you've been Sarah Davidson's student."

"She taught me a lot," Chris said. Both he and Vita had attended the crowded memorial service at the university chapel that morning.

"She was politely interested when I mentioned it to her on Friday morning," Vita said. "I even let her take another look at it. This may be inappropriate for me to say under the circumstances, but she acted as though she regretted her earlier rejection."

"She did," Chris said. "She told me so. It was an awkward moment for both of us." He remembered the conversation that Friday afternoon vividly. The day before the fire. He was sorry that Vita had encountered her, had mentioned the essay, had shown her the copy Nivens had left with him. He regretted that she had re-read it and that she had felt compelled to bring it up in what turned out to be their last real talk before she died.

"Tinker a little," Vita said, "but send it in. Show the committee that you're a serious scholar. Not just Sarah Davidson's cupbearer."

Another insult. He felt his face go hot in the car just remembering the conversation. But he would prove himself this summer. He would see that essay in print with his byline at the top: "By Christopher Nivens." He could visualize it on the creamy page, if not in *Feminist Renaissance,* then somewhere, somehow. He had worked too hard not to steer it through to publication.

But it was nice not to have to think about graduate school politics for a while, to think instead that he'd be spending his summer teaching bright students in the Arts School. The sunlight on the buildings in downtown Rockbridge was orange as he passed through the last stoplight before home. He turned left off Madison, passed the dry cleaner, and pulled into the alley that led to the parking area for his building. He took the stairs up to the third and top floor, opened the door, poured himself some ginger ale, and stood by the bay window facing the street. It was a nice apartment, only four rooms and a bit dark, but with high ceilings and furnished with sturdy antiques. The teacher who lived here was in Spain for the summer. From his window he could look almost eye to eye with the big rectangular brick school that would employ him for eight weeks. Immediately to the right of the building was a parking area, bisected by a sidewalk covered by a corrugated metal roof, open on the sides. The sidewalk led directly to the side of an edifice almost as big as the school, though more square than rectangular, and much more ambitious architecturally, with false Gothic arches for windows and gargoyles lining the roof. It was the old Lyceum Theater, originally a vaudeville house, then a movie palace, and now the property of the Arts School. It looked grand and romantic in the lemony-orange light of late afternoon. Even as he watched, a man who looked like an ex-Marine emerged from the building with a can of paint, locked the door behind him, and followed the covered walkway only twenty feet toward the school building before he turned away from Nivens and entered the sole car in the parking lot. He drove off after gunning the engine, a noise Nivens heard faintly through the leaded glass of his window but could see easily because of the cloud of exhaust. That, he guessed, was Alex Mason, the drama teacher whose ex-wife married Ramsey Paxton. So it looked as though Alex might be a workaholic. Also a paint thief. Perhaps Chris should go down to his car and get his binoculars. There might be quite a drama unfolding in front of his windows this summer.

He would not speculate on the possible flaws of his new colleagues. Sarah Davidson was supposed to have taught at the Rockbridge Arts School. He would now be taking her place. He felt callous for enjoying the advantages of her death so immediately, but he had to admit the truth to himself: He was not so sorry that she was dead that he would not gladly accept the benefits. It was, after all, nothing personal. This was a professional decision, and nowhere was a place more coldblooded than a graduate English department.

He finished his ginger ale and returned the glass to the kitchen. Perhaps he should have stayed longer at the Lindsey home. The day, how-ever, had tired him. He would not be officially employed by the Arts School for another three weeks, when the summer session began, but he would start tomorrow as an observer in the classrooms. He tried heating some soup on the stove despite his utter lack of desire for food. Since the fire he'd had hardly any appetite at all, though the glimpse of Anne Lindsey's archives had made him, in one sense, quite hungry.

Nancy Gale Nofsinger pulled into the Blackburns' driveway at 6:57 P.M., and within five minutes she was in love. She was so excited when she got out of the car that she thought she might have to drive away to get something to eat first, but she fought the impulse. There would be all summer for eating. In the sunset, with coppery light settling over the city sprawled in front of her, with cicadas chirping in the trees, Nancy Gale crossed the drive and tingled with anticipation. This was where Patricia Montgomery lived. This was where Milton Blackburn lived. She admired the Tudor styling and the small, diamond-shaped panes of glass in the windows. It was just the kind of exquisite house she expected a theatrical family to live in. On her way up the flagstone walk she let her hand brush the big boxwoods that bordered the house. Part of her giddy mood, she knew, was exhaustion. She felt drained, and she ought to get herself unpacked and get to sleep. After she checked in with her new boss. And a snack.

She rang the bell and heard footsteps within. The door swung open, and there, in all his blond glory, was Tucker Blackburn, the guy she'd seen around the grounds, the one with the strong neck and the shoul-ders, the one she'd never been able to contrive a meeting with, the one whose name she'd learned from a friend, the one she would have pounced on if he hadn't been away from school so much this spring because of some accident, the guy who'd worn the cast on his leg. Tucker Blackburn. She'd practically ridden circles around him on her bicycle, but he was always with a pack of guys or some other girl. And she'd never, never even thought that such an inveterate jock would be associated with the theater. How stupid of her. How dumb. How stirring and wonderful it was to think that here he was, that the cast was off, that here in the flesh were that chin off a statue and those teeth you could wear around your neck on a string.

"Hello, Tucker," she said. He was just as surprised as she was.
"Spandex Lady," said Tucker.

Milton Blackburn sat with his wife and his younger son on their back patio at dusk and realized that they were arranged as if for a scene on the stage. At the round gray wrought-iron table, where the white stump of a candle flickered inside the clear glass chimney of the hurricane lamp, Blackburn stared straight out into the garden and the grassy hillside rising into the woods behind the house. To his right, with chair pulled out and away from the table so that he, too, faced the hillside, Richard sat and held his bowl of ice cream in his hands and between his knees, as though he had to protect it from them. Opposite Richard, to Milton's left, Patricia also sat with chair pulled out and pointed away from the house, away from Milton, sat and sipped her decaf coffee and noted aloud that the tulips had not lasted very long this spring. Had she not had the garden on which to focus, her position would have been utterly unnatural, as contrived and stagy as anything a clumsy, unimaginative director might have blocked for a cast of three. There they would be at downstage center, the audience sitting where the hillside was, the tulips and azaleas in the most expensive orchestra seats, the grass inhabiting most of the grand circle, and the trees and underbrush of the forest filling in the upper balcony. It had been years, he realized, since he'd done a play in a house with an upper balcony. Strange that it would come back to him now, as he sat here with his family, as dysfunctional as any group gathered in a Noel Coward scene, passing time before they had to get to the controversies, which would come very soon now that the meal was nearly over. Part of the awkwardness, he realized, sprang from the absence of Tucker, who had volunteered to go up the mountain with Nancy Gale Nofsinger, their new administrative assistant, to show her where she'd be living.

Richard's spoon clicked around the bottom of the emptying glass bowl of ice cream. The boy had eaten too quickly. Since he'd come home, he had been so quiet, so sad. Everything about his body suggested weariness, uneasiness, loss of spirit. Even the pine trees in the upper balcony would notice that it had not been a happy day for homecomings. What Milton Blackburn liked about directing was the sense of control he maintained over the pace and volume of a scene. He felt no such control over this one. Was there some cosmic observer now waiting to see how they'd read their lines, some watcher in the woods who had contrived to place the table here just so, who had whispered to Patricia and Richard instructions to open out the positions of their chairs? Did an invisible pen poise over the sheets of a supernatural legal pad in order to give them notes on their performance? Several years ago he had played Gloucester in a Stone Mountain production of *King Lear*. The words from his big scene in Act I had come back to haunt him so many times this spring already: *Love cools, friendship falls off, brothers divide. In cities, mutinies; in countries, discord; in palaces, treason; and the bond cracked 'twixt son and father.*

The bond between himself and Richard had started to crack months ago, January or so, when they'd first discussed Outward Bound. But it had been worse since Sarah Davidson's death. Patricia had told him about her visit to see Sarah on the day of the fire. The more he thought of her taking that trip, the more amazed he became. Why hadn't she simply called to protest over the telephone? But she was so furious over the death of Tru Lovinguth that she'd flown to Charlottesville and rented a car. Through Milton she quickly arranged interviews with some of the drama majors at the university, so that Stone Mountain could pick up her travel expenses as business. (Not even Ramsey Paxton could question the validity of her trip, since she actually ended up hiring Nancy Gale Nofsinger as this summer's expendable administrative assistant.) She even orchestrated dinner with Tucker, who was back at the university with his leg in a cast, and with Richard, who traveled from Montpelier School with his creative writing class to the Davidson home on Park Street. But the primary business on her agenda, the reason for her going to Charlottesville, was to confront Sarah Davidson.

She met with Sarah on Saturday afternoon, talked with her in that windowless basement office, where Sarah gently but firmly put off the questions about why Tru had to die. Thank goodness Sarah held firm and kept Milton Blackburn's name out of the conversation. She claimed Tru's death was best for the story line. But at age forty-five Patricia Montgomery had been in the business long enough to know that story lines could go any damn place the writers wanted them to go. She'd been very suspicious. And, when Milton asked her, she could clearly remember the electric heater in the corner of Sarah's office among all the clutter. Sarah's desktop consisted of an old door that rested on two short wooden filing cabinets for support, atop which sat the computer and disks, the loose books, the shelved books, the student papers, the stacks of mail. Sarah Davidson was an astonishing woman. If the investigators had not discerned that the fire had started from that faulty electric space heater, Milton Blackburn might have wondered whether she had spontaneously combusted, had burned herself out in a blaze of diligence.

It was unclear as to how long Richard had been downstairs in the basement that afternoon. He said it was only for a few minutes, but who could entirely believe what Richard said? He left the rest of the boys watching television in the library and wandered down to the basement laundry room, the large unfinished space between Sarah's office and Chris Nivens's apartment. He even intruded on Nivens, walked into his kitchen area from the laundry room door, interrupted the tenant at his work. It was Nivens who escorted Richard across the laundry room to the door of Sarah's office, where the discussion between the two women was about to conclude. What bothered Milton Blackburn was that Richard had seen the heater, too, and he'd remained in the office after Patricia and Sarah had adjourned their meeting and exited the office. Eventually Richard's absence from upstairs triggered a search by Oscar, who descended the stairs in annoyance and made such a ruckus upon finding him away from the rest of the group. (Not until later did they learn about the dead bird Richard had placed under the seat of Oscar's car.) But Richard lingered in the office alone for just a moment, and though he repeatedly denied to everyone that he'd even touched the heater, none of them was entirely comfortable with his answer. True, no one could recall noticing that the heater was on when Richard had left. But that sort of heater, with its glowing coils, took a moment to warm up. And why, after all, would a heater be turned on in April?

It might have started as a prank, an attempt to make the basement office uncomfortably warm. But it had ended in terrible destruction and death, and now Richard had been caught cheating in Oscar's class. Milton Blackburn knew enough about psychology to understand how a guilty conscience can lead one to perform acts that would result in punishment. And he wondered whether a dismissal from school was sufficient penance for the accidental death of a genius.

But there was that other troubling doubt, too. If the fire had been a true accident, then why had Oscar still not received an insurance settlement for the house? Why was it rumored that the Charlottesville police had not closed their investigation? What if they'd found evidence proving that it hadn't been an accident at all? For Milton Blackburn, the prospect presented a chilling dilemma. He would love to see his son exonerated from these vaguely whispered accusations. But what might he learn about Patricia? Milton knew his wife well enough to recognize one of her performances. Patricia was withholding something from him, some unknown bit of information since the fire. He had asked her about it, of course, and she had told him that she had no secrets from him. That statement alone had been an obvious lie. But he couldn't press her. He wasn't sure that he wanted to find out. And he didn't want to get into a discussion of trust and candor and openness with her. Milton Blackburn had a secret of his own.

"Coffee?" said Patricia. She held up her empty mug in an indication that she'd be going back for more. Both Milton and his son shook their heads without speaking. She stood up and walked barefoot into the house. After her shower she'd put on a green cotton peasant dress. Milton guessed it was the only article of clothing she had on. Milton fanned his chest by billowing the white pullover shirt he'd put on immediately after that awful wedding brunch. He flexed his toes in his sandals. It was time to begin.

"I've been talking to school people all day, Richard," he said.

Richard responded by saying nothing at all and placing his ice cream bowl gently on the table.

"Dr. Lane says that since you withdrew passing from your math and science and language courses at Montpelier, you may get credit for the courses just by passing the exams. We can get somebody here to supervise them for you."

Richard looked complacent enough. He was too pale and too thin, but his complexion and his eyes were clear. Blackburn had always thought of Tucker as the classically handsome son, but Richard at least had the makings of attractiveness, too.

"I can study for those exams," said Richard.

Good: he wasn't belligerent. "Your English and fine arts requirements, on the other hand—"

"Will require summer school," said Richard. "I figured."

Blackburn said they didn't want Richard at another boarding school. "We want you to stay at home this summer. I've arranged for you to have an interview at the Arts School."

"I'll do that," said Richard.

"You don't have to," said Patricia as she re-emerged from the kitchen. She carried her coffee mug atop a stack of thick, squat, gray-covered magazines, which she placed on the tabletop without comment before she sat down.

"No," said Richard. "I'll go."

"You know that Mr. Davidson will be there," said Milton.

"I'll go," said Richard.

"Alex will be on the faculty too," said Milton. "You've always enjoyed Alex."

Richard exhaled audibly, as though he were a mystic preparing for a trance. "May I be excused from the table?" he said. He left his napkin on the chair and went into the house. In a few minutes they saw the light in his room go on.

Milton spoke to the darkening garden as much as to his wife. It was still warm outside, even at 8:30 P.M. "We've had conversations that have gone worse," he said.

"He's still denying that he did anything wrong," said Patricia.

"I'm not going to force the issue now," said Milton. "He'll talk about it when he's ready."

Patricia Montgomery did not answer but rather pointed to the stack of periodicals she'd brought from the kitchen—old copies of *The Shenandoah Review*.

"What are these doing out?" she said.

He was grateful for the change of subject. "Anne Lindsey wants to resurrect the magazine," he said. "She asked me to support her request for more money from the Arts Council. I had to tell her that I could hardly remember it. But there they were on the shelf. Right next to *National Geographic*."

"Appropriate," said Patricia. "*National Geographic* is another periodical that everybody saves but nobody reads."

"I left them out for you," said Milton. "So you could remember your literary days."

She said that would be like remembering acne.

For a moment he thought the conversation was airborne, but then it thudded to the ground. "I just don't see why they had to kill Tru," she said.

Not again. "Look at it this way," he said. "You can be at home with us. You can do legitimate theater again. You don't have to get up at four o'clock in the morning.''

"I know," she said.

"You always complained when the show was filming. You always said you wanted to get back here.''

"I know.''

"So?''

"I wasn't quite ready to have my wish come true," she said. They sat in silence. "Did you know Alex is doing *Hamlet* this summer?''

"Insane," said Milton. "I'd never try that play with kids.''

"I asked about Gertrude, but I don't think he wants me.''

"Why wouldn't he want you?''

"I'd squelch his rehearsals," she said. "He'd have to act too much like a grownup with me around." She hesitated. "He did give me an idea though, Milton. I have an issue to discuss with you.''

Now Milton felt that curious mixture of uneasiness and anticipation. Whenever she had an issue to discuss, the result was invariably unpleasant, inconvenient, or expensive. But there were so many questions he had for her, so many matters about which he'd been afraid to ask.

"I want to direct the Shakespeare," she said. "I want to direct *A Midsummer Night's Dream.*''

"Seriously?" It was utterly out of character. "That's not your style, is it?'' Most members of the public thought of actors as flamboyant, extroverted, brassy, outspoken. But the truth was that for every Jane Fonda or Whoopi Goldberg, there were ten Patricia Montgomerys: people who disliked cocktail parties, press conferences, interviews, public appearances, and confrontations. When she was acting, she would do anything and say anything as her character. When she did Dotty in *Jumpers,* she took off her clothes. When they tried the all-female version of *Glengarry Glen Ross* at the Long Wharf, she spoke billingsgate and smoked cigarettes. But that wasn't really Patricia Montgomery doing those things. She had the opposite of stage fright. A stage was the only place outside her own home where she wasn't afraid.

"It would be the kind of stretch I need right now," she said. "I'll go to the library, I'll read the criticism, I'll study the stage history. I'll think it through. It will be magical.''

"Hell." He wished he had some water but didn't want to get up. "If you're looking for a stretch, why don't you try writing again?" He pointed to the stack of *Shenandoah Review*s in front of them.

"That was a flop," she said. "You don't want me to direct?"

He chose his words carefully. "You see," he said, "I've already thought through the kind of production I want, and I've talked with Jerry about the set, and I've picked the company for the parts they can play."

"I knew you'd say that," she said. She gave him the full effect of her green eyes in the candlelight. "That's why I waited so long to bring it up. I've been worried about this summer for almost a month. Ever since the fire. I need to direct the Shakespeare. I need a challenge. I need a project."

"You're already in Shakespeare," he said. "You're Hippolyta."

"I'll recast it. I want to direct."

"Okay," he said.

She didn't believe him. "You're serious?" she said.

"I'm serious."

"That was too easy."

"I'll give it to you," he said. "I've got too much to worry about already."

"Thank you," she said. She took another sip of coffee, and again the quiet descended. Even the cicadas were noiseless.

Milton wished they had some lines to run. Anything to cut the silence. "So what's this production of *Dream* going to look like?" he said.

"Happy. There's no melancholy in this play."

"Okay," he said. "What else?"

She waited a long time to articulate her answer. "It's a play about transformations," she said. "A play in which nearly everybody changes in some way or another through their encounter with magic. Bottom gets turned into an ass. Titania changes in her attitude toward her husband, the lovers change their allegiances, and even Theseus changes from a warrior to wed his wife in a more romantic key."

"I'm impressed already," said Milton.

"You should be relieved. It'll sell lots of tickets." Already she was eager to sink herself into the text of Shakespeare, into the play that would establish a new boundary in her career, into the apprenticeship that, if successful, might allow her to leave her family again for greener, more lucrative, more challenging pastures. Milton Blackburn knew that he'd just given his wife an opportunity to keep herself distracted. He wondered if she could do it. And he had to decide immediately whether he wanted to see her succeed as a director, or whether he wanted her to fail.

Behind them they could hear the faint music of *The Phantom of the Opera* coming from Richard's room.

Patricia Montgomery took a sip of coffee. "You'll need to talk to him again, Milton. By yourself."

Milton saw the first firefly of the summer floating above the lawn. "He'll be here for three months," he said. "We'll have the summer together. A lot can happen in a summer."

The firefly landed on a geranium and extinguished its light.

"I'm glad she's dead," said Patricia.

The comment confused him. "Tru Lovinguth?" he said. "You mean you've—"

"Sarah Davidson," she said.

Oh, yes, he thought. *Of course. And you can't imagine how much gladder I am than you are.*

❧

It had never occurred to Nancy Gale that the Stone Mountain Theater would literally be on top of a mountain. A short mountain, but still enough of one to have a road that started to wind back and forth on itself as soon as you left the residential section at the foot. She followed Tucker's car up the twisting route to the top and fumbled for a Wet Wipe from the packet on the seat beside her. At the crest of the hill, when the road finally flattened, she came out of the tree line. For a moment she had to blink her eyes in their sudden exposure to the strong, rich rays of the sunset. She had entered the most beautiful world she had ever seen, a world illuminated by the sunbursts of Turner and the neon colors of Gauguin. The road led for a couple of hundred yards through a small picnic ground, where the wooden tables alternated with black metal streetlamps, and across a grassy, hilly lawn to a building perched on the hillside overlooking the valley below, where the city sprawled like Atlantis. The Pinnacle Inn, home of the Stone Mountain Theater, was an L-shaped, three-story wooden structure with a covered veranda running all around. The clapboards were yellow, the shutters and trim an elegant maroon, and the dark slate roofing shingles a deep gray going to black. Caught in the orange sunlight, the beams glinting

majestically on the windowpanes, the building beckoned like a romantic tavern from another century.

As her car drew nearer she could see that the Inn did not lean out
over a cliff, as it had originally appeared, but that a long grassy lawn
fell gradually away on its far side down the mountainside. She followed
the dirty Toyota in front of her and tried to remember whether this was
public or private property. There was something about how the railroad
leased land to the local Arts Council, which then allowed the theater
troupe to rent from them. Who cared. Tucker Blackburn was so gorgeous. She followed his car another hundred yards and took a fork
leading to the right-hand side of the building, where there was a small
parking lot. They parked side by side, their cars facing a raised concrete
platform that led to a large garage door. She got out of her Saab and
entered the warm May air.

"The real parking area is up there," Tucker said. He pointed behind
them, toward a wooded area farther along the mountaintop. "We can
park here at the loading dock to get out your luggage." On the loading
dock, accessible to the parking area by three concrete steps, an old
metal canister of gasoline and some tools sat against one wall.

"Is someone here?" she said.

"Shouldn't be," said Tucker. "But don't worry. You won't have to
spend the night in the building by yourself. I'll be here."

Let me have him just once, she thought, *and I'll never eat another
doughnut again.*

The Pinnacle Inn. Nancy Gale was in one of those time-travel
adventures.

"This is the scene shop entrance," said Tucker. "We'll go in another
way." She followed him up to the wooden veranda and turned right,
toward the valley. The view here was spectacular, starting with the
darkening lawn that sloped down the hill for a hundred yards to the
tree line. To her left, where the trees began, sat a white concrete amphitheater, looking in the fading daylight like a vision of something
from Greece or Rome. Beyond the amphitheater a thick border of forest
stretched all the way down to the city. And below the woods was
Rockbridge itself, its lights and roads spread up and down the valley
like a secret empire. There were more mountains in the distance. Already a few stars had appeared in the royal blue sky.

Tucker unlocked a double door in the center of the building, then entered and disappeared into darkness. She heard the clicks of light switches inside and saw spotlights illuminate the gates to the amphitheater. Small lamps at knee height lit the way down a path from the Inn to the outdoor theater.

"Our house is directly in front of you," said Tucker. "It's a half-mile straight down the mountain beside the trail."

"What trail?" said Nancy Gale.

"There," he said. She could just see the opening in the trees about fifty yards to the right of the amphitheater. *Show me,* she thought. But instead he steered her inside. The Pinnacle Inn was bigger than it appeared outside. High ceilings, round globes in the lamps, brass door-knobs, burgundy floral carpeting, a broad staircase just in front of them. Nancy Gale felt a sexy, giddy thrill.

"You don't have to show me everything tonight," said Nancy Gale. "Just the essentials."

If his grin were any wider, he'd be decapitated.

Immediately to Nancy Gale's left were two new metal doors, one opening into the interior wall, the other, propped open by a wooden wedge, leading straight down a dark staircase. Tucker started with the door in the wall. "Backstage," he said. "Soundproofed, supposedly." He tugged on the door, which opened with a pneumatic whoosh, and limped his way into the darkness. Then he found a switch and turned on the worklights. By contrast with the ivory walls and plush carpeting of the hallway, backstage was stark, a solid black. The ceiling rose perhaps twenty feet into empty fly space. Beyond where they stood in the right wing, the small stage thrust its way into more darkness.

"House lights, too," said Tucker. He twisted a rheostat on the wall, and the auditorium came into view.

It was charming. Or rather it was going to be charming. He showed her where the seats would go. "All black upholstery," he said, "even the armrests for the seats. Chairs on three sides of the stage." He pointed out the glass windows of the light and sound booths across the back and indicated the path of the two aisles, which would come in at diagonals from the corners of the room.

"It's so small," she said.

"Three hundred seats," he said.

"It's so intimate." She could have stepped from the edge of the stage into the lap of someone sitting on the first row. The stage itself seemed scarcely bigger than a badminton court.

"This room was once the lobby, the dining room, and the kitchen for the old inn," said Tucker. "A year ago it was a bunch of little offices."

She sat down on the dusty new wood of the stage. "Couldn't we wait here for a minute?" she said. "There's just so much potential in this one place." She flashed him her best smile, and he bounced one right back at her.

"Don't you want to see downstairs?" he said. "The laundry room, the costume room, the dressing rooms, the props storage area, the green room?"

"Sit down," she said.

He sat next to her with his scarred leg sticking out straight on the stage. His baggy gray shorts allowed her to see the blond hair on his good leg. She could even get a peek at his green boxers. "I'm ready to go to work right now," she said.

He tapped the sides of his shoes together, the way guys did sometimes if they had some spare energy to burn. "We have to clean out the green room tomorrow," he said. "The workmen stuffed it full of old props during the renovation."

He was so cute. "Okay," she said. "Then when do I start on the administration part?"

Tucker looked at her with an amused sympathy that started a gyroscope spinning inside her. "You'd better understand," he said. "I'm an administrative assistant, too. I cut the grass. We'll be doing everything. Costumes, props. Helping the custodian. I'm the groundskeeper. And you're the house manager. That means you're in charge of concessions, working with the cook to order food for the cast, and living quarters. We're the slaves on this plantation."

"So you'll help me with everything?" she said. She hoped she didn't sound too much like some damn belle.

Tucker didn't hesitate a bit. "Sure," he said. "We'll get together a lot."

She checked the expression on his face. "Starting when?" she said.

❦

The King of the Pranksters was exhausted. It had been the longest day he could remember, starting at Montpelier in Lane's office, and now ending up here. His parents had not yelled at him, and it wasn't until after the non-yelling that he realized how braced he'd been for a scene. But it was as though all of them, Richard and his mother and his father, had instinctively avoided any kind of hostility. He knew why. It was because they were all afraid of discussing more than they wanted to be revealed.

He lay on his bed with the ceiling light glaring into his eyes like an interrogation lamp, but he was too tired to get up to turn it off. On his headphones he played the soundtrack to *The Phantom of the Opera*. When his father entered the room, Richard knew that he should have turned off the light and closed the door and pretended to be asleep. But he lay there with his eyes open and watched his dad close the door behind him. It was time for them to have their real talk.

It was a meeting that Richard regarded with equal portions of hope and dread. He'd been hating his father for months now, and he was tired of the part. He kept trying to forgive him, wanting to forgive him. But he couldn't. On his feet his father still had on those damn plastic flip-flops he loved to wear in the summer. His father immediately turned out the ceiling light and turned on the softer desk lamp in its place. Then he sat down on the opposite bed. Neither Richard nor his father spoke. There were times when they used to talk about everything, when Richard could laugh about something Tucker had misspelled, and Tucker would laugh, too, and then he'd stick one of his gym shoes over Richard's mouth and nose and tell him to breathe. When Richard was a little kid he would talk to his dad about the way the girls at school wore bras even when they didn't need them, about how he wanted to be a famous actor, about how he was going to take over the Stone Mountain company someday and run it with Tucker and have nothing but world-famous stars in the company. He would ask about why his mother was away so much and why they never took a normal vacation to the beach like other families. He'd protested when they'd wanted to send him to boarding school, but he'd gone, because his dad had said that it was best for him. He and his dad had talked. Now they didn't. Richard wouldn't participate. He would leave the room or he would answer in monosyllables or he would shout and break something. He had spent fifteen years of his life loving his father and not even one year hating him.

His father reached over and turned off the tape of *The Phantom of the Opera*. He held in one hand the same periodicals Richard's mother had carried out to the dinner table tonight, all with identical gray

covers. Richard pulled off his earphones. Here it came. That was the
signal for conversation to begin.

"I thought you might like to see these," said Milton. He handed
Richard the magazines, five of them. *The Shenandoah Review*. It looked
very boring.

"Why would I want to see those?" said Richard.

"Mrs. Lindsey was the editor. If you're going to attend her Arts
School, you might want to see the kind of work she likes."

Richard took the magazines and dropped them onto the top of his
desk. "Thanks," he said.

"If you don't want them, I'll take them back to the study. Your
mother once had hopes of contributing to that publication. She used to
try a little fiction."

Then Richard could see what he was doing. "So since we're on the
subject of fiction writing," he said, "why don't we talk about my honor
violation? Is that the idea?" What a cheap opening. He could not permit
himself at any moment to lose his temper.

"That was the idea," said his father. "I guess it was a bad one."
He took a minute to stack the magazines neatly on a corner of Richard's
desk. "Maybe I could start this scene over?"

Richard didn't say anything. His father stared at him. Richard stared
at the floor. His father looked away first.

"What happened to the posters?"

"I threw them away," said Richard. "I'm sick of them."

"And the bedspreads? Did you throw those away, too?"

"They're in the dresser."

Dad nodded as if he agreed with the decision. "Richard," he said,
"should I send you to a therapist?"

Boom. That was not what he had expected. "Lane's been talking to
you," said Richard. "You think I'm crazy."

"I think you're my son, and I love you. And I want to help you get
out of whatever rut you are in."

You got me in it, thought Richard. *You cannot get me out. Thank
you so much for the offer, though.*

"Dr. Lane suggested that we have you tested for drugs."

Richard was overwhelmed by how far off base they all were. "I'm
not on drugs, Dad." He couldn't even drink a beer without puking.
The thought of drugs was ludicrous.

"I've never thought you were. I'm just telling you what it's come down to. You've just been tossed out of school for a completely un-characteristic act. You're withdrawn. You lie around the house. These are classic signs of depression.''

Whoa, what do you know, a diagnosis. "So," said Richard. "You want me to go to Western State? You going to have me fitted for a straitjacket?''

"You're going to the Arts School, Richard. But I wonder if you should get some counseling this summer.''

"No," said Richard.

"I may have to insist.''

"You may have to fuck off, Dad," said Richard. "You got that?'' He made it so easy to get mad. He set himself up. Richard couldn't resist the temptation. "If you'd just stop insisting on so many things, maybe everything would be a lot better.''

"What does that mean?''

"It means what I said.''

"Give me an example. It's not my style to push you, Richard. I don't think I've forced you to do what you didn't want to do.''

"You did last March.''

At least his father didn't sigh. "That's true," he said. "I insisted that you try the Outward Bound program. Is that what this is about? You made it quite clear that you did not want to go. And you've made it quite clear again and again that you resented having to.'' It was his mother's idea. She'd met somebody whose son and daughter had both done the program. Outward Bound was supposed to help your self-esteem, help you grow up, make you more mature. And Richard supposed it had taught him a little about how much he could endure physically. But he'd hated it, hated the vision quest business, hated being away from all the action, hated having to turn down a trip to Florida with Ralph Musgrove and some other guys from school. And he'd asked his father to intervene on his behalf, and his father had said no. He'd told Richard to go. On the night before he had left, Richard had left the water running in his bathtub and flooded it. He'd let the air out of his father's tires. He'd unplugged the freezer in the basement, which was one of his pranks they hadn't discovered for a week. He had done plenty to punish his father for making him go. "It was only for two weeks, Richard. Is that what's destroyed fifteen years between us?''

"It's been other stuff," said Richard.

"It's been everything. Richard, it's been everything I do. I can't do anything to suit you. I can't communicate with you. And school. Your life at school has gone to hell this year. I can't ignore all that, Richard. I want to help you."

"You can't."

"Why not? What's wrong, Richard? What's happened?"

Richard waited a long time before he spoke. "You should have controlled me more," he said. "You should have raised me so that I wasn't so bad."

Milton Blackburn wondered whether he was at last going to hear a confession. "This business at Montpelier, Richard. Was this some sort of punishment for me and your mother?"

He had said enough. "What difference does it make?" said Richard. "I've told you the truth. You don't believe me."

"It's not quite that simple. I want to believe you. I want to believe everything you've said. I want to be able to walk up to Oscar Davidson and punch him in the nose for manufacturing a plagiarism case against you. But when I look at what I know about Oscar, and when I look at what I know about you, I can't believe you, Richard. You've deprived me of the opportunity. And I find that very upsetting. You will be living at home this summer, Richard. You will not be permitted to get your driver's license. You will give me a chance to recover my faith in you. I resent its loss."

Richard knew that the options were not negotiable. No driver's license still. He'd be thirty years old and still unable to drive. The old King of the Pranksters would have worked himself into a rage over that announcement. Most of Richard's friends had been driving for months now. But Richard was too tired to argue. He'd thought for a minute there that the old fire still burned, but it had been just a flicker.

"Let Alex be my counselor," said Richard. "Or Tucker. I don't want to go to some stranger."

Dad didn't know how to react. "We can start with them," he said. "Show me some signs of improvement, Richard. We'll put the professional counselor on hold." It was a concession that Richard would have appreciated if he had allowed himself to feel gratitude toward his father.

"If I get into the Arts School," said Richard, "I will show you what I can do."

It was such a beautifully ambiguous piece of wording. He would sleep tonight. He would rest. And then he would start to plot his revenge on Oscar Davidson, on Lane and the Montpelier crowd, on his parents, on them all. Only Tucker would be exempt. Tucker had had enough already.

❧

For Tucker, the whole tour was surreal, a living fantasy. It was Spandex Lady herself, here in the flesh, summoned up by some magical spell as soon as Moonie had deserted him. She smelled so earthy. She looked so inviting. He throbbed with desire as he took her back into the hallway and showed her the kitchen, new and shiny, with a space beside the sink still empty. "No dishwasher," he said. "In the meantime, Dad bought us some Ivory liquid."

At the end of the hall were the public rest rooms, the offices, and the rehearsal studio. The box office was not much bigger than a closet. The main office, for Milton Blackburn and a secretary, was small and cluttered, more crowded than it should have been because it had a safe the size of a small refrigerator in one corner. The new beige carpeting had to be cut around the black metal block.

"Left over from the railroad," Tucker said. "We couldn't move it, so we left it." He showed her how the door to the safe would swing closed but would not lock. "It's completely worthless for security. I'm lucky Dad didn't ask me to live in it." *Stop babbling,* he thought, *just ask her to lie down across the top of the safe with her feet on the floor, her back on that cool metal.* To distract himself, he kept moving and talking. Next to the office was the rehearsal room. "Used to be the old library of the Inn," he said. "We kept the fireplace. Unfortunately, we also have a few support columns to dodge." They saw the high ceiling, the shuttered windows, and the three wooden pillars that would interfere with movement.

From there it was upstairs to the living quarters. The stairway was open up to the top step, where it ended at a metal door marked PRIVATE, which led into the dormitories for the company. There were fourteen bedrooms ready for occupancy. Eight baths, most of them shared. "We're in the men's wing now," said Tucker. "The women's wing is your way to your room, but the men should have no reason to walk through yours." *Except to see you,* he thought.

It was very hot upstairs. He explained that there wasn't enough money for air-conditioning the living quarters yet. "The vents are here, but we need another unit to handle the load," he said. "We're looking after the public areas for the moment." She used her hair to fan the back of her neck. The decor was simpler here, no floral carpeting, but rather the industrial beige they'd seen in the office below. The doors, however, were handsome, of recessed wood and fitted with old-fashioned glass doorknobs and old-fashioned keyholes with keys in the locks. Tucker pointed to the second room from the end, Room 8.

"This is my room," he said. "Some people have to share a bedroom, but since we're administrative assistants, we get private ones. I have to share a bath. But you get a private bathroom, too."

They returned to the top of the stairs, opened another new metal door, entered the women's wing, and stopped in front of Room 4. Tucker turned the key in the lock and handed it to her. "Go ahead," he said. "You're home." The room was simple and clean—a small box with pale yellow walls, a hardwood floor, a single bed, a new dresser, two lamps, a closet, two windows. It was even hotter than the hallway. Tucker managed to get both windows open for her. He was sweating when he finished.

After carrying her luggage upstairs from the loading dock, they drove their cars up to the big public lot, fifty yards from the Inn. The lot was not paved, but was simply a flat area of mountaintop, cleared of trees and covered with grass. The breeze was cool and fresh.

"It's large enough for four hundred cars, I hear," said Tucker. "We've never had that many. Maybe this year." Nancy Gale could hear the hope in his voice, and she thrilled to be a part of the team. It was full night now, but the air was full of moonlight and starlight and lights from the city below. The trees blocked her view of the Inn from here. It was like waiting on a landing strip for a flying saucer. She was here on a lovely plateau, alone except for two cars and Tucker Blackburn. The place was so quiet and so beautiful. So many stars overhead. A light, sweet breeze lifted her hair. She felt as though she ought to take off her clothes. But she didn't.

"There aren't any muggers up here, are there?" she said.

"Not in this park," Tucker said. "You could go across town and find some.'' The path from the lot to the Inn was paved and lighted. They saw no one on the short trip back. Nancy Gale stood on the veranda in the moonlight while Tucker gave her a key to the front door of the Inn.

"The key to your room is still upstairs," he said. "You'll probably never need it. I don't lock my door."

She locked eyes with him in the moonlight.

"I ought to check back in at home," said Tucker. He received her message. "Eventually."

"Well," said Nancy Gale. "I guess it's time for bed."

It was not so much a matter of running up the stairs as it was flying, moving faster than Tucker had moved in months, not really touching the runners or putting his weight down on the floor, not aware of any limp or pain, cognizant only of Nancy Gale's hand as she pulled him along. And Tucker thought foremost about how he could remove his clothes most efficiently, and then thought of how smooth her skin was against his in the moonlight, and then thought of how urgently, crucially important it was that they get this done now. And then, for a little while, he thought of nothing at all.

Afterward, when he left her room, Nancy Gale locked the door, remade the bed with clean sheets, and took a long shower. Then she turned out the lights, stood by the open windows in her nakedness, and breathed the night air. She could unpack in the morning. This was going to be a very strange summer, she thought, as she opened the bag of pretzels and popped a few into her mouth. She looked out on the moonlight catching the white amphitheater and the dazzling lights of the city below as she ate. She finished half the bag of pretzels before she went to the bathroom for some water, which she drank at the window while she finished the pretzels. As she ate, she heard the door on the floor below open, heard the unmistakable limp of Tucker Blackburn climbing the stairs. She noted with pleasure that he opted for his own room and not a return to hers. There was a time and a place to indulge every sort of appetite. She folded the empty bag carefully and placed it into the bottom of the simple trash receptable by her bureau.

Then it was time for her to throw up.

Ramona Lindsey was dreaming about Sarah Davidson when her mother woke her. She'd fallen asleep in the den with a book in her lap. All that alcohol in the afternoon at the brunch had lifted her into giddiness and then dropped her into slumber. Her mouth tasted dry and her head faintly ached. It was dark through the windows outside. She checked her watch. A little after 10:00. The house had been quiet all evening except for those two times the phone rang with nobody on the line when she answered. She hated that kind of call. She'd heard that it meant some burglars were checking to see whether you were at home before they came over to rob you.

"Moonie," said Anne Lindsey. She jiggled Ramona's leg, and Ramona became irritated.

"All right," she said. "I'm awake. I wish you'd call me Ramona."

Her mother still had on the same clothes she'd worn to the party. Ramona could smell wine on her breath. "Have you been in the archives tonight?" said Anne Lindsey.

Then Uncle Oscar was also in the room. He carried a glass of ice water in one hand and *The Shenandoah Review* from the kitchen in the other. He stood by the brass lamp next to the crystal figurines. The light from the lamp emphasized the bags under his eyes. His hair, unkempt and floppy, looked as tired as Ramona felt. "Have you?" said Uncle Oscar. "Have you been in the archives?"

"Yes," said Moonie. Ramona. She had to get into the habit of thinking of herself by that name. "Chris and I looked in for a second."

"Stay out," said Anne Lindsey. "And for goodness' sake, don't be taking your friends in there."

"Okay," said Moonie. She was awake now. She didn't understand what the big problem was.

"Especially not Chris Nivens," said Uncle Oscar. He had been drinking with dinner tonight, wherever they'd gone. Both of them had.

"Why not?" said Moonie. "I would have thought Chris would be an exception. The way he lived with you and everything."

"He was a tenant," said Uncle Oscar. "And he's like every graduate student, eager for success."

"He wanted to see Aunt Sarah's work," said Moonie. "I thought he was entitled."

"Nobody is entitled," said Uncle Oscar. "That includes you."

Her mother could see that they were sounding too harsh. "We just want to get Sarah's papers properly sorted out," she said. "They might have some academic value."

"Okay," said Moonie. She'd been delighted by Chris Nivens for so much of the day, so good-looking, so intelligent. But then he'd gone by 5:30. She wondered if he'd found her too immature, too shallow. He was obviously not interested enough to stay. She thought involuntarily of Tucker, then forced herself to dismiss his image. It was over with Tucker.

Uncle Oscar handed Anne Lindsey a glass of water. "We don't mean to fuss at you, Moonie," he said.

"Call me Ramona," she said. "I'm going to bed." She walked out of the room without touching either of them. This was not going to work. She was too old to be living at home. Nineteen years old tomorrow. The cake, just iced, waited in the kitchen. She should be living in her own place, or even in another city, off in Nantucket or somewhere with friends from school. It tortured her to stay here as a kind of crown jewel of the Anne Lindsey collection. And yet she felt a tiny thrill of pleasure at knowing that she lived in a house containing some materials that Chris Nivens might like to see. Those old files had been around for years, but she had never developed any curiosity in them until now.

※

Alex Mason dialed Anne Lindsey's number at 10:15 P.M. This time Moonie did not pick up the extension. Anne answered all by herself.

"Hello?" she said.

He let the silence linger.

"Hello," she said again.

He said nothing.

"Alex, I know this is you," she said. "Cut it out."

He was so startled to be named that he spoke to her. "Sorry," he said. "I'd just bitten off a piece of banana when you answered. I had to swallow it."

"I'll bet," she said.

"You might be interested in my news," he said.

"What's your news, Alex?"

He wanted to parcel it out. "It's about the manuscript," he said. "Sarah's manuscript has turned up."

Anne was openly contemptuous over the telephone. "I know that," she said. "I was with Oscar when he presented it to Ramsey."

"What?" Alex did not follow. He had not yet told her that he had the manuscript himself, that he'd just received it from Patricia Montgomery this afternoon, that it was in his car. She did not give him time.

"I was there," she said. "At the brunch. I already know."

"Oscar Davidson found a copy of the missing manuscript," said Alex. He couldn't believe the timing.

"Thanks for the news, Alex. Now can we stop playing with the telephone?"

He was speechless. She was not. "Next time, Alex," she said, "write me a note at school. I don't want you calling me at home anymore. Is that clear?"

He went out to the car to check his glove compartment. The manuscript was still there. He brought it into the house, and then he dialed the Blackburn home. Patricia Montgomery answered the phone.

"Alex," she said. "Well done. You're so efficient."

"So you heard?" he said carefully.

"Milton told me," she said. "I can't talk about this long. He's upstairs with Richard now, but he still doesn't know I kept the manuscript. All he said was that Oscar announced at the brunch today that he'd found it. Bravo to you."

"I thought you'd be pleased," he said.

"How did you manage?" she said. "You must have gone straight to the brunch after you dropped me off. How did you get it to Oscar?"

"Ah," said Alex. "You have your secrets. Let me have mine."

"I have to go," she said. "Milton's coming."

So they hung up, and Alex Mason found himself the sole possessor of a manuscript that nobody needed anymore. It was supposed to have been his great gift to Anne, his wonderful surprise. He was to have found it in his desk at the Lyceum this afternoon while he was cleaning out a drawer. But he'd been robbed of the opportunity by only a matter of hours. It was a magnificent irony, that yesterday the world had no last essay by Sarah Davidson, and now there seemed to be plenty. At least he got credit with Patricia for delivering it, even when no credit was due. Perhaps she could do him a favor someday.

He thought about throwing the text away, but he didn't. Anne's handwriting was still in the margins. Maybe he could pretend that she was writing those notes to him; he could read the essay and enjoy vicarious contact with her. Maybe he'd even find some more manuscripts at school and start his own collection. For fun he curled the whole packet to see if it would fit into the empty paint can, but then he decided that was silly, and he uncurled it again. Ramsey's appointment to the head of the Arts Council made him nervous, and so he had taken the paint can from the theater this afternoon when he'd left. He would keep it at home for a while.

By 11:00 P.M. Sunday night Alex wore nothing but his underwear shorts. He saw himself as Jim Palmer, modeling underwear in a magazine spread. Everyone told him that he had the face and the body of a thirty-year-old. Fine. Now if he could only live the life of a teenager. He had been to bed and had gotten back up three times tonight already to check the can again. It was in his kitchen, on the table atop some newspaper. The inside of the pail was dry now, not even a hint of dampness. But so what. He wasn't going to be able to pack it until tomorrow at the earliest.

He sealed the lid on tight, then placed the can among the cleaning materials beneath his kitchen sink. It would be safe enough there, and easily portable if he had to move it in a hurry. Now it felt safer. Now he could go back to bed. Now he could turn his attention to more productive activities, like how he would handle the gravediggers' scene in this summer's production of *Hamlet*. Alex loved working in the theater. It was such a manageable world. He had so much control there, unlike this world, where his life was so remarkably unpredictable. Real life was a terrible place to spend a lot of time. It was a place where, no matter how hard he worked on his tapestries, somebody else, some unnamed other, seemed determined to unravel them all the way back to thread.

❈

At a minute before midnight, Ellen Spencer sat up in bed and startled her husband. "The house is on fire," she said.

He lay beside her under the blue striped sheets and held a book under his reading lamp. "What house?" said Matthew Spencer.

"We've got to get Paul," she said. She jumped out of bed and began to search frenziedly through the drawers of her bedside table.

"What are you looking for?" he said. The long green T-shirt she wore as a nightgown looked good with her red hair. He closed his book and watched her with half amusement, half sympathy.

"The key," she said. "The key to the basement office. He's down there. Paul's down there."

"We don't have a basement office," said Matthew.

"It's on fire," she said. "We have to get him out."

"You're dreaming," he said.

Then she woke up. She caught herself kneeling beside the bed, saw the expression on his face, noticed the open drawers. "Damn," she said. She shut the drawers and rolled back onto the bed. Matthew dropped his book and massaged her shoulders.

"It always happens when you stay up the night before," he said.

"This one was so real," she said.

"Tribulations of the lady cop," said Matthew. "I'm going to tell all to the tabloids when you're head of the FBI."

"It's so embarrassing," she said. "It's so out of control."

He rubbed her shoulders. She relaxed.

"Tell me," he said. "Where's the fire?"

"It's all fading," she said. She rolled over toward him and looked at the ceiling. "We were up at the Stone Mountain Theater. You, Paul, and I. And they were doing a play about the death of Sarah Davidson."

"The Charlottesville woman," said Matthew.

"The dead professor," she said. "Only this time she wasn't dead yet. She was hiding upstairs at the Stone Mountain Theater, and I knew that, somehow. And I went up to the attic and found her there. She was nice. But she told me to get out, that the fire was about to start and that my son was downstairs in her office."

"Did she tell you her death was accidental?" he asked. "Or was she murdered?"

"Murdered," said Ellen. "In the dream, she was definitely murdered."

"By her husband?" said Matthew.

Ellen stared at the ceiling for a long time. "Yes, it was the husband, wasn't it?" she said. She stared some more. "I just wish I could remember why."

PART II

---❈---

A Midsummer Night's Dream

RICHARD dismounted from the city bus and started walking immediately toward the front of the school building. There was something morally uplifting about riding the bus. His father had offered to drive him to school every day, but he'd said no, he'd use his own money to take the bus. Penance was a pain in the ass, but at least it kept him out of the car and away from the sermonettes. Moreover, riding the bus gave him a chance to formulate his plans for revenge. He had already accomplished Stage One by enrolling at the Arts School. The problem now was that he had no inkling as to what Stage Two should involve.

Richard was experiencing a kind of psychological crisis, an inner conflict, a clash of two options. On one hand, he really wanted to stop being the evil, dark villain and become the hero. He wanted to change his reputation. He wanted to repent for his sins of the past without going through a full confession. He wanted to be good. So he'd thrown away all his dirty books and magazines (though he knew where he could get more at the bus station), cut his hair, and started to jog. He and Tucker were even fiddling with a way to set up a weight room at the Inn. On the other hand, he had lost none of his hunger to get even with Oscar Davidson. He wanted the man to pay for Richard's departure from Montpelier School, and he wanted him to pay till it hurt. Some little voice whispered that a true hero would not besmirch himself with more plotting and pranking and tricks, but Richard squelched the voice by arguing that Davidson was evil, that punishing the wicked was a true act of heroism.

The sun was hot and bright in mid-June. Classes had been going for a week now, and they were as bad as Richard had imagined. He carried a geeky little spiral notebook in his hand and a couple of pens out of sight in his pants pockets. It was weird to be going to public school again after all these years, though it wasn't really a public school, sort of public, but sort of not, and he hadn't known what to expect. Would there be bullet-dispensing machines in the bathrooms, or what? He wore shorts and a knit shirt, socks and his running shoes, which already looked tired. He exercised every day, and now that he was riding the bus to school, he'd be getting more exercise. The walk to the bus stop in the morning wasn't bad, because it was all downhill. But in the afternoon, after the bus dropped him off at the foot of Canterbury Lane, he had to walk all the way up to his house, and then he had to take the trail up to the theater. It wasn't that far, but it was steep as hell.

8:15 in the morning. That was another pain in the behind about riding the bus. He'd gotten up an hour ago. Fifteen minutes to get dressed and eat breakfast, ten minutes to walk to the stupid bus stop, five minutes to wait, and then thirty minutes to get here, when a straight shot in the car could do it in less than ten. Hell, he could jog it in thirty minutes. Maybe he would, if he noticed that the students here were bohemian enough not to object to his smelling like the inside of a jockstrap.

At the concrete steps to the old brick building he melted into a stream of students arriving for the homeroom period starting at 8:25. There weren't that many artsy-looking types, considering that the place was called an Arts School. Most of the guys wore clothes like his, and most of the girls looked like your normal everyday run-of-the-mill females, not rock star wannabes or models.

Except for Rebecca Taylor. He'd met her on the first day, the six-foot black girl in dreadlocks who'd bumped into him at the door when one of her friends got her laughing about a drawing in a magazine.

"Scuse me," she'd said. She was an inch taller than Richard. She was the tallest girl he'd ever seen.

"That's okay," he'd said.

"You got a big dick?" she'd said.

"What?"

"I said, 'you gotta be quick,' " the girl had said. "My apologies, white bread. What you playing?"

Richard hadn't understood anything she meant. She talked so fast. And she was so damn tall. Thin and tall.

"What's your instrument?" she'd said. "You're music, right? Drums?"

Then he'd caught on. "No," he'd said. "Writing. Composition."
You had to specialize in something at the Arts School.

"Com-po-si-shun," she'd said. Her friends, all of them white girls,
told her to shut up and come on. "I'm into writing, too," she said.
"I'm a playwright."

Then she'd disappeared, only to turn up later in both of his English
classes. The way the Arts School worked, you could specialize in two
courses—dance, instrumental music, voice, acting, dramatic literature,
composition and creative writing, painting and drawing, or sculpture.
Richard studied dramatic literature and creative writing. You also had
to do some kind of "lab" work after school related to one of your
courses, so Richard was working as stage manager for the production
of *Hamlet*. He didn't want to do acting, but he knew all about stage
managing. It wasn't so bad. And he liked working with Alex Mason,
who'd been in a bunch of Stone Mountain shows before and was maybe
Richard's favorite adult.

There were a couple of people he'd recognized from sixth grade, the
last time he'd gone to school in Rockbridge, but they clearly did not
remember him at all. His first-period class, which on the summer schedule lasted two hours, was English composition. There were eleven other
students in the class. Their teacher was Oscar Davidson.

That was the only reason Richard had signed up for the course. He
wanted proximity to his target. But what could you do to get revenge?
Life wasn't like some television show, where people pulled out a gun
and started shooting. Richard was willing to wait for his opportunity.
So far he had been the model student. He took his seat in the institu-
tional-gray classroom with the dark tile floor and spun his notebook on
the surprisingly clean desktop as he waited for the bell to ring. Rebecca
Taylor appeared in thirty seconds and took the seat next to his. She
had beads in her hair and wore sandals with gladiator thongs. It had
taken him almost an entire day after meeting her to realize that she was
nice and not scary. After she sat down, she pulled a tangerine out of a
paper bag.

"You want some breakfast?" she said. She pulled off part of the
peel and offered Richard a wedge.

"I've eaten," he said, but he took the slice. The tangerine was sweet
and good. She offered him her paper bag and told him to spit the seeds
into it. Her eyes looked faintly yellow this morning, and she winced

when she ate the fruit herself. Richard asked her if she felt okay.

"Fine," she said. "Just sleepy. I had to work till ten last night." She worked at a discount store in Rosalind in the evenings. "Then I stayed up reading this."

She pulled a book out of the stack on her desk. It was *Sally Galloway* by Oscar Davidson, a bright red jacket with the name in purple script, and a drawing of a dark-haired woman staring straight into your eyes. "I hate to tell you," she said, "but it's pretty good."

Richard took the book from her and opened to the first page. *For Sally Galloway the smell of peppermint always brought back memories of that first Christmas at Belle Isle.* He read the rest of the opening paragraph and leafed through the short opening chapter.

"You see?" said Rebecca Taylor. "It grabs you."

"I think it's boring," said Richard, but he had to admit that he'd like to know more about Sally Galloway's first Christmas at Belle Isle. As he returned the book to her, Davidson came into the classroom with his briefcase, saw them with the tangerine, and made them throw it away. What had been interesting to Richard this week was to see how quickly the others in the class had caught on to Davidson's garbage. Rebecca Taylor gave him as much hell as Richard ever had at Montpelier. Davidson had already tossed her out of the room once for disrespect and had given her zeroes on half her assignments.

"Mr. Davidson," said Rebecca Taylor, "can we skip journals today?"

"No," said Davidson. It was like a conflict between a tedious documentary on black-and-white television versus a three-dimensional color video. Davidson was so damn dull. The white shirt, the blue trousers, the sleeves rolled up two turns precisely, the dark tie, the hair parted down the middle as if he were Dylan Fucking Thomas or somebody, while Rebecca Taylor had a scarlet scarf on her head, a rainbow dress, dangling turquoise earrings, and her beads. She was funny as hell and smart, too. In fact, everybody in the class was pretty damn smart. Smart enough to catch on to the fact that their teacher was worthless.

"Let's start with some sample fiction," said Davidson. For a second Richard felt the panicky lurch of being unprepared, but then he remembered that it wasn't his turn until tomorrow. Every damn day, the exact same routine. Two people were supposed to bring a sample of some other writer's work to read at the beginning of class. It was supposed to inspire everybody or something, but what it did, as everybody in the class recognized after three days, was to eat up the clock so that Davidson didn't have so much work to do. Tomorrow Richard and Rebecca Taylor took their turn.

"Which one of you would like to read?" Davidson asked the two students responsible for today. Peter Nance raised his hand. He was a guy Richard did not know very well. He was very quiet and serious. New plaid shirt, little string necklace visible through the open collar, lizard skin watchband, short dark hair, very tidy handwriting that looked almost like print. He was okay. The guy cleared his throat, kept his notebook flat on the desk in front of him, and clasped his hands below, out of sight.

"The air is still and cool," he read, *"and it is not yet ten o'clock in the morning, and yet already my palms are moist as I begin what I hope will be the best summer I've ever experienced. Some people suffer from allergies, others from acne, and still others from bad luck. A good portion of our population has a propensity for finding every banana peel tossed onto the sidewalk. My particular curse has always been the sweaty palm. For as long as I can remember, my hands have betrayed me whenever I've been excited or nervous, regardless of the temperature. I have to fold a piece of paper to use as a blotter sometimes because my hands have started to gush so much. When I was younger, I thought that I'd been cursed, damned by an anonymous god who had wounded me in the spot I most wanted to be healthy. And yet I've come to appreciate my malady. I like to pretend that the perspiration flowing from my hands is the water that will nurture my writing. I like to think of myself as providing my own irrigation system for my imagination, so that I can carry with me always the materials that will sustain my prose as I pursue my goal of becoming a writer. This morning, for example—"*

He read for five full minutes. Richard watched Davidson, whose eyes were focused on nothing. The teacher wasn't even listening. Richard got Rebecca Taylor's attention and pointed to Davidson with a quick jerk of his head. She caught on immediately. When Peter Nance finished, Davidson just said the usual—"Very nice. Any reactions?"—and almost went ahead with the journal writing assignment, since there were never any reactions. But this time Rebecca Taylor raised her hand.

"I liked the metaphor of the fishbowl," she said. There had been nothing about a fishbowl in the passage.

Davidson hesitated. You could see that he didn't know how to play it. "Yes," he said finally. "That worked very nicely." Yes. They had him.

Richard raised his hand. "It seems weird that Charles Dickens would write about a fishbowl." There had been no indication that Dickens was the author of the piece, but no matter. Richard's comment was just the kind of line the guy loved. "You think that Americans in the twentieth century are the only people who enjoy keeping aquariums?" he said. "Why should a fishbowl be such an oddity in Victorian England?" It was almost too easy.

Everyone else in the class understood what they were doing and started to help out.

"That was from *Great Expectations,* wasn't it?"

"The description of the piranha was cool."

"I couldn't follow the rape scene."

"When he pulled out the machine gun, I thought I was going to faint."

Until even Davidson realized that not all that stuff could have been in the passage. "Okay," he said. "We've got some comedians in the class. If you can't take a passage from Dickens seriously, then perhaps you need some extra homework."

Peter Nance, who had sat quietly through all of it, raised his hand. "The passage wasn't by Charles Dickens," he said.

But Davidson was quick at backpedaling. "I never said your passage was from Dickens," said Davidson. "I just told the class that it was sad if they couldn't take Dickens seriously. In case somebody ends up reading from Dickens later on." It sounded so lame. "Yours was much more modern. Obviously twentieth century. Was it Joan Didion?"

Peter Nance said that he wrote the passage himself. Richard was awed. *Propensity. Nurture. Malady.* The polish, the phrasing, the metaphor. He regarded Peter Nance with respect and a little pity now. Here was a boy with some real talent. And he had to get Oscar Davidson as a teacher. Sure enough, all Davidson could focus on was the negative.

"You were asked to read the work of somebody else," said Davidson. "You didn't do the assignment."

Rebecca Taylor raised her hand. "Seems to me it's harder to write something—"

"That's enough out of you," said Davidson. He went on in the typical lecture about observing policy, blah blah, do as you're told, get busy with your journal writing, don't forget about your homework. He turned it all back onto the students. And the one area of class that Davidson didn't hesitate to exploit was homework. In one week they had already read the entire text of *A Midsummer Night's Dream* and had started on *Hamlet*. If you signed up for composition, then you were automatically placed in the dramatic literature course as well, the theory being that the literature would give you something to write about and the writing would make you a better reader. Richard suspected that it was a holdover from the days when Davidson's wife taught the literature course and teamed up with her husband. This summer the teachers were having orgasms over the fact that two Shakespeare productions would be available this summer, so the students were naturally going to read the plays and write about them before they saw them performed. Richard would be sick of both productions by the time they finally happened.

"For tomorrow," said Davidson, "keep working on the draft of the essay you're writing on the Shakespeare play. You'll turn those in to me on Friday."

"Why to you?" said Rebecca Taylor. "The assignment is for Mr. Nivens."

"We're team grading," said Davidson. "You know that."

It was such a bite. Their teachers were grading every major essay twice—Davidson for form, Nivens for content. They had the first one due next week, but they had to turn in rough drafts beforehand. For grading.

"We can write about anything?" said Rebecca Taylor.

"Anything intelligent you have to say about *Hamlet*."

"Mr. Davidson," said Rebecca Taylor, "we're writing about *A Midsummer Night's Dream*."

"Fine," he said. "You'll be writing about *Hamlet* eventually." You couldn't tell with Davidson whether he really didn't know what the assignment was—which was hard to believe, even for him—or whether he'd been genuinely confused. He was so skilled at evasion.

"And don't forget to write in your journals the answers to the questions I gave you."

"Oh, Massa Davidson," said Rebecca Taylor to Richard but loudly enough for the teacher to hear, "let my people go. These journals are getting downright boring, honey."

That was enough for another minilecture. Then Davidson went too far. "A scholarship student ought to show a little more gratitude for the chance to be here. We aren't paying you to be rude."

You bastard, Richard thought. A student's financial status should never become an issue in class. Rebecca Taylor didn't show that he'd rattled her, but she did pull out her notebook and started to write without speaking. Davidson unfolded his newspaper and told the rest of the class to get out their journals and get busy. The look that Davidson gave them was so venomous that even Richard looked away. The class turned silent. Richard began to write in his notebook—something mindless, pointless, dull, safe. While he wrote, he glanced up at Davidson, who stared at the newspaper flat on his desk. Richard knew he wasn't reading. He would be brooding over Rebecca Taylor. And while Richard wrote about summer humidity and thunderstorms and other boring crap, he waited patiently for an idea.

❧

Patricia Montgomery took her legal pad and her books and her pens to the backyard to work. It was too warm, yes, but it was also sunny and bright and alive with growth, as opposed to the chill, air-conditioned shade inside. Milton had done well with the lawn this spring after Tucker's accident had left such a scar on the hillside. That was one remarkable quality about places. You could let them collapse and go wholly to seed. But they were always renewable. The dustiest lot, littered with broken glass and weeds, could become a playground again in time. The landfill could become a park; the graveyard, a garden. A place could survive almost anything.

It was people who were so fragile. For four months her son Richard had been desperately unhappy. Tucker, by contrast, could cope. Tucker was the one to whom it had happened, and Tucker, therefore, had retained his sense of himself. He knew what he was bearing, and he knew that it was bearable. But Richard, almost like a masochist, seemed to be the one whose pain they could not assuage. It was as if he wished the damage had occurred to his legs, as if he could have been the victim, as if he resented Tucker for getting hurt. Richard must have envied the attention and the admiration Tucker enjoyed, as well as the way his brother responded to trouble. Richard's problem, she knew, was that he was scared he'd be found wanting if he ever got put to the test.

On the warm surface of the thin grille tabletop she looked over her line breakdowns for *A Midsummer Night's Dream* and reviewed the rehearsal schedule for the morning. There were only eight scenes in the whole play, but that meant some would be very long, with lots of entrances and exits and miniature scenes to schedule for rehearsal. Multiple marriages, swapping of love partners, a bungled production of *Pyramus and Thisby,* a magical herb, invisible fairies. The mischievous Puck. How did Shakespeare ever sort out such a plot?

From what Patricia had read—and she'd read a lot—this play was one of the very few for which no one could find an earlier source, aside from the Pyramus and Thisby myth in Ovid. It was, in a sense, one of the few plays Shakespeare had not plagiarized, though no one in the Renaissance would have understood the concept of plagiarism had they heard it. For Shakespeare and his contemporaries, the world was full of wonderful stories already. It was up to the playwrights and poets to write them down, or re-write them, re-tell them until they got them right. Surely, Shakespeare would have said, we don't have to stoop to making things up. In his day, the word "original" meant that a work was based on an identifiable origin, as opposed to springing fresh from one's own mind. There were even those who claimed that the man from Stratford named William Shakespeare was not even the author of the plays, that the very name Shakespeare was a pseudonym used by the Earl of Oxford. According to the Oxfordians, the world's greatest playwright borrowed one man's name and other people's stories. But whoever it was who wrote these marvelous plays apparently did invent the plot of *Dream,* in one of his earliest explorations of the relationship between theater and reality. Milton came outside with a cup of coffee. He had on a dress shirt with no tie and casual slacks—his work clothes.

"You don't want to change your mind?" he said.

"No," she said. "I've got to do this."

He sat down at the chair across from her. "The two most difficult elements in directing—"

"I know," she said. How many times had she heard it? "Knowing what you want and being able to explain what you want. I know what I want in the show."

"I have no doubts about that," he said. He took a sip of coffee and waited for her to address the unspoken obvious. She had to admit that so far she had struggled to explain her vision to the cast. Directing was terrifying. And exhilarating. She had no lines to memorize, no character to assume. She was instead telling others where to stand and how to read their lines. She liked it. She enjoyed seeing a scene take shape. It was just that she had such a difficult time conveying her impressions to the actors. With some of the experienced ones, like Radley Smethurst, the task was not so difficult. Radley could take Helena and deliver instinctively what Patricia wanted. But the younger ones, the novices like Hugh Bickley, were game but becoming increasingly frustrated by their failure to satisfy her and by her failure to articulate her wishes. From the first day, when they'd read through the text and made their cuts, Hugh Bickley had not been able to grasp her reading of the text.

"What do you mean by baggage?" he'd said.

"Baggage. Luggage. Material to carry around. Portable prop-erty."

"You mean literal or figurative?"

"The literal is the figurative," she'd said helplessly, and wondered how anybody could make sense of her groping for clarity. But she kept trying. "We have all the troubled characters carrying around their psychological baggage," she'd said. "Only it will appear as real baggage to the audience. Theseus has a hangup about war, for instance. He'll carry a sack with him until he gets to the woods in the fourth act, where he'll have it taken from him by the fairies."

"Isn't he the duke? Why would the duke carry his own luggage?"

She was convinced that it would work. Titiania and Oberon are fighting over the custody of a child. They have their own baggage carried off by Bottom. Demetrius is carrying a torch for Hermia. Helena loves Demetrius. The characters could represent all such concerns through sacks or pouches or backpacks they carry until their problem gets resolved. Through the various encounters in the woods, the principals free themselves of their psychological problems. She wanted to use the setting to her advantage, with lots of exits up and down the aisles and from behind the boxwoods. They would string white Christmas lights in the trees and the bushes behind the stage for the final scene when the fairies invade the palace. It should look lovely. But her actor doubling as Theseus and Oberon couldn't handle her interpretation.

"I will be more assertive today," she said to Milton across the table.

"Do you want me to come down again?"

"No," she said. "Let me try it alone. It's going okay."

"Why don't you try some more physical exercises with the cast?" said Milton. "A little screaming and shouting could loosen them up."

Get mad at your props, she thought. *Scream at the scenery.* She knew lots of devices. "Maybe we should spend a morning on warm-ups," she said.

"We're a bit behind schedule," he said. They opened in four days.

"We'll be ready," she said. "I know I can do this. Let me try it, Milton. I need to try it."

He would not renege on her now. "Of course," he said. "It will be marvelous." And even though he looked her square in the eye when he said it, even though his voice remained hearty and strong throughout his speech, the twitching of his fingers betrayed him. He didn't think she could do it. He didn't think she could get the play out of her head and onto the stage.

"I'm going to surprise you today," she said. "Today we're going to have a breakthrough."

He barely listened, rather stared at the hillside in front of them. "We could get a good price for this house," he said.

She put down her pen. "This house is your inheritance," she said. "No. We've poured enough money into the Stone Mountain Theater."

"We're so close."

"Leave it up to the Arts Council," she said. "It's their responsibility to find the money."

"They aren't looking," he said. "Ramsey told me yesterday that their first priority was the Arts School."

She resented having to give up her morning with Shakespeare to discuss money. "Be patient," she said. "We've got enough for the outdoor theater. The indoor theater can wait until fall. Let's think about art for now."

"You can't have art without money," said Milton. "Don't tell me you don't know that."

She knew. "How bad is it?"

"If we had to pay our cast anything, we couldn't go up," he said. "Construction on the inside of the Inn has stopped, with the stage unfinished. If we don't make money with *Dream,* we don't complete the season."

"We are not selling this house," she said.

"I just think Ramsey's unwilling to siphon any more money into

Stone Mountain because he sees it as our personal toy. If he believes that we're really sacrificing—''

"We've sacrificed," she said. "I've got enough money for us to live for the summer. If we had to pay Richard's tuition at Montpelier, then I'd have to get a job." She hesitated. Neither of them had stated what both of them knew: that Richard's departure from boarding school had been much to their financial advantage. "Would you like to see me selling cars on Channel Ten?" A local advertising agency had asked if she would do some commercials for Rockbridge businesses. She had turned them down.

"I want you here so you could have a real job in a real theater," he said.

"And if we're a hit in the amphitheater this summer," she said, "we can finish the stage inside the Inn."

He sat in the sun and imagined what it would be like to have their money problems solved. "What about the Consultants business?"

"I'll try anything," she said. "Though I see the Consultants as a nickel-and-dime kind of money-maker as long as we're tied to Rockbridge." She didn't like the way that sounded and tried to soften it. "I think we're better off investing in this show."

"Okay," he said. He tried to smile. "After all, we do have four days."

She did not smile in return. "A lot can happen in four days," she said. "You'll see."

※

Ellen Spencer sat at her desk at the police station and looked over O'Shea's notes again. She'd read them a million times. It sounded like a very sad accident. Sarah Davidson had died upstairs in her bedroom, lying on her bed fully clothed, lying on top of the bedspread, as anyone might. She'd been wearing earphones, so that she couldn't hear the smoke detectors. Perhaps she had even fallen asleep. She had left an electrical heater on downstairs in her office, and the heater had caught a poster on fire, and the flames had fallen onto some papers on the desk, and the wooden filing cabinets had caught, and then the house had gone. With the help of the leaky gas pipe in Chris Nivens's kitchen. It would be so easy to write it off as an accident if it weren't for the gas part. And yet Nivens had complained about smelling gas in his apartment earlier in the week. They'd had it checked.

She read it all again. She had to commend O'Shea for the thoroughness of his notes. He had everything down, even the names of the books by the dead woman's bedside: novels by George Eliot, Amanda Cross, and Ellis Bell. Sarah Davidson had been reading a historical romance by Emma Prynne when she died. Ellen Spencer had read that book herself. She'd enjoyed it. Knowing that Sarah Davidson had read it made the dead professor seem more accessibly human. She wasn't just a reader of scholarly materials, but of down-to-earth, regular books. It would be very nice to explain how she had died. Or whether anyone had killed her. O'Shea's files provided no help except for an extensive list of suspects.

Patricia Montgomery had gone back to her hotel after dropping her son at the Davidson home after their dinner together. She had stayed at the hotel for the rest of the evening. The hotel was on the downtown mall, about a mile from the Davidson house. The average person can walk a mile in twenty minutes. But then how would Montgomery get into the house? She could have rung the doorbell. Davidson would have let her in. So Montgomery is going to have an argument in front of several witnesses in the afternoon, then walk back that night in an area where lots of people could see her and recognize her, and kill Sarah Davidson because she wanted to stay on a soap opera? Ellen supposed it was possible, but try to sell it to a prosecutor.

Then you have Nivens, who has access to the whole house through the basement. He could easily get into the office, turn on the heater, go upstairs and kill Davidson, then run back to the gym, where lots of people saw him. But why? Both Nivens and Sarah Davidson have written essays on *A Midsummer Night's Dream*. Nivens wants his essay published and figures that *Feminist Renaissance* in Chicago would be a good starting point, since it's published the work of Sarah Davidson in the past. In fact, it's to his professional advantage to be associated with her. So why would he kill off Sarah Davidson? To eliminate his competition? That would leave him only a couple of thousand other Shakespeare scholars to go. He could burn up all his clothes, his books, and his belongings, and kill the woman he'd worked with for two years, kill the woman who had bought him an extra year of funding from the English department. For what? Because she hadn't liked his essay?

Because she'd told him to find another thesis adviser? Which adviser he had, in fact, found? No, no, no.

O'Shea had even attached a copy of Nivens's essay: "Love as Metaphor in *A Midsummer Night's Dream.*" Ellen was not a Shakespeare scholar. She looked it over but didn't find much of interest. The title itself seemed to have nothing to do with the opening paragraph or anything else, but then when did they ever? Nobody really read these damn things, did they? And just this morning she'd received from Oscar Davidson himself a copy of his wife's last essay, the one everyone had thought was missing. It was also about *A Midsummer Night's Dream,* but there the resemblance to the Nivens monograph stopped. "The Bottom of the Dream," this one was called, "by Sarah S. Davidson." Damned if it wasn't just as confusing and convoluted as the one by Nivens, though on a completely different topic. She could remember in college reading studies of literature by professional critics, and she didn't think the experience or the clarity of the essays had improved since she'd graduated. It was as though these professors all used the same coded words for communication, a language that only other Shakespeare specialists would understand. But she could follow them well enough to see that the essay by Nivens and the essay by Sarah Davidson took two different approaches to the play.

She called Charlottesville and, by some miracle, found Casey O'Shea at his desk. "Tell me about Nivens," she said.

"The tenant," said O'Shea. "A nice guy. Very serious about schoolwork. Only child, very independent. Parents divorced when he's a kid; the mother gets custody. She leaves him some money when she dies a few years ago. So he's not hurting financially, though he's not rich. He sure as hell didn't gain anything from the fire."

She was more interested in a detail of the insurance claim filed after the fire. "Davidson told the insurance people that Nivens would have been moving out in June," she said. "But Nivens claimed to be planning to live in the basement for another year."

O'Shea said he didn't see any significance.

"The significance," she said, "is that Nivens was apparently unaware that his landlord expected him to move. Oscar Davidson says Nivens was to be leaving the graduate English program and moving out of town. Nivens and this Professor Vita in Charlottesville say no such thing."

"So why would Davidson want the basement empty?"

"It's where his wife kept her office," she said. "Would Davidson need for some reason to get rid of a possible eavesdropper?"

They couldn't find anything worth pursuing.

"And what about the headphones?" Ellen said. "Sarah Davidson was reading with her headphones on."

"Because she was a slow reader," said O'Shea. "She listened to a tape, and she read the text along with the tape."

"Yeah," said Ellen. "But this note says she was reading a historical novel called *Scottish Queen Mary* by Emma Prynne. I called a local bookstore. That title isn't available on tape."

"You can get tapes of any book," said O'Shea. "Companies record them for anybody who will pay."

"But we don't know whether she had such a tape or not," said Ellen. "It melted."

"It gets to you, doesn't it?" said O'Shea. "It's hard to let go."

"I'm watching," she said.

"Somebody is bound to screw up eventually," said O'Shea.

"Yeah," said Ellen. "I just hope that it isn't me."

She hung up and looked at the advertisement in today's newspaper.

GRAND OPENING

STONE MOUNTAIN THEATER

SUMMER SEASON AT THE PINNACLE INN

A MIDSUMMER NIGHT'S DREAM
by William Shakespeare
June 20–July 12

MAN AND SUPERMAN
by G. B. Shaw
July 15–August 9

THE SECRET GARDEN
(Rockbridge Premiere of the New Musical)
August 12–30

TICKETS STILL AVAILABLE FOR GALA OPENING NIGHT
COCKTAILS AND DINNER BEFORE THE PERFORMANCE
Sponsored by the Rockbridge Arts Council
Ramsey W. Paxton, Chairman

Special Souvenir Program Featuring the Last Written Work
of Rockbridge Native Sarah Stewart Davidson

Sarah Davidson again. *She's everywhere,* Ellen thought. Her name seemed to be everywhere you looked.

It was almost as though she were still alive.

❧

Associate producer of the Stone Mountain Theater. It had sounded so glamorous. Nancy Gale Nofsinger had even been naive enough to think that she might have her own desk, if not her own phone extension or her own office. Instead she turned out to be nothing but an overworked slave for Milton Blackburn and his awful wife. She had to live in a room that stayed as hot as a catalytic converter and served as some sort of convention center for houseflies. Plus she had all those chores. Rearrange the props room. Wash the dishes. Make sure there were plenty of light bulbs in the halls. Answer the phone. Mail these letters. Take notes on the blocking for this scene.

And the strange part was that she loved it.

The reason was Tucker Blackburn. She got up at 7:00 in the morning to ride her bike, and, by the time she returned, Tucker was likely already to be working. She'd be back in an hour, and he would have already spiked off the rehearsal space for the day or swept the veranda or carried a new light down to the amphitheater or ridden that mower he used on the hillside every week. Tucker was such a piece of work, like a modern centaur out there on the mower with his shirt off, or, when he dismounted, like what's his name, the god that limped, Vulcan. She timed it so that she'd arrive for breakfast when he did, just after 8:00, when the sun was still so bright and the air wasn't so terribly hot, but she'd still have a glow from her biking, and she'd sit on the bench in that little staff dining room and sip on one little eensy weensy glass of orange juice and maybe nibble on half a banana (she knew

how phallic a banana could look if you handled it the right way, but
she thought resorting to that sort of cheap device was tacky), while
across the table Tucker would still be puffy-eyed and sort of puppy-
looking with his hair unbrushed and his face so smooth or, on some
mornings, just glinting with little golden stubble on his cheeks, and she
would talk very casually about last night's rehearsals or what a workaholic his father was or how talented his mother was (she usually left
Richard, the little brother who was your basic pest, out of the
conversation).

And Tucker would grin and respond. It didn't take Nancy Gale long
to realize, however, that she was not the only female in the dining
room to whom he paid attention. He'd keep his eyes on Nancy Gale
for most of the time, but then there would be those little darts, those
glimpses, those slips when he thought she wouldn't notice. It was obvious that he was conscious of that mousy, pouty little whiner they'd
hired as the cook's assistant. She was an infant, only nineteen years
old, a stumpy little dwarf (well, no, but compared to Nancy Gale), and
just as cool and businesslike as a whore off-duty. Nancy Gale had spent
the first two days thinking Tucker was calling her "moody," which
was certainly appropriate, but then it turned out her name was Moonie,
a nickname for Ramona, isn't that cute, isn't that just charming for that
short-haired child who needed a stepladder to reach the second shelf
of the pantry and who repeatedly gave Nancy Gale orange juice that
hadn't been properly shaken, and she knew the little bitch was doing
it on purpose. Moonie—who insisted that everyone call her Ramona—
would sigh and whimper and generally act as though she'd been having
her period for a solid decade and would pay no attention whatsoever
to Tucker, whereas here was Nancy Gale right across from him with
the sweat trickling down her bare top into her very nice cleavage
(which she knew he noticed), while Tucker would pretend to be talking
directly to Nancy Gale as his eyes jumped back and forth to follow
Ramona around the room like she was about to pay his allowance.

On Monday, when Ramona was clattering plates on the other side
of the partition, Nancy Gale asked him about her. "She's so sweet,"
said Nancy Gale. "I mean, she has such a sweet face."

"Yeah," said Tucker.

"Has she worked here before? You seem to know her so well."

Tucker said that he'd known her a long time.

"But I wonder why she seems so unhappy," said Nancy Gale. "She just seems to stay in such a bad mood."

"Her aunt died a couple of months ago," said Tucker. "I think she misses her. Remember Professor Davidson?"

Stupid bitch, she ought to be in rehab or something and not spoiling everybody else's mood up here. Nancy Gale knew that it didn't have anything to do with a dead aunt. It was Nancy Gale herself who triggered Ramona's foul temper. Ramona was jealous of her success with Tucker. That had to be it. Of course, Nancy Gale could never say so.

"I don't think she's acting this way just because of the fire," said Nancy Gale. She had to whisper now because Ramona had stopped making noise in the kitchen. "She acts like she's sick."

What do you know, she'd finally said something that got Tucker's attention.

"She doesn't want to work here," said Tucker. "She's just doing it because she doesn't want to let down my dad."

"I mean lovesick," said Nancy Gale. "Doesn't she have a boyfriend?"

Tucker was not happy. "Yeah," he said. "She dates one of Richard's teachers."

Then why, Nancy Gale wanted to scream into the rafters, why why why didn't she get herself a job down at the Arts School?

"You ready to leave?" she said. She finished her watery orange juice.

"Not yet," said Tucker. He had a quarter of a muffin and a thoroughly plundered grapefruit rind on his plate. He was acting a little cool this morning. Maybe she should start letting him spend the whole night with her. But she didn't want to wake up next to him—to see him drool or to smell his sour breath. She didn't like to sleep with somebody else in those little beds.

"See you for lunch?" she said.

"Okay."

Before morning rehearsal she ate a package of Oreos in her bedroom. But today in the bathroom, after the usual ritual, she found another fly. This time, however, she heard it enter, heard its buzzing at the ceiling. She looked up at the acoustical tiles and spotted a small hole, the diameter of a pencil, through which she could see daylight. That wouldn't be the roof, she realized, but another floor. The attic.

She returned to the hallway and approached the life-sized portrait of Sarah Siddons that hung at the intersection of the hall leading from the men's wing to the women's wing. Enclosed within a large, rectangular gilded frame, the painting depicted the actress wearing a long silky gown and pointing her index finger at some unseen object to her right, her face registering surprise and horror. Nancy Gale pulled the hinged portrait aside to reveal a modern metal door behind it. Tucker had shown her how to reach the attic on their second night. There was no knob on the door, but only a deadbolt lock, which she opened with her passkey. Beyond the door was a staircase, which she mounted into greater and greater heat. It was stifling up here. The floors were plain wood, the walls chipped plaster, and the windows smaller than those on the floor below. A series of rooms, most of them floored simply with beams opening onto ceiling tile for the rooms below, led off the hallway. In that hallway were a couple of cans of paint, a broomstick, two cinder blocks, and some lumber, including three large sheets of thick plywood.

At first she assumed they were construction materials abandoned when the Arts Council under Ramsey Paxton decided to delay further construction on the Inn for a year. Then she noticed the small round fan and the long extension cord among the materials. Maybe somebody was concealing some inventory from this Ramsey Paxton. All she ever heard people here talk about was money, money, money. If money was god, then you'd have thought Ramsey Paxton was Satan himself. Any time there wasn't money to do anything, the litany of Ramsey Paxton complaints began. She'd only seen the man a couple of times, but he seemed pleasant enough to her.

She found the hole over her bathroom in one of the unfinished rooms off the hall. This room had no floor, either, but it did have the beginnings of one, some plywood sheets over the rafters. The ceiling was angled sharp but rose to a high peak at the roofline, and an open beam ran clear across the width of the room. With some redecoration and some ventilation, it might make a nice Alpine-style bedroom. Carefully crossing the unfinished floor, she saw that the beginnings of a bathroom were roughed in over her own bath. Resting on one of the floor joists was a half-eaten ham sandwich. Several flies buzzed in the air. And there in the floor—in what would be her ceiling—was a little hole. She didn't like the idea of a hole. She dragged one of the sheets of plywood from the hall across the room and into the bathroom area, where she found it was too big to lie flat on the small floor. The hole still remained.

She looked around for a scrap of paper with which she could pick up the sandwich, but the place was clean except for the sandwich itself. Finally she picked it up with two fingers of her left hand—fingers that never went down her throat—and took it with her to the floor below. She locked the door behind her and closed the Sarah Siddons portrait back to its guardian position. This floor was actually cool in comparison with the attic. Then she went to her bathroom, threw the sandwich into her toilet, and washed both hands carefully. After they were clean, she dabbed a small bit of toothpaste onto one finger. Climbing onto the toilet seat, she sealed off the hole with the white paste. It worked all right. If she saw anyone going up there, she would have to make other arrangements. For now, however, her domain was sealed off. It was time for morning rehearsal, and Patricia Montgomery did not like for her to be late. Tucker Blackburn was easy company. His mother, like nearly every other female Nancy Gale knew, was a bitch.

❧

Rehearsal this morning took place in the amphitheater because the air outside was still cool enough. Patricia Montgomery assembled the company at 10:00 A.M., a crew of fourteen eager young actors, most of them recent college graduates, a few of them undergraduates. Though the sun was bright, the white concrete retained its nighttime chill and dampness, protected by the shadows of the boxwoods. Tucker had the hedge clippers out for the boxwoods this morning while Patricia prepared the group to run the scene. The show opened in four days. By this point they should have been able to speed through their lines in triple-time, but they were so uncertain of themselves that you would have thought it was their first day off-book.

And where was her stage manager?

Nancy Gale Nofsinger showed up at precisely 10:00, just as they were beginning Scene 2 of Act IV, when Theseus and Hippolyta come upon the young lovers sleeping in the woods. Nancy Gale pulled out her pen and her legal pad and sat silently beside Patricia, who chose to ignore rather than to glare. Little Miss Nofsinger still had not learned that she was to arrive early for a 10:00 call. The girl was enthusiastic and diligent enough, she supposed, but Patricia Montgomery did not like her. She was not sure of whether she disliked Nancy Gale for her scrupulous clock-watching or for her obvious interest in Tucker.

Hugh Bickley, who doubled as Oberon and Theseus, stood obediently on the stage with the actress playing his queen and the actors of his entourage behind him on the stage. He wore shorts that ended below his knee, high-topped basketball shoes with no socks, and a Washington and Lee sweatshirt with the sleeves cut off. He carried an empty pillowcase. He ran across the playing area, and Patricia Montgomery immediately stopped him. This was pathetic. How could Milton have hired a kid this weak for a company known for its high standards? He had the looks perhaps for a young lover, but not for a king. Hairless hands, huge black eyes, head slightly large for his body. He was handsome and earnest, but too intimidated by her demands.

"Let's try this again," she said. As an actress, she never minded a director who asked her to repeat a section, so why was she so self-conscious about directing someone else to do the same? She'd promised Milton that she would be more assertive. They were running out of time. She pointed to the chunks of scenery that her tech crew had carted down this morning. "You enter between the rocks there. Don't step into that spot. That's going to be the pool for our waterfall." She got the young lovers to lie down in their spots again. Hugh Bickley entered to center stage, and she stopped him.

"No," she said. "Not those rocks. These. There isn't room between these others. That bag you're carrying is going to be huge."

They tried it again. "Okay," she said. "But remember that what you're carrying is heavy. That's part of the comedy."

"Like this," said Bickley. He let his shoulders slump.

"No," she said. She had to think herself into carrying something that weighed a lot. "It's more in the legs." She took the empty pillowcase from him and lugged it across the stage. It appeared to weigh a ton.

The other performers watched them in silent impatience. Even Tucker at the back of the seats had stopped his snipping with the shears to watch their work.

"Make it look heavy," she said. It was so damn easy to do, so difficult to explain. Richard could do it by instinct when he was five years old. Hugh Bickley tried it again, his legs clumsily pounding the smooth concrete.

"Okay," she said. "That's coming. We'll work on it ourselves this afternoon." Everyone present could see that it was not coming at all.

She tried a different direction, lining everyone up on the stage and telling them to imagine an invisible box in front of them. "Get angry with it," she said. "Kick it. Pick it up and shake it. Throw it as far as you can." It didn't go very well. So then she tried talking to them about the various dreams encountered in the play. It was easier for her to talk about the text than about their individual performances.

Always lurking in the back of her mind, however, was the reminder that they opened in four days. The scenery wasn't finished. The costumes weren't done. Their light bulbs had not arrived. The programs hadn't even gone to the printer yet. The actors were listless and uncertain of themselves. Her Puck was shaky with his lines. Her Oberon and Theseus couldn't handle his props. Four days.

Then Milton walked down to announce that Bernard, their cook, had just resigned.

"Why this time?" she said. They'd worked with Bernard for years. Resignations from Bernard were as frequent as full moons.

"Pilfering," said Milton. "He says he's sick of getting his food stolen from the kitchen."

But that would have to be Milton's problem. She had a show to put on.

"It's your problem, too," said Milton. "Moonie needs some help in the kitchen today. I need to borrow Nancy Gale."

Patricia Montgomery would not relinquish Nancy Gale. The girl had just arrived; she would not be leaving. "Take Tucker," she said. "He's more expendable."

And she couldn't help noticing that Nancy Gale Nofsinger, who'd heard every word, looked rather unwell.

❂

Tucker loved to watch the rehearsals. He had the hedge clippers down at the amphitheater ostensibly to trim the boxwoods, but the boxwoods looked fine. He wanted to watch.

His mother knew what kind of production she was after. He just wished that she could express her vision more clearly to the performers. They weren't seasoned professionals. They weren't members of Equity. They were people like Tucker who thought they might want to pursue a career in the theater. Tucker had once considered such a life, but he'd forced himself to abandon the dream two years ago when he'd managed to get accepted to the university. After the accident in March, he had assumed that fate had agreed with his decision. This morning his leg was stiff and sore, even after the routine of exercises, but he knew that it would limber up in the course of the day.

Tucker wanted to be on that stage so badly. It had been two years since he'd been in a play, two years since he'd left high school for college, and he'd decided that he had a choice between acting or reading. It took him so long to finish even one page. He got tapes of the books, even the textbooks, and he read along with the tape on his Walkman. But it was a slow process. The advantage was that he didn't have to do a lot of rereading. Once he had it, he could remember it. Of course, writing it down without misspelling half the words was something else again. Professor Davidson, who was learning disabled herself, had been a particular inspiration to him with his studies. She'd been the one to recommend the university. He'd heard that she might have escaped from the fire in her house if she hadn't had her own Walkman on. She hadn't been able tohear the smoke detector.

His father stood on the steps of the amphitheater and talked quietly with his mother. That meant there was some sort of problem. This morning his dad had already changed into clothes for a formal meeting: seersucker sports coat over a tieless shirt, olive trousers, and socks on with his shoes. Tucker had realized long ago that he would never be as tall as his dad. Tucker's height had come from the Montgomery side of the family, as had his hair. It was Richard who would look more like Milton Blackburn, tall and dark. Richard was already taller than Tucker by half an inch. It was the only advantage he could see the kid having. He felt sorry for Richard. The guy was envious and angry and unhappy and all those other unpleasant characteristics you associate with adolescents. Richard was always looking for attention, and Tucker supposed that was partly his own fault. Well, not fault. Tucker didn't feel guilty about it. But he could recognize that all the special schools and accommodations granted him during his childhood might have made Richard feel somewhat deprived. Dad had always been fair to them, it had seemed to Tucker. Mom had been a little detached. But since this cheating incident, relations between his parents and Richard had stretched to a polite distance. He and Richard got along okay, but he suspected that part of the reason was that Richard wanted to show their parents that he was capable of rapport with somebody. Plus, it was odd to see what Richard would allow as public knowledge and what he wanted kept secret. This business with the weight room, for example. Nobody was supposed to know that they were setting up a weight room in the attic. Getting real weights would have brought too much attention, supposedly, so they were rigging up their own system with paint cans.

And Spandex Lady. Ever since she'd arrived, Richard had not said one word about her. He must have known what Nancy Gale and Tucker were up to, but he didn't ask about it, didn't mention her; he practically pretended she wasn't there. Tucker guessed his brother was envious. Richard had never had a steady girlfriend. Tucker could remember being that horny, but that had been a while ago.

He watched his father interrupt rehearsal by leaning over Patricia Montgomery and speaking into her ear. Finally she stood up. The sun was bright in her hair. Beside her Nancy Gale sat with the same corona of sunlight around her own hair. He had touched that neck last night. He looked away and cut some more boxwood. His attraction for Nancy Gale Nofsinger was waning. She was a nice person, and she was a fabulous partner, but they seemed to have reached the limit in their relations. Though she would never let him stay overnight from the beginning, he'd only realized for the last couple of nights that he didn't especially want to. There was something perfunctory and obligatory about their clandestine meetings in one bedroom or the other each evening. For the first time in his life, he had the uncomfortable and demeaning sense that he was being used as a sex object.

Besides, it was driving him crazy to have Moonie working here for meals, to have her so close, to be able to talk to her (but not to talk to her), to be able to touch her (but not to touch). For the last couple of nights with Nancy Gale, he'd imagined it was Moonie with him. He and Moonie had never done it. There'd been a lot of girls with whom he had, but not with Moonie. Even back last summer when they'd gotten serious, back when he was giving her tennis lessons, back when the sweat would pour out of both of them and drench their shirts and

heat their faces, they had drawn the line at the ultimate intimacy. Now
he feared that he'd never have even a memory to enjoy.

His father walked back up the steps and this time approached Tucker.

"You need to help us out inside," said Milton Blackburn. "Bernard
has resigned."

"Again?"

"Yes," said Milton Blackburn. "Until he comes back, I need you
to help Moonie in the kitchen."

The old lurch in the heart chamber again. Was it a sign, his being
forced into proximity with Moonie until the cook got over the latest
temper tantrum? Tucker responded with the opening speech of Theseus
in the play:

> Now, fair Hippolyta, our nuptial hour
> Draws on apace. Four happy days bring in
> Another moon; but O, methinks, how slow
> This old moon wanes . . .

Milton Blackburn appreciated his recitation. They walked up the
sidewalk to the Inn together, Tucker taking a few more steps to compensate for his limp. He was grateful that his father did not slow down
his pace for him. The grass was freshly cut, and the fine gravel on the
walkway crunched under their shoes.

"You know the whole play, don't you?" said Milton Blackburn.

"Every word," said Tucker. " 'Love looks not with the eyes, but
with the mind.' Don't you think that's a line about dyslexia?"

They talked on the way up the hill about why people did fall in love
with some persons and not with others.

"I suppose there is a sort of enchantment about it," said Milton
Blackburn. "A magic herb that gets squeezed into the eyes."

Tucker found Moonie in the kitchen washing dishes. He burst in
upon her with a voiced fanfare—"ta-da!"—and his hands outstretched
like a performer's. But she greeted him with a silent glare and threw
him a dishtowel.

Love could be an enchantment. But it was also a kind of madness.
According to all the notes he'd taken in school and all the commentary
he'd heard about Shakespeare during the past eight summers, the cure
for love-madness was to relinquish all ties to the beloved. Tucker told

himself that he needed to treat his work in the kitchen as a business arrangement, another part of his job. But when he sniffed Moonie's balsam shampoo, when he glanced at her perfect backside, when he glimpsed the moment one of her delicate hands absently rubbed at those flawless curves under her T-shirt, when he remembered what he had once known of her and had lost—her smile and her affection and her conversation—he felt himself go almost ill with regret and desire. He felt his stomach heave, as though he might be sick.

✂

He had a twenty-minute break between classes. Richard found Rebecca Taylor by the drink machines, where she sipped on a Diet Coke and ate another tangerine. It was odd to see her standing alone, since usually she spent recess with a large group. But today in her fury she had isolated herself. Davidson's public announcement that she was a scholarship student had hurt her more than she'd shown in class.

"He's a jerk," said Richard. "Don't worry about the guy."

"Man had no right to put me down like that," she said. "You're on scholarship, you're supposed to have that confidential. Nobody is supposed to know."

He felt sorry for her. "You going to do anything?" said Richard.

"I might," she said. "You offering any ideas?"

"I'm just offering my professional advice," said Richard. "You want to watch out for Davidson. Don't get on his bad side."

She finished the Coke in one long swallow. "That's so typical," she said. "You boys think women can't cope on our own."

He told her about being dismissed from Montpelier because of the honor violation in Davidson's class. She was shocked.

"Why you taking his class again?" she said. "You're crazy."

"I want revenge," said Richard.

Rebecca Taylor wiped her eyes with the back of her hand. "I'll tell you what you want," she said. "You want to make sure you're in class tomorrow."

She would say no more.

✂

Anne Lindsey lived by the checklist, and by mid-June she was pleased with how many items she'd been able to eliminate from her agenda.

There was the funeral, of course. Late April, in Rockbridge as she had wanted, simple, dignified, quick, lots of people. But the last thank-you note went into the mail yesterday, and that meant the funeral was officially over.

Then there was the will. Oscar got the insurance money. Not that he needed it. He already owned the house in Charlottesville, what was left of it, and the land it was on, and the other houses, and the apartment here in Rockbridge and all the furniture. Moonie got some cash and would have had some china and crystal had they survived the fire. There was a little silver for her. Most of the books that would have come to them were destroyed. That was one of the many heartbreaking elements of the fire, the terrible loss of Sarah's library.

Anne had inherited all the publication rights. Oscar had not liked that, but it was fair. Anne had been the lifelong editor for Sarah Davidson. It had become as much a matter of superstition as habit for Anne to proofread the final version of whatever Sarah was writing. Anne had a degree in literature as well, but she knew, even before she took her orals, that she was no intellectual match for her brilliant younger sister. That was all right. She'd done for Sarah what she could—correcting the spelling when Sarah was younger, and then, after the spell-check devices on the computers became more sophisticated, reading mainly for homonym errors and perhaps a logical loophole on rare occasions. Sarah's dyslexia was profound, but it was also the stuff of legend. She didn't allow a couple of crossed mental wires to slow her down, and she could prove to her similarly hampered students that there was no correlation between intelligence and learning disabilities. Anne Lindsey had edited well for her sister. On the last monograph, the one on *A Midsummer Night's Dream,* she'd penciled in several suggestions in the margins about the organization of the argument. It was too bad that the manuscript was lost. Not that it would have brought much money—maybe fifteen dollars a page, plus a few hundred if somebody like Bloom decided to reprint it in a collection. It was a matter of principle. She would like to see Sarah's last work in print—her real work, not this travesty Oscar was palming off on Ramsey as a trick. And, even given the four scholarly books, all still in print, and the reprints of the various reviews and analyses, the rights to Sarah's scholarly publications would scarcely give Anne more than some extra pin money. The real profit lay in the popular stuff Sarah wrote under her pseudonyms—the television series and the novels.

Now she had to confront the matter of Ramsey Paxton. When he strolled into her office and dumped the stack of manila folders and ledger books onto her tidy desk, she felt like clawing him. What a smug bastard he was. Ramsey's ego was as inflated as his belly and his cranium. His round head perched like a walnut on top of a potato, a talking walnut with wiry black hair and wearing an expensive dark suit. She had given him the tie himself. She wondered if he even remembered—whether he'd worn it by accident or chosen it to humiliate her further.

He dumped his load of manila folders and record books onto her desk and then sat down in the scalloped plastic chair that shuddered under his weight. "Not bad," he said. "You keep good records."

Ramsey had a voice like a football coach's and the condescension of a film star. *What could possibly make him so sexy,* she wondered, and she could come up with nothing except his own self-assurance. Yet sexy he was.

"I do have one question about Milton Blackburn's fee," he said.

"Only one?" she said.

His eyes were too close together, but instead of making him look cross-eyed or comic, they gave his stare more intensity. "Is this tone necessary?" he said.

She'd betrayed her annoyance. "Harriet seems to be feeding you well," she said.

He didn't blink. "I never made you any promises," he said.

"You accepted my invitations to dinner," she said.

"For a while," he said.

"You never told me you were dating Harriet."

"She wanted the divorce to be final," he said. "I respected her wishes."

"You asked me to keep our meetings a secret," she said. "I thought it was because of your pending appointment to the Arts Council. It was just to keep Harriet ignorant."

Ramsey said that was preposterous. "Harriet knew I was seeing you. It was business."

"Alex dated while they were separated," said Anne. "At least he had the integrity to do it in public."

Ramsey shrugged. "As I said, I never led you on."

"You used me to get yourself onto the Arts Council," she said.

"As I recall," said Ramsey, "you were quite opposed to my nomination as chairman."

That had been afterward. In January, when she'd had such a crush on him—and that was the only word for it, a damned schoolgirl crush—she'd brought him onto the board. It was like bringing Mordred into Camelot.

"You're not going to cut my budget, are you?" she said.

He produced the one folder that he had not dropped onto her desk. "I told you already," he said, "I have a question about Milton Blackburn's fee."

"A hundred dollars," she said. "He comes once a month and gets a hundred dollars."

"Who approves his payment?"

"Alex and I do," she said. "I approve all expenditures for the city budget, and Alex for the Arts Council. Milton gets fifty dollars from the city and fifty more as a subsidy from the Arts Council."

"So he gets two checks," said Ramsey.

"Yes. For fifty dollars each." She said it as if she were talking to someone with Alzheimer's. He knew that the Arts Council supported visits by lecturing artists. Why belabor the point?

"So who are the Stone Mountain Consultants?" said Ramsey Paxton.

She knew it was going to be like this when Ramsey was appointed chairman. Every little *i* dotted and *t* crossed. She knew how thorough he was from personal experience, from those times in January she'd ask him over and he'd walk from his home so that no one would see his car in her driveway, back when she worked to get him onto the Arts Council, when she thought he would be her ally, back before she realized that all he wanted was dinner.

"That's some other thing," she said. "That's the name of his company."

"His company is the Stone Mountain Theater," said Ramsey. He pulled out an invoice from the folder. "These have been coming in to the Arts Council treasurer regularly," he said. "Five of them since January." She looked at the invoice. Stone Mountain Consultants. 1137 Roanoke Avenue in Rockbridge. Five hundred dollars. It was approved by Alex Mason.

She was embarrassed not to know more about it. "Maybe it's not even Milton's," she said. "I don't know. You'll have to ask him. Or Alex."

"Is that a typical expenditure for a high school drama department?"

His ignorance made her furious. "You have no idea of how much good drama costs," she said. "Of course it's a typical expenditure. Has Alex exceeded his budget with the Arts Council?"

"No," said Ramsey.

"Have I exceeded mine with either the Arts Council or the School Board?"

"Not that I can see."

"Then what's the problem?"

"The problem is that I wonder about this fee," he said. "Who are these people? What are they giving us? If it's Milton Blackburn, why do they have an office all the way out on Roanoke Avenue?"

She hated being unable to answer his questions. "These could have no connection with Milton at all."

"Find out."

"Why?"

"Because if it is Milton Blackburn, then he might be double-dipping," said Ramsey. "He gets a grant from the Arts Council anyway. If he invents a company and inflates a bill to the Arts School for the same services, then he gets two allocations for one piece of work."

"Why don't you call Milton and ask him?" she said.

"I will."

"Or, better yet, why don't you just walk over to the Lyceum right now and ask Alex?" she said. "I'm sure he could clear it all up for you."

She was delighted to see that even Ramsey Paxton could hesitate at some suggestions. "I'd rather not do that," he said. "I just married the man's ex-wife."

She couldn't resist. "So what's he going to do?" she said. "Castrate you?"

Ramsey stood up. "What you should worry about," he said, "is what I'd do to him."

What a ridiculous line. What a macho, swaggering oaf. It would be so easy to pick up the telephone and bash his face with it. Last winter, when he had told her that he'd be marrying Harriet in April, she had thrown a dictionary (abridged) at him. Today she was determined to keep her temper.

"Let me use your phone," said Ramsey.

"I need this phone," she said. "There's one in the teachers' lounge."

"I'll be back," said Ramsey.

She lifted the telephone receiver and pretended to be searching through her Rolodex for a number until Ramsey was clear of the office. All right, all right, she would have to talk to Alex about this Stone Mountain Consultants business, but she ranked that conversation at the bottom of her priorities. She had a meeting of the curriculum committee at 11:30 and a conference with the performing arts teachers at 2:00. There was so much she had to do, so much on which she needed to concentrate. But seven minutes after he'd left, she still stewed over Ramsey, and she trembled with suppressed fury over the way their meeting had proceeded. She still wanted him. Somehow, in spite of all his arrogance and his fault-finding and his suspicions about her trusted colleagues, she retained her desire for him. No matter how many times she'd rubbed with erasers, blotted with ink, coated with white-out, and pressed the "delete" button, she could not remove his name from her list.

The letter from *Feminist Renaissance* arrived with the morning mail. During recess Chris Nivens walked across the street from the Arts School to check his mailbox in the vestibule of his apartment building. And there it was, not a brown envelope containing the manuscript and a pre-printed rejection slip, but a letter of acceptance. Enthusiastic acceptance. It had taken them only nine weeks to decide—very little time. They were going to publish his essay next spring. That was so far off. But he could show this letter to Professor Vita. He could certainly use this news to his advantage with the people in Charlottesville.

Chris Nivens stood with the letter in his hand and felt his heart pound the way it hadn't pounded since the night of the fire. It had actually happened. He had taken a chance, and the chance had paid off. They were going to publish the essay. He, Chris Nivens, was going to have a credit in a national scholarly periodical. He felt a curious mixture of euphoria and shame. What would Sarah Davidson say if she were here now? That he'd taken advantage of his opportunity to work with her? That he'd used her name to get a reading after she had told him that she hadn't liked his work? He pushed the misgivings aside. He had done plenty of research on *A Midsummer Night's Dream.* He was entitled to use what he had gathered. He was a professional, and he was about to have his intelligence and creativity confirmed by a respected outside authority. He felt as though Destiny itself had sent him a note of approval.

He walked back to the classroom building to consider how to handle this news. Should he advertise it? His instincts told him to tell nobody. No need to boast. Just let it quietly appear next spring. The people who needed to see it would see it. But it might appear rude or arrogant for him to conceal the news, especially from Anne Lindsey. Why should he be secretive? He found the decision removed from his control when he returned to his classroom and found a note from her on his desk: *See me immediately.*

Ramsey Paxton was in Anne Lindsey's office when Chris arrived. They stopped talking the moment he opened her door.

"Oh, yes," said Anne Lindsey. "I wanted to ask you about this." She handed him a blue telephone message slip. "You got a call from Baltimore this morning," she said.

Chris took the slip and read the number. "I don't know anybody in Baltimore," he said.

"That's why I wanted to see you," she said. "He identified himself as your father."

Chris felt his euphoria disintegrate. "What a cruel trick," he said. "Please don't accept any more of these. I told you already. My father is dead." He folded the message and stuck it into his back pocket.

"I wasn't sure of how to react," she said. "You think it's some sort of practical joke?"

"Probably," he said. "A very un-funny one. Richard Blackburn just wrote an essay about his favorite pranks. I thought that Richard and I got along well."

"Don't jump to conclusions," she said. "It could just as easily have been Tucker."

Chris should have thought of that himself. Tucker, who once dated Ramona, was the one with the motive. Both Ramsey Paxton and Anne Lindsey looked at him sympathetically, Ramsey Paxton with his huge head turned in the chair, Anne Lindsey with her hands folded neatly in front of her. Destiny had brought him here to tell them his news. He would do so.

"I don't think this letter is a joke," he said. He showed them the acceptance from *Feminist Renaissance*. Letterhead stationery. Postmark Chicago. Both were excited.

"Damn," said Ramsey Paxton. He read with half-glasses propped onto his huge head. "We ought to print your essay in the program, too."

"No," said Chris Nivens. "I don't want that."

"It's a wonderful accomplishment," said Anne Lindsey. "I hope you'll let me read it."

"Sure," he said. He had no intention of letting her read it.

"Why can't we print it in our souvenir playbill?" said Ramsey. "It's the right play. We could have complementary essays, both of them connected with the Rockbridge Arts School. Very prestigious."

"No," said Chris Nivens. "This summer is for Sarah Davidson. I don't want to compete with her. Besides, I'm not sure the magazine would want to publish it if it had already appeared in a souvenir program."

"Well," said Ramsey. "I might call this *Feminist Renaissance* outfit and ask permission."

"Please don't," said Chris Nivens. He already regretted his announcement. He had misread the signs. "I seriously do not want my essay published alongside that of my teacher."

Ramsey Paxton would not let go. "What if I write and ask for a blurb?" he said. "You know, like what you see on the back of paperback books? Get the editor up there just to say something nice about it, so we can advertise it for you."

So you can further impress the high rollers at your champagne feast, Chris Nivens thought. "I don't see the necessity for that," he said.

"Leave it to me," said Ramsey Paxton.

Chris Nivens found Oscar Davidson in his classroom stapling together strips of paper. So far this summer he had worked cooperatively with Oscar Davidson, though he had not grown any fonder personally of the man he considered a dilettante. But Nivens thought it was politically wise to tell Davidson the news.

"Congratulations," said Oscar. He was not especially warm in his delivery. "Look what I've got."

It was the proofs for the playbill. There was the essay, the essay attributed to Sarah Davidson, the essay Oscar had shown to him at the wedding brunch and then again three weeks ago. Chris had grave suspicions about the authorship of this essay, but he had not divulged them to Oscar. He had not told him that it simply did not sound like Sarah's voice. He had kept silent. Perhaps that was the wrong strategy, but what was his alternative? What proof did he have that Sarah had not written this manuscript? His reaction was pure instinct, and yet it was enough to keep him from asking for a credit in the byline. He did not want his name associated with this mediocrity.

"I like the typeface," said Chris. The monograph ran in two columns across three pages.

"Are you going to show your essay to our students?" said Oscar.

"No," said Chris Nivens. "I'm not circulating it until it's published."

"Paranoid?" said Oscar.

"It's important to me," said Chris.

"What if we give them this one?" said Oscar Davidson. "They might enjoy seeing a model analytical essay before they have to write their own. I've already made copies."

"Why not?" said Chris. "I'm sure Sarah would be pleased to know that we were teaching with her work."

He tried to keep the irony out of his voice, to keep from sounding dubious or suspicious. From Oscar's bland facial expression, Chris thought that he had succeeded.

※

If he made a list of the worst things that could happen to him, like, say, getting caught beating off or not being allowed to drive a car until he was fifty, having to attend two English classes at the Arts School would have to rank in the top ten. Richard couldn't believe what a jerk Davidson had been in class this morning, but that was typical. He'd almost forgotten what it was like to be in one of Davidson's classes: the boredom, the bullying, the big vocabulary getting thrown around the room, the busywork. It was so obvious that Davidson did not like teaching. Why didn't he just stay home and write novels?

It was now 11:15 A.M., second period. Time for his class in dramatic literature taught by Mr. Nivens. Richard had been ready not to like him. After all, he was the guy who'd snaked Moonie from Tucker. Also the guy who'd lived in the basement of the Davidsons' house as tenant. He was taking the job originally designated for Mrs. Davidson, and Richard had assumed that Nivens would be like Oscar. The thing was, though, Nivens seemed pretty good. He'd taught before, but only college freshmen in a composition class. So he wasn't trying to act like a know-it-all, even though he made it clear that he wasn't a rookie. He wore a plaid shirt with the sleeves rolled up and a solid blue necktie and clean jeans and tan buck shoes. He was trim and athletic and relaxed. He sat on the front of the desk and talked a lot with his hands. He smiled a lot. And what Richard especially liked was that his glasses, old round wire-rims, were identical to the ones Richard wore himself. With his short, dark hair, he was almost the older brother Richard could have had instead of Tucker. Or an image of what Richard could grow into himself.

"We're doing *Hamlet*," said Mr. Nivens, "because that's the play Mr. Mason has chosen to direct here at the school." He held up the two Signet paperbacks with colorful covers, both of them quite familiar by now to the students. "And we're reading *A Midsummer Night's Dream* because we'll have a chance to see a production at the Stone Mountain Theater. Richard's dad is getting us tickets." He looked at the back row, and Richard sat up.

"They're not the greatest pairing of plays we could have," Mr. Nivens said. "*Hamlet* is a revenge play, and it might have been more interesting to read *The Tempest* along with it. I don't suppose we could get your dad to change his season, could we, Richard?"

"It's my mom who's directing the play," said Richard. He hated this sort of attention. It was hard not to be the class clown if the teacher kept reminding everybody that you were there.

"Still," said Nivens, "*A Midsummer Night's Dream* has a wonderful plot. You've got the court of Theseus and Hippolyta." He hopped up and started to make a list on the board. "And you've got the young lovers, who are falling in and out of love with each other. And you've got Bottom and the 'rude mechanicals,' who are putting on their own play. And finally, you've got the fairies, who are invisible to all the human beings on the stage."

He stopped and looked at the list he'd drawn. "And I guess, now that I think about it, *Hamlet* might be an interesting play to study with this one after all. In *Hamlet* you've got a ghost, and you've got young lovers, and you've got a marriage between a king and a queen, and you've got people putting on a play." He jiggled the chalk in his hand and thought for a second. The classroom was silent. Then Mr. Nivens turned to the students and grinned.

"Sorry," he said. "What I was doing was thinking about some connections I'd never made before. That's what I want you to do." He sat back down on the front of the desk. "And that gets back to the assignment you have for Friday. I'll read for content. Mr. Davidson will read for form. And in the spirit of cooperation," he said, "Mr. Davidson has offered to let you see his wife's very last essay. The one that will be used in the playbill for the Stone Mountain production later this month."

He handed them photocopied pages of program proofs. Richard stuck his into his book bag without looking at it. What a terrible assignment. Then Rebecca Taylor spoke up.

"Is this a punishment?" she asked.

Richard thought she was awesome.

After class Richard dropped by Alex's office for lunch, as he had every day since school had started. The office was a little cubicle backstage at the Lyceum Theater, a little room in the stage-right wing about the size of three telephone booths. Alex wore his painting overalls, splotched with every possible color, and leaned back in his chair with his feet on the desk while he drank a Mountain Dew and ate two bananas. Richard took the swivel chair with the wheels on the legs. He liked to bump around in the tiny office. Sometimes he'd even roll out on the stage. The Lyceum was the perfect theater for *Hamlet*—a gigantic old movie palace with its Gothic design, stonework, arched doorways, ribbed vaulting in the ceiling, stained glass, false spiral staircases, and gargoyles along the proscenium, with two magnificent monsters' heads at eye level on either side of the stage. It seemed ridiculous to sit in such a place while he ate a peanut butter and pickle sandwich and potato chips.

"I'm still not used to bringing my lunch to school," said Richard. "That was one thing about Montpelier. The food was horrible, but at least they fixed it for you."

Alex asked him whether he was going to eat in the office all summer.

"Maybe," said Richard.

"Haven't you made any friends yet?"

"Not really," said Richard. "Sort of. There's this one girl who's unbelievable."

"A girl?" said Alex. "That's a good sign."

"Not really like a girlfriend," said Richard. "More like a friend who happens to be a girl."

"Both of my marriages started like that," said Alex. He threw his banana peels into the green cylindrical trash can and wiped his hands on his overalls. Then he started to shuffle the papers on his desk. "How'd you like to direct *Hamlet* all by yourself?"

Oh, no. It was another typical bitch session from Alex. He was always complaining about bad luck or unfair treatment or long hours or low pay. Richard knew never to take him seriously. "I'd cut it down to the last act," said Richard. "That's the only place with any action."

Alex found a pencil stub and started wearing it down on the back of a notebook. "You might just come to school some morning and find me gone," he said. "Out of here. I get so tired of all the hassles. I'm ready to roam."

Alex was always ready to roam. He'd been threatening to leave Rockbridge every month for six years.

"What happened this time?"

Alex said it was the usual problem with tightening money from the Arts Council. "They're threatening to cut my budget after already approving it. I could seriously say bye-bye to the bunch of them."

Richard said he'd go with him.

"You, my boy," said Alex, "have not paid what are known as dues."

"I've paid plenty," said Richard.

There was a beat of silence between them.

"Things going okay at home?" said Alex.

Richard shrugged his shoulders. "I guess," he said. "I'm not grounded or anything. Mom and Dad are so busy that they don't really check on me that much at night. I don't think they're used to having me around like this."

Alex didn't push the conversation. He opened his notebook with the *Hamlet* text on loose-leaf pages and started to look through the scenes they would rehearse this afternoon. Richard unzipped his backpack with one hand and pulled out the essay Mr. Nivens had given them in class this morning. It was very dull reading, especially for a theater program.

After five minutes, Richard quit trying. "I can't take any more," he said.

"What are you reading?" said Alex.

"Mrs. Davidson's essay for the program," said Richard. "Homework for Nivens."

"Love and its connection to the theater," said Alex. "Romantic love as an analogy for the relationship between the audience and the actors."

"I haven't gotten to that part yet," said Richard.

"It's in the first paragraph, Lazy One," said Alex. "I thought Tucker was the one with the reading problem in your family."

Richard looked at the first paragraph again. "No," he said. "You're the one with the reading problem. Or maybe you're just trying to bullshit me."

"Let me see that," said Alex. He read the first column of the page proofs. Then he reached into the bottom drawer of his desk and pulled out a brown mailing envelope with a typed essay inside. He read the program proofs, then read some pages from the envelope, then the program proofs again. He put both down on the cluttered desktop and looked genuinely confused. "This is very strange," he said. He picked up the pages he had pulled out of his drawer and handed them to Richard. "This is Mrs. Davidson's original essay," he said. "It's completely different from that thing in the program."

Richard recognized the envelope immediately, but he said nothing before he examined the pages carefully. He read enough to confirm that the two essays were different. "Where'd you get this?" he said.

"I'm not supposed to tell," said Alex.

"You got it from my mother," said Richard.

"I'm not supposed to tell you that," said Alex. "Let the record show that I did not. But how the hell did you know?"

Richard loved the way Alex treated him as one of his peers. He'd heard his parents criticize the guy for being in "arrested development," but Richard thought more adults ought to have their development arrested if they could turn out to be as much fun as Alex. "She had this kind of envelope with her when we left the Davidsons' house that night," said Richard. "Intelligent guess."

"You remembered something that trivial from two months ago?" said Alex.

Richard didn't want to discuss his memories of the night of the fire. "So what are you doing with it?" he said.

Alex explained about his commitment to return the essay to Anne Lindsey. "Only when I called last month, she said Oscar had already found a copy. So I figured it hadn't been lost. And therefore Anne didn't ever need to know about this particular copy. I'm very protective of my lady friends."

"You count my mother as a lady friend?"

"She's a friend," said Alex. "Sometimes. And she's a lady."

"Sometimes," said Richard. "So now we've learned that the essay in the program isn't the lost essay after all. Does that win us a prize?"

Alex didn't say anything. And his silence got Richard wondering what he was missing. "Isn't this just a misunderstanding?" said Richard. "Haven't they just found another essay she was working on and turned it in by mistake?"

"I wonder," said Alex. "These are Anne's pencil marks in the margins. She edited this manuscript."

"Meaning?"

"Meaning she would certainly realize that this thing in the playbill is not the same essay she'd edited."

Richard could tell that something very important was about to happen, but he couldn't tell what. The air was different in the office. It was the air that he always breathed when he and Alex were about to launch one of their classic pranks.

"Tell me what happened in Oscar Davidson's class at Montpelier," said Alex. "Tell me about the cheating."

"I didn't cheat," said Richard.

"You've said that before," said Alex. "Tell me exactly what transpired."

It was the first time Alex had asked to hear the details. So Richard told him about getting taken to the honor council. The assignment had been to write a short story, so Richard had written one on his computer, had printed it out, and had turned it in with his honor pledge signed on the title page, according to instructions. When he got to the honor council, however, his signed title page was all that remained of his original work. That signed title page was attached to a short story that someone had taken and retyped from a library book—a book that Richard had checked out from the library two days before the assignment was due. "I swear to you, Alex," said Richard, "I didn't cheat. Nobody else believes me. I don't blame them, I guess. But I didn't. It was Davidson who retyped the story. It had to be."

"If you wrote a story on your computer," said Alex, "wouldn't it still have been there? Didn't you save it?"

"Of course I saved it," said Richard. "But they said I could have written it after I got accused. You can change the dates on a computer file. Anyway, Davidson said the story on my computer disk wasn't the story I turned in."

Alex rubbed the short hairs on the top of his head. "Why would Oscar want to frame you?" he said.

"Because he didn't like me," said Richard. "Davidson and I never got along. I used to do stuff in his class. I put a dead bird under the seat of his car once. Somebody else ordered a bunch of skin magazines in Davidson's name and address. He didn't believe me when I said I hadn't done it."

"He assumed you had," said Alex. "Interesting." He thought it over. "And for that he would drive you out of the school? Could Oscar really be that big a bastard?"

"Yes," said Richard.

Alex studied him. "Yes," said Alex. "I believe he could."

Richard loved it. Maybe he could even convince his parents.

Alex looked at the two essays on his desk. "What in the world could they be up to?" he said.

"They're cheating," said Richard. "They've told Mr. Paxton that they found the lost essay, but they're trying to pass off another one in its place."

"Why?" said Alex. "I don't see any reason they could benefit at all. They don't get any money or credit or prestige." He looked at the two essays again. "But the essays are clearly different. It just makes no sense."

Richard suggested that they give both copies to Rebecca Taylor so that she could publish them in the school newspaper. Alex said no.

"We have to," said Richard. "It's a fraud. Davidson deserves to be publicly humiliated."

Alex shook his head. "I'm thinking of Mrs. Lindsey now," he said. "I'd rather not embarrass her."

Richard couldn't believe it. "Why not, Alex?" he said. "Is this chivalry or something? You don't owe her anything."

"True," said Alex. "But it does give me some leverage with her. You can understand that, can't you?"

Richard had to admit that he could.

"I'm going to ask her about it today," said Alex. "There's got to be some simple explanation. If there were two essays by Sarah, Anne will want to have this one back again."

"What a waste," said Richard. He could feel the idea arriving: It was just around the corner, just out of sight, but it was close, he could almost smell it, and he could tell that it was gigantic—a huge colossus of an idea, lumbering its way along the back alleys of his imagination, approaching the public plaza where his mind stood now, waiting, watching for it, knowing that it was very close. And then he saw it. He gasped at its magnificence.

"What are you thinking?" said Alex.

"I know what we can do," said Richard. "This is better than tying all the door handles to the dressing rooms shut. This is the ultimate."

"You're not making this essay public," said Alex. "At least not until I get a chance to discuss it with Anne."

"No, no," said Richard. "This is a private joke. I have a draft of an essay on *A Midsummer Night's Dream* due on Friday. Here's an essay. It seems like an obvious match."

"You would turn in Sarah Davidson's essay as your own?"

"Of course," said Richard. "I can type it over on my computer so that Mrs. Lindsey's comments aren't visible."

Alex was not impressed. "Aside from relieving you of the burden of actually doing your homework," he said, "what possible good would that do?"

"I'll do my homework," said Richard. "I'll turn my real essay in to Mr. Nivens for grading. I'll turn in the fake one only to Mr. Davidson."

"And?"

"And Davidson reads the essay. He'll have to know that I didn't write it. No high school kid could write something like this. With luck, he'll accuse me of cheating again."

"You want him to accuse you again?"

"Yes," said Richard. "Because this time Mr. Nivens will have another essay, my own work. And when they compare, then Mr. Nivens will see that the two essays aren't the same at all."

Alex said he still didn't understand.

"Come on, Alex," said Richard. "It will be a repeat of what happened in May at Montpelier. I turn in one essay, and Davidson produces another one. But this time Davidson will be the one to get nailed. He'll be accusing me of cheating with one of his wife's own essays. Her supposedly lost essay. It'll be up to Davidson, not to me, to explain where that essay has come from."

"Aha," said Alex. He played with it for a while. "I like that. 'The play's the thing wherein I'll catch the conscience of the king.' " Davidson would have two choices after he read Richard's draft. Either he'd have to keep quiet—and think that he was deliberately letting a student get away with plagiarism this time—or he'd have to confront Richard and have his own deceit become public knowledge.

"But why would he show Nivens the essay?" said Alex. "If you produce the real Sarah Davidson essay, won't Oscar know better than to advertise it? He'd have to explain what the hell he was doing with this other thing in the playbill."

Richard was on a roll. "There's a chance that he might not even recognize it as his wife's. The guy is so out of it in class. He might not even have read his own wife's manuscript."

"You're hoping for a lot," said Alex. "But if he does decide to accuse you again, he will certainly bring into question the entire cheating incident at Montpelier."

They talked about various scenarios. "If he shows it to Mrs. Lindsey," said Richard, "then I'll need you to get involved. To tell her that you approved what I did. If he shows it to Nivens, then Nivens will probably recognize it. That could be the best."

"And the most embarrassing for him."

"Mr. Nivens probably won't make a big public scene," said Richard. "He's sort of friends with Davidson and Mrs. Lindsey."

"And what if Oscar reads it and just grades it without saying a word?" said Alex. "What if he doesn't take your bait?"

"Then I'm no worse off than I am now," said Richard.

Alex handed him the brown mailing envelope containing the original manuscript. "You'll be careful with this, won't you?" he said. "Anne will be grateful to get it back when all this is over."

Richard stuck the packet into his backpack and zipped up the top. "Do you think we could embarrass Mr. Davidson into resigning?" he said.

"Don't get too optimistic," said Alex. "You'll probably end up doing a lot of work for nothing."

"We'll see on Friday," said Richard.

But by Friday their plans would change.

Richard was only trying to help. He kneeled on the forestage of the Lyceum, where Alex pulled up old tape that had been painted over on the stage.

"You're in my way," said Alex. He had been impatient all afternoon. "Try over there."

Richard didn't understand what had put Alex into such a bad mood. This was going to be their greatest prank ever. With luck, Davidson would be absolutely deep-fried, but Alex didn't want to talk about it, didn't want to talk about anything except getting the stage cleaned up. Richard worked the stubborn tape on the boards with his fingers. The wood of the stage pressed into his knees. "I hate doing this," said Richard.

"A stage manager never complains," said Alex. He worked in a T-shirt and his overalls.

Richard picked at the old tape, which came off the stage in tiny bits. "I don't see the point, Alex. This tape doesn't matter."

It was 4:30 in the afternoon. Rehearsal had just ended. "Dust the gargoyles," said Alex. "Be careful of the trap."

Richard stood up and walked to the stage-right gargoyle head. In order to get there he had to skirt an open pit, three feet square, downstage right. It opened into a storage room beneath the stage, now dark. Richard could still see the surface of the scaffolding that Alex had rolled beneath the trapdoor from the room below.

"That's not much of a grave," he said. It looked more like a hatch for ship cargo than a grave for Ophelia.

"I have to get the other door open," Alex said. "It's stuck."

The gargoyle head on the stage-right side of the proscenium was twice the size of a human's and was made of what looked like rough stone. Its grin sat at Richard's eye level. He stuck his fingers into the open mouth as far as he could reach. The head jiggled a bit on the wall. "It's hollow," he said.

"Of course it's hollow, Richard. It's removable."

Richard lifted the head from the metal bracket that held it to the wall. It was heavier than a bowling ball. He pulled it over his own head and couldn't see anything.

"Put it back," said Alex. "Don't do that." But it was too late. The extra weight on his shoulders pulled Richard off balance, and he backed into the wall. The gargoyle head chipped a large piece of plaster away. Alex got mad.

"Just go home," he said. "Go now."

"I can fix it," Richard said. He lifted the gargoyle head to replace it on its bracket. The chipped spot in the wall was the size of a plum.

"Leave it," said Alex. "Just leave."

So he left. Hell, it could have been worse. He could have fallen into the open trapdoor and smashed the head to bits.

It was cloudy when he emerged from the theater, but he didn't want to wait for the bus. He jogged home and left his books in his bedroom before he continued up the trail to the Inn. It opened just off his back-yard, on the uphill side of the house, a small opening in the trees with a threshold of scree and gravel washed down during rainstorms. Richard ran up the red gulley and dodged tree limbs on his way. He didn't have to stop once, even though it was half a mile, almost straight up the mountainside. He was really getting into shape.

His face was hot and his pores gushing when he emerged from the woods. A roll of thunder sounded in the distance. To his right the amphitheater was empty. They would be rehearsing inside because of the change in weather. Straight ahead was the Inn. He could see the open window at the attic level where he and Tucker had started to rig up their weight room with paint cans and a broom handle and some cinder blocks. It had been so easy. Unused construction materials were everywhere.

He went to the rehearsal room on the main floor in the hope of finding Tucker. Though he was breathing hard and sweating, it would not take him long to recover his wind. A few heads turned when he opened the door, but then they ignored him. The actors were used to seeing him there. The one that gave him the dirtiest look was Nancy Gale Nofsinger, Tucker's new girlfriend. Spandex Lady. She was very good-looking, but not especially friendly. The cast was rehearsing the same damn scene as yesterday. Or rather they weren't rehearsing, but were watching his mother work with one guy, that spastic Hugh Bick-ley, who just couldn't manage to make what he was carrying look heavy. He had a huge canvas sack that he'd filled with what looked like foam rubber, and he kept trying to get his body language to convey weight. Dumb ass.

Richard left the rehearsal room and went upstairs. His passkey got

him through the Sarah Siddons door leading up to the attic. As far as
he knew, nobody in the company was aware of how to get to the attic
except for him and Tucker. Thunder boomed outside, and at once a
rain shower began to pummel the roof. Not wanting to add even a
degree to the heat, Richard didn't bother with the light switch, but
simply maneuvered in the dim light spilling into the hall from the
windows. In the hot hallway, he found the plywood and the rest of
their supplies. It looked as if Tucker had been up earlier today to move
some of it. Richard dragged two sheets of plywood into the nearest
room for additional flooring, then arranged two cinder blocks on end
about six feet apart. He opened another window and appreciated the
breeze that the rain brought. Below him the world was all shades of
gray. He felt cozy here in the attic as the rain fell outside. He took the
plank that Tucker had found down in the scene shop and laid it across
the cinder blocks. Before he started his actual workout, he plugged the
fan into the wall and turned it on, aiming at the bench he'd just built.
But the fan didn't work. He tried another socket with the extension
cord. Nothing. He quit trying and just opened the windows wider for
maximum ventilation. Then he got the broom handle, hung a paint can
on each end, and lay down on his back to do some presses. It wasn't
so much the weight, Tucker said, as the repetitions. Richard was tired
after twenty. He tried to keep the handle balanced as he sat up, but his
left arm dropped, and the paint can slid off and onto the plywood with
a loud bump.

"Hey," he heard in the room below. It was a woman's voice. He
stayed perfectly still, hot and sweating in the heat of the attic, the sloped
ceiling over his head permitting heat to rise, but not to escape. In
dismay he heard the portrait door swing open, heard a key in the lock,
heard footsteps approach his room.

It was Nancy Gale Nofsinger. She still carried her clipboard and had
on a bright pink T-shirt. Her hair was pinned up off her neck. "You
little Peeping Tom," she said.

"What?" said Richard.

"Get out of here," she said. He put down his homemade barbells
and tried to explain.

"It's just to work out," he said. "Tucker knows about it."

"Then why didn't Tucker tell me?" she said. "Go on. Get. Take all
this with you." She made him carry the two cinder blocks while she
took the paint. There were no lights on anywhere. They'd had another

power failure. That was why rehearsal got cut short and why she happened to go upstairs.

He descended the stairs and had to wait by the pay telephone while she checked to see if its phone line was clear.

"We've lost a line downstairs," she said. She put down the paint long enough to make a note on her clipboard. "Your dad wants a complete list of problems. For the contractor." The pay phone was working. They continued to the main floor and turned to walk toward backstage and the scene shop, but she made him go to the rehearsal room. While he walked along the main-floor hallway, the lights came back on. He could hear the refrigerator in the kitchen hum back into life.

"We're going to let your mother see this," she said.

Richard felt like dropping the blocks on the stupid bitch's foot, but he went on into the rehearsal room, where the lights shone but didn't seem sufficiently bright. The room was empty. Nancy Gale put down the paint, and he put down the heavy blocks gently on the floor. His arms ached.

"What's with you?" Richard said. "What's your problem?"

"Tucker warned me about you," she said. "You were the one who punched that peephole, weren't you?"

Richard didn't know what she was talking about. "If I was over your room, I'm sorry," he said. "I only wanted to help my physique."

"You only wanted what?"

"To help . . ." said Richard. He felt like such a little kid. "To build up my body. I'm trying to get into shape." He gestured stupidly at his running shoes.

Nancy Gale Nofsinger looked at him and lost the edge of her anger. "Put this stuff away," she said, pointing to the paint cans and the cinder blocks. "I don't want any gymnasium over my head."

Patricia Montgomery opened the door to the rehearsal room. "You two clear out of here," she said. "Hugh and I need the space." She shut the door without entering.

"Look," said Nancy Gale Nofsinger to Richard, "I understand about physiques. But stay out of the attic, okay?"

She had turned actually nice about it. Richard now could perceive why Tucker hung around with the Spandex Lady. "I wish I'd known there was a peephole," he said.

She reacted the right way and gave his upper arm a little squeeze.

"I'm going to take that as a compliment," she said. Then she left him. Richard was alone in the rehearsal room, his heart still fluttering from her touch. But quickly he turned his attention back to all the materials they had just carried into the room. The idea that came to him was so simple, so elegantly tidy. He carried the cinder blocks to the large canvas sack that Hugh Bickley had been using for rehearsal and pulled out a couple of squares of foam rubber. Then he placed the cinder blocks inside and stuffed the foam rubber back in on top of them. The sack sat on the floor as it always had.

Richard was on his way out of the room with the paint cans when his mother ushered in Hugh Bickley, who looked like a kid who'd been asked to stay after school.

"Get mad at that prop," said Patricia Montgomery. "I want to see you channel your anger."

Richard went to the door but lingered so that he could watch. It was obvious that his mother had just had a private harangue with the actor. She'd come up with one of her bullshit devices for inspiring him and had brought him in here to try it out. Hugh Bickley walked confidently to the canvas sack, grasped its top with both hands, and yanked up with all his strength. The sack did not budge, but Hugh Bickley fell screaming to the floor.

"My back," he shouted. "I've broken my back."

It turned out that he had not broken his back. He had only ruptured a disk between two of the lumbar vertebrae. But he was out for the summer.

"Richard," his mother said.

"Richard," his father said.

"I was only trying to help," Richard said.

><

For Richard it was just evidence that trying to be good was a waste of time. Trouble was inevitable, and it was inevitable because he was bad. The logic was irrefutable. Now his mother was furious with him for what she called sabotaging her show. As if it hadn't been anything but an accident. But he had to wonder about accidents. He'd heard people say that there was really no such thing as an accident, that whatever happened to you was something you subconsciously wished for. Maybe he'd planted those cinder blocks in the sack hoping that something would go wrong. But that would mean that Tucker had wanted to fall off the lawn mower last March and ruin his leg, and Richard knew that wasn't true.

He sat banished to his room at home. The glow from his desk lamp was soft and yellow on the new navy blue bedspreads. He had to work on his own rough draft of the critical essay assigned for Nivens's class, plus retype the other essay Alex had given him. He pulled out his backpack and extracted the manuscript from its envelope, then started to copy it into his computer. This was going to take a long time. After half an hour he got discouraged and put the essay away. It wouldn't work anyway, probably. Nothing he did ever worked out right.

Still, it was a great idea, to goad Davidson into another accusation. Richard did want his revenge. He imagined his father and mother coming to him in tears, begging forgiveness for their lack of faith in him, groveling, apologizing, buying him a car and stuff. He went back to his typing and daydreamed about Nancy Gale Nofsinger. The way she'd looked at him on her way out of the rehearsal room this afternoon. The way she'd understood about his wanting a good physique. The way she'd squeezed his arm. Like she'd been sampling some merchandise.

Typing was too boring. He wasn't in the mood. For tomorrow in Davidson's class he and Rebecca Taylor were supposed to bring in more published fiction to read to the class. He wondered what she had in mind and came close to calling her up. But she'd be at work. He stood up and looked around for something appropriate. There were the Hardy Boys books on his shelf. No. He wanted to come in with something nobody would have heard of. He tried a paperback mystery or two, but they didn't sound literary enough. The catch was to find something that sounded half-decent but wasn't famous. He knew that Davidson hated to look ignorant in front of the class. Once at Montpelier last spring, he had thrown a guy out of his room for correcting his use of the subjunctive mood. He tried the old copies of *The Shenandoah Review* that his father had left in here last month. Obviously, with the spines this smooth, nobody had read them since they were printed. The table of contents was right on the cover, so you could see right away what was inside.

When he got to the issue printed eight years ago, he stopped. The title of the third story was "The Trials of Sally Galloway," written by somebody named C. Y. Anderson. Sally Galloway. The name of the character in the title, of course, had to be a coincidence. This story appeared eight years ago, and Davidson's book had been in print for only twenty-four months. But, just out of curiosity, Richard opened the stiff pages and found the beginning. Then he nearly died.

For Sally Galloway, he read, *the smell of peppermint always brought back memories of that first Christmas at Belle Isle.* He read the rest. It was the opening chapter of Davidson's novel, published in a literary magazine six years before the novel appeared. And the author was somebody else.

Richard trembled with the same excitement he would have felt at opening King Tut's tomb. He was tempted to call Tucker at the mountain, to run downstairs and show his father, show his mother, show them all. But he forced himself to wait. If Davidson had plagiarized, wouldn't this C. Y. Anderson have complained by now? The title of the novel would have certainly alerted anybody who'd written a story about that character. But maybe C. Y. Anderson was from out of the state. Or dead. Who was C. Y. Anderson, anyway? Richard had never heard the name before. Quickly he searched the pages to find a biographical sketch about the contributors. It was on a page in the back. "C. Y. Anderson is a Virginian passionately devoted to classical theater," said the editor's note. The editor was Anne Lindsey.

Better and better. He knew he would use this information to his advantage. He didn't know how yet. But he had plenty of time. He would learn who C. Y. Anderson was and why at least part of Davidson's novel had appeared under somebody else's name—and in a magazine edited by the woman who would eventually become Davidson's sister-in-law three years after the story appeared. And then he would present Rebecca Taylor with the biggest news story of her journalistic career. He'd made this discovery all on his own. In this case, he'd made no promises to Alex Mason about keeping silent.

It was better than getting squeezed by Nancy Gale.

※

Milton Blackburn lay next to his wife in their bedroom. Through the white curtains the moon shone softly on the creamy carpet. They did not touch one another.

"You still thinking about the show?" said Milton Blackburn.

"I'm thinking that I tried as hard as I could to avoid playing Hippolyta," she said, "and I've still ended up doing it anyway."

They had been on the telephone for most of the evening. Their search to find someone who could double as Theseus and Oberon had led finally to Griffin Dupree in Boston, who would play Oberon alone and who would require Equity wages. The cost would asphyxiate their budget. Furthermore, his refusal to double meant that Milton Blackburn would have to play Theseus himself. In order to make the symmetry right, Patricia Montgomery would play Hippolyta opposite him. Claire Vasquez, the actress intended to double as Hippolyta and Titania, would be bumped into playing Titania alone. She was not happy with the change, but neither was anyone else.

"Why don't you try Tucker as Theseus and Oberon?" he said. "The boy can do it. And he'd come cheap."

"He can't do it," said Patricia. "He knows the lines. That's not the same."

"He can act," said Milton. "You know he can act."

"He hasn't done anything since high school," she said. "That's two years. He's had no training."

"He's had a lifetime of training. He knows more about acting than most people in the company."

"No," she said. "It's too nepotistic."

He didn't understand her argument. "You want me to play Theseus, and that's okay, but you don't want Tucker because he's too closely related to you?"

"You're closer to the age of Theseus," she said. "Your casting makes more sense."

"Your position doesn't," said Milton.

"Milton," said Patricia. "Stop it. I love Tucker. You know I do. But I can't use him in the show. I won't. Now drop it."

"Just tell me why," he said. "Just tell me the real reason why."

"He's not right for the part," she said.

"More specifically, please," he said. "Tell me why our son can't be in this show. It would save us money and avoid a begging trip to Ramsey tomorrow."

"Because this is my directorial debut," she said. "This is the most important step I've taken in my career."

"You've hired a young man sight unseen from Boston who will charge us a fortune. Ramsey may veto the idea because of the expense."

"I've talked to the actor. I've talked to people who have worked with him."

"But how do you know he'll be better than Tucker?" said Milton.

"Because," she said, "because, if you have to get down to essentials, he's got two good legs." She was angry at him for making her say it. "I don't want an Oberon who limps."

And that was the last word of the evening.

At 9:30 the next morning, Milton Blackburn tried to ignore the fact that he ought to hire more service staff. Bernard's resignation in the kitchen had meant jury-rigging the food service, and now Moonie herself had just tried to quit. Milton had begged her to stay until they could get a replacement. He sat in the office of the Stone Mountain Theater with the building around him relatively silent. The morning was sunny and gorgeous, though thunderstorms had been predicted for the afternoon. Until this summer, when they'd acquired the Inn, the company had had to rehearse in rented space downtown, sometimes at the Lyceum. They'd had access to the amphitheater only a week before the shows had gone up. Now it was theirs, but the chaos seemed to have increased. Today Marcie, his seamstress, had announced that she'd have to work overtime to make the changes to the costumes requested by Patricia. They were still waiting for a shipment of light bulbs from their regular supplier in Indiana. His fall indoor season was frozen by the Arts Council, likely to be canceled. And though it was 9:30 in the morning and their ads in the newspaper distinctly stated that the box office was open from 8:00 A.M. to 8:00 P.M., the telephone had refused to ring since he'd arrived half an hour ago.

"Why aren't they calling?" he said.

His secretary, Virginia, checked responses to the banquet scheduled for Saturday night at the desk across from his. She attached her glasses to a leash and wore them at the end of her nose, kept her hair pulled on top of her head, and held her mouth in a permanent smirk. "Just hush," she said. "You always get like this."

"Lots of people are coming for the meal," he said. "But what about the other twenty-one performances?"

"Why did you say twenty-one?" said Virginia. "You made me lose count."

He was supposed to be reading a draft for a grant request from the state arts endowment, but he couldn't concentrate. He'd never seen so many potential disasters on the horizon. He told himself to calm down. Up until this morning, ticket sales had been steady. Ramsey Paxton was right about snob appeal. Having Patricia around was good for business.

The office faced the mountaintop. For decoration he'd tacked up posters from past Stone Mountain productions on the walls. They were like the plaques on church walls that honored the dead. Through the security bars over the windows, Milton could see lush grass and a black asphalt strip winding to the tree line at the crest of the hill, where the road disappeared downward to lead past his own home before joining the thoroughfares of the city. It was like living at the end of all roads, to be here on this mountaintop where the pavement stopped at the parking area and any further progress had to be upward, into the ether and the clouds and the sunlight.

Footsteps echoed on the veranda. Soon the three seamstresses from the costume shop crossed his line of vision, two smoking cigarettes and one drinking a Coke. An invisible male voice from stage left shouted something to them, and they turned and laughed at whatever they saw. In another moment two men from the scene shop came into view, one wearing the ass's head to be used by Bottom, the other pretending to feed it a powdered doughnut.

"What the hell are they doing on break?" said Milton. He found out a moment later, when the electricity went off. Virginia was typing into her computer. "Fudge," she said. She looked across the desk at him over her glasses. "Who's running the hair dryer?"

"Nobody should be," he said. It was such a nuisance to put up with these power failures. Though they had rewired the entire building, something was not right. Their electrical contractor had promised to come, but Blackburn had seen no sign of him. He almost grabbed one of the four kerosene lamps they kept inside the safe to provide emergency lighting, then decided that a flashlight would suffice. He opened his second drawer and chose the red flashlight this time, walked out the door, past the rehearsal hall, the stairway, the kitchen and dining area, to the basement stairs. In the darkness below him he could see the light of a flashlight ahead of him.

It was the repairman. He had parked at the loading dock, come in through the scene shop and the stage, descended to the power boxes in the basement, and started to work, all without consulting with Milton in the office. Why hadn't Milton noticed his truck? The repairman had pulled the large horseshoe-shaped switch controlling the main power out from the wall and parallel to the floor, so that the connection was open. In the darkness Milton could see a bald head over gray plastic eyeglasses with lenses too small, like a child's. The man smelled like yeast.

"Don't you guys ever warn anybody?" said Milton. "My secretary lost everything in her computer."

"Sorry," said the repairman. He did not sound sorry. "I told the ones I saw. I thought all the rest of you folks was down yonder."

He was doing something to the circuit breaker. Blackburn returned to the main floor and met Virginia in the hallway. He supposed while the power was out he could still read the grant proposal outside. On the veranda he sat down on one of the rocking chairs and got stung by a bee. He stood up, found the insect with his fingers, and ground it to paste. The half-dozen employees waiting for power to resume turned their faces discreetly away before they laughed. He shot a brief glare toward the sky and wondered whether the gods were betting on how long he'd maintain his composure.

Virginia emerged from the door at the L of the building and handed him a pink message slip. "Ramsey Paxton," she said. "He wants to know about the Stone Mountain Consultants."

Milton took the paper and crumpled it. He would have thrown it into a bush if there hadn't been any witnesses around. "The Stone Mountain Consultants company is none of his business," he said. But he was afraid that maybe it was.

❈

Richard took both the Sarah Davidson manuscript and *The Shenandoah Review* to school with him. He expected to use the computer lab to continue transcribing the essay onto his disk, and he hoped to get over to the library to find out who C. Y. Anderson was. Davidson's class changed his plans. When it was time for hearing some sample fiction, Rebecca Taylor said she would read from *Sally Galloway,* by Oscar Davidson. Davidson just sat there as if he didn't care, but you could tell that he was flustered. Rebecca stood up and started to read. From his angle, Richard could see that she held a photocopied page from another book inside the volume she held in front of her. What happened next was fantastic.

"*Sally decided to wear red today,*" Rebecca read, "*so she donned her red shoes, her red stockings, her red dress, and her red scarf. Underneath it all, she wore her red strawberry-flavored underwear.*" She stopped to watch Davidson's expression, but he sat there deadpan. So she read on and on, about Sally Galloway going to a cheap motel and checking in and calling her boyfriend Carl. "*When Carl arrived, it was only a matter of minutes before all her work at dressing had gone to naught, for Carl had stripped her down to the strawberry panties and was soon plying her with his cherry-red love pickle—*"

"Wait a minute," said Oscar Davidson, "there's no passage like that in there."

"It is in the version I got," she said, and she quickly distributed pages to the class. She had played with the Xerox machine and had pasted a passage from a porn novel over a copy of two actual pages from *Sally Galloway.* All the students loved it.

Davidson, however, went wild. "Get out of this classroom," he said.

"Come on, Mr. Davidson," she said. "I didn't mean anything ugly."

He used words like trollop and cheap and smutty. But then he said something that made Richard burn. "Get your lazy behind out of my classroom now," he said.

"Mr. Davidson—" said Rebecca.

"Go to the office," said Davidson, "and clean it up."

That was when Richard exploded. "She's not your maid," he said.

"I was talking about the language," said Davidson. "Keep your mouth shut."

Richard nearly went up in flames. Rushing back to him came all the old rage he'd felt after his honor trial at Montpelier. Davidson was so deft at insulting you and then backing out on the grounds of an ambiguity. Richard wanted to kill the guy. Somehow he got through his own reading (from a book by Robb Forman Dew, which Davidson actually knew after all), though afterward Richard couldn't remember any details of his performance. He thought of Rebecca Taylor and Oscar Davidson throughout the time that his lips moved and his voice worked. There were no questions from his classmates afterward. The students were dead silent. Davidson made them go straight into journal writing, which, again, Richard pursued with a blank detachment. He wrote "I can't think of anything to say" again and again on the pages of his journal as he replayed this latest scene with Rebecca Taylor in the classroom. Richard had Sarah Davidson's manuscript. He had the frigging *Shenandoah Review* with the Sally Galloway story in it. Surely God or whoever was in charge up there had arranged for those materials to be in his possession for a reason. Surely Richard was intended to serve as avenger to Oscar Davidson. Here was the ammunition; he had to use it somehow. Going to Alex as a mediator was out of the question. Even though Alex would be sympathetic, he would balk at an action that might embarrass Mrs. Lindsey. And if Richard went to Mrs. Lindsey herself, she would undoubtedly just tell him to shut up in that mock-polite way she had of talking to him. He considered confiding in Chris Nivens, but Nivens was Davidson's teaching partner, not to mention a new teacher. Nivens wouldn't have any clout. To hell with Alex and his caution. It was time to move the game up to higher stakes.

Rebecca was gone for the rest of the class period. She'd left her books at her desk. As soon as the bell rang, Richard grabbed her copy of *Sally Galloway* and took off. You were allowed to leave the school grounds during the breaks as long as you didn't come back drunk or stoned or carrying a cartload of merchandise you'd just shoplifted. Most people just hung around the drink machines anyway, except for the nicotine addicts who either smoked or ran off to 7-Eleven to try to buy cigarettes illegally. Richard traveled with the nicotine addicts today. He knew exactly where he was going. He'd have to hurry if he wanted to make it back in time for Nivens's class, but it was only two blocks north and three west to the car dealership owned by Ramsey Paxton.

Ramsey Paxton was very busy and very dubious. He sat behind a large wooden desk in a carpeted office. On the paneled wall behind him were a Kiwanis medallion and a certificate from the Jaycees. He was such a goofy-looking man to Richard—big pumpkin head and frizzy hair—but he talked like somebody used to being in charge. He did not enjoy the interruption. "You say Oscar Davidson is guilty of plagiarism," he said.

"Look," said Richard. He showed him *The Shenandoah Review* with its story by C. Y. Anderson. "It's the same as Mr. Davidson's opening chapter." He opened Rebecca's copy of the novel and handed it to Mr. Paxton for comparison.

Mr. Paxton was not impressed. "It's obvious that C. Y. Anderson is Oscar's pen name," he said.

Richard had never thought of that. Mr. Paxton was not even the slightest bit suspicious. "He couldn't steal somebody's short story without getting caught doing it, Richard. His novel has been out for two years, and nobody has said a word."

"Can't I be the first one to notice it?" said Richard. He sounded ridiculous, even to himself. "Nobody ever read this stupid magazine when it came out."

"Nobody?" said Ramsey Paxton. "Nobody in the world? Not even the contributors or their families?" He closed both book and magazine and kept them on his desk. "I'll grant you that it's an interesting discovery. I'll ask him about it when I get a chance."

Richard hated being patronized.

"They won't tell you the truth," said Richard. "They're trying to trick you." He pulled out the envelope containing the Sarah Davidson essay Alex had given him yesterday. "This is the essay Professor Davidson wanted you to print in the program. My mother got it from Professor Davidson herself."

Ramsey Paxton took the envelope from Richard and read the opening paragraph. He was still unconvinced. "You got this from your mother, you say?"

"Mrs. Davidson gave it to her in Charlottesville. On the night of the fire. I saw her." Ramsey Paxton compared the essay to the proof for the program that he already had on his desk. Then he put the essay back into its envelope.

"And you decided just now to show it to me," said Ramsey Paxton.

"I just found out about it," said Richard.

"I see," said Ramsey Paxton. He looked very tired. "And now you and your parents want me to substitute this essay for that one?"

"No," said Richard. "My parents don't know I'm here. I don't care what's in the playbill. I just think you ought to yank the essay Mr.

Davidson gave you. He's submitting it to *Feminist Renaissance*. He told our class. He's trying to get it published as his wife's work. You don't want the Arts Council associated with some kind of fraud, do you?''

"No," said Ramsey. "I don't." He stacked the envelope on top of the book and magazine already on his desktop. "I don't know what you're up to, Richard, but I don't have time for one of your notorious practical jokes."

Richard swore to him that it wasn't a joke, but he felt helpless even as he spoke. Everything he did, everything—it always turned out so wrong. Now Ramsey Paxton was mad at him, too.

"Oscar Davidson made one of your friends angry, so you're trying to get back at him, is that it?"

"It's more than that," Richard said. "He's doing wrong."

"Didn't you have some trouble at Montpelier in Mr. Davidson's class?" said Mr. Paxton.

Richard admitted that he had.

"It was about forging a paper, wasn't it?" said Mr. Paxton.

"Yes," said Richard. "But this is real."

"I don't believe you, Richard," said Mr. Paxton.

"I can tell," said Richard. He reached for the magazine, the book, and the manuscript on the desk, but Mr. Paxton pulled them away. "I'll keep these," he said.

Now everything was all wrong. "You can't," said Richard. "Those don't even belong to me." He wanted to go back and start over. He should never have tried this. Now he'd screwed everything up.

"I'm going to sort this out when I have time," said Ramsey Paxton.

Richard begged him to return at least Rebecca's book and Alex's manuscript. He could keep the magazine containing the story. But Mr. Paxton would not budge.

"You need to get back to school, Richard."

Richard was furious and frustrated and outraged. "Mr. Paxton," he said, "I know you don't believe me. If I were you, I guess I wouldn't believe me, either. But I'm telling you the truth. I'm trying to do something right. For once. Nobody wants to consider that as a possibility. I just wish for one minute you'd forget it was me who brought you this stuff. I just wish you'd look at the evidence. I'm not trying to trick you. I hate Mr. Davidson's guts and I wish he'd go to hell forever, but

I haven't made up anything that I've told you. Look at that story. Look at that chapter. What would you have done if you were in my position?''

Ramsey Paxton did not look at the materials again, but he looked at Richard carefully. For a long time. ''Come back here at five o'clock this afternoon,'' he said. ''I'll return your friend's book to you then. And then we'll discuss these other matters.''

Richard finally left the office in despair. 5:00. He might as well have to wait until the turn of the century. He could hardly even remember walking back to the Arts School. Why wouldn't anybody believe him? Why wouldn't they at least consider that his story was true? That was the trouble with being the King of the Pranksters. You might as well lie all the time. Nobody would believe you anyway.

When he got to Mr. Nivens's class, the late bell had already rung. He would have to stay after class. He could hardly have screwed up any more. And he blamed it all, every bit of it, on Oscar Davidson.

After his class Oscar Davidson walked upstairs to Anne Lindsey's office. She was on the telephone with a parent and motioned him inside. He took the sculpted plastic chair by the desk and waited until she hung up.

''That was Rebecca Taylor's mother,'' she said. ''She's very upset.''

''Her loudmouth daughter should be expelled,'' said Oscar.

''No,'' said Anne Lindsey. ''Rebecca and I had a long talk. She said you embarrassed her in class yesterday. Talked about her financial aid package.''

''She's a whiner,'' said Oscar.

''And you made a racist slur this morning.''

''That's ridiculous.''

''She's a bright girl who needs a chance,'' said Anne. ''Maybe you'd better start being a little kinder to your students. Why do you teach anyway, Oscar?''

''Good question. Why did you hire me?''

She said he knew the answer to that one. ''Frankly,'' she said, ''you're beginning to lose your charm for me.''

''Don't you turn on me now,'' said Oscar.

''Oscar,'' she said, ''your financial gifts to the Arts School have

always been greatly appreciated. But you are not buying yourself a
personal playground here.''

"It's hardly a playground for me.''

"Or your own group therapy. Or whatever urge you happen to satisfy
from being here. Why do you want to spend so much time at high
schools, Oscar?''

"This is pop psychology out of pulp paperbacks,'' he said.

Anne said she expected him to apologize to Rebecca Taylor.

Oscar Davidson stood up. "I bought you a house,'' he said. "I gave
your sister financial security.''

Anne rose and faced him across her desk. "But we know what you
didn't give her, don't we?'' she said.

"That's vicious.''

"True,'' she said. "I'm sorry for that.''

"I'm as angry over Sarah's death as you are,'' he said. "It's been
an adjustment for me, too.''

"Just don't use it as an excuse to abuse the students, Oscar. Why
don't you take the rest of the day off?''

"I'm too professional,'' he said. She didn't think it was funny. A
few minutes later, when Ramsey Paxton called to talk about an old
copy of *The Shenandoah Review* and a new copy of Sarah's last monograph he'd acquired, she didn't think that was funny, either.

❧

For Tucker the silence in the kitchen was unbearable. Moonie had declared half an hour ago that they would offer club sandwiches and a
salad bar for lunch. That was the last word she had spoken to him. He
stood by the stove and removed the last piece of bacon from the pan,
and then he looked around for something else to do. Moonie tore lettuce
into a large metal bowl.

"Moonie—'' he said.

"My name is Ramona,'' she said.

"Okay, Ramona,'' he said.

"Not in that tone, Tucker.''

He would lose his temper in a minute. Beside him the hot bacon
dripped onto white paper towels. A fan hummed over the stove. He
walked to the metal counter where Moonie made the salad.

"I didn't ask to work here with you," he said. "It's not my fault that Bernard quit."

"It's your girlfriend's," she said. "Nancy Gale Slut. She's been stealing food since she got here."

He didn't believe it.

"It's true," she said. "Nobody else in the company has a passkey. You haven't been stealing, have you?"

"I think Bernard just makes excuses," said Tucker. He reminded her that last summer, when the company had rehearsed downtown, Bernard had quit three times. "Once was because people were using too much silverware at each meal. I don't know why Dad has put up with him."

"Because he comes cheap," she said. "And he wasn't making excuses this time. We've been missing all kinds of stuff."

"She's not my girlfriend, anyway," said Tucker. He grabbed some lettuce and started to tear it into the bowl. Moonie told him to wash it first.

"If she's not your girlfriend," she said, "what do you call her? Your milking machine?"

"What difference does it make to you?" he said. "You're the one who wanted to date Northrop Frye."

"Chris cares about something more than physical pleasure," said Moonie. "And he enjoys more than just hitting a tennis ball around or lifting weights or chalking up scores on his belt." She was furious.

"Yeah," said Tucker. "I can tell he makes you really happy."

"As happy as Nancy Gale makes you," she said. And they worked in silence, each of them wondering why, if they were now so marvelously, magically happy, their throats burned with so much bile.

❈

Because Richard and Rebecca Taylor were both late to Mr. Nivens's class, they had to remain behind when the bell rang. Nivens started by asking them where they'd been.

"I took Rebecca's book over to Mr. Paxton," said Richard. "His office. I wanted him to know what had happened." It was true enough. He'd decided that he wouldn't tell them about the discrepancies in Oscar Davidson's writing. Not about the short story or the manuscript

for the playbill. Not until he knew their significance. He'd been embarrassed already this morning at Mr. Paxton's. He did not want a
replay.

"I was in the office," said Rebecca. "I called my momma. That
man is uncool."

Nivens sat casually behind his desk, his glasses off and resting on
the books in his lap. His feet were propped up on the desktop. "Will
you read another passage tomorrow?"

"Yeah," she said. "And I have to write an apology to the class. But
I bet you fifty dollars I could fake another passage out of that book
and he wouldn't even know. The man has that attention thing."

"Attention-deficit disorder?" said Nivens. The suggestion amused
him. "I doubt that."

"My momma says it's a common problem," said Rebecca. "She's
taking psychology classes over at the community college." They
weren't in a disciplinary meeting anymore. It had evolved into a casual
conversation.

"What about your dad?" said Nivens.

She told them that her father taught biology at Rockbridge High
School but painted houses this summer because he could earn more
money. "My dad's cool," she said. "I love it when we're home
together."

"That must be weird," said Richard.

"What?"

"Nothing," said Richard. "It's just that I can't stand being around
my own dad."

"Why?" she asked, half expecting a joke.

He didn't know how to get started. "It's too complicated," he said.
"Let's just say I hate my father."

Nivens was interested. "Does he belittle you? My father used to tell
me I was stupid. Over and over he'd tell me how limited I was. Before
my mother and I moved out."

Richard thought that was horrible. What his own dad had done was
not nearly that bad. Not really.

"He called me stupid," said Nivens, "and now I'm going to earn a
doctorate and publish a scholarly article. You can turn that negative
energy into something productive, Richard. You can show him."

"Do you get along with your dad now?" said Richard.

Nivens waved the question away with his necktie. "My father is dead," he said.

"You're lucky," said Richard.

"You're full of it," said Rebecca to Richard.

"You don't know," said Richard.

"Your daddy beat you?" said Rebecca.

"No," said Richard.

"Get drunk?"

"No."

"Run around on your mother?"

"Not that I know of," said Richard.

"Neither does mine," said Rebecca. "So why hate him?"

He knew that he would never tell them everything, but he wondered if maybe they would pry it out of him. "He made me do this outdoor program last spring. Outward Bound," said Richard. It sounded so stupid, even to him.

"Poor boy," said Rebecca. "Couldn't go to Fort Lauderdale."

Chris Nivens said he wouldn't have liked Outward Bound either.

"Tucker did it when he was my age," said Richard. "He loved it." Then he told them all about the blond hero and the dark-haired villain. "Fair" and "light" were always associated with the good guy, and black was always associated with evil.

"Be careful," said Rebecca.

"It was as if by being born first, Tucker got first choice," said Richard. "I'd like to do something good once in a while. But Tucker's already there in front of me. Whatever I do, he can do better."

"You can read better, can't you?" said Nivens. "I've heard he's severely dyslexic."

"But that somehow makes it worse," said Richard. "Reading is easy for me. It's hard for Tucker. So when he does it, he's doing more of a heroic gesture."

Nivens never kept his tie knotted tight. He played with the knot. "Tucker never complains about his leg, does he?"

"Never," said Richard. He wished that Tucker would. It would make him seem more human. "I think he's worried that he'll hurt my dad's feelings, so he never, never mentions it. But I've seen him get cramps. I know it hurts him sometimes."

Nivens nodded. "Were you there when it happened?"

"No," said Richard. "I was away. I was at Outward Bound."

"Oh, yes," said Rebecca. "Where that mean old father sent you."

Richard told her that she just didn't understand. "Going to Outward Bound was what made me realize that I was bad, that's all."

They both kidded him for saying that. "You've decided to be evil?" said Nivens. "A conscious commitment?"

Richard had such a hard time explaining it. "I haven't decided to be," he said. "I just think I am." He looked at them and hoped for a contradiction. "I think I was just born that way. Born bad."

"Too heavy for me," said Rebecca. She took her books and waved good-bye as she left the room.

Nivens waited through a good silence before he spoke. "Do you feel guilty about something?" he said.

Richard wanted to tell him so badly. But he couldn't. He couldn't.

"Why do you think that you're so bad?" said Nivens. "It's more than just these pranks, isn't it?" Just a few days ago Richard had written an essay for Nivens that described and renounced all of his favorite practical jokes from the past—the tying of one doorknob to another, the salt in the sugar bowl, the dye in the shower head, tooth-paste in the mouthpiece of the telephone.

"You know," said Nivens, "there's nothing you could do that would be too terrible to name."

Richard looked at him and said nothing.

"Once you say it out loud," said Nivens, "it loses its power over you. Name your dragons, Richard. Is there anything you want to tell me?"

Yes, thought Richard. *Yes, yes, yes.* "No," he said, and their conversation was over.

✣

Griffin Dupree arrived by taxi just before lunch. It was hard to tell how old he was—under thirty, certainly, but how far under was a matter of some dispute among the company. What was indisputable was that their new Oberon was physically slight but mentally prodigious. He learned all of their names upon introduction and found something interesting to say about the characters they were playing. For the first ten minutes they liked him. Then they became better acquainted. He wore his black hair pulled straight back in a dry pompadour, carried his belongings in a shoulder bag, and removed his sunglasses only when he entered his room at the Inn, the room previously occupied by Hugh Bickley, the room sharing a bathroom with Tucker Blackburn, who showed him around.

"This room is too hot," he said. "I need an air conditioner."

Tucker explained that the air-conditioning was hooked up only for the main floor so far.

"I need an air conditioner," said Dupree. He was shorter than Tucker and several pounds lighter, but he made it clear that he was accustomed to being accommodated.

"We don't have an air conditioner."

"Rent one."

"I don't think—"

"While you're fetching it, I'll be downstairs in that dreary rehearsal hall you showed me. I have lines to review. The plane was too bumpy."

During the afternoon rehearsal, which they held inside at Dupree's insistence, their new Oberon picked up all his blocking on the first run-through and had his lines cold. Tucker left the lunch dishes for Moonie in order to rent an air conditioner downtown.

His father was insistent that he keep it secret.

"How do you conceal a window unit, Dad?" said Tucker. "Everybody's going to see it. And hear it."

"Everybody's going to want one," said Milton.

But when Tucker plugged in the rented air conditioner, the lights in the building went out.

"The breaker panel trips," said Tucker, who had to go down to the basement to reset the buttons.

"Get fans," said Dupree, who was not pleased.

Tucker unplugged the fan from its extension cord in the attic and set it up in Griffin Dupree's room.

"Not enough," said Dupree. "I need at least three."

This time Milton Blackburn gave Nancy Gale Nofsinger some cash and sent her to Wal-Mart for a couple of fans.

"Keep them a secret," he said to her.

"How do you keep floor fans a secret?" she said.

"You unload them when the rest of the company is busy," he said.

Nancy Gale was delighted to miss a rehearsal in order to buy Griffin Dupree some fans. From the first moment she'd seen him, she'd thought he was absolutely gorgeous.

Oscar Davidson found Chris Nivens reading Hamlet's fourth soliloquy aloud in his classroom.

"*Rightly to be great is not to stir without great argument,*" Nivens read to the empty desks, "*but greatly to find quarrel in a straw when honor's at the stake.*" He broke off and looked a bit embarrassed when Oscar entered the classroom. "I can't help it," Chris Nivens said. "I like it."

Oscar sat at the desk closest to Nivens's chair. "Have you distributed those program proofs I gave you yesterday?" he said.

Nivens said that he had.

"That's too bad," said Oscar.

"Why?"

"This is awkward," he said. "Can you get them back?"

"What's the matter, Oscar?"

"The matter is that Ramsey's no longer including the essay in the playbill. He's called the printer. They're pulling it."

"Why?"

"Because he found out Sarah didn't write it," said Oscar.

Chris Nivens was very interested. "Who did write it?"

"I did," said Oscar. He looked Nivens directly in the eye. "You must have had some suspicions."

Nivens said he had indeed. "I'd wondered when Sarah could have written such an amateurish piece," said Nivens. "But I never guessed you were the author. Why?"

Oscar shrugged. "I wanted to publish it," he said. "They wouldn't print it under my name, so I used Sarah's." He watched to see how Nivens would react. Nivens smiled.

"And now you'd just as soon forget the whole thing," said Nivens. "You'd rather not have our students inquiring as to why this essay is no longer going to be in the program."

"Correct."

"Especially not Richard Blackburn," said Nivens.

"Correct again," said Oscar. "Though I did write the piece. It's not as if I'm trying to take credit for somebody else's creation."

Nivens said he didn't know how to collect the essays without bringing more attention to them. "Why not let it go?" he said. "They had nothing to say about it in class this morning. It's of no interest to them.''

"Because Ramsey now has the original manuscript,'' said Oscar. "The real one. The one I thought was burned up in the fire.''

"What?'' Nivens was staggered.

"I don't want the students to be able to compare the two.''

"Where did Ramsey get it?'' Richard Blackburn had been to see him this morning. But the boy couldn't have had Sarah's monograph.

"He wouldn't say,'' said Oscar.

"I've got to see it,'' said Nivens. "Have you looked at it? Is it the real thing?''

"Probably,'' said Oscar. "He says it's got Anne's pencil marks all over it.''

"I can't believe it,'' said Nivens. "After all this time.''

Oscar Davidson was not willing to wait through his expostulations. "This could be potentially embarrassing for me and for Anne,'' he said. "I'm here to inform you of what's going on so that you can help us keep this as quiet as possible. We do not want this matter made public.''

"I understand, Oscar,'' said Nivens. He allowed himself a mildly admonitory expression. "What an idiotic stunt.''

"Tell the kids that the essays were on loan,'' said Oscar. "Just get them back somehow. In case Ramsey decides to print this other monograph.''

"Is he going to do that?''

Oscar Davidson didn't know what Ramsey was going to do. "I'm trying to smooth it over,'' he said. "Ramsey frequently listens to conversations in which money is the subject of each sentence.''

"Good luck,'' said Nivens. He waved his paperback as Oscar departed. Then he forced himself to wait a full three minutes before he fled from his classroom and to his apartment across the street. Assurances of secrecy be damned. He wanted to call Ramsey Paxton right away. But he hesitated when he saw the blue telephone message slip taped to his mailbox in the vestibule. "Call your father in Baltimore,'' it said, with a number attached. He took the slip and crumpled it into the size of an acorn. Then he reconsidered. What would happen if he called the number? What would he hear on the other end? Perhaps he should call. Perhaps it was time to put a stop to these outrageous intrusions via telephone.

But first, Ramsey Paxton.

❧

Ramsey Paxton hung up the telephone from speaking to the editor of *Feminist Renaissance,* who promised to call him back by the end of the working day. It had taken a long time to get through to the woman and an even longer time to persuade her that what he asked her to check was important. He couldn't remember a day when he'd spent so much time on the telephone. Oscar Davidson calling to argue about the essay in the program. *Too bad.* Patricia Montgomery calling to ask for more money to pay some substitute actor they'd hired. *Forget it.* A moment after he hung up, the telephone rang again. It was Chris Nivens from the Arts School.

"Is it true you're pulling the Sarah Davidson essay out of the playbill?"

Ramsey Paxton did not want to talk to Chris Nivens.

The kid was persistent. "Oscar tells me you've found another manuscript of Sarah's," he'd said. "I'd be happy to authenticate it for you."

"No, thanks."

"That essay means a lot to me," said Nivens. "I did the research. It's not just Sarah's work, but it's mine, too. You can't imagine how eager I am to see it."

Ramsey as much as told him that that was tough luck before finally getting rid of him.

3:15 P.M. Time to get out of the office and away from the phone. He collected an advertising brochure from the Stone Mountain Theater and a yearbook from the Rockbridge Arts School, left his office, and drove to 1147 Roanoke Avenue, the address listed on the invoices for Stone Mountain Consultants. It took him twenty minutes to get there, past tire dealerships, used-car lots, and eventually warehouses and shipping firms. Number 1147 was a small office building the size of a modest house, two stories high, with the numbers pasted onto the side of the building with stick-on lettering. Ramsey parked in the lot in front and noted that the shingle hanging over the glass front door was for a medical supplies company. He took the yearbook and brochure from the seat beside him, entered the dark hallway, and immediately found himself at another glass doorway with WORRELL SUPPLY COMPANY painted in tidy letters on the glass. He could see that the office was occupied. He passed it and proceeded down the hall. There was only one other door, an unmarked one, which was locked. The lights were out in the stairway, but he climbed the dark stairs anyway, his feet shuffling on the ridged rubber risers. On the second floor he found two rest rooms and a locked door painted with a sign for ANNISTON PESTICIDES, INC. He returned to the ground floor, where a middle-aged black man in a short-sleeved shirt and tie stood in the doorway to Worrell Supply Company and waited for him to descend.

"May I help you?" he said. "There's nobody upstairs."

Ramsey followed him into the bright, busy office. Inside were two comfortable chairs, between which sat a stand-up ashtray and which faced a long Formica counter. Behind the counter were three desks, two of them occupied. A black woman talked on the telephone at one, while a younger black man typed into a computer at another. A ledger stood open at the third, presumably vacated by the man who had greeted Ramsey.

"I'm Henry Worrell," he said. "You don't look like a man who needs any bandages."

Ramsey introduced himself and told him that he was looking for the Stone Mountain Consultants.

"Out of business," said the man. He was relaxed, comfortable, polite. He leaned on the counter as he talked to Ramsey.

"For how long?" said Ramsey.

Worrell shrugged. "Two or three months? Maybe four?" he said. "I really couldn't say. They never made it here."

"What do you mean?"

"I mean they never made it into business. Back around January a man came by here and told me that he'd started a company and opened an account but that it wasn't going to work out. He asked me to forward any mail that arrived."

"Forward it to where?" said Ramsey. He placed the brochure and the yearbook onto Henry Worrell's counter. This was getting very interesting indeed.

Worrell had to return to his desk and look into a couple of drawers. He returned to the counter. "To post office box eighty-seven," he said. "I've never had to use this. They never got any mail."

"Did you know the man's name?" said Ramsey.

"He did introduce himself," said Worrell. "I can't remember his name now."

"Was it Milton Blackburn?" said Ramsey.

"I honestly can't remember," said Worrell. "It was a while ago. But the man did look familiar. He was one of those theater people. I've seen his picture in the paper."

"And no mail has ever come here?"

"No," said the man. "Well, it wouldn't, ordinarily. It would go to the post office box. He was just covering his bases, that's all. In case something came to the street address by mistake."

"There has never been a Stone Mountain Consultants Company?" said Ramsey.

"Not here," said Worrell. "Not lately. We've been here for fifteen years."

Ramsey opened his brochure advertising the Stone Mountain Theatre. He pointed to a photograph on the second page. "Was it this man?" he said.

"No," said Worrell. "This guy had blond hair."

"What about her?" said Ramsey Paxton. "Could she have been disguised as a man?"

"No way," said Henry Worrell. "This was definitely a man."

Ramsey Paxton opened his yearbook from the Rockbridge Arts School and turned to the faculty section. He pointed to a face.

"That's him," said Worrell. "No doubt about it."

Now Ramsey understood why this business about Oscar Davidson's writing had suddenly come up today. It was an attempt at a smoke screen. They had contrived to send Richard Blackburn over in a last-ditch attempt at deflecting Ramsey's investigation of the Consultants account. But the Blackburn boy had revealed more than anyone could have guessed. "Alex Mason," Ramsey said, reading the name under the picture.

"Yes," said Worrell, also looking at the page. "Alex Mason. He's the one."

※

Richard looked at the clock all through play practice. Usually Alex's *Hamlet* rehearsals started at 1:30 and ran until 4:00. Theoretically, Richard would have plenty of time to get over to Mr. Paxton's office before it closed at 5:00. But today Alex was in a terrible mood, snapping at everybody and threatening to make the cast come back after dinner. Hell, the show didn't even go up for another four weeks. At last, at 4:15, Alex dismissed the group. Everybody but Richard.

"You have to touch up that spot in the plaster from yesterday," he said. "You'll find the paint downstairs."

"Can't I do it tomorrow?"

"Now."

He knew that he should tell Alex about going to Mr. Paxton's. But there was still time for him to get there. He could still retrieve his materials before Mr. Paxton went home for the day. It was possible that Alex might never know he'd been to see the guy.

"May I use the trapdoor?"

"Use the stairs, Richard."

Alex stood in a three-foot-square hole on the stage with his waist touching the stage floor. He had on a T-shirt with holes in the armpits and blue jeans open at the knees and some old paint-spattered tennis shoes, and he was sweating. These trapdoors were old and needed lubrication. He had arranged scaffolding in the storage room below, where the paint was, so that he could work on this trapdoor plus the one next to it, closer to center stage. As Alex loudly worked a bolt on a neighboring trapdoor, Richard hurried past the office and down the stairs leading to the all-purpose room beneath the stage.

The hall downstairs was windowless, the walls of unpainted gray cinder block lighted by bare bulbs overhead. When Richard arrived at the door to the storage room, he found that it was locked. Another delay. He wondered sometimes if there were some huge cosmic conspiracy devoted to ruining his life. By the time he got back upstairs to the stage, Alex had worked the other trapdoor open. Now there was a hole that looked like a grave. Alex was pleased with his efforts.

"It needs some repair," he said. "There's something sticking in this locking mechanism."

He closed the second door back, popped it open again, and then closed it once more. The hole no longer resembled a grave, but a square cargo hatch.

Richard explained that the door downstairs was locked and asked if he could use the trapdoor and the scaffolding to get into the storage room. Alex was so relieved about getting the second trapdoor open that he sounded almost apologetic.

"Sure," he said. Then the telephone in his office rang, and he climbed out to answer it. Richard lowered himself onto the scaffolding through the trapdoor with his hands on the gritty floor of the stage. It was easy to climb down the scaffold and find the paint against the far wall. The room was large, with a concrete floor, four bare bulbs for illumination, cinder-block walls. The stage overhead made a ceiling almost fifteen feet high. Alex had divided the room into quadrants. Most of the costumes on hangers and the props were in the half of the room closest downstage, closest to the audience. Facing them were tools on hooks, lumber in bins, and supplies on shelves, including paints. Lots and lots of paints.

Richard found a new can of flat black latex and carried it back to the scaffolding, which provided much faster transportation than the stairs. The paint can was heavy. He climbed up ten feet of scaffold, reached the top platform, and stuck his head through the trapdoor. Alex was still in the office on the telephone. Richard leaned down to get the paint and rested it on the closed lid of the trapdoor beside him. Then he put one hand next to the paint, placed the other nearby, and hoisted himself upward.

He progressed only a few inches before the closed trapdoor on which he was lifting himself gave way. Richard and the can of paint fell only a few feet, onto the platform of the scaffolding. But the paint bounced off and plummeted onto the concrete below, where it landed with a loud *thwock*. The lid came off, and instantly the room looked as though someone had sprayed black paint through a hose in an arc all over the back wall. The spin from its fall had given the liquid inside plenty of momentum. It was a disaster. The far wall where the tools hung had become a universe with a thousand black holes. The handsaw dripped black from several teeth onto the screwdrivers. The hammerhead was now speckled with black. The door was splattered. The paint cans on the shelf also dripped black. Richard wanted to run away. It didn't matter what he did, it always turned out badly. He was just bad, that was all. He picked himself up and climbed out of the trap to tell Alex.

It took a minute for Richard to realize that Alex's horrified expression had to do not with Richard's mishap, but with his telephone conversation.

When Ramsey Paxton called at the end of his rehearsal to tell him about his visit to Roanoke Avenue, Alex was stunned.

"This is wrong," said Alex. "This is a big mistake."

"A mistake we're going to rectify now," said Ramsey. "I'm on my way over."

"No," said Alex. "Please. There's a student here." He had to figure this out. "Let's just talk about it tomorrow."

But Ramsey wouldn't be put off. They settled on 9:00 that evening.

After he hung up, Alex reached into the bottom drawer of his desk and extracted a brown mailing envelope, one of several which he'd concealed under some notebooks. It was printed with the return address for the Arts School and was identical to the envelope Patricia Montgomery had given him when he had picked her up at the airport. From the envelope he pulled a dozen invoice forms from the Stone Mountain Consultants, all blank. Patricia had given them to him two years ago, and he had never used them.

"Now," he said aloud to the printed sheets, "what's the best thing for me to do with you guys?"

And then Richard was there telling him something about some damned paint.

❈

After his third trip to town for Griffin Dupree (air conditioner; mineral water; soft-light bulbs for his lamp), Tucker was ready to commit murder. All these chores, and he still had to work in the kitchen tonight. It was torture to be around Moonie. Ramona. When in the hell was Bernard going to decide to return to work? They were having the technical rehearsal at 7:00, supposedly, though he could tell that everything was going to be badly delayed. He was upset over his tiff with Moonie (Ramona!) this afternoon, but he couldn't decide whether to be angry with her or with himself. And then, at 4:30 P.M., just as his car approached the top of the hill and sped toward the Inn, his engine coughed. The car lurched and then died. *No, no, not now.* He was in a shady section of the road, and the dappled sunlight reminded him of jungle movies where the hero's Jeep breaks down and he has to walk. He got out of the car and popped open his trunk, where he stowed his one-gallon emergency gasoline ration. It was nearly empty itself, containing perhaps a cup or so of fuel. He drained it, and it was enough to get the engine started and over the crest of the road. He progressed through the gate to the Inn and almost to the Inn itself when the car died again. Damn it to hell. Tucker still had one last chance. He pushed the car around the curve to the right of the building and got it rolling downhill as far as the loading dock, where he parked face in toward the building. He was stuck now; the slope was too steep to push the car out. But he ought to be able to get some fuel.

The old red cylindrical gasoline canister for the mower was behind the trash cans at the end of the loading dock. Tucker hobbled up the stairs and grabbed its handle. The canister followed his hand into the air as if it contained helium. It was empty, too.

Okay, Tucker thought, *you're having what we call a bad day. But it's not over yet. A bad day can get better.*

He refused to admit that it could also get worse.

❊

"Get out of here, Richard," Alex said. He looked sick, not simply uncomfortable, but ill, as if he had just eaten something poisonous.

"Did you see—?"

"Get out of this office."

"I spilled paint—"

"Clean it up and then get out of the theater."

"Could I use the phone first?"

"No." It was not a tone you argued with.

Richard went downstairs and put on Alex's old paint-spattered overalls. He used a dustpan to scoop up the paint on the floor and replace it in the pail. A lot of it came up, maybe a third of a bucket. Then he went to the sink in the far corner of the room, wet a rag, and started to clean the walls and the workshop area. The floor looked as if it had been washed in wet charcoal.

Alex came downstairs after half an hour. "You can go now," he said.

Richard ran upstairs to the office. It was 4:55. He looked up the number and called Mr. Paxton at work to tell him that he would be just a few minutes late. The secretary said that Mr. Paxton had left for the rest of the day.

"But we have an appointment for five o'clock," said Richard.

"Mr. Paxton has canceled all appointments," she said. "Why don't you call back in the morning?"

Richard felt betrayed. Mr. Paxton had forgotten about him. He went back downstairs and found Alex cleaning off one of the cans of paint. Richard startled him.

"Go on," said Alex. "You can leave."

"No," said Richard. "Look at the wall. Look at the tools." Richard continued to work. He had paint on his hands and on his arms, but he'd managed to keep it off his face so far. He wiped off the head of a hammer. He could stay and work. He could talk to Mr. Paxton later. Before he left this theater, he would do one thing right. He would clean up.

"Richard," said Alex. "I'm sorry for shouting at you. You don't have to stay."

"Might as well finish," said Richard. "I don't want to leave with a mess behind me."

Alex looked at him as if he were the Buddha on the mountaintop. "Yes," he said. "I can understand that." He relaxed all his muscles at once, as if he were preparing for a performance. Then he walked to the paint-splattered wall and grabbed the heavy bolt cutters—the long, thick metal handles ending in a snub-nosed clip, a combination of scissors and hedge clippers. The bolt cutters were one of the few tools to escape the paint, and, after working them for a moment, Alex replaced them on the hooks on the masonite. "I wish I could clean up my own mess as easily."

They worked for another half hour cleaning up the paint. When they were finished, Alex took Richard's dirty rag and rinsed it in the sink. "Richard," he said, "thank you."

"For what?" said Richard. "I trashed your trap room."

"For helping me make up my mind," he said. "I made an appointment with a man for nine o'clock tonight. I've decided now to be here for it instead of to run away."

Richard did not understand.

"I talked him into nine o'clock so that I'd have time to get out of town," said Alex. "This time I really was going to take off."

"What do you mean?" said Richard. "Who?"

"Ramsey Paxton," said Alex. "Remember that tomorrow, won't

you? Remember that Alex Mason gave his most courageous performance at the Lyceum Theater at nine o'clock on Tuesday evening. Remember that I could have run, and I didn't. I didn't want to leave any
mess behind.''

"Have you done something wrong?'' said Richard. It was such a
weird conversation.

"At the moment,'' said Alex, "I can't think of anything I've done
that's been right.''

"I know the feeling,'' said Richard. He'd never felt closer to Alex.
"What have you done?''

"I've betrayed my friends,'' said Alex. He would not say who they
were. He would not say anything else. But it didn't matter. Richard
was already thinking ahead to 9:00 this evening. That he had learned
of this meeting had to be more than mere coincidence. He'd received
a second chance, like the one Scrooge got in *A Christmas Carol*. He
could meet with Mr. Paxton after all. He could still maybe retrieve the
papers he'd left with the man this morning.

Richard did not tell Alex that he, too, had some business with Mr.
Paxton, that he would join them for their meeting, that his luck seemed
to be changing. He didn't inform Alex because he knew Alex would
instruct him to stay away. Richard could not imagine what Alex had
done to stir up Mr. Paxton, but he didn't believe the part about running
off. Alex was like that—very theatrical, tending to exaggerate when he
described his triumphs and his failures. He couldn't have done anything
too bad, or he wouldn't have mentioned it just now. Tonight at 9:00
Richard would make a surprise appearance and find out what it was.

❦

At 5:15 P.M. Ramona should have already been up on the mountain to
fix dinner, but she'd managed a set of tennis with Chris during his so-
called lab period, when he was supposed to be supervising the student
newspaper. Tucker could start dinner. Tonight the company had its
technical rehearsal, so the cast would eat an early light snack. She was
upstairs when the telephone rang. It was Alex Mason.

"Your mother's not at school,'' he said. "Is she at home?''

Ramona shouted downstairs for her mother to pick up the line.

When Anne Lindsey came to the telephone in the kitchen, Ramona did not hang up. She listened in.

"I need to see you," said Alex Mason. Ramona suppressed a giggle. It was so funny to hear people that old talking like desperate seventh-graders.

"Alex," Anne said, "it's all over."

"I need to discuss money with you," he said. "The Stone Mountain Consultants."

Anne Lindsey did not respond immediately. "Ramsey Paxton?" she said.

"Exactly."

"Trouble?"

"Lots."

"I'll cancel dinner with Oscar," she said.

"We might need him," said Alex Mason.

"I'll cancel dinner anyway," she said. "I'm glad for an excuse."

Ramona waited until both had disconnected before she hung up the line herself. Well. More money problems at the school. And a rift in the relations between her mother and Uncle Oscar. She wasn't surprised, but it made her sad. Ramona had never witnessed anything permanent in her mother's love life. Anne Lindsey grew tired of her companions after very short periods. It had happened with Ramona's father. It had happened with Alex Mason. It had happened for years, and the history terrified Ramona as she considered her own recent disenchantment with Tucker. Whatever she grew up to be, whatever she became in adulthood, whatever form her personality finally took, Ramona dreaded only one outcome: that she would turn out to be like her mother.

⁂

At 8:30 P.M. the mountaintop was bright with activity. There was plenty of daylight lingering in the sky, but the grass had already become a dark carpet, and the tree line at the edge of the lawn was black. At the amphitheater the technical crew adjusted lights according to faint directions issued from the seats. From the porch of the Pinnacle Inn the white glow looked like the entrance to a magical kingdom that had burst open on the side of the hill. Below the dark tree line, the lights of the city had begun to appear, and in the distance, the mountains were as blue as the sea, and the clouds a royal purple cloaking a few early stars. Costumed members of the company strolled the grounds around the Pinnacle Inn, reciting lines, singing nonsense songs, concentrating on their characters. It was a magnificent night, but Milton Blackburn, walking from the porch of the Inn down the sloping path to the amphitheater, was conscious only of the passage of time. At this rate they would not be finished until after midnight.

8:32. The phone call from Ramsey had come an hour ago, and Milton had still not mentioned it to Patricia. He couldn't decide whether to bring it up now or after the rehearsal. Stone Mountain invoices, possible embezzlement, apparent fraud. It was a typical Ramsey Paxton power play, one which alluded to all sorts of improprieties but never issued a direct accusation. Ramsey loved to toss out bits of what he knew in order to get someone else to reveal more in response. In this case Milton had said nothing. Patricia had mentioned talking to Alex about the Consultants a couple of weeks ago, and Milton was worried that Alex had lured her into some potentially embarrassing scheme. It was the invoice business that particularly bothered him. Ramsey had asked them to be present for his meeting with Alex and Anne at 9:00. That was impossible on the night of a rehearsal. Alex could straighten it out on his own. But Milton wondered if Patricia was aware that some sort of trouble over the Consultants had surfaced.

8:35. He reached the boxwoods at the edge of the amphitheater. They were already over an hour behind schedule, but he'd deliberately said nothing. Patricia was coping. Technical rehearsals were always a nightmare. They'd had to fit out a costume for Griffin Dupree and find some bulbs for the fresnels at the back of the stage. One of the ellipsoidal spots had come unclamped and crashed into the boxwoods, fortunately with no damage to either, but it had meant getting the ladder out and resetting it. Now the crew was down there fiddling with more lights. The cast had started to mumble at 8:15, but too bad. He should never have agreed to play Theseus. It was such a dull, pompous part, even with all the physical gags Patricia had introduced. He wore a scarlet satin doublet, white hose, and slippers for Act I. He also wore a heavy gold chain and carried an ornate sword, suitable for the Duke of Athens.

Patricia, in her Hippolyta costume, sat in the back of the amphitheater with Nancy Gale Nofsinger. Yellow sheets of legal paper surrounded them like fallen leaves. Nancy Gale wore a wireless headphone set and spoke to the crew backstage setting lights in the boxwoods. Apparently the microphone in her headset did not work.

"I'm telling them," she said to Patricia. "They're not answering." Nancy Gale wore a thin orange T-shirt and shorts. She had tied her hair back with a rubber band, and she fanned her face with a legal sheet. "Brent! David!" she shouted into the small wire in front of her mouth. She turned to Patricia. "Nothing."

"Just go down there and tell them. We need the lights higher."

Nancy Gale ran down to the foot of the stairs, crossed the grassy verge, and jumped up onto the stage itself, where she wove her path through a half-dozen performers warming up and disappeared into the boxwoods behind. Only after she was gone did Milton see Tucker, who had been lying on the grass just behind where Patricia sat and who now rose to his feet.

"Dad," he said, "can I borrow the car? I'm out of gas."

Again. Milton should have chastised him, but he could see that his son was unhappy. "Where do you want to go?"

"Just out," said Tucker.

Milton told him the keys were in the dressing room at the Inn. "Take the can and get some gasoline when you go," he said.

"I'm going to a movie," said Tucker. "I promise I'll get it tomorrow."

Milton wondered why Tucker didn't just call one of his friends to hitch a ride, but he did not want to ask. Maybe Milton was too indulgent with Tucker. But aside from the boy's bad luck with machinery, he was an astonishingly loyal, reliable son. Milton watched him limp off through the gate in the bushes on his way up the hill. It was not like Tucker to be spending an evening by himself. He sat down beside his wife and told her that her costume made her look like a Lost Boy, with her hair under that hat.

"Hippolyta's the queen of the Amazons," she said. "She's supposed to look masculine."

He adjusted his sword so that he could settle into the wooden seat, then swatted away a mosquito. That was another problem with performing outside. You had the bugs, the airplanes overhead, the weather. People would bring flash cameras and copies of the text to read along as you went, and there would always be some squirmy child to run up and down the aisles at the most poignant moments.

Now, however, it was Griffin Dupree who ran up the aisle. He was in most of his costume and makeup, his skin painted pale blue, so that it would look positively ethereal on the stage, his hair full of glitter, his loose white shirt gathered at the waist like a swashbuckler's.

"I'm getting awfully tired of waiting," he said.

Blackburn wanted to blister him, but he kept silent. It was Patricia's show. She would have to handle it.

"I'm sorry, Grif," she said. Milton could not bear to hear her groveling. It was so undirectorial. She'd worked with plenty of pros; surely she knew how much authority she wielded. "We work with what we can at Stone Mountain," she said. "It's often a trial for all of us. Be patient."

But Griffin Dupree was not patient. "Did you know that your son Richard is trying to build a homemade gymnasium over our heads?" he said. "I think he took one of my fans."

Patricia said she would check on it. She wrote a note on one of her legal sheets.

"Perhaps we should keep Richard away from the stage area," said Dupree.

Milton had heard enough. "Richard will not disturb you," he said.

"Nobody disturbs me for long," said Dupree. He turned and strolled slowly back down to the stage.

"Why do we do this?" Milton said.

"You know," she said. And he did. As one of his colleagues had once said, it's the closest you ever get to flying. But he was not thinking about flight at the moment. He was thinking about the Stone Mountain Consultants.

"Patricia," he said, "do you have anything you'd like to tell me before we start rehearsals?"

"Break a leg," she said. She was astonishingly calm for all the chaos around them.

"No," he said. "I mean about something else."

She put down her coffee cup and her book. "Yes," she said. "We're going to have to rethink having Richard home for the summer. He's just causing trouble."

"I'll speak to Richard in the morning," said Milton. "That's not what I meant."

"What, then?" she said. Lights in the trees behind the stage came on one by one.

"Isn't it time for each of us to confess?" he said.

She turned and looked at him. "Is it?" she said.

"Don't you have something to tell me about money?"

She held her gaze. "And do you have something to tell me?"

"Yes," he said.

"Go ahead," she said.

"I'm the one who asked Sarah Davidson to kill your part," he said.

"What?" She was appalled. It was not what she had expected to hear.

"It was awful having you away," said Milton. "I asked her to write Tru out of the show."

She was speechless for only one good beat of outrage. "You prick," she said. "That's rotten."

"I've felt guilty about it ever since," he said. "We wouldn't be in such a money crunch if I'd kept out of it."

She was still absorbing it. "Why did you choose now to tell me this?" she said.

"Because it's time," he said. "Ramsey and Alex are meeting in half an hour."

"So?"

"So what do you have to tell me?"

"I'm not sure I want to, now."

"Ramsey will expect me to know," he said.

"It's Ramsey's fault that the whole thing evolved." She batted away a gnat. "I'm paying Griffin Dupree from our personal account. Ramsey wouldn't give me the money."

It was his turn for outrage. "We agreed never—"

"I was desperate," she said. "If the show's a hit, we can pay ourselves back."

"Ramsey will go berserk over our bookkeeping," he said.

"Yes," she said. "What about our bookkeeping?"

"Yes," he said. "Tell me about it."

"Tell you?" she said. "What are you doing with this Consultants account?"

He was not prepared for the question.

"You're the one running that," he said. "That's what I've been waiting for you to explain."

"Me?" she said. "You're the one with the Consultants account. I've been wondering all day why you've never mentioned it to me." She told him that Ramsey had broached the subject this afternoon when she'd called him to ask for money to pay Dupree.

"I have nothing to do with it," he said.

"Of course you do," she said. "Alex was signing your invoices."

"Alex was signing your invoices," he said.

They both caught on at the same time.

"I'd better get down there," said Milton.

"Yes," she said. "But not now. We have a rehearsal."

"It's Alex," he said. "It could be serious this time."

"Wait until your scene is over, Milton." She could be quite assertive with him, he noted. It was only the rest of the cast with whom she was timid.

Nancy Gale Nofsinger walked across the stage ringing a handbell. Time to get started. The actors who were not already onstage shuffled out of their hiding places. Patricia stood and descended to the stage. Milton Blackburn turned to run in the opposite direction until she stopped him.

"Milton," she said, "I mean it. We can't do the show without Theseus."

"I'll be here," he said. "I'm just going to make a phone call." He ran back to the office in the clumsy black shoes of his costume. He was breathless and sweating by the time he arrived. The door was unlocked. That was careless. No answer at Ramsey's home. No answer at the Lyceum. But Ramsey said he'd be meeting Alex there at 9:00. Theseus did not appear after the first scene until Act IV. If they got going right away, if he could wangle Patricia's car keys away from her, if Alex and Ramsey were still meeting, he just might be able to rehearse and still join the two at the Lyceum in his full regalia—doublet, hose, and sword.

❧

Richard hadn't exactly been banned from the Inn, but his parents had told him that they expected him to get his homework done before he approached the place again. As if he wanted to go up for a tech run-through anyway, with everybody screaming and yelling at the light man, the sound man, each other. It was the kind of evening that Richard thought of whenever somebody spoke of theater people as being like a family.

He figured it would take less than half an hour to jog the three and a half miles to the theater. He'd arrive a few minutes after nine, make sure that Mr. Paxton was there, and then wait for him to finish his meeting with Alex. It was only a few blocks to his office. They could get Rebecca's book and the *Review* and the manuscript, and then maybe Mr. Paxton would even give him a ride home. Or Alex would. Just in case he had to run back, though, he would take his backpack with him. With luck he would be back home before anybody returned from the Inn; nobody would know he'd been gone.

At 8:30 P.M. he changed into his running clothes and grabbed his backpack. On his way out he took a key with him, locked the front door, and stuck the key into his pack. Then he was off—down Canterbury Lane in the gray twilight, past the sprinklers and the smell of barbecue, past the badminton and croquet and kick-the-can games, around the people strolling on the sidewalks, down past the light and the gas station and the convenience store and on toward downtown until the buildings got taller and the sidewalks more deserted and the traffic lights more frequent. The air was warm and humid. It was an easy run, but he was hot by the time he got to the Lyceum. Having to stop at traffic lights had slowed him down, and it was almost 9:15 and full dark, though the yellow streetlamps provided plenty of light for the sidewalks.

In the parking lot he recognized three cars—Alex's Honda, Ramsey Paxton's Camry, and Oscar Davidson's Mercedes. Hell. Richard had not counted on meeting with Davidson tonight as well. He walked to the double doors at stage right and opened one of them. The lights were on inside the theater. He could see the black masking curtains and the empty vault of the fly space, but he didn't hear any voices. Alex's office was empty. The trapdoor was still open from this afternoon, and a light was on in the storage room. There was a sealed can of paint beside the open trapdoor. As he approached the trap, he could hear shuffling noises coming from the room below.

"Alex?" he called. The noises stopped. Richard arrived at the trapdoor and looked inside. He could see a man's body lying on the floor far beneath him. There was blood by his head. And suddenly there was Alex himself, hanging his overalls onto a hook on the wall, dropping a can of lubricating oil with a clunk onto the concrete floor, then leaping into Richard's line of vision, scrambling onto the scaffold, and pulling himself through the opening in the stage. Richard was scared.

"What are you doing here?" said Alex. He pushed Richard hard away from the opening in the stage.

"I came to see Mr. Paxton."

"Who else is here?" Alex's voice was loud.

"I'm alone," said Richard. "I'll go." Alex scared him. He backed off, but Alex grabbed his arm.

"Relax," said Alex. He was trembling. "Ramsey Paxton had an accident. He fell through the trapdoor. It wasn't properly secured, Richard." He looked at Richard with frustration.

The trapdoor again. Had Richard caused this accident as well? He tried to look back through the open trap, but Alex steered him away.

"Forget it," said Alex. "I just oiled the latch. How did you get in here?"

Richard pointed to the double doors.

"Great," said Alex. He reached into his pocket and gave Richard his keys. "Lock the doors now. Be sure they're secure."

Richard ran across the stage and locked the double doors. Then he pulled the panic bar hard to secure them. By the time he was done, Alex had moved to his office. He took his keys back from Richard and stuffed them into a pocket. Then he handed him Rebecca Taylor's copy of *Sally Galloway* from where it sat on the desktop.

"For you," said Alex, "with compliments of Ramsey Paxton. Though he wasn't planning to get it back to you tonight."

The book felt huge and clumsy to Richard. He stuck it into his backpack. "Did he bring *The Shenandoah Review* too? And the manuscript?"

"You didn't tell me you'd been to see him this morning, Richard," said Alex. He closed the zipper on his brown shoulder bag, lifted the bag onto his left collarbone, and pulled Richard out of the office and onto the stage. They were far from the open trapdoor. "We agreed that we weren't going to publicize any of Oscar's little discrepancies yet, didn't we?"

"Davidson deserved it," said Richard. "But Mr. Paxton didn't believe me."

"He believed you, Richard. If you could have seen him a few

minutes ago, you would have known how much he believed you." Alex ran both hands across his face and then shook them as if they were asleep. "Who knows you're here?"

"Nobody," said Richard. He was scared. "I'm supposed to be home studying."

"Why did you have to see Ramsey tonight?"

"I missed my meeting this afternoon," Richard said. "I wanted to get my stuff back."

"Your stuff? How did you know he would bring it?"

"I didn't," said Richard. "I thought we'd have to go by his office."

Alex laughed helplessly. "Beautiful timing," he said. "You're not going to need your so-called stuff now, Richard. The prank is over."

"What about my plagiarism trick?" said Richard. He moved toward the office, but Alex jerked him back.

"No," said Alex. "Listen. We have to leave." His hands were still shaking. He was in constant motion. "Are you reliable?" he said.

"Yes," said Richard.

"I have to go back downstairs for a second," said Alex. He hesitated. "No. Let's just leave now."

"But what about Mr. Paxton?" said Richard. "We need to get help."

"That's not necessary," said Alex. He realized that didn't sound right. He was jumpy and fidgety. "We have to go. We'll call nine one one when we get outside." He looked back at the trapdoor and then at Richard.

"Wait here," he said. He stepped over to the bucket of paint by the door and lifted it. Then he replaced it on the stage. "No," he said, "I can't."

Richard had no idea of what he was talking about. "Is he dead?" said Richard.

"No, no," said Alex. He was growing angry and very nervous. "I told you we'd call for help once we get outside." They heard someone tug on the double doors at stage right, the doors that Richard had just locked. They rattled.

"Somebody's coming," said Richard. Alex breathed shakily, looked across the stage at the double doors and then back at the paint can. "Maybe it's Mr. Davidson," said Richard. "I saw his car."

"We don't know who it is," said Alex. But it was enough to make him decide to bolt. He pushed Richard toward the edge of the stage. "I need a place where I can go to think in private. Let's get out of here before . . . before Mr. Paxton wakes up."

They were off the stage and nearly at the left exit door on the opposite side of the theater when they heard a knocking and a pounding on the doors across the stage. There was a shout. They could not hear the voice clearly.

"Quickly," said Alex. "Before they get inside." He grabbed Richard by the arm and pulled him out of the building through the exit door, which opened with a panic bar. Outside Alex held the handle and closed the door behind them gently, so that anyone entering the theater from the opposite door would be unable to hear their exit. They were in an alley at the side of the building. Broken glass glittered in the moonlight.

"You have to trust me, Richard," said Alex. "I've done something very bad, and now I need to get away. Do you have any money?"

It was so odd for an adult to be asking Richard for help. He was thrilled and flattered and terrified.

"I have twelve dollars," he said. He opened his backpack and gave all the money in his wallet to Alex.

Alex took the bills and put them into his pocket. Then he looked at Richard in the moonlight.

"I'll explain all this to you one day," said Alex. "He said I was going to jail. He kept yelling about jail, jail, jail, and I . . . I pushed him. He was sitting in the swivel chair, he glided over the trapdoor, it gave way, he fell through the trap, his head hit the floor, he started to bleed. And then you showed up. He's unconscious, Richard. We need to get him help."

Something was not right. Alex could have called for help on his office phone. And why would he ask Richard to lock the doors if he knew an ambulance would soon be on the way?

"What is it?" said Richard. "What aren't you telling me?"

"I have to get out of here, Richard. I can't be arrested. I won't be."

Richard couldn't believe it was real.

"I'm going away now," said Alex. "You're going to hear all sorts of bad things about me, Richard. They'll be true. Just remember that you can be bad in some ways but not bad all the way through. That's the truth, Richard."

Richard wanted so much to believe that.

"You've got Rebecca's book," said Alex. "That means people will know you were here. You understand that, don't you?"

"I understand."

"I want you to call nine one one. Just go to a pay phone on Madison Street."

"What will you do?"

"Don't ask," said Alex. He held out his hand. Richard shook it. There was something wet on Alex's hand. The touch was exhilarating.

"If they don't find the money right away," said Alex, "tell them it's in the paint can. The one on the stage." He was very nervous now, almost hyperventilating. "I was going to give Ramsey the money in person, Richard. If he hadn't started yelling, I would have given him the money back by now."

"What money?" said Richard.

"Never mind," said Alex. "Remember that I could have taken it, but I didn't."

"I'll get it and save it for you," said Richard.

"No," said Alex. "Don't get any more involved in this."

"I want to help you," said Richard.

"If they ask you questions," said Alex, "just tell them what you saw. If they ask you why you were here, you can say that you wanted to get your friend's book back from Mr. Paxton. That's true, anyway." Alex looked at him with appreciation. "How the hell did you find that short story?"

"He showed you that?" said Richard. "He had that with him inside?"

"C. Y. Anderson was just a pseudonym," said Alex. "Mrs. Lindsey told me."

"Was she here?"

"We had dinner tonight, Richard."

"What about the manuscript? What did she say about that?"

"What manuscript, Richard? It's best that you forget about the manuscript and the story. You don't remember those, okay? We aren't going to bring Mrs. Lindsey into this, right?"

A car with its radio blaring went past the entrance to the alley. Alex hitched up his shoulder bag and squeezed Richard's upper arm.

"Go now," said Alex. "You don't need to bring up Oscar Davidson's writing. You don't have to mention Mrs. Lindsey's magazine.

I'm the one who pushed Ramsey. I'm the one who took the money. That's all you need to say. Can you get home?''

"I can get home," said Richard. "Where will you go?"

"Better if you don't know where I am," said Alex. "This is very bad."

Richard felt an excitement unlike anything he'd ever felt before. "That's okay," he said. "I'm bad, too."

❈

Richard walked down the alley to the bright sidewalk of Madison Street while Alex waited by the stage door. It wasn't far to the street. When he reached the edge of the building, Richard looked back to wave, but Alex had already disappeared. It seemed impossible for him to vanish like that. Richard did not know whether he had gone back into the building or down the alley and around the Lyceum toward the parking lot for his car. Richard stepped onto the sidewalk, but then jerked himself back into the shadows when he saw a man in full, flashy red Elizabethan costume trying to get in the doors to the front of the theater. Unbelievable. It was his father. Richard stood in the alley and peeked with one eye at the front of the Lyceum. If Dad came down toward the alley, Richard would have to run in the opposite direction. But after trying the front doors, Milton Blackburn walked back toward the school, toward the covered walkway and the parking lot. As soon as he disappeared around the corner of the building, Richard ran across Madison Street. He stopped when he heard his own name coming from a window in one of the buildings opposite the theater.

"Richard." It was a stage whisper from Chris Nivens, who leaned out of his screenless front window and motioned for Richard to come up. This was not going well. He'd been free of Alex for thirty seconds and had already been caught. Richard ran to the building. It was an old brick house that had been converted into four apartments, two on each floor. In the light of the vestibule Richard turned his back on Madison Street and the Lyceum as he tried the main entry door of the building.

It was locked. He looked for Mr. Nivens's name beside the four buttons. It wasn't there. Was he in the wrong building? Richard pushed all four buttons anyway and hoped somebody was home.

"Come on," came the voice of Chris Nivens over the speaker. He was subletting the apartment belonging to K. M. Gaines. The buzzer sounded, and Richard was inside and running up the stairs. Nivens had already opened the door to the apartment when Richard reached the top. There was a reading lamp on by the window facing the street. Richard could see the Lyceum and the sidewalk to the school through the leaded windowpanes. He did not get too close to the window.

"What's the matter, Richard?" Nivens asked. He took off his glasses and scratched his stomach under his striped rugby shirt. He wore socks but no shoes. "I've never seen so much activity over there."

Richard hardly knew where to start. "I don't know what to do," said Richard. "Alex told me to call nine one one."

"What are you talking about?"

"Alex hurt Mr. Paxton," said Richard. "And now Alex has left."

Chris Nivens pulled him into a chair and sat in front of him. They were too far from the window to see the entrances to the theater. "Tell me what happened," said Nivens. "Alex hurt whom?"

Richard told him about seeing Ramsey Paxton motionless on the floor of the storage room and leaving the building with Alex. "It's something about money," said Richard.

"Alex and Ramsey had an argument over money? Money for the Lyceum?"

"Alex just told me he took some money," said Richard. "I don't know what money it was. But he left it inside a paint can. I don't know. He said he was leaving town. He didn't want to go to jail."

Chris Nivens was stunned. "I'm going over there," he said. "There's money inside a paint can?" He reached for his shoes, which had been kicked off under the coffee table in front of a corduroy-covered sofa.

"Maybe my dad's already inside by now."

"I saw him," said Chris Nivens. "You didn't come together?"

"I don't think he knows I'm here," said Richard. "I don't see how he could. I never told anybody."

"Why are you down here?" Nivens jumped up and looked for his keys. "Why are you so sweaty?"

"I ran," said Richard. "It was my chance to see Mr. Paxton again. I wanted to talk to him after I'd screwed up my conversation with him this morning." He would not tell Chris Nivens about the short story or the essay manuscript or the stunt he had wanted to pull with his own essay assignment this Friday. It was too complicated. There wasn't time. And Alex had asked him to avoid those topics.

Chris Nivens found his keys on the bookshelf by the door. "You're still upset over what happened in class this morning? Oscar's treatment of Rebecca?"

"I don't know what I'm upset about anymore," said Richard.

Through the open window they heard a siren approaching on the street outside. Both of them went to the window in time to see a fire truck race down Madison Street and pass them by. Richard saw no activity at the theater across from their window. His father had disappeared. In the parking lot he saw that Oscar Davidson's car was now also gone. Ramsey Paxton's car was still there. So was Alex's.

"Maybe Alex hasn't left yet," said Richard.

Chris Nivens guided him back to a chair and made him sit down. "Do not make any phone calls," he said. "I'll call an ambulance from over there if we need one. You wait here."

"I'm going home," said Richard. "I don't want to be a part of this."

"If the police come, you have to be a part of it," said Chris. "You have to tell them what you saw."

"Why the police?" said Richard. "Why can't we just call an ambulance now?"

Chris Nivens knelt and grabbed him by both arms. "Nobody wants trouble," he said. "Stay here, and don't call anybody. If I can reason with Mr. Paxton, maybe we won't have to involve the police. But don't leave."

"You'd better go," said Richard. "I don't think you can reason with him."

Chris Nivens headed for the door. "Richard," he said, "is Mr. Paxton hurt badly?"

"I think so," said Richard. "I think he's dead."

❖

Anne Lindsey was not accustomed to being out of control. She sat in her own kitchen and wept, wept helplessly, while Oscar Davidson used a dishtowel to blot the blood on the hem of her dress. He had already wiped her hands clean, as one would a child's.

"What have I done?" she said. "What have the two of us done?"

It was 9:45 P.M. "Calm down," said Oscar. "Everything's taken care of."

"Taken care of," she said. "There's going to be scandal and shame and prison. I'm going to lose my job."

"No, you're not." He took pleasure in watching her hysteria, in being the one to think rationally. "You weren't there. Neither of us was there."

"Of course we were there," she said. "You think Ramsey won't tell what happened?"

"Ramsey won't say anything about either one of us," said Oscar. "Trust me."

"What did you do in there? What did you tell him?"

"I asked him to leave your name out of it," he said. "He was in a good bit of pain at the time."

She still shook with sobs. The glass of whiskey Oscar had poured for her sat untouched on the counter beside her. "Poor Ramsey," she said. "I'm so ashamed. Poor Alex."

"Yes," said Oscar. "Poor Alex."

"Shouldn't we call the theater?" she said. "Or the hospital?"

"No," he said. "What reason would we have? Let them call us. We were working in the school building, we left at nine-twenty-five P.M., we saw nothing unusual, we did not go near the Lyceum Theater."

"Why would Ramsey go along with such a story?" she said. "It's impossible."

"He never saw who shoved his swivel chair," Oscar said. "His back was turned."

"Of course he saw me," she said. "He was looking right at me."

"He's willing to forget," said Oscar. "I promised Ramsey we'd get him the money back. Ramsey's always ready to listen to talk about money. Especially when some seems to be missing."

"The money was in that damn bucket of paint," she said. "I told you that before you went over."

"But you never saw it, did you?"

She had not seen it. Alex had said it was inside the paint bucket, and she had believed him. "Why didn't you call anyone before you left? How could you just leave him there on the floor?"

"I couldn't call. We weren't there, remember? Besides," said Oscar, "he made me angry in the end. He wouldn't cooperate about my writing."

"You bargained about that, too? You've got terrible timing, Oscar. He was hurt badly. He was out cold."

"He was awake when I arrived," said Oscar. "And he had a very bad headache. Of course, Ramsey had a lot of head to ache."

She was still crying. "This will never work," she said. "What if Milton saw us?"

"He didn't see us. If he did, he saw us in the parking lot. It's all right. Nobody saw us."

"We should go down there. I want to check on Ramsey."

He tossed the dishtowel into the sink and held her. "It's over," he said. "Put on your poker face."

She shook her head. The tears had begun to dry. "There's still going to be the trouble over Sarah's manuscript," she said.

"That's nothing," he said. "We can weather that. It's *Sally Galloway* we want to protect."

She fought off a new fit of weeping. "Oscar, you're so damn stupid. It's a miracle nobody has found out before now."

"Careful," he said. "Be very careful, from now on, about the aspersions you cast."

"Alex knows," she said. "He asked me about it at dinner. I tried to put him off by telling him C. Y. Anderson was a pseudonym."

"Alex has other problems," said Oscar. "He wasted no time in getting away, I might note, though he did take the time to lock all the doors. You should have heard the obscenities Ramsey shouted at me when he heard me walk into the theater. At first he thought I was Alex coming back." He paused. "Or you."

"All right," she said. "I was irrational. But I wanted to push him away from me, that's all. I'm a fool. You'll hear me say it forever."

"And yet you expect me to continue to be your lackey," said Oscar. "Perhaps it's time for a change in our contract."

They regarded one another in silence.

"Alex loves me," she said. "He did this all for love."

"An unfair comparison," said Oscar. "Love is so much more glorious than money."

Chris Nivens stood in the basement storage room of the Lyceum Theater and looked around him in horror. The paint-splattered overalls were
on the hook where Alex kept them, but they were smeared with fresh
blood. On the floor was more blood. A fresh can of black latex paint
sat on the smooth concrete surrounded by blood, one string of black
paint running down the white side of the can and into the sticky red
pool. Nivens felt like vomiting. He had vomited after the fire, after he'd
seen the wreckage of Sarah's house, and he felt like vomiting again.
He went to the sink and ran water over his hands and splashed his face.

On the floor in front of him Ramsey Paxton lay dead. His face was
down on the concrete, his eyes bulging, his mouth open in what had
been his final scream. All the fingers from his left hand were cut off
and scattered around the room like wine corks. Two fingers from his
right hand were missing as well. The bolt cutters used to remove the
fingers were wrapped in some of the same rags Richard had used that
afternoon to clean up paint.

Nivens tried to suppress his nausea and backed out of the room. He
left the lights on, and he walked, deliberately and rationally, up the
stairs and to the small office Alex Mason used, where he picked up the
telephone and called the police. While he waited, he looked again at
the empty can of paint he had carried from the stage into the office.
The police would undoubtedly be angry at him for touching it. But
Richard had mentioned money, and Chris Nivens had seen no money.
Nivens had only the vaguest sense of what had transpired between Alex
Mason and Ramsey Paxton. He felt certain as he spoke to the police,
however, that Providence was somehow at work here. It was no accident that he had been watching out of his window tonight and had
called Richard over. The preceding events were all part of some grand
metaphysical scheme, and while Nivens had no inkling of how this
cosmic drama would work itself out, he was confident that fate had
brought him here deliberately. Had he been a believer, he would have
called it a religious experience.

***

The detective's name was Ellen Spencer, and she had thick red hair
that was going gray and was cropped short just below her ears. She
had a round face and a firm mouth. She wore a yellow blouse and a

dark skirt, and she served as navigator of the conversation, steering it back onto course whenever Richard took the rudder. At 11:00 P.M. she sat with him in the worn lobby of the Lyceum on a padded bench and asked him questions. Everything he told her was true. But he did not tell her everything.

"Why were you down here?"

"I wanted to get a book belonging to a friend of mine."

"What book?"

He told her about the incident in class that morning involving Rebecca's reading of *Sally Galloway*. "I didn't think Mr. Davidson was fair to her. I took the book to Mr. Paxton to complain, since he's the head of the Arts Council."

"Why did you have to take him the book? Especially since she'd been reading from another story altogether?"

Good question. "I wasn't thinking," said Richard. "It seemed important at the time."

"Why didn't you go to the principal? To Mrs. Lindsey?"

"She likes Mr. Davidson," said Richard. "Mr. Paxton didn't." The sweat had dried on his face, but not on his shirt. Alex had asked him not to bring Mrs. Lindsey into the story tonight. He would try to observe Alex's request.

"How did you know anyone would be here tonight?"

"Alex told me that he'd be meeting with Mr. Paxton," said Richard.

"And you got the book back?" He had already shown her the contents of his backpack. "Why would he bring this book to a meeting with Alex Mason if he didn't know you were going to be here?"

Richard wasn't sure. "He knew Alex and I were friends," he said. "It would have saved time tomorrow if he could just leave it for me."

She took a lot of notes and had a tape recorder going. He told her about walking in and seeing Alex through the trapdoor. She wanted to know a lot about that part. "Was Mr. Paxton moving?"

"No."

"Could you see or hear him breathing?"

"No."

"Did you tell Mr. Nivens that you thought he was dead?"

"Yes."

"Have you ever seen a dead person before?"

"No," said Richard.

"Did Alex Mason tell you that Mr. Paxton was dead?"

"No," said Richard. "He said he was unconscious. He said we had to leave before he woke up."

"Was Alex Mason nervous?"

"Very."

"Did he have anything with him?" said Ellen Spencer. "Any luggage, any packages? Any papers?"

"Yes," said Richard. "He had his shoulder bag."

She nodded very slightly.

"Did he tell you where he was going?"

"No."

"Did you see anyone else while you were down here?"

"Yes," he said. "I saw my father." He told her about almost running into Milton Blackburn on the sidewalk.

"Why didn't you speak to him?"

"I didn't want him to know I was here," Richard said. "I was supposed to be at home studying."

"And then you ran across the street to Chris Nivens's apartment?"

"Yes."

"And did you see anyone else?"

"No," said Richard. "But when I first got here, Mr. Davidson's car was in the parking lot. And when Mr. Nivens and I looked out of his living-room window, the car was gone."

"What time was that?"

"I'm not sure," said Richard. "Nine-fifteen, nine-thirty."

"And you left that apartment when we arrived."

"Yes," said Richard. "I was there about twenty minutes."

"How long?"

"Fifteen or twenty minutes," said Richard. "In all. Counting my conversation with Mr. Nivens."

She made another note. "You're sure it was that long?"

"Yes."

She ran him through the history of how long he'd known Alex, and how well. "Do you know why Mr. Mason would do this, Richard?" she said. "Any idea at all?"

He told her about the paint bucket and the money. "He said Mr. Paxton threatened him with jail," said Richard. "And I was supposed to tell him that the money was in the paint can."

She sent a uniformed policeman off to fetch the pail of paint from Alex's office. "This can?" she said.

"I guess."

"This can is empty," she said, and she showed him. "Any idea why Mr. Mason would mislead you like that?"

He couldn't explain at all. Alex had seemed so convincing. It was a great performance.

Ellen tapped her notebook with the eraser of her pencil. "I have one more question to ask you, Richard," she said. "Why did Alex Mason let you go?"

That was one question that had never occurred to him. "I don't know," he said. "I guess because we're friends. Alex would never hurt me." And yet he had a very great suspicion that there might have been another reason. He had to wonder whether Alex had let him go so that Richard would tell his story a certain way. Alex wanted some facts omitted and some facts included. He had asked Richard not to mention Oscar Davidson's writing, and so Richard hadn't. And it was a justifiable decision. As far as Richard could tell, neither the Davidson manuscript nor the Davidson short story had anything to do with Ramsey Paxton's death. There was no logical reason to bring them up, to go through the embarrassment of explaining the trick he'd planned to play on Mr. Davidson, to talk about how he'd been ready to counteraccuse his teacher of committing plagiarism. He'd told the police what he'd seen, he hadn't told any lies, and he hadn't betrayed his friend's request. He should have felt good. But he didn't. He could make a great guess as to why Alex had let him go. Alex had let him go because he'd known that Richard was on the side of the bad guy.

❖

At 11:35 P.M., five minutes after Richard Blackburn went home with his father, Chris Nivens told Ellen Spencer that he had a confession to make. They sat in the lobby of the Lyceum while the team of investigators dusted and photographed the stage area.

"I didn't call the police right away," he said. "It took me a while to get into the building, first of all. My key is new, and it jams in some of the locks. I had to try a couple of doors before I got in."

She waited for him to tell it at his own pace.

"But then," he said, "when I got inside, I thought I was the victim of some elaborate practical joke. I didn't see Ramsey. I didn't see anything unusual at all. Richard had said the trapdoor was open when he and Alex left the theater."

"Wasn't it?" The boy had told her the same story.

"No," said Chris Nivens. "It was closed. And then I saw the paint bucket on the stage, and I opened it. It was empty. Richard had made a significant issue of some mysterious argument over money concealed in a paint can. So then I really started to wonder." He told her about reading Richard's essay about all the pranks he and Alex had orchestrated. "But I'd seen Ramsey's car in the lot, so I knew he had to be around somewhere. I shouted for him, I got no answer, I looked around the theater lobby and the seats. Only after all that time did I go downstairs to check the storage room. That's when I found him. I'm sorry about the delay."

She asked him how the trapdoor happened to be open when the police arrived.

"It fell open on its own," said Nivens. "When I walked out of the office after I'd called you. It spooked me worse than anything."

"Barely latched? Or rigged like a booby trap?" she said. "What do you think?"

He didn't know enough about trapdoors to say.

She consulted her notes. "What do you know about the Stone Mountain Consultants?"

"I don't know the Stone Mountain Consultants," said Nivens. "I've never heard of them before."

It was Anne Lindsey who told them about the Consultants account. They called her at home, and she arrived close to midnight, looking sick. She looked even sicker when she heard about the fingers that had been cut off by a tool in the storage room. Nivens wondered if she had left Ramona at home by herself.

"Alex told me about the Consultants tonight," she said. "We went out for dinner. He said he'd set up a fake account in the name of a company Milton and Patricia had discussed incorporating a few years ago, but had never followed through." She told them that Alex had confessed it all to her and that he'd planned to confess it to Ramsey: how he had billed the Arts Council an extra $500 for each of Milton Blackburn's visits to the Arts School and then had cashed the checks himself. "He kept the money in a paint can," she said. "Don't ask me why. He wanted money to spend on his shows here. And maybe on me. He loved me. He did. I never gave him a chance to spend it."

Ellen Spencer asked her to run through her activities after dinner.

"We came here to the school," said Anne Lindsey. "Alex and I came here to the Lyceum. After Ramsey arrived, I left the Lyceum and went to the classroom building, where I found Oscar. He took me home."

"You left? When they were talking about embezzlement?"

"Alex asked me to leave," she said. "So I did. I thought he would call me at home to tell me what had happened. So I got a ride with Oscar."

"At what time was this?"

"We got home a little after nine-thirty," she said. "It's just a few minutes' drive."

"And this meeting proceeded amicably while you were there?"

"Yes."

"What changed the atmosphere?"

Anne sat with her hands clasped in her lap. She shook her hair, damp with sweat on her forehead, before she replied. "Ramsey can be very abrasive," she said. "He may have threatened Alex with legal action."

"Isn't that what you expected?" she said.

"No," said Anne Lindsey. "I think we were both optimistic that Ramsey would let it go if he returned the money."

"Do you know where the money is now?"

"I already told you," she said. "He had it in a can of paint. Apparently he wanted something he could hide both at school and at home."

Ellen said they had looked through every can of paint in the building and found nothing.

"Did you look upstairs and downstairs?" she said. "In his office?"

"Everywhere," said Ellen. "There's nothing in any can of paint but paint. Or air."

"That son of a bitch," said Anne Lindsey.

Everyone thought she was talking about Alex Mason.

At midnight Richard sat in his bedroom with his father. Richard had taken a shower and wore his boxers and a T-shirt. His dad was dressed in the kind of pullover shirt Richard associated with Colonial Williamsburg.

It was as it always was when Richard was alone with his dad. He could remember that he had once loved this man more than anything or anyone in the world, but he couldn't find the emotion anymore. It was as though he'd misplaced it or outgrown it, like a belief in Santa Claus. But it wasn't as simple as discarding an old childhood illusion. Richard couldn't let go of his father. The affection he'd once felt had been replaced by pain, and he found himself daily thinking of his father with a nagging, stinging hurt. It was what he recognized as hatred. He'd heard at school that the opposite of love was not hatred, but indifference. The restoration of love seemed impossible, so now he strove for the indifference that would free him from this searing anguish, this sore, this recollection of what once they had shared and could not ever share again because Richard could not allow it. When he was a child, he'd been able to go to his father with any problem, and his father had always been able to make it okay. All that had vanished. His father had taken sides, the side against Richard. From that decision all the agony had sprung.

Richard sat with his most indifferent expression on his face, but he was not feeling indifference. Part of him despised the sight of a grown man coming to him so deferentially, asking permission to enter his room, failing to mask the hurt and the uncertainty on his own face. And part of Richard, the part he sought to vaporize, wanted to go to this man on the bed and seize him and tell him every horrible secret he knew. But he couldn't. He couldn't do that. There were some secrets too horrible to name.

"Richard," said his dad, "I would go to jail for you. I would go to hell for you. I would do anything for you."

Richard looked away.

"Richard," said Milton Blackburn, "what are you not telling me? Do you know where Alex is?"

"No," said Richard.

"What was going on between you?" said his father. "Why did he let you get away?"

"I don't know."

"You had nothing to do with the death of Mr. Paxton, did you?"

"Of course not." Richard was shocked at the suggestion. "I just . . ." He reminded himself of Tucker, unable to find the words to finish his own sentence.

"Just what? What did you do?"

Richard was annoyed at himself for not controlling the conversation better. It took him a long time to come up with a logical answer. "I helped Alex get away. I helped him get away by giving him time."

Milton Blackburn moved closer to Richard. "That's not bad of you," he said. "I understand. He was your friend. He was my friend, too, Richard."

"But friendship doesn't last, does it?" said Richard. "Nothing lasts. You can't count on anything. Like you. I can't count on you."

"Richard," said his father. "Please, please tell me what I've done. Please."

"Why were you down there?" said Richard. "Why did you go?"

"Because I wanted to help Alex. I wanted to help him straighten out this mess with the money."

"You said you couldn't get in. But you have a key. Everybody who works there has a key."

Milton Blackburn shook his head. "Tucker had borrowed my car," he said. "His own car had run out of gas. I had your mother's keys. She doesn't have one for the Lyceum."

Richard was half relieved and half disappointed that he had not caught his father in a lie. "I'm tired," he said.

Milton Blackburn did not go. "Accuse me," he said. "Name the crime I committed against you."

But Richard would only repeat what he had already said. "You took her side, Dad," said Richard.

Milton Blackburn did not understand.

"You took Mom's side about Outward Bound," said Richard. "I didn't want to go, and I counted on you to support me. And you took her side. I expected it from her. But not from you. You made me go."

Blackburn pulled Richard around so that he could not look away. "Is that all?" he said. "Richard, I did it because I thought it was the best thing for you. Is that all there was?"

"No," said Richard. Could he go on? "There was Tucker's accident."

"What about it?" said Milton Blackburn. "What about Tucker's accident?"

"I wasn't here for it," said Richard. "I was away." It felt lame even as it emerged from his mouth. "If you hadn't made me go, I would have been here."

Milton Blackburn said he still didn't understand.

"It might have been me on the mower that day," said Richard. He was clumsy in his wording. "Maybe if I'd been here, the accident wouldn't have happened to Tucker."

"Richard," said Milton. He reached out to hug his son, but Richard pushed him away.

"I'm tired," said Richard. "And you have to rest for the show. Now we've talked. Leave me alone."

His father sat, speechless, for several long moments. Finally he stood and touched Richard's hair on his way out. He shut the door behind him. Richard wondered how much longer he could use Outward Bound as his crutch for avoiding the real confession. What he had done was horribly destructive. It had been an accident, yes, but it was nevertheless his fault, and it was too awful to tell to anyone. They would despise him for certain if they knew. It was a funny thing about pain, Richard thought. He had always heard that misery loved company. But it didn't help a bit to know that somebody else was hurting just as much as you were. The pain was all his, his private stock, and he nearly crumpled onto the floor before he shook it all away, the way a dog shakes off water, and went to bed.

❊

While classes were canceled at the Arts School on Thursday, activity flourished at the Stone Mountain Theater. There were reporters, there were telephone calls, there were troubled members of the Arts Council coming by to assure Milton Blackburn that the festivities on Saturday night would go on as scheduled ("as Ramsey would have wanted," they said), there were the people coming to measure for the tent on the mountaintop lawn, there were rumors galore. But in the kitchen, the routine was tediously ordinary. Meals had to appear on schedule.

Tucker and Ramona worked in silence. Both of them had been up late the night before listening to news of Ramsey Paxton's death and Alex

Mason's flight from the city. Tucker had gone to a movie by himself, something he hardly ever did, a movie that had turned out to be the same movie Ramona had chosen to attend with two of her friends. It had been embarrassing for all of them, and Tucker had left without seeing the end. Moonie would say this morning only that her mother was devastated over what had happened at the Lyceum. She said it as if it were Tucker's fault. The pouting was just about to drive him off the mountain. But he couldn't drive. His car was still out of gas.

Tucker's job for lunch today was to slice ham and chicken. He had a sharp knife but couldn't find a fork big enough to hold the ham on the cutting board.

"Could you fork me, please?" he said to Moonie. Ramona.

"Shut up, Tucker," she said. "Is that wit?"

"I need a fork," he said.

She reached into a drawer and handed him a two-pronged serving fork.

"Thank you," he said. He couldn't stand this atmosphere. He stuck the fork into the ham until both prongs disappeared and sliced for several minutes in silence.

"I knew this would happen if we worked together," she said. "You don't understand anything about subtlety or beauty or the eloquence of language."

"*I am, my lord, as well derived as he,*" said Tucker, "*as well possessed; my love is more than his; My fortunes every way as fairly ranked (If not with vantage) as Demetrius; And, which is more than all these boasts can be, I am beloved of beauteous Hermia. Why should not I then prosecute my right?*"

At least he'd managed to surprise her. He put down the knife and got as close as he could without touching her.

"Tell me I don't know what all those words mean," he said. "Tell me I don't know. I can live those words. I can act them. I can say them. Chris Nivens can read them in a book and tell you the . . . the . . . whatever you call it—"

"The etymology."

"The etymology of every one," said Tucker. "But that doesn't mean I don't understand."

She looked at him with only a clinical interest. "You've memorized the whole play, haven't you?" she said.

"Every word," he said. He had never done anything like that before. Not on that scale.

She pulled out two loaves of bread and began to make sandwiches. "What are you trying to prove?" she said.

"I don't know," he said. "Maybe that I'm good at something. I never had the incentive to try it before."

"Don't go for sympathy, Tucker," she said. "It's degrading."

He would not go back to the cutting board. "Moonie . . . Ramona. Tell me what I did that was so wrong. Why are you so furious?"

"Because you should have cared more," she said. "You could have."

"Me?" he said. "Why did you leave?"

"I had to," she said. "You ran me off."

"That's not true," said Tucker.

"Why didn't you let me see you for a month after the accident?"

"I was sick," he said. "I felt bad. I looked bad."

"You didn't want me to look at you, did you?" she said.

"No," he said. "Is that so strange?"

"You thought that I wouldn't like you anymore because of your leg."

"I didn't want you to see me as crippled," he said.

"I never did," she said. "Never. Not that way. Why, for our first time together, did you take me back to the tennis courts? It was awful."

"I wanted you to see that I hadn't given up," he said. "I wanted you to see that I'd be just as good as new."

"So I had to watch you get mad at the ball, mad at the tennis racquet, mad at yourself," she said. "You didn't have to prove anything to me. It was insulting that you thought so. You must have thought I was awfully small."

It was true. "I was scared," he said. "I thought if all we had to do was sit around and talk, we'd run out of things to say. I thought I'd be boring and stupid."

"So every time we were together, it was talk about physical therapy and how much you can lift now and how fast the doctor says you're going to be well. As if all that mattered to me was your body. I got sick of it, Tucker. And Chris was interesting. He still is." The last words hurt the most. "And he doesn't have to prove himself with people like Nancy Gale Nofsinger," she said. "He doesn't have to advertise his virility. Last night he had to work. So we didn't go out. I understood.''

Tucker went back to the ham and chopped out pieces the size of postage stamps. "You really like him," he said.

"He's not like anybody else," she said. "Actually, I think I'm in love."

"I am, too," said Tucker. It cost him a lot to speak. "But not with Nancy Gale."

She finished making a sandwich and rested her arms on the table. "I'm sorry, Tucker," she said. "It's a sweet line, but I don't think you mean it the same way I do."

He put down the knife and walked out of the room. Ramona continued to make sandwiches in the quiet kitchen. It was a full thirty seconds before she started to cry.

Richard ordinarily would have slept in on a day when classes were canceled, but he woke up early and couldn't get back to sleep. The phone started ringing early, as did the doorbell. But his father told all the reporters that Richard was unavailable for comment, and he sent Richard upstairs to his room whenever somebody came to the door. It was boring, and he especially hated his room because his computer was here. It was a reminder of schoolwork. Technically speaking, he should have been working on the draft for his essay. Any normal teacher would extend tomorrow's deadline, but he didn't trust Oscar Davidson to give him any break whatever. So he sat down to work, even though all he could do was stare at the screen. He thought not of Shakespeare, but of seeing Alex at the theater, of seeing Ramsey Paxton lying motionless on the floor of the storage room, of talking to the police and to his father. He fell asleep in his chair and woke up at noon. The sun was bright outside.

A few minutes later he jogged up the trail to the Inn to snag a sandwich for lunch from Tucker. It was terribly hot. Richard dripped with sweat when the two of them went out on the veranda to eat.

"Shouldn't you be working?" said Richard. "Aren't you supposed to help Moonie?"

"She'd rather work by herself," said Tucker.

The air over the city was hazy with humidity. The air glowed with heat, even under the shade of the veranda.

"Too hot," said Richard.

They retreated inside but avoided both the noisy dining room, where the performers ate, and the kitchen, where Ramona worked. The secretaries occupied the office. Some actors ran lines in the rehearsal room. Richard and Tucker finally settled on the stage of the theater itself, accessible through the soundproof door off the main hallway. The air in the theater was comfortable. The stage was finished, and all the seats were installed, surrounding the small thrust stage on three sides. Tucker turned on a few work lights, then sat with Richard against the back wall, directly at center stage. With the empty seats in front of them, Richard felt as though they were performing something avant-garde, like *Waiting for Godot*.

"This is my favorite spot in the building," said Tucker. "You know what I wish? I wish I could be in the first show performed here. If it ever happens."

Richard asked him what the holdup was. "It looks finished now. Finished enough."

Tucker leaned forward from his seat on the boards and flipped open a metal lid recessed in the floor like the top of an oversized shoebox. Inside should have been plugs for lighting. Instead the box was a deep and empty metal coffin in the stage. "No wiring," he said. "No wiring anywhere. It's always money."

"Why can't Mom just pay for it?" said Richard. He closed the top to the wiring box so that it was again flush with the fresh-sanded wood. "Or Dad. They have plenty of cash."

"No, they don't," said Tucker. "Haven't you noticed that Dad does all the housework himself?"

"What happened to all the money?" said Richard.

"It was expensive for her to live in New York," said Tucker. "And they have bills."

"Like what?"

"Like our tuition. And doctor bills."

Richard didn't want to pursue it. He tried a ham and cheese sandwich with a little lettuce. It tasted dry, and his Coke was warm. He asked if there had been many reporters up here.

"All morning," said Tucker. "I can't believe you saw a dead body."

"It looks just like a live body from far away," said Richard. "I didn't see the fingers or anything."

"Could you tell Alex was weird?" said Tucker. The police still had not caught him. He had left his car in the lot at the Arts School and had simply vanished. The theory was that he had taken a bus out of town.

"No," said Richard. "He seemed sad, that's all. And scared." It was so strange to think about it. "He really fooled me. I wasn't scared of him. I was just scared of the situation. Even at the end, when he was running off, I felt like we were friends."

Tucker finished his Coke and crushed the can. "All my life I've had friends," said Tucker. "I always thought that once you were friends with somebody, you stayed friends forever." Richard had never before heard him sound so mournful. "I always thought Moonie and I were . . . you know. Special. I always thought she'd be available. But it's like we never knew each other. Everything we had, everything we shared, that's all in the past. I'll probably never have another conversation with her."

A couple of actresses came through the hall door to their right, crossed to the stage, and walked directly in front of Richard and Tucker. They smiled but kept walking to the left wing, where they pushed on the sliding door of the scene shop and passed on through, then closed the door behind them. Richard and Tucker watched them disappear.

"You want to work out?" said Richard. "We could set up another weight room upstairs."

"Not today."

Richard suggested that Tucker do something about filling up his gas tank so that he wouldn't have to borrow their dad's car again.

"I should do that," said Tucker. He did not move.

To their right the door to the hallway opened and Griffin Dupree entered the wing. "Here they are," he said. "Edgar and Edmund in person." He carried a Diet Pepsi can and wore loafers with no socks. His shoes sounded like taps on the stage as he crossed to them. "You got a tape player that also records?" he said to Tucker.

"Yes," said Tucker.

"I need it," said Dupree. "I'm working on my voice."

Tucker said he could use it.

"I want it moved into the rehearsal room," said Griffin Dupree. "Cooler."

"So move it," said Tucker.

Griffin Dupree used a foot to flip open the lid to the empty metal light box in the stage. He finished off his Pepsi and dropped the can inside, as though he were throwing it into the garbage, and then he neatly closed the lid with his foot. "I'm here to act," he said. "Not to move furniture. Now get the tape player without a fuss and make Mommy and Daddy very happy." He turned and walked off the stage and through the door he'd entered. It closed with a pneumatic whoosh.

"What a jerk," said Richard. He reached into the empty light box and retrieved the Pepsi can.

"Don't," said Tucker.

"Don't what?" said Richard. He stood up and stretched his legs. Tucker sat on the stage with his bad leg slightly bent.

"Don't even think about pulling some prank on him," said Tucker.

"Why not?" said Richard.

"Because he's all mine," said Tucker. But he continued to lie on the stage.

❧

Oscar Davidson was on the telephone with Anne Lindsey at 3:00 in the afternoon. He had been awake for two hours.

"I'm telling you that Ramsey was alive when I left the theater," he said. "He was very much alive. And he had all his fingers."

"Why should I believe you?" she said.

"Why should I kill him?" said Oscar. "Or torture him? It wasn't my wife he married."

"Why would Alex leave and then come back?" she said.

"To get rid of the Blackburn boy," said Oscar. "He had to shake the kid before he went back to finish Ramsey off." He painted the entire scenario for her. "He kills Ramsey, closes the trapdoor in the stage to conceal the body, and then bolts. He can't use his car because it's too easy to identify. So he heads on foot for the bus station." It was time to shift from this tedious subject. They had been over and over the same material for half an hour. "We're eating dinner here tonight," he said. "To celebrate the departure of Ramsey Paxton."

"No," she said.

"And to mourn the fate of my poor essay."

"No," she said.

"Yes," he said. "I have to insist."

"I hate this deception," she said. "I hate all this sneakiness. Why don't we just tell the police we were there?" she said.

"Go ahead," he said. "Tell them about how you pushed Ramsey on that rolling swivel chair. Tell them about knocking him unconscious. They'll be fascinated."

She was helpless. "I only wanted to push him away," she said. "I didn't know the trapdoor would give way. If you had heard any of what he said to me, you would understand."

"Maybe that's why Alex killed him," he said. "He didn't like hearing Ramsey abuse you."

"And what about the money?" she said. "You didn't see any money in that paint can?"

"How many times are you going to ask?" he said. "No, I didn't see any money. Do you want me to swear it in blood?" It was easy to lie to her. He had removed the cash from the paint can last night as soon as he'd entered the theater. There had been very little time for him to accomplish all that he needed to do, very little time for him to finish with Ramsey and get out before the Blackburn boy could send Chris Nivens from across the street. But it had worked. Now everyone, even Anne, believed that Alex Mason had taken the cash after killing Ramsey Paxton.

"I'm not well," she said. "I can't come tonight."

"Seven-thirty," he said. "Bring some wine." He wasn't used to telling women what to do so forcefully. It was wonderful to control Anne so absolutely. Even better than a class full of students.

❈

Alex Mason emerged from the swaying rest room on the bus feeling only marginally cleaner. The towel he'd bought at the Farmville stop at 5:00 A.M. helped for a while, but he was going to need a bath soon. And another change of clothes. He'd been able to withdraw two hundred dollars from his personal account using the automatic teller machine. He'd borrowed twelve from Richard, and had had forty-four on his own. He still had two hundred six dollars on him, but that would not last long. He'd been riding in a circle around the state of Virginia all night, trying to decide what to do. Should he turn himself in? Or should he get across the country? The indecision was torture, as was the bus. It bounced and shimmied as it gathered momentum down the narrow, rolling highway. He checked his shoulder bag in the rack overhead, took his seat on the aisle, tried to sleep, and wondered what was happening in Rockbridge.

The police by now would have extracted from Richard a description of Alex's clothes. The T-shirt and baseball cap, which he'd purchased at 6:00 A.M. in a bus terminal and which he now wore, would possibly confuse a casual observer, but he knew he would be recognized eventually if the authorities were looking for him. The Rockbridge police probably knew by now that he'd taken a cab from the bus station to the truck stop outside of town. It had been easy from there to hitch a ride north, but he hadn't wanted to go too far. He'd switched to buses at Winchester and had ridden southeast for a time. Now he was heading vaguely north again. It was time for another switch.

When they stopped in Charlottesville at 3:30 P.M., Alex got off the bus to find something to eat. At a newsstand he bought a Rockbridge newspaper, and he took it with him back to the bus, where he drank a cup of orange juice and ate a raisin cinnamon bun. He turned immediately to the second section, for local news, and scanned it for reports. Nothing. Maybe they had managed to keep it all away from the police. But then he turned back to the front page and was stunned to see the article below the fold on page one:

BUSINESSMAN SLAIN AT ARTS SCHOOL

Ramsey R. Paxton, 38, philanthropist, civic leader, and businessman, was killed last night at the Lyceum Theater in what police termed tentatively a ritualized, cult-like murder. Physical mutilations on the body, discovered last night by a teacher at the school, indicated that Paxton had been tortured before he died.

Police seek for questioning Alexander Mason, 42, head of the drama program and instructor at the Arts School.

It went on to give the details. He read the entire article three times. He was trembling. It was horrible, horrible.

There was no photograph of him in the paper. And nothing about Anne.

And nothing about the money.

※

Carrying a small jug of kerosene for the emergency lamps in her hand, Nancy Gale emerged from the office of the Stone Mountain Theater at precisely 5:00 P.M. Most members of the company stood outside on the veranda enjoying the view. Some had gone to walk or jog, and some ran lines one more time in various corners of the Inn. Tension was usually high at the first dress rehearsal. It did not help that the director was also an actress and their chief patron was dead.

She strolled down to the kitchen, which was locked, but from which she could smell some sort of soup cooking. It was too risky to try a visit now, not after all the uproar over stolen food. She left the kerosene in the scene shop and then went upstairs to the men's wing, where she knocked on Tucker's door and entered without waiting to be invited. He lay on his bed naked except for his underwear, flat on his back, his hands locked behind his head. When she entered, he glanced up, and then looked back at the ceiling.

"I don't think so," he said.

She thought that was rather insulting, considering that she was the one giving him the benefit of her company. There were others she might have chosen. "What's wrong?" she said.

"Not so loud," said Tucker. He pointed with an elbow toward the bathroom, where she could hear water running. Griffin Dupree was in there.

It made her angry that he would lie there so casually with her in the room, as if she were one of his buddies from school. She sat down on the end of his bed and started to massage one of his feet. He pulled it away.

"No," he said.

"Aren't you supposed to be fixing dinner?" she said.

"It's cooking."

"I can help you."

"Thanks anyway."

She was going to lose her temper, she could tell that she was going to explode, but she didn't want to do that. "Something bothering you?" she said.

"Give me some time to myself," said Tucker. "I need to think."

That was it. "It's nice that you'd try something new," she said. She walked out of the room and slammed the door behind her, then knocked at Dupree's door loudly enough for Tucker to hear. Arrogant pig, lying there so lazily. Let him listen through the walls.

Griffin Dupree answered the door with a towel around his waist. He had no hair on his chest anywhere. He was gorgeous, simply gorgeous.

"Hi," she said.

"Sorry, dear," he said. "Wrong tree."

"I just thought you might want to talk," she said.

He shut the door in her face.

Nancy Gale was seething. Stupid selfish male bastard children. She went back to her room and finished off two tubes of Saltine crackers. Then she found a box of cookies and some peanut butter. But even after she'd finished it all, even after she'd finished the marshmallows, she hadn't had nearly enough.

❈

Thursday had been so tedious for Ellen Spencer. She'd had to go to the two banks Alex Mason had used for his Stone Mountain Consultants fraud, cross-check the payments from the Arts School and the Arts Council, look for the money. Everything worked out tidily, except that the money had disappeared. It wasn't in any of Mason's accounts. Wasn't in his home, which she and a team had searched. He must have taken it with him. Twenty-five hundred dollars. That was not very much money to kill a man over, but she'd seen people die for less.

They'd spent a lot of time at the Lyceum Theater working with the trapdoor. The door appeared to work perfectly. No faulty latch, no sticking. It had just been lubricated, in fact. How had it been rigged to pop open as Chris Nivens had said? Why would anyone bother? And who had closed it? The Blackburn boy had been certain that the door in the stage floor had been open when he had left the theater with Alex Mason. Yet it had been closed a few minutes later when Nivens entered in search of the body. The Blackburn boy had admitted that Alex Mason had wanted very much to return to the basement before they had left. So he must have returned to the theater after saying good-bye to Richard Blackburn in the alley outside. But for what purpose? To steal the money? What if Ramsey Paxton had not been dead when the Blackburn kid arrived, but only unconscious? Would Alex Mason risk returning inside to finish Paxton off after he'd told the boy to call 911? And why take the time to cut off his fingers? Ramsey Paxton had married Alex Mason's ex-wife. Was there a sick grudge at work here? And was there anybody else who could have been inside the theater? Milton Blackburn claimed that he had no key, that he'd knocked in vain at the doors of the theater and then had departed in frustration. Anne Lindsey and Oscar Davidson both said that they'd left the school building together and had driven straight to the Lindsey home. It must have been Alex Mason. Still, the questions bothered her.

When she finally got home at 7:30 P.M., Ellen Spencer was very tired. Matthew had prepared them a Caesar salad with grilled chicken for dinner, and they deliberately avoided talking about the death of Ramsey Paxton over their meal. Afterward, however, when Matthew refused to let her help with the dishes, she went to the television room, where he'd refolded the morning paper she'd never taken the time to read. She picked up the paper with interest, curious to see how badly the press had butchered the Paxton murder story. But it wasn't the news pages that she remembered later.

She found it mixed in with the movie ads. There was the advertisement again for the Stone Mountain Theater, exactly the same text she had seen earlier in the week except for one crucial change at the bottom:

TICKETS STILL AVAILABLE FOR GALA OPENING NIGHT
COCKTAILS AND DINNER BEFORE THE PERFORMANCE
Sponsored by the Rockbridge Arts Council
Ramsey W. Paxton, Chairman
Special Souvenir Program

Matthew walked in with Paul on his shoulders. Paul wore a bald wig that made him look exactly like his father. They were good at figuring out how to make her laugh. She simply didn't laugh long enough.

"What now?" said Matthew. He squatted down so that Paul could dismount and run off to look at himself in the bathroom mirror. She showed him the ad in the newspaper.

"It's different," she said. "What happened to 'Special Souvenir Program Featuring Sarah Davidson's Essay' et cetera? I saw it just the other day."

Matthew sat beside her and put an arm across her shoulders. "You're thinking what now?" he said.

"I'm thinking maybe Sarah Davidson's death was somehow related to money after all. Ramsey Paxton's seems to have been."

"How can you connect Sarah Davidson with Ramsey Paxton?" said Matt.

"Because of the personnel," said Ellen. "We have Oscar Davidson and Anne Lindsey at the Arts School when Ramsey dies. We have Chris Nivens, the graduate student, discovering the body and living across the street from the scene. And the Blackburns. We have the wife in Charlottesville on the night of the fire, we have the husband at the theater on the night of the murder, and we have the son."

"The son," said Matthew. "This is not sounding good."

"Yes," said Ellen. "The son was there both times. Charlottesville in May and here in Rockbridge last night. Inside both rooms where the trouble started. Inside both buildings where somebody died."

"You think the boy is a killer?"

"I think he's not telling me something," she said. "Aside from that, I don't know. Maybe it's all some gigantic conspiracy. Why would they change this ad? It had to be changed during business hours yesterday. Before Paxton died."

Matthew took the paper from her and folded it neatly on the coffee table. "Overload," he said. "You've done enough detecting for one day."

"It's worth checking."

"Sure," he said. "Tomorrow."

She let the magic word act as a blessing on the remainder of their evening. Tomorrow. Fatigue washed over her so unexpectedly that she thought she might sleep right there on the couch. There would be nobody in the business office at the newspaper now anyway. She would have to check it tomorrow. Newspaper ads were constantly changing.

It was probably nothing.

❧

Ramona was ready for a romantic evening on her only night off from work. As soon as she'd heard that her mother was going to Oscar's for dinner, she had called Chris to cancel the restaurant reservation and come to dine there.

"All week I fix food for the masses on the mountain," she'd said. "Tonight I can cook for two."

Now it was nearly 8:30, still amazingly early and amazingly light outside. She and Chris had finished the pasta they'd fixed together for dinner and finished the wine he'd brought, and now they turned toward other matters. They still had not switched on any lights in the house. But they could see perfectly in the waning daylight. In the kitchen Ramona held him by two belt loops. She turned her head up to his, and he bent down and kissed her. He took her hands, one by one, and kissed her palms. And now for business.

Chris pulled a toothbrush out of the back pocket of his trousers and laid it on the counter next to her keys.

"What I want you to do," he said, "is to go upstairs and wait for me."

So this was the way they did it, older guys, more experienced. "You'll find me," she said.

Upstairs she opened the doors to the sleeping porch and saw a spiderweb in the corner. The whole room was dusty and hot from the day's sun. Back inside, in the air-conditioning, she felt faintly frantic. Which room? Her own, with its canopy bed? Her mother's? The guest room, with the soft mattress? There was something not right about all this, her being upstairs, his being down. They should be together. But she knew what he was doing. Brushing his teeth, getting ready for her. Maybe he was taking off all his clothes down there. Maybe she should do the same. But damn, she had to go to the bathroom again already. Was it the wine?

She came out of the bathroom and heard nothing. She pulled off her shoes, then her shorts and her underwear. Her shirttail ended at mid-thigh. She could not bring herself to take it off as well. She would let him do it for her. She left her clothes at the top of the stairs on the floor. Maybe she should leave him a trail to the guest room. Maybe they could just use the couch in the study.

"Chris?" she called. She heard nothing.

She moved quietly down the stairs, the thick white carpet cool on her bare feet. He was not in the living room, not the dining room. He was not in the kitchen. She moved on to the back wing of the house. He was not in the television room. The door to the study was, as usual, closed, but she tried the knob anyway. It was unlocked. She opened it and saw Chris immediately. He was going through the filing cabinets behind her mother's desk.

His head jerked up from the open drawer at the sound of the knob turning. He spoke before she could say anything. "I told you to wait upstairs," he said. He looked at her attire. He spoke with regret.

"What are you doing?" she said. She crossed the room to stand next to him.

"I had to look," he said. "I had to see."

"This is private," she said. "I told you no." She was becoming more and more appalled.

He grabbed her by both arms and held her close to him. "Your mother and your uncle are up to something," he said. "I want to find out what it is."

"They are not," she said. She was confused. She was very angry and at the same time unwilling to believe that this was not simply some game.

"They are," said Chris. "Oscar Davidson was trying to pass off an essay of his own as something by Sarah. Your mother went along with the charade. I want to know what they're doing."

"Why didn't you just ask Mom if you could see the files?" she said.

"Because I don't trust her," he said. He still had hold of her arms. She squirmed free.

"You'd better go," she said.

"Not now," he said. He turned back to the filing cabinets. The top drawer was full of manila folders. There were a few stationery boxes in the back. "I am so close. This is everything Sarah Davidson ever wrote."

Ramona pushed the drawer so that it closed. "This is wrong," she said. "You had this all planned from the first. Didn't I pass out quickly enough from the wine?"

He turned to her and tried to hold her. She stepped back, but he reached her anyway. He put both his arms around her back and pulled up to him hard. "Don't think I didn't care about you," he said. "I do. It was just so tempting for me. I just got impulsive."

He hurt her. It was no longer pleasant to be close to him. "Let me go," she said. She tried to push away. He hurt her arms.

"Not when we're this close," he said. He took one hand and reached up under her shirttail to fumble at her.

"No," she said. She shouted. She kicked and pushed at him, but he kept groping, touching, searching. She shrieked and scratched at his face and hit him with her one free hand and suddenly he released her.

Both were breathless.

"I'm sorry," he said. "I'm sorry. I've had too much to drink. I've been too obsessed by this business of Oscar's essay. I'm sorry. Let me stay."

"No."

He hesitated, and she thought for a moment that he was going to lunge at her. But he didn't. "I'll go," he said.

She kept her voice calm and strong. "First give me my keys," she said.

He reached into his pocket and gave her the keys. She checked to make sure they were all there.

"Let's just forget this," he said. "Okay? I never wanted to upset you. I really did want to meet you upstairs."

"Get out," she said.

"Don't tell Anne," he said. "She'll fire me."

"Get out," said Ramona. She was calm and strong.

He left the house and drove away. Ramona checked all the doors and made sure they were locked. She returned to the study and tidied everything, closed the drawer, locked the room.

And she still didn't break down. She dialed from memory the number for the Stone Mountain Theater, knowing that he would not be there, knowing that she'd get the recording, hoping that somebody would hear her message and pass it on to him and that he would come. She knew what she would say into the answering machine.

She knew the instant she started to dial. *Please tell Tucker to call me,* she'd say. *Please tell him it's urgent. Tell him I'm sorry. Tell him it's me.*

It's Moonie.

Tucker sat in the office at the Stone Mountain Theater and watched the light fade outside. The box office was supposed to close at 8:00 on nights before the season opened, but it was nearly 8:30, and Tucker still had not turned on the answering machine. If anyone called, he'd talk. So far ticket sales for *Dream* were going okay. Linda, the nighttime box-office manager, had told him that business had been steady all evening. She was relieved and grateful when he told her that he'd sit in for her. She was happy to leave him there in the office, though she wasn't sure why he was doing this for her, and neither was he. The dishes were washed in the kitchen. He ought to borrow somebody's car and get the gasoline canister and get his car running again so that he could get the hell out of here. But sitting behind the barred windows was almost like being in jail: He felt as though somehow he deserved to be here.

It seemed much lighter outside than here in the office. Posters appeared only as rectangular patches on the walls, file cabinets as vague geometric shapes, the trays for sorting mail as dim replicas of futuristic parking garages. Tucker could have turned on a light, but he didn't want a light on. He didn't like to read for pleasure, and if you weren't going to read, there was no need to have a light on. The door to the hallway was closed. As far as he knew, he was the only one in the building, but he'd left the door closed when the company had moved down to the amphitheater for rehearsal. Air circulated past the painted bars across the open windows, and he felt the pleasure of privacy. If the company came back to the Inn, they wouldn't know he was in here. They wouldn't ask him why he wasn't out on a date. Strangers over the telephone were much better for conversation, because they didn't ask any personal questions.

He had blown it with Moonie. He hadn't trusted her enough to like him with a crippled body. Hadn't trusted himself enough to be likable. And he probably shouldn't have. He wanted to be an actor, but his own mother wouldn't hire him even when she was desperate.

The phone rang for a reservation. Party of four, next Wednesday night, two students, two adults. He was very careful to get the Visa number recorded properly and the information correct. It took great concentration for him, as did reading the number back and reading back all the other information, expiration date, home telephone number, address. He was glad for the need to concentrate. He wanted a project that would take him out of himself, that would get his mind off Moonie.

Tucker was not in the habit of feeling self-pity. It wasn't his manner. If things went badly, so what, they'd get better tomorrow, other people had it worse, that was the way life was—he'd go through the whole litany of clichés as a way of avoiding the black dog of despondency. It annoyed him to see Richard turning so sour and so gloomy, so full of self-absorption and unpleasantness. Hell, Richard had so much in his favor. He could read without thinking about the fact that he was reading. He could write without wondering how many words he'd just misspelled in each sentence. He could think quickly and cleverly. And he'd been doing better about getting himself physically fit. He was stronger, healthier—almost as healthy as Tucker had once been. Tonight Tucker felt sapped, drained, bloodless. He could not believe that he'd ever been attracted to the Spandex Lady. Nancy Gale. It had actually been fun there for a while.

The phone rang again. He checked his watch. It was 8:35. Maybe he'd stay in here until 10:00 or so. Dad would be grateful for the extra orders.

"Stone Mountain Theater," he said.

Instant adrenaline surge when he heard her voice.

"Please come," she said. "I don't deserve you, but I need you here. I need a friend, Tucker."

"What happened?" His heart nearly drowned out her words.

"Just come," she said. "I'll tell you."

He remembered to turn on the answering machine after he hung up. Careful now. He felt for his keys in his pocket. So what. His car was out of gas. He could borrow his mother's. Or his father's. Hell, he could go on foot. He burst out of the office and ran down the hallway toward the back veranda. But he noticed in passing that the kitchen door was open. The kitchen was supposed to be locked. He stopped and ran back and closed the door without looking inside the room. Then he thought about it. He wondered. He opened the door again and switched on the light.

Nancy Gale crouched by the refrigerator with a bagel in her mouth and two bags of doughnuts in her hands. She looked like an animal surprised by headlights, ready to flee. She dropped the doughnuts on the counter and spit the bagel into the trash can. Her chin and her arms trembled. Tucker was surprised by how sorry he felt for her.

"Relax," he said. "I won't tell."

She closed her mouth tightly in silent humiliation.

"Let's do each other a favor," said Tucker.

"Like what?" she said, and for a moment both of them thought she was going to be sick. But she held it in.

❊

Nancy Gale Nofsinger drove up Canterbury Lane so fast that she scared herself. She was so angry that she was shaking. She should turn on her headlights at this hour, but she could see enough, see the dim houses, see that there were no children on the street. It was a quarter to nine. She was mortified. She'd have to resign. She couldn't possibly finish the summer season now. Tucker Blackburn had said he wouldn't report her to his father. He'd said he'd talk to her about it later. He'd been so fucking nice about it. But he knew. He knew. And in exchange for his silence, he'd made her engage in the most humiliating, degrading act a man had ever asked her to perform.

He'd asked her to drive him down the mountain to Ramona Lindsey's house.

Ooh, she could kill him now. She really could. He'd actually made her chauffeur him, made her ease his travels to the home of that sassy little tease. He was so into all these little power games, sick little attempts at control and manipulation, and she'd consented. She'd taken him.

She turned onto Canterbury Lane and nearly rear-ended a cab that was pulled over two houses down from the Blackburns'. She screeched to a stop and scared the hell out of both the cabby and his passenger, who actually ducked down behind the seat for protection. Okay, okay. She switched on her lights and pulled around them. It was awful. She would have to go back to the theater and pack. She would have to drive to Atlanta alone. All she'd wanted all summer was a little companionship, a little sense that there was something inside her that others found appealing. And she was still hungry.

She passed the Blackburns' house and saw the lights on. Richard was home. Why not? She stopped, backed up, pulled into their driveway, and knocked on the door until he answered.

"You got anything to eat?" she said. "I'll explain if you let me come in."

"What do you want?" said Richard. "I'm busy."

"I want a snack," she said. "Will you humor me?"

He took her back to the kitchen and let her rummage through the refrigerator. She took out a liter of Coke but left everything else.

"No," she said. "Too much fruit, too many vegetables. I'm in the market for junk."

He showed her the pantry, where she took a bag of potato chips and a package of chocolate chip cookies.

"The patio looks lovely tonight," she said. "Why don't we dine outside?"

"I'm working upstairs," said Richard. "I have a paper due tomorrow."

"Just fifteen minutes," she said. "Long enough for me to say goodbye."

Tucker sat with Moonie on the couch in the living room. She had her clothes back on, except for her shoes, and she sat with her legs folded up under her and her body cradled inside Tucker's left arm. She had stopped apologizing. She drank a glass of ice water.

"I should have known better," she said. "Somebody that old, somebody that bright. He didn't want to go out with me. He just wanted to get to Mom's archives."

Tucker had heard of the phenomenon, though he had never understood it. Premedical students sabotaging their classmates' lab work.

Graduate students hiding reserved books in the library so that nobody else could use them.

"He's hungry," said Tucker. "He's really into the politics of academia."

"Aunt Sarah was never like that," said Moonie.

"Of course not," said Tucker, but he wondered if, in her very early days, she might have been.

"I really think he was drunk," said Moonie. "I know I was. I know it now. I still am, I guess, though I don't feel it."

Tucker told her to keep drinking water.

"I wonder if I led him on," she said.

"Don't say that," said Tucker.

"You've told me girls can be teases," she said.

"Sure," said Tucker, "but the guy has always got self-control. Or should have. I'm going to kill that asshole when I see him next."

"No," she said. "He's humiliated as it is. That's enough."

She took another drink of water. The yellow glow from the lamp by Tucker glistened in the blond fuzz on his legs. The scar was nearly invisible in this light. "He said Mom and Uncle Oscar were up to something bad," she said. "I think he was trying to spare my feelings. He was trying to find out without getting me involved. That shows a certain amount of integrity, don't you think?"

"I think you're very generous," said Tucker. He didn't move. He loved the warmth and the weight of her body against his.

"He didn't really hurt me," she said. "He was as confused as I was."

"Bull," said Tucker.

"He did leave when I asked him to," she said.

"He'd better have," said Tucker. "Moonie, the guy broke into your mother's private study."

"I know," she said. "But I've been thinking. What if there is something? He said they were trying to pass off one of Oscar's essays as one of Aunt Sarah's. Even back when Aunt Sarah was alive, Mom and Oscar spent so much time together. He came to Rockbridge every summer for his job at the Arts School."

"This is your mother," said Tucker. "For crying out loud, Moonie. Are you going to believe this stuff from some guy you've known only a few months and who practically rapes you?"

"I don't know my mother," said Moonie. "I just live with her sometimes."

Tucker asked her what she wanted to do.

She picked up her keys from the coffee table in front of her. "We've got some time," she said. "Why don't we look?"

"For what?" said Tucker. "I'd rather sit here."

"We'll know if we find it," said Moonie. And in just a few minutes, they did.

❦

It was dark outside, but the stars were bright overhead. A slight breeze stirred the leaves of the surrounding trees, and the cicadas on the edge of the lawn chirped. Nancy Gale and Richard sat at the round metal table, she on one side, he on the other. All the food lay untouched on the grille of the tabletop.

"It started during my junior year of high school," Nancy Gale said. "I was fat back then. Not enormous, but fat. I used to work backstage at the plays and dream about playing all the leading roles. I also used to fantasize about having sex with the drama teacher who directed the plays. I used to dream about that a lot. You probably think about sex all the time too, don't you?"

"Just about," said Richard. She looked so pretty and so sad sitting in the metal chair, her wrists propped on the armrests, her head against the back of the chair as if she were expecting a collision.

"After we did *Anything Goes* one winter, we had the usual cast party at somebody's house. It was a big deal after those shows— pizza, ice cream, sandwiches, cake. I think the parents all thought if they fed us enough we wouldn't do any drugs or alcohol. Ha ha. I showed up at the party with a pint of Southern Comfort in my shoulder bag. Can you imagine that? I used to drink it with Sprite."

"Gross," said Richard. He had no idea of what Southern Comfort and Sprite would taste like, but he could tell by her tone how he was supposed to react.

"So as usual at the party I was Little Miss Food Suction. I mean, I was practically eating two things at a time, you know, get a sandwich and put it on top of a piece of pizza and then sprinkle peanuts all over some ice cream? I was putting the food away. And there was this guy there, a junior, who had a car and who was really good-looking. I had the hots for him so bad.'' She told Richard about how she let the guy know she had a pint of liquor in her bag, and suggested maybe they could split it if he gave her a ride home. ''So the guy says, 'Sure, sure, you get us some food to take and I'll go get the car, I'll meet you at the foot of the driveway.' So I'm subtly wrapping up pizza in a couple of napkins and slipping it into my shoulder bag when Mr. Epes, the director, asks to speak to me outside. I'm like dying. He takes me outside in the cold and he tells me that I don't need all that extra food and that maybe I should consider our hosts, and all that. And then he says, you have such a pretty face, Nancy Gale. You'd be so pretty if you'd just lose some weight.''

Richard guessed what happened next. ''So then he reaches into your shoulder bag to get out the pizza and finds the liquor.''

''Wrong,'' said Nancy Gale. ''He doesn't look into my bag. He goes back into the house. But I'm so embarrassed that I just leave without even getting my coat. And I get down to the bottom of the driveway, and the guy is waiting for me. His car's running. You can see the exhaust in the cold air from the lights outside the house. And I have to go around the car to get into the passenger side. But before I do, he rolls down his window and says, let's have a sip right here. And I'm so dumb, I'm looking into his car and it looks like he's got a bunch of blankets on the passenger seat. And that gets me even more excited. And I get out the bottle and give it to him, and he opens it and takes a big swallow, and he says, 'Thanks, pig, why don't you go back to the trough?' And then his friend pops up from the passenger side, and his other friend starts laughing in the back-seat, and they screech out of the driveway with my liquor bottle.'' She sat still for a long time, remembering it. ''And then I walked over to the curb, and I heaved out everything I had in my stomach. It was a lot. And I'll never forget that feeling. It was wonderful. It was the feeling of being completely drained, of having all the tension and the trouble purged out of my system. And that was how I learned how to lose weight.''

Richard had never known anyone who would trust him enough to tell him a story like that. He was the King of the Pranksters, and he would be likely to use it for a practical joke. But he didn't want to make a joke of this memory for Nancy Gale. He surprised himself by wanting to protect her.

"I hope those guys had a wreck," he said.

"No," she said. "They're all doing just fine." She sat up and put her elbows on the table. She fiddled with the package of potato chips, but she did not open it. "And now Tucker has caught me. He was the one single person in the whole world who I didn't want to know about this. And he knows."

"I guess I understand why you didn't want me lifting weights over your bathroom," said Richard.

She looked across the table at him. "I was scared that you'd find out and tell Tucker," she said. "I was scared that you'd tell everybody. Hey, guess what, Nancy Gale is bulimic. See? I even know the clinical term for it. I've read all about it. I'm supposedly ruining my digestive system."

"Why don't you stop?" said Richard.

"That's hard," said Nancy Gale. "I've tried. But I don't want to go back to being fat."

"That teacher was right," said Richard. "You are pretty."

She sat back then and smiled at him. "I was so wrong about you," she said. "I thought you were such a nerd when I first met you."

"I thought you were a bitch," said Richard. It was funny to both of them.

"You know," said Nancy Gale. "It's horrible to have Tucker know, to have the news out there in the world. But, in a way, it's a relief, too. You know what I mean?"

Richard was afraid to answer.

"Haven't you ever had a secret that you didn't want anybody to know?" she said. "But once it gets found out, you don't have to hide it anymore."

Some secrets are easier to live with than others, Richard thought. He envied her.

"Maybe I can do it this time," she said. "I told Tucker that I wouldn't steal any more food. Maybe I should start eating a real breakfast and riding my bike more."

"You can," said Richard.

"What's wrong?"

"Nothing," said Richard.

"You're crying," said Nancy Gale. She got up from her chair and crossed over to him, knelt by his seat. "I've been doing all the talking. You're just as upset as I am, aren't you?"

"I'm okay," said Richard.

"Is it Alex Mason?" she said. "He was your friend."

"It's not Alex," said Richard. "It's nothing."

She stayed where she was. Her face was very close to Richard's. He could smell her sweet scent. Her eyes were bright in the moonlight. "It must be awful to be Tucker Blackburn's little brother," she said. "To see all the women throwing themselves at him."

"I don't mind," said Richard.

"He's good-looking," said Nancy Gale, "but so are you."

"No," said Richard. "You said yourself I was a nerd."

"You're different," she said. "You look different. Your shoulders are broader, your skin is better, something. I don't know. Your legs are sturdy, not spindly. You've got a nice face."

Richard felt some tiny compartment in his loins open that he hadn't known was there. There was some kind of electricity generating. Nancy Gale touched his hand and pulled him upright. She took off his glasses and laid them on the tabletop, and then she kissed him gently. He held his arms out to his sides. He didn't know what to do. She pulled him to her and kissed him again. Then he tried to return her kiss, but she stepped away, off the patio and past the garden into the carpet of grass. That was that, Richard thought, but she was stepping away only to get off the concrete patio and onto a softer surface.

"Would you like to say good-bye properly, Richard? I don't think I'll be able to tell this to anybody else. Over here," she said. As Richard watched, she reached one arm behind her, made a quick motion, and then stepped out of her dress. Another blur of motion, and she stood naked before him. He picked up his glasses from the table and put them back on. Then he walked to her, afraid to blink, afraid to miss seeing anything. She stopped him when he was a foot away.

"Take off your shirt," she said. He took it off and dropped it into the grass.

"Now sit down," she said. He sat and watched with exquisite excitement as she carefully removed one of his shoes, then the other. He reached for the button on his shorts.

"Wait," she said. "Lie back." He lay back on the grass and felt the cool, gentle blades on his skin. She leaned over him and kissed him again, her breasts brushing his chest. He surged to grab her, but she sat up. ‘‘Not yet,’’ she said. She reached down and unbuttoned his shorts. Then she pulled them off. His boxers next. Once again he moved to embrace her, and she gently pushed him back down on the grass. She leaned over and kissed him again.

‘‘What if I take my hand and do this?’’ she said, rubbing her palm across his chest.

‘‘I like that,’’ he managed to choke out.

‘‘And what if I do this?’’ she said. This time she massaged his belly.

‘‘Yes,’’ he said.

‘‘And this?’’

‘‘Uh-hum.’’

‘‘And this?’’

Richard did not want to speak.

‘‘And what if I do this?’’ she said.

Oh, oh. Oh.

One entire filing cabinet was devoted to the works of Sarah Davidson. Tucker and Moonie discovered quickly that the works were arranged chronologically, starting at the bottom drawer, so that the top drawer contained the most recent work.

‘‘This stuff goes all the way back to high school,’’ said Tucker. He pointed to the labels on the drawers. ‘‘She wrote so much.’’

‘‘She wrote constantly,’’ said Moonie. ‘‘It was impossible for her not to write.’’

Within each drawer, the files were arranged by category: BOOK REVIEWS, CRITICAL ESSAYS, BOOKS IN PROGRESS, FICTION, MISCELLANEOUS. Tucker asked for the two smallest categories, which happened to be FICTION and MISCELLANEOUS. He stacked the file folders on the desk in front of him and opened the top one. It was a short story set in Richmond. In the margins and between the typed lines were Anne Lindsey's penciled corrections and changes.

‘‘I didn't know she wrote stories,’’ said Tucker.

‘‘She wrote everything.’’

In the lower left corner of the cover page were Sarah Davidson's name, her address, and the word count for the story. Her last name and the page number were in the upper left corner on each page of the manuscript. But the title page itself suggested that somebody else had written the story. "Touring Church Hill," said the title. And just beneath it: "by Heidi Crawford."

"Does your mother proofread things by people other than her sister?" Tucker asked.

"Not that I know of." Moonie systematically pulled out each folder in the drawer, glanced at it, and then replaced it. Tucker felt so stupidly slow in comparison. But he had to interrupt her.

"I don't understand this," he said. "There are two names on the title page, your aunt's and somebody else's. Is this Heidi Crawford one of her students?"

Moonie looked down at the story. "That's one of her pseudonyms," she said. "Aunt Sarah didn't like to use her own name on fiction." She explained that the author's real name went into the corner of the title page while the pen name floated under the title. "I remember this one. It was in *Redbook* three or four years ago."

"Why wouldn't she want credit?" said Tucker. "If I got a short story published, I'd want everybody to know about it."

"Not if you wanted to be taken seriously by other professors," she said. "Aunt Sarah had to be careful not to make herself look too shallow. She'd leave her own name on a short story if it went to a place like *The New Yorker* or *The Atlantic,* but as far as I know, she never got anything published there. She told me once that she had a trashy mind for fiction. She didn't want to cheapen her scholarly work by having it associated with mass culture magazines."

"I never thought of her as a snob," Tucker said.

"It's not snobbery, exactly," said Moonie. "It's practicality." She replaced another folder in the drawer. "I wonder if you've just found what Chris was looking for. Maybe he wanted a list of Aunt Sarah's pseudonyms. For a chance to collect all her fiction or something. Do a study. Whatever they do in graduate school."

Tucker thought that made sense. "Was he in the fiction section when you caught him?" said Tucker.

"I can't remember," she said. "I don't think so. I think he was somewhere toward the front of the drawer."

Tucker put down that file and opened the next one. It was another short story, again edited by Anne Lindsey in pencil, again with Sarah

Davidson's name in the corner, but this time the listed author was Katherine Wells. He read the first few lines. This one was set in Washington, D.C. Tucker wished he could read the rest of the story. It started quickly, with a woman finding some guy's credit card in the stairwell of the Washington Monument. But if he read every story, he'd never get through the pile.

"Do you remember this one?" he said. " 'Alarms and Excursions'?"

"It's about a shoplifter," said Moonie. "That's old, too. I read it when I was fourteen. In *Cosmopolitan* or somewhere like that." She finished with her section of the top drawer and moved down to the second one. "This is harder than I thought," she said. "Maybe there are some letters hidden in here or something."

Tucker went through two more file folders, both of which contained short stories. In the fifth one, however, he found something else. It was the story line and first-year projection for a soap opera series called "Eden, Pennsylvania." The first name he saw on the page was that of Tru Lovinguth.

He read the first page carefully. Then the second. It took him a long time to pull the words into sentences. "Wait a minute," he said. "This is *Adam's Garden*." He showed the sheaf of papers to Moonie. "Didn't Chris know about that? Was that the big secret?"

"I doubt it," said Moonie. "The word was out after your mother lost her job."

She closed the second drawer to the filing cabinet and reopened the first one.

"There must be something else in here," she said. At the back of the drawer were three boxes for stationery, plain white cardboard lids over plain gray cardboard bases. She lifted them out to see whether a missing folder might be on the bottom of the drawer. There was nothing.

Tucker took the boxes of stationery from her and laid them on the desktop beside him. "Your aunt sure as hell used a lot of stationery," he said. The boxes were the size for full standard-sized 8.5" by 11" typing paper, the kind of stationery used by businesses. "Maybe it does involve letters in some way."

"Maybe it involves nothing," said Moonie. "Did you ever think of that? Maybe that's just the excuse Chris gave me when I caught him going through Mom's archives. He could have just wanted to get his hands on the complete works of Sarah Davidson.''

Tucker lifted the lid from the box closest to him. Inside was no stationery at all, but rather more fiction in a tidy stack. Lying on top was the manuscript of a short story. ''The Trials of Sally Galloway,'' read the title page. ''By C. Y. Anderson.'' And in the corner of the page, Sarah Davidson's name once again, in the space where the author's name would be. Tucker picked it up. He had not read the story, but he recognized the character in the title.

''What about this?'' he said. He showed her the story. ''Your uncle seems to have borrowed a name from your aunt.''

''Let me see that.'' She looked at the title page, then at the introductory paragraph. ''Oh, no,'' she said. In the rest of the box, beneath the ten pages of story just extracted, lay the manuscript of *Sally Galloway,* the novel. Tucker stared at the title page himself to decode the words more deliberately. In the center was certainly the familiar title, *Sally Galloway,* and under it, centered, ''A Romance by Oscar H. Davidson.'' Then his eye caught the name and address in the lower left-hand corner of the page. Sarah Davidson, it said. He looked carefully. Sarah Davidson. Oscar Davidson was listed as the author, but Sarah Davidson's name and address were at the bottom of the page.

They caught on at the same time.

''The novel Uncle Oscar wrote wasn't the one that got published,'' said Moonie. ''Aunt Sarah just used his name for a pseudonym.''

''She and your mother let him take credit for Sarah's work,'' said Tucker. ''They never told anybody.''

''Why would they keep it a secret?'' said Moonie.

''Richard will go berserk,'' said Tucker.

❄

Richard stood in the front doorway and watched Nancy Gale back her car out of the drive. He wanted to follow her up the mountain. He wanted to be with her forever, to touch her hair, to feel her skin, to reinvestigate her body slowly and deliciously. And yet, strangely enough, he also wanted never to see her again, ever. He feared that they would never again be able to share the sort of experience they had shared tonight. What he and Nancy Gale had learned was something no other people in the world had ever known before. Richard had never been in love until now. He had lusted and he had fantasized, but he had never before known what it was like to be so consumed by that other, to feel so fulfilled by someone else, to find strength and beauty inside himself because she had found strength and beauty there, because she, who was so wonderful, had deemed him worthy enough of her. He could exult in the grandeur of what had passed between them.

The night was warm and fragrant. He latched the screened door on the front of the house, then closed and bolted the wooden one. His parents would have killed him for leaving the front door unlocked like that, but so what. How utterly trivial a complaint. He walked to the back of the house and out the kitchen door, where he looked once again at the spot on the lawn where they had been. Not a trace. All their clothes were back on. No remnants. The grass was as smooth as it had always been. It might have never happened. But it had.

The telephone rang and summoned him back to the house. It was Tucker. For a minute Richard was afraid that his brother had found out, that he was angry, that he was going to retaliate. Tucker, however, had called for another reason. It took Richard a moment to register what he was hearing.

"You mean Davidson didn't write that novel?" said Richard. "His wife wrote it? He cheated?"

"Easy," said Tucker. "It was her decision. She probably did it to be nice to him."

Richard reacted as though they had just found buried treasure. "Can you bring it over here?"

Tucker had to consult with Moonie. "She says nothing ever leaves the archives."

"Just for a few hours, then," said Richard. "On loan. Just long enough to copy some pages."

Moonie agreed.

Richard wasn't even sure of how best to use the information. "Let's not spread this around," he said. "Let's think about how we want to go from here."

"Rich," said Tucker. "You didn't cheat in his class, did you?"

Richard liked the first taste of vindication. "Will you come by the house later on?"

"Much later," said Tucker. "Moonie and I have some visiting to do."

Richard hung up the phone. How the hell would he ever go back to school now? How could he concentrate on anything? This was the best day he'd ever had in his whole life. It was just what, an hour or so ago, that he was working on his homework. It waited for him upstairs. But he was different now. He was not the same person who had sat down to type. He knew things. He was experienced. He was wise. Yet up the stairs he went, giddy in his manhood, determined to finish the work he had to do, the work required for children at school, the work that was so beneath him but that he would finish anyway because he was big enough to comply. Because his older brother had given him nuclear weapons to use against Davidson. There would be no mere pranks from Richard Blackburn. The King of the Pranksters was deposed. He was into serious adult-level revenge now. Something worthy of his new station.

But, damn, if Tucker were only here. Richard found himself grinning alone in the house, grinning when there was nobody there to see it. What a night. He wanted to scream and yell and jump up and down and high-five and tell Tucker about every little detail about Nancy Gale, and yet at the same time he wanted to keep it private. He didn't want to call her tonight. He was scared of breaking the spell, scared he would wake up.

Although the hall was dark upstairs as he walked to his room, he didn't need the light. He knew the way. He entered his room and saw the red glow of the switch for his surge protector bar into which his computer was plugged. Aside from the faint gray glow from the windows, there was no other light in the room. He reached for the light switch on the wall, but his hand never made it that far. He saw and felt a form rise up from its seat by the door. A hand reached out of the darkness and grabbed his wrist, yanked him into the room, and slammed the door. Then he was up against the wall struggling but helpless, pinned there by an arm against his windpipe.

"Don't make a sound, Richard," said the familiar voice.

It was Alex Mason.

The lights were hot and painfully bright in the amphitheater on top of the mountain. Milton Blackburn had found his costume too heavy last night; tonight it was both heavy and tight. After his scenes at the beginning of the play, he sat in the darkened seats in discomfort and took notes on Shakespeare's Act III, during which the young lovers switch roles and allegiances because of Puck's magic herb. He had to admit that Griffin Dupree was quite wonderful as Oberon—dignified, intelligent, regal, and somehow not quite human. When Dupree declared himself vexed with Puck, Blackburn believed him. The rest of the cast, however, lost energy as he performed. The grander their fairy king was, the flatter and slower was everyone else. He mentioned it to Patricia, who sat three seats away and also took notes.

"Why are they so dead when he's on stage?" Milton asked.

"Because they hate him," she said. "He keeps telling them that they're just a bunch of amateurs."

He bristled but did not reply. Patricia had done nothing to defend the cast from Dupree's complaints. By her silence, of course, she suggested that his criticism was justified. It was another way of getting at Milton, who had hired the company this winter and spring. Ever since she had learned that he had requested her removal from the cast of *Adam's Garden,* she had been distant and peevish. She had not raised her voice or made any threats, but rather had simply withdrawn into her own concerns. She had become another version of his son Richard, his son who had left him. He didn't know how to get through to either of them. He was more depressed over his family relationships than he was over the death of Ramsey Paxton.

At the break Griffin Dupree hopped off the two-foot elevation of the stage onto the grassy verge between the first row and the concrete. He stepped out of the bright lights and into the shadowy seats two yards below the two observers.

"I ordered a refrigerator for my room," he said. "The food here is deplorable."

"We're not paying for a refrigerator," said Milton. Half expecting a contradiction from his wife, he glanced at Patricia, who silently listened from her seat. "That's too extravagant."

"I'm not asking you to pay for it," Dupree said. "I'm telling you that they had a terrible time delivering it. Your son's car was blocking the loading dock."

"It's out of gas," said Milton.

"Chop, chop," said Dupree. "It's been there for over twenty-four hours. Is everything in the South this slow?"

"He's been very busy," said Milton. "He'll move it when he can."

Dupree turned to Patricia. "Are you doing notes tonight? This cast is as slow as Tucker. You might remind them that I'm on time-and-a-half after eleven o'clock."

Patricia said she could do his notes now.

"I don't need any," he said. "I'm really on tonight. Too bad the others can't keep up."

"You're right," said Patricia. "You've been splendid."

He beamed. "Is that all?" he said. "Nothing more? Didn't you like that business with the herb?"

"Loved it," she said. "There's just one little quibble."

"Yes?"

She leaned forward so that he could see all her perfect teeth. "If you say anything derogatory about either of my children again, I'll cut off your balls and play Oberon myself. Would you care to test me?"

"Patricia—"

"Get back to that cast and try to be civil. It'll be the biggest stretch of your career."

He left. She looked over at Milton, who had no idea of what she was about to say next. Was it his turn now?

"You know," she said, "he's an awful human being, and they are a green cast, and it's horribly hot to work out here." Somehow she did not sound angry. He wasn't sure of how to respond.

"I know," he said. "I'm sorry."

"Don't be foolish," she said. "It's exhilarating. For the first time in my career, I'm in control. I've never enjoyed anything more in my life." Then she stood up and kissed him. Within thirty seconds she'd put her attention back on the rehearsal, but Milton noted with some pleasure that his costume, for the first time since he'd put it on, felt much lighter. It was actually quite comfortable after all.

Dinner with Oscar Davidson turned out to involve a lengthy cocktail hour, fresh seafood and vegetables, and good white wine. At 9:30 P.M. they sat across from one another at the formal dining room table, the kind of table at which Anne and Sarah had never sat when they were growing up. The white linens and fresh flowers were lovely in the soft glow of candlelight. Anne Lindsey had no stomach for any of it, including her host. She had sipped half a glass of wine by the time he was ready to open a second bottle. But during the two hours she had been there, she had at least regained her composure.

"You know, Oscar," she said, "you do have a gift for creativity. For making beautiful things."

He wore a starched cotton dress shirt and a beige silk jacket, and he acknowledged her words with a raising of his wineglass as he chewed on salmon steak.

"But it's all so sick," she continued. "It's all so perverse. Sarah thought she was giving you some inspiration when she offered to put your name on *Sally Galloway*. You seemed grateful."

"Faustian bargain," he said. "How was I to know that people would then be screaming for a second book?"

"But why didn't you write one?" she said. "You had a manuscript. You could have revised it. Instead you just went soft."

"I could never keep pace with Sarah," he said. "Neither could you."

"But you do have the urge to create," she said. "You can't squelch it. The essay you wrote for the program. That was an act of creation, Oscar. Not a professional one, but a good try. So why can't you write on your own?"

He drank more wine, ate more fish. "It's too hard to be that good," he said. "It's too much work."

"So you piddle around with theater playbills and schemes to make children miserable in school. Why are you so hostile to your students, Oscar? Why do you dislike them so much?"

"I don't dislike all of them," he said. "Just some."

"Just the ones who challenge you," she said. "That's why you dislike Richard Blackburn so much, isn't it?"

"I dislike Richard Blackburn because he burned down my house," he said. "Isn't that valid enough?"

"You've convinced yourself of that story," she said. "There's no evidence."

"Hardly," he said. "Look at the kid. Look at the way he behaves. He's got something gnawing at him."

"Not arson."

"Not intentionally," said Oscar Davidson. "Of course not. He was just playing one of his practical jokes. But the heater went bad. And Sarah died. He killed your sister.''

"Perhaps. It's an awful burden if that's true.''

"It's true. And he's paid.''

She could guess what he meant. "You did manufacture that cheating incident, didn't you? You typed out the story yourself and then attached his cover sheet.''

"He learned who was in charge,'' said Oscar.

"Did he?'' she said. "I wonder if he learned to despise authority. Or to embrace wickedness if he wants to prosper.''

"I got control of the class,'' said Oscar.

"It was all a big amusement for you, wasn't it?'' she said. The smell of the food in the room nauseated her. "You wanted to publish your own essay in his father's playbill as a little twist to your private joke, didn't you? You would accuse the boy falsely at school, and then you would manipulate the boy's father into publishing your own fabrication.''

"You were perfectly willing to help,'' he said.

She watched him eat. "You didn't do it because of the fire, did you? Not entirely. You did it because you felt like creating some pain.''

"I did it to teach him a lesson,'' said Oscar. "The schoolroom is the one place I know where a teacher can exercise absolute control.''

"Richard won't always be in the classroom,'' she said. "And after this summer, you won't be in mine, either.''

"I will if I want to be,'' he said. "That was the deal.''

She was fed up with the deal. She was fed up with salmon steaks and pouilly-fuissé and steamed asparagus and shiitake mushrooms. "When you came along,'' she said, "both Sarah and I thought we'd met the fairy-tale prince who liked to play the charming rogue. You offered her the huge house in Charlottesville, the apartment here in Rockbridge. You paid for Moonie's education at boarding school and bought me the big house in Canterbury Hills. We thought you were the most generous man in the world.''

"It sounds generous to me,'' said Oscar.

"And it was,'' she said. "I want to be fair. But talk about your Faustian bargains. Whose soul has gone to the devil, Oscar?''

"You got what you wanted,'' he said. "I gave that huge grant to the Arts Council. You got to run the kind of Arts School you wanted.''

"And in exchange for that,'' she said, "all I had to do was hire you part-time. Did you make a large gift to Montpelier for the same arrangement?''

''I wanted a place to work,'' said Oscar. ''A place where I could do something.''

''When Sarah died,'' she said, ''I actually felt sorry for you. I'd always considered you charming. Your cynicism was amusing to me. I enjoyed the sardonic repartee. In your own way, Oscar, you can be very seductive.''

He took another drink of wine and poured more. ''Seductive,'' he said.

''Attractive,'' she said. ''I've enjoyed your companionship. I don't mind the platonic part. But you've gone sour, Oscar. *Lilies that fester smell far worse than weeds.*''

''Shakespeare again,'' he said. ''Sarah was more married to Shakespeare than she was to me.''

''But she stayed with you, Oscar. She kept hoping you'd come to life.''

''You think I didn't want the same thing?'' he said. ''Why do you think I wanted to marry her? I wanted to be inspired. I wanted to find some energy. Sarah was the liveliest person I'd ever seen. It's almost as though she's still alive, the way she dominates our conversations.''

''But she isn't.'' Anne Lindsey had no more appetite for his company. ''I'm going home now,'' she said. She stood up. ''I will not serve as your companion any longer.''

''You can't just abandon me,'' he said. ''We share too many secrets.''

''Write a book about them, Oscar,'' she said. ''Ramsey is dead. Alex is a fugitive. They were people who meant something to me. If you want the house back, take it. I'd rather have my dignity. I can't go on with this mock relationship anymore.''

''What kind of relationship do you want?'' he said.

''I think I'll start by developing one with my daughter,'' she said. And she left.

❖

Alex let Richard breathe on the condition that he would not shout. ''Just give me five minutes,'' he said. They stood in the dark of Richard's room with Richard's back against the wall. Alex held his wrist.

"Relax, Richard," said Alex. "I'm not here to hurt you. I just want you to listen to me."

It was still hard to breathe because he was so frightened. He had to think. He was the King of the Pranksters, after all. He could devise some way to get out of this.

"Listen to me," said Alex. "I did not kill Ramsey Paxton."

Richard did not speak. He wondered if he might get to the door. The window was impossible.

"I didn't," said Alex. "I didn't cut off any of his fingers. I didn't bash in his head with the bolt cutters. You saw him. There was nothing like that."

An idea emerged. Worth a try. He would have to be an actor. Have to pretend. "Yes," said Richard. "I remember now. You're right."

Alex yanked him over to the windows, where he pulled down the shades and then turned on the desk lamp. He let go of Richard's arm but moved to a place between Richard and the door.

"Don't patronize me, Richard," said Alex. "You were transparent that time. Good instinct, but an unsuccessful performance. Not enough conviction in your voice. Richard, I'm telling you the truth."

Alex had not shaved. He had stubble under his chin, and his clothes were wrinkled and smelly. "I'm guilty of a hell of a lot," he said. "But not murder."

If only somebody would come home. Maybe rehearsal would end early. Tucker was at Moonie's. "How did you get here?" said Richard. "I thought you were far away."

"I took a cab here from the bus station," said Alex. "We almost got rear-ended by that woman who came to see you."

Richard felt his face going hot.

Alex allowed himself a fragment of a smile. "I didn't watch," he said.

He let Richard sit down on one bed. Alex sat on the other and rubbed his eyes with his knuckles, as if he were a little boy trying to stay awake. Richard was not prepared for such a gesture of vulnerability. Alex, clearly exhausted, lost some of his threat.

"Why are you here, Alex?" said Richard. "Why aren't you in Canada or somewhere?"

"Because," said Alex, "when I found out Ramsey was dead, I wanted to look you in the face and tell you that I did not kill him. I didn't want to write you a letter or call you on the phone. I wanted to tell you in person. What you think of me matters, Richard. We're friends. If I get arrested five minutes from now, at least you'll know.''

Richard really wanted to believe him. The guy looked as if he were playing some modern-day *Prisoner of Zenda,* or maybe an undercover cop. He looked like the character who would be the hero. But Richard was having a hard time buying what he said. He wanted to accept Alex's story, but he couldn't. Not all the way. What Alex was doing was so crazy, a grand gesture out of a stage tradition nobody believed anymore.

''Why did you steal that money?'' said Richard.

Alex shook his head. ''I don't even know. I thought at the time that I was doing it for Anne. I was building a reserve we could use at the Arts School. Then I told myself that I was doing it for myself, so that I could entertain Anne on a level she was accustomed to. She would find me attractive again. I think mainly I did it because I thought of it. It was another silly prank that got out of hand.'' He told Richard that he never would have tried it if he'd known that somebody as scrupulous as Ramsey Paxton would be taking over the Arts Council. He had cashed the checks, then withdrawn the money from the bank and stored the cash in an empty paint can. ''I knew I'd get caught,'' he said. ''I was ready to run. But I never spent any of the money, Richard. I never spent a penny of it. The most I stole from the Arts Council was the interest that money would have earned, which I can repay. When Ramsey came down to the theater, I had fully expected to return it all. I really thought he'd be nice about it. He wasn't.''

Richard tried to believe him. It was a horrible prospect. ''If you didn't kill Mr. Paxton,'' said Richard, ''then who did?''

Alex hesitated. ''First, tell me what happened to the money,'' he said.

''I told the police about the paint can,'' Richard said, ''but it wasn't there when they checked.''

''No,'' said Alex. ''There was no mention of it in the newspaper article.'' He stared at Richard hard. ''Somebody took it,'' he said, ''to make it look as though I did.''

''Who?''

''Somebody who knew it was there,'' said Alex.

Richard felt his uneasiness returning. ''Not me,'' he said.

''Of course not,'' said Alex. ''Don't you remember the knocking on the door when we left?''

"That was my father," said Richard.

"No. It was Oscar Davidson."

"It was my dad," said Richard. He explained about Tucker's borrowing Milton Blackburn's car keys. "I saw him at the front doors right after. He told me himself he was there. He told the police. But he didn't have his key. That's why he didn't get inside."

Alex thought about it for a minute. "All right," he said. "Oscar must have arrived immediately after your father left."

"Mr. Davidson said he never went to the theater that night," said Richard. "Why do you keep mentioning him?"

Alex would not answer directly. "Here's my problem, Richard. I'd like to see Ramsey's murderer caught. I'd like to stop being a fugitive. But if I talk to the police, they'll arrest me. I don't want to go to jail. And I'm afraid that I'd make a very convenient defendant in a murder trial."

Richard hardly heard him. He was thinking of Oscar Davidson. And of why Oscar Davidson would show up at the Lyceum after Ramsey Paxton got hurt. "Mrs. Lindsey lied to the police," Richard said. "She was there when Mr. Paxton fell, wasn't she?"

"Leave her out of it, Richard."

"She was there the whole time, wasn't she? Maybe she's the one who pushed him."

Alex stopped him. "She was there," he said. "After the trapdoor gave way under him—it was an accident, Richard—she ran to get Oscar from the classroom building, where he was waiting. That's why I was so shocked to see you. I'd expected Oscar. And that's also why I was so eager to get you out of there. I didn't want you to know that anyone else was present. The publicity and the scandal were supposed to involve only me."

"But what good could Mr. Davidson do?" said Richard. "By that point, Mr. Paxton was lying on the storage room floor."

"Oscar was supposedly going to call for help after I left. And return the money. And make an additional donation to persuade Mr. Paxton not to implicate anyone else."

"Meaning Mrs. Lindsey," said Richard.

"We're not bringing Mrs. Lindsey into this anymore, Richard," said Alex. "I don't expect you to understand."

And yet Richard could understand. If Richard had a chance to do something for Nancy Gale, he would make the grand sacrifice. He would be her Cyrano, would relinquish his happiness to protect hers. There was such a thing as a love that would not die. He thought of his father.

"You don't even know for sure that it was Mr. Davidson at all, do you?" said Richard. "You just want me to think he's guilty."

"I want the truth revealed," said Alex. "It was Oscar who killed him. There's no need to drag anyone else into it."

"Why would Mr. Davidson kill Mr. Paxton?" said Richard.

"Because Ramsey wouldn't publish his essay in the playbill," said Alex.

"He would kill over that?"

"Ramsey Paxton was as angry over the essay as he was over the money," said Alex. "He accused me of perpetrating a fraud with that, too. He did check on it, Richard. He did end up checking out your story. He believed you enough to call the magazine in Chicago where Oscar was sending it."

Richard was simultaneously gratified and appalled. "One little magazine article?" said Richard. "And Mr. Davidson would kill somebody for it?"

"Publication, ego, pride. Manipulation. Power game. Who knows?" said Alex. From his shoulder bag he pulled out the familiar brown envelope and handed it to Richard. Inside was the manuscript of the Sarah Davidson essay Richard had taken to Ramsey Paxton. "Surprise," said Alex.

Richard held the envelope gently in both hands. He was almost scared to keep it. Every time he had touched it, something awful had happened. "Mr. Paxton did bring it to the theater that night," he said. "Why'd you take it with you?"

"Because its discovery would have meant another embarrassment for Mrs. Lindsey," said Alex.

True or not? It was so hard for Richard to read Alex. "Can't you just turn yourself in and tell the police? Now that somebody's dead, can't you show them this manuscript?"

"No," said Alex. "The police would say that I was using the manuscript to distract them." He reminded Richard that he was guilty of embezzlement and fraud, that he had the motive and the opportunity to kill Ramsey Paxton, and that Richard himself was an eyewitness who saw him with the motionless victim.

Richard wouldn't accept his answer. "Why don't you write the police a letter and tell them about Mr. Davidson? Or I'll go. I'll tell them I did see Mr. Davidson at the theater. I'll tell them everything.''

"They'd never believe you," said Alex. "You've already had a chance to name everybody you saw. They'd think it was just another of your attempts to hassle Oscar." He paused and looked at the envelope in Richard's hands. Then he looked at Richard. There was a long silence.

And somewhere during that silence, Richard realized why Alex had come back. "You're not just telling me this so that I can keep it a secret, are you?" said Richard. "You're not just here because you want to tell me face-to-face that you're innocent. You want me to do something, right?"

Alex almost smiled. "Now I'm the one who's been too transparent," he said. "You're right, Richard. I want to see if we can trick Oscar into making a confession. Will you do it?"

Richard was not at all sure of what was happening. Part of him suspected that Alex wanted to frame Oscar Davidson for the murder of Ramsey Paxton, that Alex wanted to use Richard to set the guy up so that Davidson would have to take the blame for somebody else's crime. Richard was thrilled by the audacity of it all. But part of Richard truly wanted to believe that Alex was unjustly accused, that he had returned here to set the world right, that it was Oscar Davidson who was guilty.

"What do you want me to do?" said Richard.

"Just help me get him out here tomorrow," said Alex. "I'm going to spend the night in the woods behind your house. You can give me some food. I'll be okay. Get me Tucker's tape player, the one that operates on batteries. Get me a spot where I can talk to him tomorrow, privately, after everyone else has left for the rehearsal. We'll talk about Ramsey's death. I'll ask him for money and promise to leave. After we're gone, you'll pick up the tape and take it to the police. By the time they get it, I'll be gone."

It sounded logical enough. But it could also be only part of the truth. Alex might want to go one-on-one with Oscar Davidson for other reasons. Before he responded, Richard concentrated on his delivery. He had to sound as though he were fully convinced of Alex's innocence. "How do I lure him out here?" said Richard.

"You use this manuscript," said Alex. "He'll want to know how parts of it end up in the draft you'll turn in to him tomorrow. Tell him you've got the original at home. That's why I brought it back here.''

''There's a better way,'' said Richard. He told Alex about the phone call from Tucker. ''He's been posing as a novelist, but he hasn't published any fiction himself. Tucker's bringing me a few pages tonight.''

''We'll use it all,'' said Alex. ''Anything to get him near me.''

Richard wondered how much of this to believe. How much was Alex manipulating him? How guilty was Oscar Davidson? How dangerous was this latest prank they were plotting? Where was the side of the angels?

And then, deep within him, he heard the voice of the Prankster Muse, the song of inspiration breaking forth in a melody of ideas. Note upon note rang out in this private concert, this opera of opportunity, this intricate symphony of serendipitous circumstances. It was an outrageous scheme, but he had to try it. Forces outside his control had collaborated to provide him the opportunity to pull off the grandest stunt of them all. He could get his revenge on Oscar Davidson and still—perhaps, maybe, possibly—get a chance to play the part of the hero.

Alex asked him what he was thinking. ''Are you willing to try it? It's the biggest favor I've ever asked you, Richard.''

''No,'' said Richard. ''I have a better idea.''

PART III

The Phantom of the Opera

ELLEN Spencer was back in her office by 9:15 on Friday morning, but she did not bother to call the newspaper office right away. Waiting on her desk were the telephone records dating back three months for Alex Mason, Ramsey Paxton, Anne Lindsey, the Blackburns, the Stone Mountain Theater, and the Davidsons. Somebody had spent a long time identifying the names associated with each number. She found nothing of interest in the Lindsey telephone log. Then she tried Ramsey Paxton's and Alex Mason's. She was especially interested in the calls made from home and office telephones during the week before the fire in Charlottesville. There were lots to check. She hoped to establish some connection between Ramsey Paxton and Sarah Davidson. Or between Alex Mason and Sarah Davidson. She was frustrated to see that neither man had made any telephone calls to Charlottesville during the entire period.

But there was something. Ramsey Paxton had phoned one number in Chicago three times on the day that he was killed. It was the only number in Chicago ever called on either the home or the office lines, and it was the same number each time. It belonged to a periodical called *Feminist Renaissance*.

She knew that name. She pulled out her file on the Sarah Davidson death and began to look once again through all of O'Shea's carefully recorded details. Time of death. Autopsy report. The book by Emma Prynne Sarah had been reading before she died. The earphones she'd been wearing. O'Shea's interviews with the principals. And there it was in the back—the bibliography of scholarly publications. *Feminist Renaissance* had published more monographs by Sarah Davidson than any other periodical. And Ramsey Paxton had called the place three times on the day he died.

By now it was nearly 10:30. She would not allow herself to become excited yet. First she dialed the number for *Feminist Renaissance* and identified herself.

"I don't remember speaking to a Mr. Paxton," said the woman who answered the telephone. "He probably talked to one of the editors."

Ellen Spencer asked if she could have the names of the editors, which the woman provided. "A few are in the office now," she said. "But they're in a meeting."

Ellen told her why she was calling and requested that she interrupt the meeting. In a few minutes a man picked up the telephone. "I didn't talk to Mr. Paxton," he said. "He talked to Sally. The editor-in-chief. It was some question about a manuscript."

Still she wouldn't let herself get excited. "What manuscript? A manuscript by Sarah Davidson?"

"It was something about Sarah," said the man. "But I'm thinking Mr. Paxton believed this essay was written by somebody else. You'll have to talk to Sally."

Sally Jobe, the editor in chief, was in Cincinnati at a conference. She was expected back in the Chicago office on Monday. Ellen left a message at her hotel in Cincinnati. But she did not wait for her to call back. Instead, she immediately called the business office of the newspaper to ask why they had omitted the plug for the Davidson monograph in their most recent advertisement for the Stone Mountain Theater. It took four changes of speaker before she found a woman who could tell her.

"Ramsey Paxton himself telephoned in the change Wednesday afternoon," said the woman. Two days ago. The day of his death. "He said we were to drop all references to Sarah Davidson because her article was no longer going to be in the playbill. We barely made deadline, but we got it changed."

"Did he say why?"

"No." The woman wanted to ask Ellen questions about Paxton's death, but Ellen had other calls to make. She tried seven printing firms before she found the one doing the program for the Stone Mountain Theater.

"That's right," said Richard Lynne, who ran the company. "Ramsey called me yesterday afternoon and told me to yank the Davidson piece. We were about to go to the camera. I told him he'd still have to pay for the typesetting."

She could feel how close she was. "Do you have any idea why he would make such a change?"

"Nope," said Lynne. "He just said he wasn't going to take a chance on it."

"Take a chance? What kind of chance?"

"He didn't explain," said Lynne. "Ramsey was very thorough, but he wasn't the type for chitchat. Have you guys had any luck looking for Alex Mason?"

She did not talk to him about Alex Mason. She hung up the telephone and sat for a minute. Then she decided that it was time for her to make a visit to the Arts School. Classes had resumed this morning, and she'd be able there to speak face-to-face with the people she most wanted to see. Before she left, she went back to her files and pulled out two essays to take with her: "The Bottom of the Dream" by Sarah Davidson, and "Love as Metaphor in *A Midsummer Night's Dream*" by Christopher Nivens.

❦

Oscar Davidson sat in an uncomfortable chair made of molded yellow plastic in Anne Lindsey's office. Ellen Spencer, the policewoman with the red hair, sat in a similar chair a few feet away. Anne sat behind her desk. Oscar and Anne competed to see which of them could explain about the essay in the playbill first.

"It was all my idea," said Oscar. He knew the advantage of a strategic confession. "I was trying to get my own work published."

"I didn't see any harm," said Anne. "It was wrong, of course."

"I'm surprised you didn't know about it already," said Oscar. "I told Chris Nivens just the other day. Asked him to collect all the essays from his students so that we wouldn't have any confusion on our hands."

"We really weren't trying to hide anything," said Anne Lindsey. "Not permanently."

Oscar said he was in part trying to make a satirical comment about name recognition. "Ramsey would take the monograph if he thought Sarah had written it, but he wouldn't take one by me," he said. "It was a private joke." Ellen listened with a stone face.

"I had once dated Ramsey," said Anne. "I liked the idea of his looking foolish. We were going to tell him after the program came out.''

''Well,'' said Oscar. ''We were going to tell him after *Feminist Renaissance* rejected it.''

''Which they would have done,'' said Anne. ''I'm convinced of it.''

Ellen got a chance to ask a question. ''But you didn't know whether it was going to be accepted or not? You hadn't heard from the magazine?''

''I hadn't,'' said Oscar. ''I expected to in another couple of weeks. That's how much earlier Chris Nivens had submitted his own essay, and he just heard of his acceptance this week.''

Ellen was not entirely taken with their answers. ''But you willingly turned in this sample to me,'' she said. She indicated the manuscript titled ''The Bottom of the Dream'' on the floor at her feet. ''You misled the police.''

Their embarrassment was obvious.

''And how did Mr. Paxton find out about this forgery of yours?'' she said.

''I wouldn't call it a forgery—''

''How did he find out?'' she said.

''He saw another manuscript,'' said Oscar. ''Or he said he'd seen another manuscript. One that was supposedly the original. He got suspicious, I suppose.''

She asked him what he meant by the original.

''The essay that Sarah wrote for the playbill earlier this year,'' said Oscar. ''He said he had a copy.''

''Where did he get it?'' asked Ellen.

''I don't know,'' said Oscar. He looked at Anne.

''Alex Mason had it,'' said Anne. She looked straight ahead at Ellen. ''He told me that night at dinner.''

''And where did Alex Mason get it?''

''He wouldn't say,'' said Anne. ''He could be so damned irritating.''

''Have you seen this other manuscript yourselves?''

They both said no.

''So we have no way of verifying its authenticity unless it turns up again?''

They said that was true.

''Any idea where this manuscript might be now?''

"I think Alex took it with him on the night he left town," said Anne. "Why?"

"Because he didn't want you to find out about our attempt to pass off Oscar's essay as one of Sarah's," she said. "You found out anyway."

Ellen reached down for the other essay at her feet. "Would you recognize the original Sarah Davidson essay if you saw a copy?"

"Yes," said Anne. "I edited it. I can remember it very well."

"Is this it?" She handed Anne a copy of Chris Nivens's essay, "Love as Metaphor." She had taken care to cover the name of the author on the manuscript.

Anne reacted immediately. "It's the same title," she said. Then she read further. "But not the same analysis at all." She skimmed through the entire monograph. "No. This is nothing like Sarah's. It sounds like the one Chris Nivens wrote. Sarah told me about it. She didn't like it."

"And how do you like it?"

Anne shrugged and returned the manuscript to Ellen. "It's better than Oscar's," she said.

Ellen sat with her legs crossed and doodled on the edge of her notepad. Her tape recorder ran on the desk in front of them. Finally she spoke. "You have your sister's work at home, I believe," she said to Anne.

"Yes," said Anne. "I have all her manuscripts. Plus the materials from her office at the university."

"Correspondence?"

"Some."

"Would you be willing to let me look through those files?" said Ellen. "I'd like to see what's there."

"You won't find anything of interest," said Anne.

"May I look?"

"Yes," said Anne. "I can meet you this afternoon."

Oscar squirmed slightly in his seat and tried to catch Anne's eye. She kept her look stubbornly on Ellen.

"What about now?" said Ellen. "Can you leave the school?"

Anne hesitated. "I'd better not," she said. "I have a meeting with some parents in half an hour. But I could meet you after lunch. Before the funeral." Ramsey Paxton's memorial service was scheduled for 3:00.

Ellen thought about it for a good little while. "Okay," she said. "We'll make it one-thirty." She took her tape recorder and left. Oscar waited until he was sure she was gone. He did not want the police looking into the archives.

"Let me go over there now," he said. "I want to move the *Sally Galloway* materials."

"She's going to find out, Oscar," said Anne. "It's going to be known."

"It doesn't have to be," he said. "What's the harm in my moving the box out?"

"Because she's probably calling right now for some patrolman to go sit near my house and watch to see if either of us tries to sneak in there," she said. "Do you think the woman is a fool? She's going to find nothing. There are hundreds of pages. She doesn't care who wrote *Sally Galloway*. Nobody cares."

"I care," said Oscar. "The one single shred of respect I get around this town is for being a writer. I don't want to lose it."

Anne did not answer.

Oscar could feel himself losing control. "This is important," he said.

"Not to me," she said. "I won't point it out to her, Oscar. But if she asks, I'm going to tell her."

"Are you going to tell her you pushed Ramsey Paxton over that trapdoor?"

"I might," said Anne. "I might tell her everything."

It was disheartening for him to see her so implacable. "That would be awfully cruel to Alex," he said, "after he's worked so hard to keep your name clear."

"Don't you dare take the high moral ground," she said. "Alex has kept your name clear, too."

Oscar turned to go. "Be sensible," he said. "She thinks she's onto something with this silly essay. It's going to lead nowhere. But she doesn't need to know about the novel. She doesn't need another connection between Ramsey Paxton and us."

"What does that mean?" she said.

"It means that I went back into the theater that night to do your dirty work, and Ramsey ended up dead."

"Is that a confession, Oscar?"

"Of course not," he said. "It's just a preview of the way the police like to think. We've come up with our story, Anne. We have to stick to it.''

"Why?" she said. "Why can't we just tell the truth?"

Oscar looked at her with dismay. "Listen to yourself," he said. "Are you that far gone? You know why we can't tell the truth."

Anne Lindsey took a long time to answer. "Yes," she said, "I suppose I do."

❧

Friday at school was the most excruciatingly tedious day Richard had ever spent. They'd missed a day of classes, so supposedly the teachers were going to catch up on their course work, but everybody wanted to talk about Alex Mason and the murder of Ramsey Paxton and the blood on the floor of the Lyceum. All the students wanted to go into the theater, which the police said was closed until after classes were over this afternoon. The production of *Hamlet* was canceled, so the crew and the cast scrambled for other lab activities. Richard signed up for the school newspaper with Rebecca Taylor, though of course Mrs. Lindsey told them that they could print nothing about the "unfortunate incident" in the paper. She also held a special assembly to offer to the student body the facts about what had occurred on the day before yesterday. However, since she didn't allow questions afterward, the rumors still circulated. His classmates practically mobbed Richard, who had slept maybe two hours the night before but was so high on adrenaline that he didn't feel any fatigue.

In Davidson's class Richard tried not even to look at the teacher. The man was obviously hung over—red-eyed and sweet-breathed. There was some confusion among the students as to whether the drafts of the essays were still due today, since classes had been canceled yesterday, or whether all assignments were postponed until tomorrow. Davidson's response was to tell everybody, even the five people who had finished their drafts, that they could have the entire two hours of class to work on their essays. So typical. Richard spent the class period trying to look busy in the library. He could not possibly concentrate on schoolwork at this point. Between thoughts of Nancy Gale and thoughts of Davidson's not being the author of *Sally Galloway,* he replayed his conversation with Alex. He'd decided that Alex was probably insane. But it didn't matter. Davidson was going to get his own punishment tonight.

Richard had not found time to write his own analysis of the play. He had a few half-formed ideas down, but he had been unable to develop them over the past two days. At most he had half a page's worth of gibberish about Shakespeare. He didn't care. What he had done to flesh out the draft, to make it at least look presentable before anybody started to read it, was to type a couple of pages from Mrs. Davidson's essay into his essay, to surround the whole damn package with quotation marks, and to footnote the entire mess with the words Alex had told him to use: "From an unpublished manuscript by Sarah Davidson." But to make sure that he got Davidson's attention, he prefaced everything with an epigraph: *For Sally Galloway, the smell of peppermint always brought back memories of that first Christmas at Belle Isle*. And he identified the source as "The Trials of Sally Galloway," by C. Y. Anderson.

At break the air was oppressively humid, and the sky was white with haze.

"Thunderstorms tonight," said Rebecca. She had on a lime-green shift and matching scarf on her head. "You want to go hear some music? I got tickets to the concert at the civic center."

Richard appreciated the gesture. "I can't," he said. "Not tonight." He was dying to tell her what he was up to, but he couldn't. She wouldn't believe it anyway.

"Big date?" she said.

"Sort of." He could reveal enough to keep her from thinking that he just didn't want to go. "I'm putting on a show of my own tonight. You think Davidson reacted to you? Read the newspapers tomorrow."

"That right?" she said. They were standing by the drink machines near the cafeteria.

"Remember Hamlet? When he decided to put on a play to catch the guilty king? That's me tonight."

"Hamlet was stupid," she said. "Why didn't he just march in and stick a knife in Claudius and get it over with?"

"Because he wasn't sure," said Richard. He tried to imagine how Hamlet must have felt when he learned that Claudius, the man he already hated, might have been the murderer of his father. "At that point Hamlet wasn't sure if the ghost was from heaven or from hell. That's why he put on his play. As a test."

"You selling tickets?" she said.

"Private affair," he said. "But you'll hear about it."

"Oh, sure," she said. She thought he was kidding her. "You remember what happened after Hamlet put on his play, don't you? That was when the king decided to kick his butt."

During the next period, the students got to talk to Mr. Nivens about his discovery of Ramsey Paxton's body. Unlike Mr. Davidson, who said nothing about the incident at all, Mr. Nivens was candid and answered all their questions about what he'd seen. They loved the part about the cut-off fingers.

"So kinky."

"So sadistic."

"So grisly."

At the end of class Richard turned in the draft of his essay to Mr. Nivens with a little nod. Nivens was friendly enough, but he didn't strike up a conversation and just stuck the essay into the pile with the others. Tucker had told Richard about what happened with Moonie. That was a shock for Richard—Nivens was a teacher, after all—but he could sort of understand. After Nancy Gale, Richard could understand a lot more. He felt so wise. He felt so confident. He felt so utterly in control.

It was such an illusion.

❧

On Friday afternoon the weather grew even hotter and more humid. Weather reports on the radio called for thunderstorms in the afternoon and evening. It was crucial that the weather be good. Patricia Montgomery wanted to use the amphitheater for her rehearsal. Milton Blackburn, harangued by the Arts Council, wanted to risk no damage to the vast green-and-white-striped tent being set up on the public lawn. And Richard Blackburn very much wanted the company to be out of the Pinnacle Inn after dark. If they had to rehearse inside, he would not be able to pull off the production of his own.

After lunch he found Davidson packing up his briefcase in his classroom alone. Richard closed the door to the classroom and stood in the doorway.

"What is it?" said Oscar Davidson. He looked tired and flabby and fat.

"I know all about you," said Richard.

Davidson hardly glanced at him and continued to pack. "Tell me what you want or leave," he said. "I'm busy."

"I know you and Mrs. Lindsey tried to pass off a fake essay to the playbill for the theater," said Richard.

"So what?" said Oscar Davidson. "Everybody else knows, too. Get out of here." He went back to his packing. It looked as if he were cleaning out his desk.

Richard had expected some resistance. "I know about *Sally Galloway*," he said.

"What do you mean?" said Davidson. He continued to pack his case.

"Look at my rough draft," said Richard.

Davidson found the drafts and read the first page of Richard's. "This proves nothing," he said, pointing to the epigraph. "C. Y. Anderson was my pen name."

"You're lying," said Richard. It was the first time he'd ever said such a thing to an adult. "Look at the back pages." Attached to this copy of the essay were photocopies of the first three pages of the manuscript of the novel. Sarah Davidson's name was on the title page. Anne Lindsey's pencil marks were legible in the margins. Richard had not included copies of these pages in his packet for Chris Nivens. "Tucker and Moonie got into the archives last night. They took some pages of the manuscript. I know you didn't write it."

Davidson stood like a hunter behind his desk. Richard was glad that there was an entire classroom between them.

"You're a vindictive little bastard, aren't you?" said Davidson.

"You haven't written anything," said Richard. He pulled out another photocopy of the title page of *Sally Galloway,* run off that morning in the library. "I'm ready to give it to Rebecca Taylor," he said. "The school newspaper circulates to the Arts Council. I think Rebecca would write a good editorial about you."

Davidson still didn't move. "There's nothing illegal about what we did," he said. "Sarah didn't want her name attached to a popular novel. She used mine. So what?"

"So you've been selling yourself as a published novelist all this time," said Richard. "You're about to become exposed as a fraud, Mr. Davidson. You'll be a joke. Unless you do what I say."

"I'm not going to be blackmailed by the likes of you," said Oscar Davidson. "Get out of here. No one's going to listen to you. We won't permit the publication of that sort of rumor in a school paper."

"What about in a real newspaper, then?" said Richard. "I bet there are lots of people who'd like to know that it was your wife who wrote the novel you've been claiming all this time."

"I don't care," said Davidson. But Richard could see that he did.

Richard gave him a moment to consider his alternatives. "I guess you can read about yourself in the news," Richard said. He turned to go.

"Wait just a minute," said Davidson. He looked very troubled. He sat down. "What do you want from me?" he said. It was not quite the voice of acceptance. But Richard was thrilled that they had proceeded this far.

"First," said Richard, "you will write a letter to the headmaster at Montpelier telling him that you are very embarrassed, but that you found the story I'd submitted to you in the spring. You don't know how my name got on that other story, but it was such an unfortunate event, blah blah. You want to clear my name. Yackety yak. You can word it right."

Davidson looked relieved. So far it sounded easy. "I could do that," he said.

"Second," said Richard, "you will drive this letter to the Pinnacle Inn at precisely nine-fifteen tonight. That's after dark. You will not arrive early. You will not bring anyone with you. You will meet me in the office of the building with the letter so that I can read it. You will not discuss this meeting with anyone. The cast will be rehearsing down in the amphitheater. We'll have privacy, but there will be people nearby. Do you understand?"

"That's rather Byzantine, isn't it?" said Davidson. "Why then? Why there? What are you scheming?"

Richard had to answer very carefully. "That's when I'll be free," he said. "I'm supposed to be working earlier."

Davidson tried to work up a smile. "Are you suggesting that we might be able to clear up all our misunderstandings? Maybe it's not too late for us to be friends, Richard." He was so affectedly nonchalant. It was terrifying to see that he actually cared. Maybe Alex was right. Maybe Davidson had killed Mr. Paxton. Richard had never been so close to such a dangerous person before. He felt as though he were making a homemade bomb.

"All right," said Davidson. "I'll write the letter. You'll give me the manuscript. You and Tucker and Moonie will keep quiet about *Sally Galloway*. Is that your offer?"

"That's the offer," said Richard. "You help me, I help you."

"Haven't you already submitted a copy of these papers to Mr. Nivens?" said Davidson. "He's going to read them and know everything."

"I left off the back pages," said Richard. "If he asks about C. Y. Anderson, I'll tell him I found the story in an old copy of *The Shenandoah Review*. He won't care. All he'll want to see is the manuscript of the Shakespeare essay. Which I also have."

"I'd like to get that, too," said Davidson.

Richard said that he would have everything up on the mountain. "Remember," he said, "you can't tell anybody that you're coming."

"And you won't tell anyone either," said Davidson.

They agreed on 9:15 sharp as the time for their rendezvous.

"May I go to lunch now?" said Davidson. He was scarier when he was friendly.

Richard wanted to fly out of the place before Davidson changed his mind. But he couldn't go yet. "I'm not finished," he said. "There's one more thing."

❧

Ellen Spencer found what she was looking for in the top drawer of Anne Lindsey's archives. She squatted uncomfortably on the thick carpeting with her notepad balanced on her lap and a stack of stationery boxes on the floor, while Anne Lindsey knelt beside her and offered answers to her questions. As soon as Ellen opened the stationery box, as soon as she saw the names on the title page, she knew that she had found their evidence. She knew with absolute certainty that Sarah Davidson had been murdered in Charlottesville. The trick was not to look too excited by her discovery. Anne watched her carefully. Ellen deliberately put the box aside, made a few notes, and then returned to it with studied nonchalance.

"This one," she said. "Do you have any correspondence on this one?"

"Certainly," said Anne. She pulled open the bottom drawer and extracted a thick file folder, then opened it on her desk. Ellen gratefully stood up to allow the blood to return to her aching legs. The file rested neatly on the green blotter. Inside were letters from a New York publisher and clipped reviews from newspapers.

"This is one of your sister's pseudonyms?" said Ellen.

"Yes," said Anne. "She used it only once."

"And who knew?"

"Nobody," said Anne. "One of her colleagues in the history department actually assigned the novel as parallel reading in his course. Sarah was thrilled."

"Her husband knew, of course," said Ellen. Casually, cautiously.

Anne hesitated. "I'm not sure that he did," she said. "This was fairly recent work." She explained that Sarah was aware of the way her prolific output bothered Oscar. "In the last couple of years, she played down her work when they were together. She told me that he got depressed whenever she published something new, so she just stopped telling him."

Ellen acted as though she couldn't buy it. "That's unbelievable," she said. "Somebody could publish a book and not have their spouse know about it? Aren't there phone calls, packages back and forth in the mail? Don't publishers send out advance copies? Aren't there autograph parties?"

"Sarah kept her office downstairs," said Anne. "She had her own bedroom upstairs. She didn't want publicity when she wrote under a pen name."

"Still," said Ellen. "It's incredible."

"I'm not saying that he didn't know," said Anne. "I'm just saying that it's possible. Sarah was a remarkably thoughtful person." She spoke to Ellen without a blink. The policewoman deliberately looked down at her notes. She didn't wanted this to look like an interrogation.

"Was it your sister's habit to read her own books after they were published?" she said.

"No," said Anne. "By then she was sick of them. She was on to the next project."

"And what about reading tapes?" said Ellen. "Would she ever get one of her own books recorded?"

Anne thought it was an odd question, but she shook her head emphatically. "Never," she said. "Dyslexia is a strange condition. She would get tapes of books that required her strictest attention, but there was no need to record her own work. She could read. And she could read her own work more efficiently than she could somebody else's."

For the sake of appearances, Ellen went through the rest of the files. The only essay on *A Midsummer Night's Dream* she found was one that had appeared in *Shakespeare Quarterly* in 1988. There was no sign of anything more recent. She finished her search in an hour.

"Is this everything of your sister's?" she said.

Anne hesitated just a fraction too long. "Everything I've got," she said.

Ellen waited. She'd learned long ago that silence was sometimes the most effective means of extracting information.

"That is," said Anne, "we lost a few items in the fire."

Give me a motive, thought Ellen Spencer. *Just give me a motive.* In looking for information about the death of Ramsey Paxton, she had found the crucial detail about the death of Sarah Davidson. Exactly where the hell had Alex Mason been on the night of that fire in Charlottesville? Had he really been here in Rockbridge? Just how carefully had anybody checked on his whereabouts? It would be so tidy if she could find one perpetrator for the two deaths, but it appeared now that she sought two separate killers.

She could see a logical explanation for the phone calls to *Feminist Renaissance* after all. Ramsey Paxton had learned of the fraudulent essay submitted by Oscar Davidson, had pulled it from the playbill, and had called the magazine to inform them of what he had learned. She just couldn't build that into a motive for Oscar Davidson to kill the man. A murder because of an unpublished essay? It wouldn't work. It especially wouldn't work given the timing, given that Ramsey Paxton had already done the damage by the time of his death. The essay was not going to be published. There was no way to undo the decision, and it simply wasn't that dire a loss for Davidson. If he wanted to get it published, he could always resubmit his essay under his own name somewhere less prestigious. She would follow up with the editor of *Feminist Renaissance* just to confirm her understanding of the facts. However, it appeared more clearly than ever that Ramsey Paxton had died not because of any manuscript, but because of the Mason embezzlement. Now she was desperate to find some connection between Mason's theft and Sarah Davidson. Or rather with someone connected to

Sarah Davidson. The woman in Charlottesville had been murdered. If Ellen could find out why, she felt certain that she could identify both killers.

She restrained herself from running to the car when she left the house. As soon as she got to the office, she would call Casey O'Shea in Charlottesville. He would love it. It had turned out to be the headphones after all. Sarah Davidson had been wearing headphones while she read *Scottish Queen Mary* by Emma Prynne. It had seemed peculiar, and yet, as O'Shea himself had pointed out, it was possible to get a recording of any book on tape. But Ellen had just seen the manuscript for *Scottish Queen Mary* in the Lindsey archives. Emma Prynne was one of Sarah Davidson's secret pen names, a pseudonym known only to her sister. And no matter how dyslexic Sarah might have been, she would never use a recording to read a book that she'd written herself, a book that nobody had known was hers, a book that her murderer had placed into her hands as a ruse before leaving her unconscious on the bed to die in the flames.

Anne telephoned Oscar Davidson as soon as Ellen left her home. He was not in a mood to converse.

"You're going to be late for the service," Oscar said. "You're going to make me late as well."

"Oscar, it wasn't there. The manuscript of *Sally Galloway* wasn't in the archives."

"How about that," said Oscar. "And you're going to pretend that you don't know where it is?"

"I have no idea," said Anne. "I nearly choked when we opened the top drawer. It's disappeared."

Oscar told her that it hadn't disappeared at all. "Little Ramona and her lover of the week found it and took it," he said. "They've given it to Richard Blackburn. Who happens to be putting me through his own little adolescent version of the Stations of the Cross."

Even before she had fully comprehended what he told her, she giggled. It was the first giggle in what seemed years for Anne Lindsey.

"Enjoy yourself," said Oscar. "This is unacceptable. All agreements between us are off."

"I hope so, Oscar."

"What if I happen not to show up for work on Monday?" he said.

Anne found everything he said to be strangely hilarious. "Exactly what's Richard asking you to do?" she asked finally.

"Never mind," he said. "I will not tolerate this treatment. From him or from you."

"I think you will, Oscar," she said. Then she indulged in one last mad folly by hanging up on him.

❧

After the memorial service for Ramsey Paxton, Moonie came home to take a nap. She woke up suddenly at 4:30 P.M. when she heard someone in the room with her.

It was her mother, embarrassed to be caught staring. "You look so much like Sarah," said Anne, as if that would explain her presence.

Moonie lay on top of her favorite quilt in the four-poster that her grandfather had made. Anne, both discomfited and determined, stood at the foot of the bed. She had changed from her dark dress for the church service and wore her favorite yellow. The white curtains at the windows billowed with the strong breeze. The air outside was gray, and the light in the room was dim. Rain was inevitable.

"Okay," said Moonie. "I know what you're here for." She got up and closed the windows. She liked the fresh air before a thunderstorm, but Anne did not like the windows open when the air-conditioning was on. Moonie returned to the bed and sat on the quilt Indian-style.

"It wasn't that," said Anne. "I was just watching you sleep. I used to watch you sleep when you were a little girl. It's been so long since I did that."

Moonie could not remember hearing such a tone from her mother. She supposed that the funeral was the cause. Then Anne surprised her again by sitting on the end of the bed and facing her. Her mother never came into this room except to inspect it.

"Do you have to work tonight?" said Anne.

"I have to serve the food," said Moonie. "And clean up. Somebody on the Arts Council has hired a caterer for this last dress rehearsal."

"I thought maybe we could eat together here," said Anne.

Moonie was stunned. She could not remember when they had eaten a meal together—just the two of them, just for fun. "Is something wrong?" said Moonie.

"Not anymore," said Anne. She paused and rubbed her hand gently on a patch of quilt. "Oscar told me that you went into the archives. Richard has wasted no time in using the material you gave him."

Moonie prepared herself for the inevitable lecture. Her mother surprised her once more.

"I'm glad you did it," said Anne. "I'm sick of secrets." She told her all about *Sally Galloway:* how she and Sarah had discovered the advantage of using pen names while Anne was editing *The Shenandoah Review,* how her struggling periodical received hundreds of submissions but so few good ones. She stumbled on the practice of publishing several of her sister's short stories under different bylines; in one issue, there had been three different stories by Sarah, all credited to other names. After the marriage, when Oscar was working so hard on his own novel and Sarah cranked out her own work so effortlessly in comparison, they felt sorry for him. Sarah offered to share her inventiveness, turned one of her early short stories into a novel, and gave it to him.

"Why did it have to be so hush-hush?" said Moonie. "Why couldn't you even tell me?"

"There were several pseudonyms Sarah wanted secret," Anne said. "It had nothing to do with her affection for you. By then it was English department politics. And it was love for Oscar. She wanted him to get the attention. Now that she's dead, Oscar doesn't want to relinquish that attention."

"It's so childish," said Moonie.

"He has lots of money," said Anne, "but what he wants is to feel important." She pointed to his recent attempt to publish an analysis of *A Midsummer Night's Dream,* his impulse to see his own work in print. "I think he sees it as some bizarre form of poetic justice, using Sarah's name the way she used his. But he's conceded on this one. He's calling *Feminist Renaissance* to withdraw the submission."

Moonie could think of nothing generous to say about her uncle.

Anne reached over and took Moonie's hand. "How much more awful do I have to seem before you move out?" she said. Her hair was light and delicate in the dim light from the windows.

Moonie was tempted to withdraw her hand, but she didn't. Her mother's fingers were cool and smooth. She thought of Chris Nivens last night. "I'm not all that eager to move out," she said. "Eventually. No deadline."

Anne said she understood. "I just hadn't realized until recently how much I liked your company," she said. "When Sarah died, I wasn't prepared to feel so lonely here."

"But I'm away at school all year."

"I know," said Anne. "It's just been this summer, coming home and knowing there was somebody else in the house."

The telephone beside the bed rang. It was Tucker. Anne Lindsey stood and waited while Moonie completed the brief conversation.

"I have to go up the mountain," said Moonie. "They're moving the dress rehearsal inside because of the weather. They need help."

"Tell them they can use the Lyceum," said Anne. "The police have cleared it."

Moonie doubted that they would want to move everything downtown for one rehearsal. She pulled her white sneakers out of the closet and started to put them on, and then she stopped, surprised by the strong, moist breeze that eddied around her. She turned to look, and she was startled and touched by the sight of her mother, reopening the windows and letting the fresh air into the room, where it caught the hem of her dress and made her appear to be floating.

"Before you go," said Anne, "we need to discuss something else." Then she sat on her daughter's bed and told her everything.

※

At 7:30 P.M. the wind picked up and blew hard, and the first faint rumblings of thunder stirred in the distance. At his apartment on Madison Street, Chris Nivens took off his shoes and stretched his legs on the easy chair by the bay window in his living room. He loved days like this one, when he was inside and safe from the elements while nature was about to put on a show. He was embarrassed about his behavior with Moonie. He'd written her a note of apology, to which she had not yet responded. No matter. He was ready to forget her. She was only an undergraduate kid, after all. And he'd been able to determine that in fact there was no manuscript of Sarah's last essay in the files. He would have to consider other locations. Thunder sounded overhead, like an armored truck passing through the dark gray sky. Even the weather acted out every now and then.

On his lapboard was Rebecca Taylor's draft for her research paper. Conventional, unexciting stuff. She played with the old chestnut popularized by Olivier that Hamlet was a man who could not act until desperation drove him to it. Solid enough, he supposed, but there were so many more interesting ways to read the play. He wrote a final suggestion on the bottom of her last page, and then he tossed the essay into the pile with the completed papers. The next in the pile was Richard Blackburn's.

Chris Nivens began to read first with boredom, then with confusion, and finally with recognition. He looked quickly through the rest of the essay and then back at the opening lines. Trembling, he dialed Oscar Davidson's telephone number. No answer. He forced himself to calm down and think. Richard obviously wanted him to see this work. He tried the Blackburns' home number. No answer. Then he tried the Pinnacle Inn. Nancy Gale Nofsinger answered the telephone.

"Is Richard there?" he said. "This is Chris Nivens. His teacher."

"He's around," said Nancy Gale. "I don't know. It's very confusing up here right now. We just had a power failure."

She hung up. He put on his shoes as the first drops of rain hit the window, grabbing his umbrella on his way out the door. Then he came back for his binoculars. His mind could work very fast.

❧

Pulling the main trip-hammer for the electrical current was the only ploy Richard could devise at the last minute. The company was coming into the Inn for their rehearsal because of the weather, and he couldn't have that. He'd never be able to pull off his play with all those people around. As he had hoped, when they checked the circuit breaker in the basement, they never bothered to look and see if the power itself had been turned off. They checked the breaker panel, and all the circuits were still on. The big horseshoe-shaped handle for the main power circuit lay flat against the wall, as it should. Nobody noticed that its handle was pointed down instead of up.

There would have been enough confusion before a dress rehearsal anyway. Now the place was in chaos. Milton Blackburn had called Anne Lindsey in desperation. Yes, she had said, you may use the Lyceum. They were all part of the Arts Council family anyway, and the police had cleared the Arts School theater this afternoon.

Upstairs people in costumes bumped around in the dim light. Somebody in the office found a couple of flashlights and, in the office safe, the kerosene camping lanterns, cylindrical and glass enclosed, two of which they set up at the top of each stairwell, one to the basement and one to the second floor. Silhouettes bobbed in the dimness until they reached the corona of bright light cast by the lanterns, and then faces came suddenly into illumination as if in an Old Master. In the kitchen Moonie and Tucker helped the caterer pack the last of the dishes from dinner by candlelight. Outside rain splattered the building ferociously, and lightning flashed like a strobe across the landscape. It was hard to recognize anyone in the dim light and the confusion as the members of the cast gathered costumes, props, shoulder bags, and umbrellas to drive down the mountain to the Lyceum.

Upstairs Richard slipped into Tucker's room in the men's wing. He could hear Griffin Dupree groping around by candlelight in the bathroom. Downstairs sounded like intermission at the circus. There was enough light from the window for him to see Tucker's bureau. He found the key ring right away and took it. *Sorry, Tucker,* he thought to himself. *I've screwed you over too many times already.*

But the King of the Pranksters was on a roll.

❦

Chris Nivens reached the Pinnacle Inn at 7:45, at almost the exact moment as the peak of the storm. Rain lashed his windshield and defeated his wiper blades. His headlights were useless in the gray light, and lightning served more to blind him than to illuminate his way.

He did not know that Oscar Davidson was a quarter mile behind him, also ascending the mountain.

He pulled around to the side of the building and parked beside Tucker's Toyota near the loading dock. It gave him a slight pang to think that Tucker and Moonie would be here, but he had more important matters to consider. He rushed out of his car and was soaked before he could get his umbrella open. On the veranda, looking out over the violent storm in the valley below, several actors clustered in makeshift ponchos made from plastic sheeting.

"Where's Richard Blackburn?" Chris shouted over the noise of the storm. Even under the shade of the porch roof, the wind blew rain onto the boards and slickened them. No one in the group knew.

He ran inside and looked in the office, in the rehearsal room, in the kitchen and dining areas, even backstage, which was pitch dark and into which he simply shouted Richard's name, with no response. There were people everywhere, but he could not find Richard. On his way back to the loading dock he nearly collided with Tucker and Moonie.

There was only a moment of silence. "I'm looking for your brother," he said. "It's very important."

"He could be anywhere," said Tucker. Moonie said nothing, but she held his eye.

"Where? Where most likely?" said Chris. "I've looked all over this floor. Is there a bottom level?" He was soaking wet and desperate. Tucker could almost feel sorry for him, almost consider him a decent guy who had bad timing.

"Try upstairs," he said. "He likes to hide in the attic sometimes. Behind the picture of Sarah Siddons. There's a door. If you need a key, there's one on my bureau."

Chris Nivens ran up the stairs. In the shadows cast by the kerosene lamp he saw the portrait of Sarah Siddons. He pulled it open on its hinges and saw the metal door beneath. The door was locked. He pounded on it.

"Richard," he shouted. The thunder cracked outside. He could barely hear himself.

If Richard was up there, Chris would need a key to get in. Tucker said there was one on his bureau. He looked at the row of eight doors in front of him. Which one was Tucker's? He felt like quitting. But he didn't. He tried every room in the men's wing. Some of the doors were locked. In the others, there were no keys on any of the bureaus, desks, or tables. As he finished his search, he heard a thump overhead. There was indeed somebody in the attic. But he could not get up there without a key.

Nancy Gale and Richard were in the actors' green room in the basement of the Inn. Overhead was chaos. Here the vinyl couch was hot and sticky, and they could barely see with the one flashlight they had.

"We'd better go separately," said Richard.

"You first," she said. He left the flashlight with her, grabbed an armload of costumes, and exited up the basement steps, eerily bright with the light of the lamp at the top. She gave him a minute to get down the hallway to the front door, where the cast members would be pulling up their cars, and then she grabbed another load of costumes and followed. She felt faintly guilty for her behavior. Was it guilt for her pleasure with Richard or her revenge at Tucker?

Upstairs she left her costumes in the chair by the office door and sneaked up to the second floor to wash her face. Her bathroom was very dark, creepy even with the flashlight, but after only a few seconds of groping she found the spigot.

Then she heard the floor creak overhead. That little schemer was upstairs. She knew she was supposed to be helping with the transfer of supplies to the Lyceum, but she wanted to peek at what Richard was doing. Was he eavesdropping on her? Or spying? She reached into the pocket of her jeans for her keys and remembered that she'd left them on the table beside her bed. Nobody at the Pinnacle Inn locked their rooms except when they were in them. But when she left the bathroom to look, she couldn't find her keys on the table or the dresser or in the pockets of yesterday's jeans. Damn. She'd lost her keys. Nancy Gale was not usually so careless. Overhead she heard another soft bump.

She proceeded with flashlight in hand down the hall to the attic door. When she pulled back the Sarah Siddons portrait, she could see that the inner door was not latched. In a second she was inside the stairway. Someone was clearly moving around up there, but the noise stopped when she closed the door behind her.

"Don't worry," she called. "It's just me."

She aimed the light onto the steps in front of her and ascended to the very hot attic. A couple of windows in the upper hallway were open, and the cool breeze and rain blew in. She left the windows open for the necessary ventilation. Down the hall to the familiar door. A turn of the knob. She walked into the room and lost her breath.

A male body hung by the neck from the central rafter, tied with the brown extension cord for the now useless fan. Her flashlight beam caught protruding eyes and an extended tongue and a terribly red face. She started to scream, but she never could finish, because something hard hit her in the back of the head, and then she was gone.

Chris Nivens found Richard in the office by the telephones. Outside, the actors and materials were nearly loaded into the cars, but there was still plenty of turmoil inside. Richard sat at his father's desk. After all that searching, all that frantic searching, the boy was right here in the midst of everything. He had one of the lanterns on the desk and sat quietly by the telephone.

"Richard," Nivens said. He entered the office and shut the door behind him. Immediately it was opened by an actress looking for a makeup kit. This time Chris left the door open. "I need to talk to you," he said.

"Not now," said Richard. "I've got phone duty." A stupid answer, but he was nervous and eager for the building to empty. He still had to rig up the tape player and turn the power back on. He could do so only after the cast and crew departed.

"Richard, I've read your draft," said Nivens. He sat in a chair next to the desk and pulled it up close. "Do you have the complete manuscript of Sarah's essay?"

Richard looked to see if anyone was listening. Everyone was too frantic to pay attention to their conversation. "Yes," said Richard, "but we can't talk about it now."

"Where did you get it?"

Richard regarded him impatiently in the commotion around them. "I got it from Alex."

"From Alex? He mailed it to you?"

"Don't ask me that," said Richard. He did not want to tell lies to Chris Nivens. But perhaps he should have.

"Is he here?" said Nivens. He kept his voice low. "Do you know where Alex Mason is?"

Richard tried to stand up. Nivens pushed him back down. Richard fought to keep his temper. "I can't discuss it now," he said. "I'll tell you about it tomorrow."

"Richard," said Nivens, "this manuscript is very important to me. I was Sarah's student. I did the research. I'd thought it was lost. Won't you let me see it?"

"Not till later," said Richard. "I need it here."

"It's here, then? Just for a minute. Just let me see one of your photocopies."

"There are no photocopies," said Richard. Another actor came into the room, looked around, and left. Outside, people with umbrellas climbed into cars with the headlights switched on.

"It's material you've received from a suspected murderer, Richard. Don't your parents want you to show it to the police?"

Richard told him that his parents weren't aware that he had it yet. "They'd be the last to hear," he said. "Not even Tucker knows. He thinks I'm just up here to be helpful."

"Just let me take it to town to copy it."

"No," said Richard. He was losing his patience. "I need it for Mr. Davidson."

"He's coming here? Oscar Davidson?"

"That's right. At nine-fifteen. Everyone's got to be gone by then. Including you."

"Is he coming alone? What are you up to?"

"He's supposed to come alone," said Richard. "What difference does it make? Please. Don't stay. You'll spoil everything. I'm sorry, but I really don't want you here."

"Then why did you dangle so many prizes in front of me?" said Nivens. "Who is this C. Y. Anderson you mentioned in your draft? What have you found out?"

It was tempting to tell him, but he couldn't, not with Alex upstairs. He couldn't risk having the police come before they'd had their chance with Davidson. Richard had to get Nivens to leave. He offered a compromise. "I'll call you at ten o'clock," he said. "I'll call you at home and tell you everything. Give me until then, please. I've got to work this by myself."

Chris considered the possibilities. "All right," he said. "Are you sure you'll be all right here alone?"

"I'll be all right," said Richard. "I'll be fine."

"You'll be here by the phone?"

"Yes," said Richard. "It's where my parents expect me to be."

"Who else knows about this, Richard?"

"Nobody," said Richard. "I wish I hadn't told you." But he worked up a grim smile when he said it.

Chris Nivens left the office. He walked out the back veranda, ran through the rain to his car, and drove away. 8:15. Oscar would be up there in an hour. All right, all right. Again he had the strange sense that Providence was at work. It had been no accident that circumstances had arranged for him to stumble into this scene. Chris had very little time to prepare himself before it was time for Oscar's rendezvous. It tortured him to have to leave the Inn, to depart from this place, to give up his vigilance for even a few minutes, but the boy undoubtedly would watch to see whether his car proceeded over the crest of the road and down the mountain to town. Besides, it was unlikely that Richard would wander into a dangerous area as long as so many people were there. Chris Nivens would have to risk leaving, at least for a few minutes, long enough to find a telephone from which he could call Anne Lindsey. Even before he carefully steered his car past the first wet curve in the road, he knew what he would do.

Tucker took Moonie to his room upstairs at the Inn while he got his rain jacket. She wore a bright blue shell with a hood. His was green. The hall was quiet, the rain outside falling steadily in a shower. The wind and lightning had stopped, and the thunder was rolling off into the mountains.

"It'll be back," said Tucker. "We never have just one thunderstorm here."

"You're an expert on meteorology, too?" said Moonie.

He didn't turn on a flashlight, but let the gray light from outside illuminate his room. It never occurred to him to search for his keys. His car was still out of gas.

"Guess what Mother said to me today," said Moonie. "She asked me if I'd like to go to the beach with her in August. Anne Lindsey. Can you believe it?"

"Your Aunt Sarah was always nice," he said. "Why shouldn't her sister be?" He found the green nylon jacket in the closet and pulled it on over his head.

"It's incredible, Tucker. You should have heard what she told me about herself and Uncle Oscar. She's going to talk to the police tomorrow."

"The police?"

"She's waiting till tomorrow so that any newspaper reports will come out after the opening of your parents' play."

"What the hell has she done?" said Tucker.

"I'll tell you in the car," she said. "Hurry up."

"I don't see my tape player," said Tucker. "Dupree said he'd returned it."

She opened the bathroom door and cut through to Dupree's room. "What do you suppose Richard has done to bring Chris up here?" she said.

"Probably something to do with his schoolwork," said Tucker. He followed her into Dupree's room. The bed was neatly made, but there was clothing strewn across the entire surface of the bedspread. "Dupree is a weird housekeeper," he said.

Moonie looked into the closet. All the shirts were stuffed into a garment bag. "He hasn't even unpacked yet," she said. "Where is he, anyway?"

"Where the hell is my tape player?" said Tucker. He looked under the bed, then stood up and checked the drawers of the dresser.

"Let's go," said Moonie. "I've got to get some dry clothes before I work at the Lyceum. Did you see how wet Chris was?"

Tucker slammed drawers. They were all empty. "I wonder if Richard has included Nivens in whatever he's planning for Oscar."

Moonie said she was too timid to ask either teacher why he was here. "Chris was in such a rush," she said, "and Uncle Oscar wouldn't even speak to me. He just walked out through the scene shop."

"Oscar?" said Tucker. "I didn't notice him. You mean he's here tonight?"

"I saw him just a minute ago backstage. He did not look happy."

They left Dupree's room after confirming that the tape player was not there.

"Damn him to hell," said Tucker. "It wasn't in the rehearsal room either. That guy's lost my box. I'd like to kill him."

"You'd have to queue up for the chance," said Moonie.

❖

The huge Lyceum Theater downtown was dark, looming like a derelict cathedral, when the first cars pulled into the lot. Patricia Montgomery received minimal protection from her umbrella as she ran through a new downpour to the covered sidewalk connecting theater with school. The smooth concrete was wet and slick, but she did not slip. Tucker, his hair damp and sticking to his face, waited for her outside the double doors at stage right.

"I didn't think it would be locked," Tucker said. Several others from the lot ran toward them. "Can you get in?"

"I think so." She pulled out her key ring and began to search. Though the key was unlabeled and she hadn't used it for months, she found it quickly.

"I didn't know you had a key," said Tucker.

"Of course I have a key," she said. "Anne Lindsey gave it to me herself two years ago when I was doing those readings with the acting classes." The key jammed in the lock, but when Tucker jiggled and twisted it, the lock eventually surrendered.

A few minutes later, the theater crawled with activity. Some performers lolled in the chairs for the audience, others strolled the aisles in costume and recited their lines, others stretched on the boards of the stage. Patricia Montgomery directed the crew in the placement of platforms and masking tape. They would have to do the show without much scenery. But at least they would get a run-through. If they could ever get started. There was no apparent sign of the recent police investigation, except that everything was dusty. She asked one of the stagehands to find a mop.

Tucker came out of Alex's old office angry. "Richard says that he hasn't seen Nancy Gale since we left," he said. "I thought she was more reliable." He did not tell his mother that he had noticed some food missing this afternoon.

"Not now," said Patricia Montgomery. "Help get the stage set, Tucker. Where's Moonie?"

"At home. Changing. She'll be down in a minute."

"Where is Milton?" she said. "And Griffin Dupree? Were they in the same car? Were some people delayed?"

Tucker said he didn't know. One of the stagehands in a white T-shirt uncoiled a rope and twisted it around the gargoyle head at stage right, then ran it back to a pole along the far upstage wall. He and Tucker took strips of muslin and hung them over the taut rope to make a kind of forest through which the actors could enter. It looked like hell, but Patricia Montgomery did not comment. Music blasted too loudly over the public address system, then sank to an inaudible level.

Bad dress rehearsal, good performance, she told herself. But where was the rest of her cast? Where was her husband?

Oscar Davidson stopped at the Exxon station on the Jefferson Parkway at 8:50 P.M. He parked under the covered pumps for self-service, opened the deep trunk of his car, and began to fill the gasoline canister there, the canister that he had taken earlier from the loading dock at the Pinnacle Inn. A young attendant approached in a blue shirt with his name, GRIGGS, in a white oval over one pocket. The rain had nearly stopped. Water dripped from every surface, and puddles shimmered in the amber streetlights. Lightning flashed silently in the distance.

"Rain really cooled things off, didn't it?" asked the young man. He was tall and knock-kneed. "You hardly ever see old cans like that any more. Most of 'em nowadays are plastic. Guy was in here a little while ago with a plastic jug. Funny, you can go two or three days without ever seeing anybody wanting to fill up a can, and then you get two in one night. You live out in the country? Most people that put that much gas in a can live out in the country. What's that, five gallons? That's heavy. You can hurt your back getting that much out of the car. You think that storm's going to come back? I get off work in ten minutes. Just my luck to get caught in a gully-washer. You want me to check under that hood for you?"

Oscar Davidson held the nozzle of the gasoline pump inside the mouth of the red gasoline canister. "What I want," he said, "is for you to shut your fucking mouth."

Oscar Davidson was sick of all human beings under the age of thirty. He would not be at school tomorrow. In his apartment his bags were packed and waiting for him to return from this last bit of business with Richard Blackburn. He wondered whether he should have called Chris Nivens to see how Nivens had reacted to Blackburn's rough draft. But it didn't matter. He was leaving. Nivens would not be a problem for him.

Tonight he would say good-bye to the whole pack.

Milton Blackburn entered the Lyceum Theater soaking wet and furious. Patricia had the cast assembled on the stage. A couple of hands tried to adjust some lights overhead to illuminate a dark spot at stage left. She stopped talking when she saw him. He preempted her question.

"Griffin Dupree won't be able to make it tonight," he said. "He said he was tired of amateur theatricals and was leaving town. He's already gone."

Patricia was flabbergasted. "So soon? So abruptly?"

"It was the power failure that did him in," he said. "But I think the real reason is that he couldn't stand having you bite him back." He raised his hands helplessly. "So now we have no Oberon."

The voice came from the right wing, a clear and lively delivery of Oberon's first line in the play: *"Ill met by moonlight, proud Titania."*

It was Tucker.

Moonie was in her bedroom when the telephone rang. She picked it up on her own extension.

It was Chris. He was very agitated. "Look," he said, "I owe you more apology than what you're going to get. And I don't mean to sound abrupt now. But I really need to talk to Anne. Is she there?"

Anne was there. She picked up the telephone downstairs. Moonie covered the mouthpiece and listened to the conversation.

"I think there's a big problem brewing," said Nivens. "Can I come by to pick you up?"

"You can come by to talk," said Anne Lindsey. "Why do we need to go out?"

"We need to go up to the mountain," said Chris Nivens.

"Why?" said Anne. "They aren't rehearsing up there. They're using the Lyceum."

"I know," said Nivens. "I was up there myself. But we need to go. Oscar is going to be there soon. We need to get there before he arrives."

Anne Lindsey did not speak for several moments. "Why?" she said. "What has Oscar done? What's this about?"

"I'm not sure," said Nivens. "But there are lots of hiding places up in the Inn. And I think Richard Blackburn has tricked Oscar into making a rendezvous with Alex Mason."

❖

Finally everybody was gone. Richard worked his way back to the basement with a flashlight and turned the power in the building back on.
He was so keyed up by what was about to happen that he thought he
might be sick. At the top of the stairs he extinguished the last of the
kerosene lanterns. He could go up and get Alex now, or he could wait.
He decided to wait. It was possible that the actors might have forgotten
something for the Lyceum and would send somebody back for it. Even
if they did, though, and saw that the lights were back on, they would
still hold the rehearsal downtown. It would be too much trouble and
too late to try to move the whole cast back up to the rehearsal room
at this point of the evening. However, if somebody came back for an
overlooked item and saw Alex, then there would clearly be trouble.
Better to delay until the last possible moment.

He took his backpack with him and went outside through the front
entrance to check the park for traffic. Not a sign of anyone. He did not
see in the distance the car parked under the trees at the crest of the
road. He did not know that he was being observed. He walked along
the covered veranda across the front of the building and around to the
loading dock. The rain had stopped, but water still dripped from the
eaves. Tucker's car was ghostly in the early darkness. Richard could
see a few leaves pasted to the windshield and hood like smallpox scars.
He vaulted the railing of the veranda and jumped onto the dock itself,
where he raised the garage-type door to the scene shop. There he found
the bolt cutter, long and worn and heavy, like the offspring of pliers
and scissors, in the bottom of the tool box. He flexed the little finger
of his left hand, tested it against the edge of the tool. It would not feel
good. He also took a pair of work gloves and placed them into his
backpack.

He moved toward the office by way of backstage, which he
reached by sliding open the large door between scene shop and stage.
At the hall door, just before he left the boards of the stage for the
carpeting of the Inn, he looked back at his path. Both scene shop
doors remained open, so that he could see the dim whiteness of
Tucker's car outside. He hoped that the escape route he had left
would not invite Davidson to enter from the direction of the scene
shop and the stage, but it really didn't matter. The guy would end up

in the office anyway. Richard carried his heavy backpack down the hall, past the kitchen and dining room to the now brightly lighted office. He tested the door to the safe. It opened easily, and he quickly grabbed Tucker's tape player from inside, where he had concealed it that afternoon. From his pack he removed the thick box containing the novel manuscript and stuck it into the safe. He did the same with the brown mailing envelope containing the monograph on *A Midsummer Night's Dream*. Then he concealed the bolt cutter and the gloves in the middle drawer of the desk.

A problem arose with the tape player. He tried plugging it into an extension cord and placing the machine under the desk. That position didn't work because he would have to reach down too clumsily to turn it on. He tried putting it into a drawer, but that was awkward, too, with the cord leading out. Finally he decided to stow it behind the filing cabinet. He'd just turn it on when Davidson drove up. There was a sixty-minute tape on the cassette. That would be plenty of time. He checked his watch. Almost 9:00. He looked out the window. What would ordinarily have been a faint twilight was now complete blackness because of the storm clouds overhead. Thunder continued to rumble in the distance. He was pleased to see that there were no headlights on the road, no unwanted visitors.

Now what about the packages he had just left in the safe? Chris Nivens had given him reason to reconsider his original plan. Richard had told Oscar Davidson this morning that he would give him both documents, but he now regretted his generosity. Why not save Mrs. Davidson's monograph for Nivens, who really wanted to see it, who really had a stake in its preservation? Richard opened the safe again, pulled out the flat brown envelope containing the *Dream* monograph, and walked it back down the hall and through the heavy soundproof door to center stage, where he placed the envelope into the small metal light box recessed into the floor. It fit neatly along the bottom of the thin metal coffin. Through the two open doors of the scene shop he could hear the rain dripping in the darkness outside.

Time to go upstairs for Alex. Everything was working on schedule. He left backstage and proceeded to the second floor. As soon as he stepped onto the staircase, the car parked behind the trees at the crest of the road started its engine, then rolled without headlights toward the Pinnacle Inn.

The telephone at the Lyceum rang in the middle of the first scene of Act II. The stagehand who answered it came down from the Lyceum stage and found Milton Blackburn sitting next to his wife in the audience.

"It's Moonie," said the stagehand, who had on a dirty white T-shirt and was a student at the Arts School. "She says it's important."

"So is this," said Blackburn. He was watching his son onstage. Tucker was remarkable. He was letter-perfect with his lines, and though his mannerisms were a bit forced, he had the instincts down. The gene pool was not dead in his sons.

"She sounded upset."

Blackburn grudgingly stood up and followed him through the archway in the aisle and up the stairs to the stage office. He picked up the receiver at the exact moment when Tucker backed into their makeshift wall of dangling muslin and lost his footing. Tucker grabbed at the rope overhead to hold himself up. The rope held. But the gargoyle head to which it was attached did not. Down it crashed, smashing on the stage. Tucker crashed as well. Everything stopped.

Patricia Montgomery rushed down to the front of the house. "Are you hurt?" she said.

Tucker was not hurt at all. Only embarrassed.

"Let's just do it without the forest," said Patricia. "This rehearsal is a debacle anyway."

That was when one of the stagehands started shouting about the money.

"Look," he said. He was a kid with red hair and braces. He held up two fistfuls of cash. "It was inside the gargoyle."

"Milton," said Patricia Montgomery. "Come and look at this." She turned to the office. "Milton?"

But Milton was gone. They estimated later that he had only a four-minute head start on the police, who burst into the theater while Patricia was still trying to restore some order to her dress rehearsal. The police, however, required much longer than four minutes to determine where to proceed from the Lyceum. They knew the man they wanted, but they didn't know where he had gone. Ellen Spencer had finally talked to the editor-in-chief of *Feminist Renaissance*.

Richard pulled open the portrait of Sarah Siddons and unlocked the
door to the attic. The first thing he noticed, with some irritation, was
that the overhead bulbs were on. Outside it was full dark, and anyone
from the parking lot would immediately notice lights in the windows
of the top floor. This was stupid of Alex. He should have been smart
enough to turn them off. Lightning flashed outside as Richard reached
the top of the stairs. A massive clap of thunder followed, so close that
it startled him. Instantly the rain started again, a couple of warning
drops, and then like a shower head with the water turned on all the
way. The breeze through the windows helped to reduce the heat a lot.

"Alex?" he called. "It's showtime."

He turned to walk down the hallway at the top of the stairs and
pushed open the door to the hideaway room. "I hope you ate well,"
he said. "I stole a hell of a lot of food—" He stopped. Alex was
hanging from a rafter in the ceiling. Alex. His unfocused eyes and
protruding tongue seemed to be mocking Richard, as if it were a game.
He swung gently in the breeze from the open window.

Richard was paralyzed. Suicide. Why? When? The body swayed
gently in the breeze. He had never seen a dead body before. Not so
close. It was unlike anything he'd experienced on stage or in the movies, the three-dimensional wet smelly horror of it. He felt his heart do
a drumroll and his belly ride a trampoline, and he knew that he should
do something—cut him down, call for help, run away. But all he could
do was to stare in frozen fascination. Why would Alex change his
mind? Everything was all set. Soon Davidson would be here. What
would Richard say to Davidson now? Alex was going to be Richard's
ghost beneath the battlements. Alex was going to be his protection.
Now Alex was hanging there, dead. Richard took a step into the room.
The harsh glare from the bulb overhead exaggerated the lines in Alex's
face. He couldn't take his eyes from that face.

Then he heard the moan. Behind him, crumpled up in a bundle, was
Nancy Gale. She lay on her side in a fetal position, and her hands
trembled violently. She had a black eye and blood on her mouth. There
was blood on the back of her head and on the floor.

"Richard," she said. Sort of said. Whispered. He moved to kneel
beside her.

"I thought you were him," she said. "Get out of here. Get help. He's coming back."

Her hair covered one eye. He pulled it back. It looked as if there was no eye because there was so much blood.

"Who?" he said. "Who did this?" The rain poured down and the thunder crashed.

"Get out," she whispered. "He's coming back."

Every molecule in his body told him to flee. But he could not leave without helping Nancy Gale. "Who?" said Richard. "Who's coming back?"

And then the lights went out.

❖

Oscar Davidson drove his car back to the Pinnacle Inn and turned on the wipers when the rain returned. The lights in the Inn had just gone out, all at once, obviously the result of another power failure, unless Richard Blackburn had them rigged for some sort of special effect. Let him rig them. Oscar had a good flashlight in the glove compartment. Little bastard was going to get more than he'd bargained for. He drove around to the side of the building and saw the white Toyota parked by the open door of the loading dock. He pulled in beside it, grabbed his flashlight and his umbrella, and emerged into the darkness and the pouring rain. He opened the trunk of his car and appreciated the light from the courtesy lamp inside. Might as well get this over with. He reached in and pulled out the canister of gasoline. That blabbering idiot at the gas station was right. It was heavy.

❖

Richard felt his way back down the attic stairs. He shook so hard that his arm thudded against the door frame when he reached the bottom. It was absolutely black inside the Inn except for the frequent lightning flashes that gave him colorless glimpses of his surroundings. Think carefully. There was a pay phone on the wall just a few feet away. You didn't even need to deposit money to call the operator. Lightning flashes through the windows gave him occasional glimpses at the hallway. He could see the gleam of the black plastic. Be calm. Careful.

He lifted the receiver and was grateful to hear a dial tone. The phone smelled like peppermint. He felt for the buttons. Operator was at the bottom, wasn't it, in the middle. He pushed the button and heard the call begin to ring. He tried not to think about what was upstairs.

"Operator."

"Hello," Richard said. "Please, please call the police. I'm at the Stone Mountain Theater—"

"Operator."

"Yes," said Richard. "I need help. Call the Rockbridge police."

"Is there anyone on this line?"

She couldn't hear him. Maybe you did have to deposit money. Flustered and trembling, he found a quarter in his pocket, got a new dial tone, deposited his money, and pushed the button again. Hurry up, hurry up.

"Operator."

She couldn't hear him. It was the same with 911, even when he shouted. He felt something gooey on his chin and wiped it off, then smelled it. Toothpaste. Somebody had clogged the mouthpiece of the phone with toothpaste. Impatient now and frantic over the time he'd wasted, he forced himself to think. There was a phone downstairs in the office. That one worked. He'd used it himself during the evening. There was a lantern at the top of the steps. But where were the matches to light the kerosene in the burner? The matches were in the kitchen. Lightning showed him the lantern, and he groped for it in the darkness, groped his way down the stairs. Be calm. Just get to the office, get to the phone, call the police, call the Lyceum, call everybody.

He reached the bottom of the stairs. Okay. Off to the right, a couple of steps up the hall. He found the kitchen door. It was locked. The thought of wasting time to fit a key into the lock drove him crazy. Call the police. Then get your damn matches. The electricity could come back on any minute anyway. Rain fell with furious pounding outside. Lightning flashed again, and Richard saw the open door to the office down the hall. He walked in that direction, toward the doorway that he knew was there, and he hoped for another friendly lightning bolt to guide his way. He still held the darkened lantern in his left hand.

Just as he got to the doorway, the lightning flashed again. In that moment, Richard wanted to be dead. He saw in the brief flash a man with his back turned to the doorway. The man stood upright in the office from where he had been leaning over the safe. Then it was dark again. The unlit lantern in Richard's hand clattered against the wall.

He dropped it. He heard a shout from the office, heard footsteps following him. He turned and ran back into the darkness, past the kitchen door, to the end of the corridor, to the doors opening onto the back veranda or to the stage. It was so dark, like running inside a cave. He collided with the outside door, found his bearings, and turned the knob, but it wouldn't open. He pulled and pulled, but the door would not open. The deadbolt was thrown. He needed his keys, but just as he reached for them, he felt hands grope and then connect with him and grab him hard and tight and hug him close. Richard screamed and fought and kicked.

"Be quiet, Richard," said Chris Nivens, his mouth at Richard's ear. "Do you know where Oscar is?"

The door from backstage swung open, admitting damp, cool air, and a bright flashlight beam hit both their faces.

"Well," said Oscar Davidson. "What have we here?"

###

Milton Blackburn drove through the driving rain and wished he could fly. What in heaven's name was Richard doing? What on earth had possessed the boy? He didn't really think that Alex would hurt Richard, assuming that Alex really was in town, and why wouldn't he be, where else would he be—Alex, who always talked about leaving Rockbridge but never, never did?

He skidded on one curve up the mountain and forced himself to slow down. But if his car ended up in the trees, he would still get out and crawl to get to the top of this mountain. The one thing he should have done, he realized, was to call the police. It was mindless to fly out of the theater without even picking up a phone, but he hadn't thought to call, had thought only of action, of moving, of getting to the top of this hill. He could call them from the Inn. No police could have gotten here faster than he would, anyway.

At the crest of the hill, through the laboring wipers, he could see that the power was still out. What bothered him was that he saw no lantern light in the windows of the Inn. No. There was a flicker of something in the office window. He roared down the road and pulled up in front of the Inn. He got out in the pouring rain and ran the thirty yards to the front veranda, mounted the steps, and pulled on the knob to the office. It was locked. He got out his keys and worked the knob, but the door would still not open. It was tied somehow. He moved to the barred windows and saw nothing but darkness in the office. He was about to move away, to try another door, when his glass paperweight came through the pane of glass to his left, collided with one of the metal bars, and fell to the soggy porch floor. Milton was frightened and startled by the noise, but he recognized the voice coming through the hole in the glass.

"He's got your son," shouted the man trapped inside the office. "He's got Richard."

"Thank you, Oscar," said Milton Blackburn, and he went to try another entrance.

Richard Blackburn and Chris Nivens were in the dark hallway just outside the door to the office of the Pinnacle Inn. Locked inside the office were Oscar Davidson and Anne Lindsey. Richard was not sure whether Mrs. Lindsey was still alive or not. Nivens held Oscar's flashlight in one hand and Richard's left thumb in the other. Two of Richard's fingers on his left hand were already broken. The broken fingers had swollen into painful sausages, and his thumb ached from the degree to which Nivens was bending it.

"All right, Richard," said Nivens. "We're not going to waste any more time. I think you've seen what I'm willing to do, and I'm not going to dally any longer. Where's the other manuscript? I don't give a damn about the novel."

"It's in the next room," said Richard. "It's on the stage. In the box for the wiring." His fingers were hot and throbbing with pain. He had seen Anne Lindsey's hand protruding from the half-open door of the safe at the moment when Nivens had ripped the telephone out of the socket and bashed Oscar Davidson with it. Nivens had stolen the flashlight after kicking Richard and dragging him out of the office. Then he'd used the telephone cord to tie the office doorknob to the one for the outside door, so that neither door could be opened. Richard choked with fear. "You don't have to hurt me anymore."

"We'll see." Nivens tugged him along, down the hall, past the kitchen and the dining room and the door to the back veranda, past the door to freedom. They went through the door to the stage.

There was a lantern on the stage burning with a very bright light.

Milton Blackburn, dripping water from his crimson costume, crouched over the lantern to adjust its filament but stood up when they entered. Nivens held on to Richard's thumb and pushed him to a point five feet from where the lantern burned. Its light caught the red metal glow of a canister of gasoline resting nearby.

"Let him go," said Milton.

Instead, Nivens increased his pressure on Richard's thumb. Richard cried out. Nivens pointed the flashlight at the red can of gasoline.

"What are you doing with that?" he said.

"I didn't bring it," said Milton. "Let Richard go."

"Mr. Davidson brought the gasoline," said Richard.

"Why?" said Nivens. He pushed on Richard's thumb.

"I made him bring it for Tucker's car. So Alex could drive away."

"Don't talk, Richard," said Milton. "Let him go, Chris."

"All right," said Nivens. He released the thumb and twisted Richard's arm as he threw Richard onto the hard wood of the stage. The pain in Richard's shoulder was enough to take his breath. He thought of a chicken leg getting ripped from its thigh as he lay with his face on the floor.

Milton Blackburn bent down to examine his son. "Dad, don't," said Richard as Milton rolled him over, but it was too late. The flashlight came down hard on Milton's head. And again. The power of the collision broke the flashlight. Milton fell to the floor next to Richard. Chris Nivens threw the splintered plastic tube into the seats for the audience, strode to the scene shop, and picked up a four-foot crowbar from one of the workbenches. Richard cried out an inarticulate moan. Milton started to move, slowly, but as he pulled himself to his feet, Nivens swung the crowbar like a baseball bat into his knee. Blackburn grunted and fell back onto the stage, and then Nivens raised the bar again. This time he broke Blackburn's foot. Milton screamed with the pain and rolled onto his back. Richard watched him silently.

"That takes care of Dad for a while," Nivens said. He picked Richard up. Nivens's face was half shadow in the glare from the lantern. His breath was hot on Richard's face. Outside, the rain continued to fall. The thunder cracked. Richard waited with dread for what would come. He had to think. The King of the Pranksters could not run out of tricks.

"Now," said Nivens. "At last. Where, exactly, is this manuscript?"

"It's in that metal box," said Richard. He was horrified by what he had seen in the last half hour. Here, indeed, was the face of evil. It was not a face that he knew. "I'll help you. You don't have to kill me, too."

"Yes, I do," said Nivens. "You know that I do, Richard. Fate delivered all of you to me this evening so that I could solve all of my problems at once. *There's a divinity that shapes our ends, rough-hew them how we will.* The manuscript, please." He needed only to squeeze Richard's left shoulder to send him into pain.

"There," said Richard. He pointed to the metal opening in the boards at rear center stage.

Nivens knelt on the stage, opened the lid, and extracted the envelope. He pulled out the contents. He read enough to see that it was the original manuscript of Sarah Davidson's last essay, complete with Anne Lindsey's commentary in the margins. Richard let his left arm hang by his side. He limped over toward the canister of gasoline, bent his knees, and lifted it slightly off the floor with his good right arm. He strained as he lifted it and grunted, then replaced it gently on the floor.

"Why?" said Richard. "Why was it so important to you?"

Nivens sighed as if they were in class and Richard had just asked a question to which the answer was obvious. "I'd rather not discuss that right now," he said. "Let's just say that I consider this manuscript mine by right. This is my research she used." He watched Richard carefully to make sure that he did not try anything. Milton Blackburn lay on the stage gasping. "It wasn't until Paxton's fifth finger came off that I was convinced he hadn't told anybody he'd found out."

Richard shuddered. He had given Nivens the chance to kill Ramsey Paxton. He had told him that he thought the man was dead. Richard truly was bad. He would never be the hero. And Alex, who had kindly left his overalls downstairs so that the guy could keep the blood off his clothes, had been doomed to die as the fool.

"Let's burn the place down," said Richard. "Then we can get out of here."

Nivens looked at him with something like admiration. "Why should I let you join me?" he said.

Milton breathed unsteadily. "Run, Richard," he said. "Run away. Get out of here."

Richard knew that he could not run. "I want to help you," he said to Nivens.

"Why?"

"Because Davidson will die," said Richard. "He set me up. He accused me of cheating. I was all ready to make him look like the murderer. I was ready to have Alex cut off one of my fingers and then blame it on Davidson."

Nivens leafed through the manuscript to make sure that all the pages were there. "I was wondering what you were up to," he said. "I should be grateful. You've made it so easy for me to clean the entire blackboard at once."

Thunder boomed outside. Through the open doors of the scene shop they could hear the steady pounding of rain. "The weather doesn't matter," said Richard. "This place will still burn, with enough gasoline."

"Oh, I know it will burn," said Nivens. "It's a shame you don't have a natural gas line in the stove here to help it along."

Richard found it eerily thrilling to be so close to somebody so wicked, to be carrying on a conversation with the man who had just crippled his father.

"You were at the gym when the Davidsons' house burned," said Richard. "You were at the library at the university."

"You ought to know yourself that it's easy to jog from one part of town to another," Nivens said.

"Let me help you get out of here," said Richard.

"Why?" said Nivens. "Why do I need you? You're going to see the fire, Richard. But from inside."

"No," said Richard. "I can help you get away with it. I can tell the police the same story that you do. I can tell them Alex came back, and he got Mrs. Lindsey and Mr. Davidson here, and he killed them and then he killed himself."

"What about Nancy Gale Nofsinger?" said Nivens. "And your father? What are you planning to do with them?"

"They can burn, too," said Richard. He glanced at his father, who was sweating silently where he lay on the stage. Blood oozed out of his foot on the stage. "I don't care about them."

"I find that hard to believe," said Nivens. "This is your father."

"I hate my father," said Richard. He fought to keep from crying.

He limped over to his father's broken foot and kicked. The stomp of his shoe boomed on the stage floor. Milton looked at him with silent, horrified surprise before he shuddered and gasped in pain. Richard walked back to Nivens. He stood beside the gasoline canister.

Nivens looked at him with a new fascination. Almost respect. Then he shook his head. "Sorry, Richard," said Nivens. "I don't buy it. Nobody hates his father that much." He grabbed Richard's left arm again. Richard shrieked with the pain.

"I do," said Richard. "I hate him enough to burn him up. To burn down this whole damn place. I hate him enough to lie for you. You'll be doing me a favor. You'll let me have a life without him around."

Nivens let him go. "Why?" he said. "Why do you hate your father so much?"

Richard reached for the canister of gasoline. He lifted it with a strain. "Because he made me go to Outward Bound last spring," he said.

Nivens shook his head. "Wrong answer," he said. "Insufficient grounds."

"He made me go to Outward Bound," said Richard, "and I didn't want to go. And so I let the air out of his tires, and I unplugged the freezer." He made himself go on. He looked down to make sure his father could hear this.

"No, Richard," said Milton Blackburn.

"And I loosened one of the wheels on the riding mower," said Richard. "I thought it would just fall off in the driveway. But it didn't fall off until Tucker was on the hill. I did that to my brother. I crippled my big brother. And it was all my father's fault."

Tears were streaming down both Blackburns' faces.

Nivens considered it. "Yes," he said. "That's got to be true."

"It's true," said Richard.

"Richard," said his father. Then he said nothing.

Nivens looked at Richard with new appreciation. "Perhaps we're soul mates after all," he said.

"I brought a photocopy of the manuscript, too," said Richard. "You have to lift the light box out to see it. You can get it if you want. Before we start to spread the gasoline."

"I was going to use kerosene from the lamps," said Nivens. "Gasoline is much better."

He leaned down to open the lid again, and that was when Richard

raised the canister of gasoline high off the floor with his one good arm
and swung it downward as hard as he could. The canister was empty.
Richard hit Nivens in the head and stunned him the first time. He
knocked him out with the second swing. He opened a bloody wound
with the third.

"That's enough," said Milton Blackburn. He dragged himself toward his son on the stage. "That's enough, Richard. You don't want
to kill him."

"Yes, I do," said Richard. But he stopped. And then Richard was
down beside his father, kneeling gingerly, his one useless arm by his
side, his broken fingers gnarled and painful, and he hugged his father
as hard as he could.

"How about that, Dad?" he said. "He believed me."

"Of course he believed you," said Milton. "The acting genes aren't
dead in my sons." He held his son gently. Richard sobbed out loud as
his father strained to speak. "Richard, Richard, what a performance."

"I'm so sorry, Dad," said Richard. The only story he could think
of to distract Chris Nivens had been the true one. "I'm so sorry."

"Be still," said Milton Blackburn. "Richard. Richard. You were
good."

❈

Thirty seconds later the police arrived, having learned of Milton
Blackburn's destination from Ramona Lindsey. Even before the first
uniformed officers could get into the building, the lights came back
on. Anne Lindsey, who was pulled disoriented from the inside of the
safe, and Nancy Gale Nofsinger, who was semiconscious, shared the
first ambulance. Richard knelt by his father, who lay supine on the
stage, and waited with the policewoman, Ellen Spencer, for the next
ambulance to arrive. Chris Nivens was gone, removed to a police car.
Oscar Davidson sat, sick and silent, in the first row of seats in the
theater.

Milton Blackburn, who felt only physical pain, looked at his son
with pride and wonder. "We'll have to tell Hugh Bickley how well
you carried the empty gasoline canister," he said. "I truly, truly
thought it was full."

Richard shook his head. "That was part of the deal. Mr. Davidson
was supposed to fill it up and then pour it into Tucker's tank."

"I almost ruined the performance," Milton told Ellen Spencer. "When Richard gave me that stage kick, I didn't catch on at first. I was afraid I'd waited too long to react."

"I thought I'd really hurt you," said Richard. He adjusted the raincoat serving as pillow under his father's head. "I guess I had."

"I should have guessed about Tucker's accident," said Milton.

"I couldn't tell anybody. It was too horrible," said Richard. "He'll hate me now."

"You know better than that."

They didn't say anything for a while. The work lights were harsh for their eyes. There were lots of police coming and going from the room and talking with Ellen. She passed along some of the information to Richard and Milton Blackburn, loudly enough for Oscar Davidson to hear, though he had not said a word since he had sat down in the auditorium.

"Mr. Nivens has regained consciousness and has started to talk," she said. She told them what she had heard. "He felt desperate. As he saw things, Sarah Davidson had turned on him. She had helped him through the first two years of his graduate work but was ready to wash him out of the program at the end. He saw the dream of his lifetime about to disappear."

Milton asked why. "Aren't there other graduate schools? Couldn't he get a degree somewhere else?"

"Of course," she said, "but it was a matter of self-image for him. He'd always wanted to prove to his father that he wasn't stupid, that he was an intellectual. He wanted not only success, but sensational success. To be closed out of his program after two years was to him the ultimate humiliation. He couldn't bear to start over and face the possibility of a similar result at another school. And he couldn't stand the thought of his father finding out."

"But his father's dead," said Richard.

"No," said Ellen. "His father lives in Maryland. They've been estranged ever since Chris's mother died in an automobile accident four years ago. If anyone asked, he said that his father was dead. He wanted no contact with him. But he did want that degree, and he didn't want the news to drift back to his father that he'd been unsuccessful at the university." She condensed the rest: how Chris Nivens had written his own analysis of *A Midsummer Night's Dream,* how it had been rejected by Sarah Davidson and every other professor who'd seen it, how

Nivens had convinced himself that the Davidson monograph, which he had helped research, was rightfully his. So he took a gamble and copied the disk containing the essay from Sarah Davidson's office, printed out his own version, and submitted it to Professor Vita, who liked it. Then came the troublesome part. Nivens had hoped that Vita, who was something of a loner in the English department, would keep the contents to himself. But Vita saw Sarah Davidson in the elevator on a Friday morning and described enough of this brilliant new essay to arouse her suspicions. She went to Vita's office and read the essay, her own essay, which Chris Nivens had submitted under his own name. On that Friday afternoon she confronted Nivens at home, informed him that he would have to move out, that he would have to withdraw the essay and leave the university.''

"She didn't tell anybody what he'd done?" said Richard.

"No," said Ellen. "She wanted to give him a chance to leave quietly. Without scandal. She only told her husband that they'd need to find a new tenant."

"She didn't even let on to this Professor Vita?"

"She was good at keeping secrets," said Ellen. The rest of the story was easy to follow. Nivens could not bear the thought of leaving in shame. He considered himself betrayed by a woman to whom he had given all his energy. He knew that Oscar Davidson would be busy on Saturday night with students from Montpelier, so he waited until Sarah Davidson was alone in the house, jogged back home from the gym two miles away, and knocked her unconscious on her bed, where he placed into her hands one of the books by her bedside. He did not know she had written it as Emma Prynne. He then started a fire in the basement, loosened the coupling on the gas line into his stove, jogged back to the gym.

"Even at that point, he had no intention of publishing the essay," said Ellen. "He was just using it out of desperation, a way of continuing his career. But then, after the fire, when it appeared that all copies had been destroyed, Vita had told him to publish it. He'd been unable to resist. And when *Feminist Renaissance* accepted it, he'd felt as if he'd been given a blessing by Providence itself."

Milton Blackburn asked her why she'd never thought to look at Chris Nivens's essay.

"I did," she said. "He gave a copy to the police in Charlottesville.

Only it was the other essay, the one he'd actually written, the one that wasn't any good. I even showed it to Anne Lindsey, who could only confirm that it was an essay that her sister Sarah had never written. Now Richard has given us the real Sarah Davidson essay, the one that her husband had hoped would disappear.''

They looked over at Oscar Davidson, who sat with his eyes rigidly focused on the far wall. Richard tried to imagine a man's hunger to be published somehow, somewhere, even if his work appeared under his wife's name. The ambition was like a disease.

Ellen continued to talk, as though she were telling them a story before bed. ''After the fire Nivens offered his services as an employee in the summer Arts School. He knew that Sarah had already printed out the essay and sent it down to her sister, so he needed to be here to make sure that there weren't any stray copies in the archives.''

''But, copies or no copies, Anne Lindsey had read it,'' said Milton Blackburn. ''She'd edited it. She would have recognized it in print.''

''Maybe,'' said Ellen. ''He was willing to risk it at first. There was a chance that she might not even see the issue next spring. Besides, he had several months before publication to figure out how to get rid of Anne Lindsey as well. Tonight gave him a chance. He wanted to pin it all on Alex Mason. He even used Alex's name over the telephone with Anne so that her daughter, who he knew was eavesdropping, would hear him.''

Richard still did not fully understand. ''But why,'' said Richard, ''after it turned out that there was a manuscript of the real Sarah Davidson essay after all, why didn't Nivens just call the magazine and tell them that he'd changed his mind? He could say he didn't want them to publish it. He could say he wanted to revise it some. Wouldn't that have been easier than killing everybody?''

She said Nivens had persuaded himself that such a route was impossible. ''Professor Vita would have told him to submit it elsewhere,'' she said. ''He was afraid that it would look suspicious for him not to be publishing such a brilliant paper. And he was also worried that his failure to publish might change Vita's mind about advising him.''

It made a crazy sort of sense to Richard. Nivens had to publish. But if he published and then one of his readers saw an actual copy of the manuscript with Mrs. Davidson's name on it and with Mrs. Lindsey's editing in the margins, he'd be nailed. He'd be revealed as a plagiarist, and he'd be tied to the death of Sarah Davidson. Richard felt over-whelmingly tired. He looked over at Oscar Davidson, who still did not speak or move.

"Why did he kill Mr. Paxton?" said Richard.

"Because Paxton learned from *Feminist Renaissance* that he'd stolen Sarah's work. He telephoned them to check on the phony Davidson essay, but while he was talking, he asked about the Nivens piece, too. The editor read him the opening paragraph of the essay Nivens had submitted for publication, and it matched up word for word with the manuscript you'd given him. She read me the same paragraph tonight. I caught on for the opposite reason—because it didn't match the Nivens essay we had in our files."

"So why didn't Mr. Paxton tell the editors at the magazine that Nivens was a phony?"

"Because Ramsey was too thorough," she said. "He wanted to make sure that you and Alex weren't trying to pass off a Nivens essay as the work of Sarah Davidson. He wasn't sure where the liars were. That was one reason he brought the manuscript and all the books to his meeting with Alex: He had lots of questions." She paused. "You should have told us what you'd learned about Davidson's writing, Rich-ard." She was not angry at him.

"I didn't think it mattered," said Richard. "And Alex asked me not to bring Mrs. Lindsey into it."

"We need to talk to Mrs. Lindsey about her story, too. But we know most of what happened." She explained that Nivens had been observ-ing the Lyceum Theater carefully to see when Ramsey Paxton departed. He had hoped to get the manuscript from him that night, if possible. That was before he'd realized there was an emergency, that Ramsey had already talked to the magazine in Chicago. So he'd gone to the Lyceum after leaving Richard in his apartment, had been shocked to hear detailed accusations from Ramsey Paxton in the theater basement, and had used the most expediently violent means he could find to make sure that no one else knew of what Paxton had learned. "He realized that the police would want to know why he had taken so long to call, so he invented a story about the trapdoor being closed when he arrived. He figured it wouldn't hurt. He already had Richard waiting to testify that Ramsey Paxton had looked dead earlier. When he couldn't find the manuscript in the theater, he assumed that Anne had taken it home to her archives."

Milton Blackburn asked why he had killed Alex in the attic room.

"That was apparently unplanned," Ellen Spencer said, "but Nivens was a talented improviser. When he entered the attic, Alex actually tried to restrain him. Alex was afraid that Nivens would go downstairs and immediately report him to us. But Nivens convinced him that he had no such intentions, reassured him enough for Alex to let down his guard. When Alex turned his back, Nivens killed him. He realized that it was to his advantage to have Alex die. It would look as though the bereaved killer had taken his own life. Even if Nivens couldn't orchestrate an inferno that would kill off everyone who might threaten him, he was better off with Alex dead. Alex had read his manuscript. Alex was a threat to him."

"Wasn't I a threat to him?" asked Richard. "I'd read the manuscript, too."

"Yes," she said. "But there wasn't such a rush for you. He said nobody would take you seriously. Not as seriously as Alex."

"Alex," said Richard. He was still stunned that the man was dead. "Why did Chris kill him and not kill Nancy Gale?"

"He thought he had," she said. "He almost did."

"How did he get up to the attic in the first place?" said Richard. "I'd locked that door."

"He found the keys in Nancy Gale's room," she said. "He'd gone up to the attic expecting to find you, not Alex. Otherwise he never would have been so careless as to leave the door unlocked behind him. Once he'd jumped Nancy Gale, he used her keys to relock the door on his way downstairs. And he squeezed her toothpaste into the telephone mouthpiece."

The old toothpaste trick. Chris Nivens was so smart, so quick.

"How did he know that I wouldn't go upstairs sooner?" he said.

"He didn't," she said. "It was quite difficult for him to leave you in the office after he'd already killed Alex and left Nancy Gale upstairs. But he felt as though some divine supernatural plan was at work for him. He guessed that he'd have time to leave the mountain, fetch Anne Lindsey, and return before you went upstairs. Then he could watch the windows through his binoculars to see whether you had discovered the bodies. If you had, if he saw the police or signs of a big panic, then he could simply drive on down to the Inn with Anne Lindsey and shake his head over how sad it all was. And if you hadn't found the bodies, if there were no alarms ringing when he got back, then he could go for the whole package. Kill everybody at once.''

"Why did he wait?'' said Richard. "Why didn't he just come on down and get me before Mr. Davidson drove up?''

"Because he had to make sure that Oscar would show,'' she said. "He didn't maul Anne Lindsey until he saw Oscar's headlights. Timing was everything. He said you almost got away from him in the dark.''

She turned to speak to a uniformed officer who had just entered from the scene shop area. The second ambulance was approaching. Richard and his father would be leaving soon.

Milton Blackburn said he could have prevented the whole affair. "If only I'd known about Patricia's key when I went to the theater that night,'' said Milton. "I didn't find out she had one until tonight.''

Richard tried to digest it all. "If only the manuscript had burned up in the original fire,'' he said.

"The manuscript was essential,'' said Ellen Spencer. "We would have had a hard time proving our case without the manuscript.''

Milton said it was Sarah Davidson, back from the dead, who finally provided the means for justice to be done.

They looked over at Davidson. He was listening to every word. He glared at them and breathed in long, deep shudders.

Ellen appeared to notice him for the first time. "We found the missing cash tonight at the Lyceum,'' she said. "What about that, Mr. Davidson? According to what your sister-in-law tells us, you're the one most likely to know how it got there.''

It took what seemed like a long time for him to speak. "I wanted it to appear as though Alex had stolen the money,'' he said finally. "When I entered the theater, I wrapped my jacket around the can so that I wouldn't leave any fingerprints. Then I transferred the cash to one of the gargoyles and showed the empty paint can to Ramsey, who was just coming to. I told him I would replace the funds myself and add a little more if he would just be fair to Anne and me. He was agreeable to keeping Anne's name clear. He knew she hadn't meant to hurt him when she shoved him toward the faulty trapdoor. But he wouldn't reconsider publishing my essay in the playbill. I left him in the basement with a wet rag on his neck. He had a headache, but he was all right.''

Ellen worked on her notes. Richard heard one quick burst of siren from the second ambulance outside.

Oscar Davidson spoke again to Richard. "I was ready to leave town after tonight anyway. I couldn't have tolerated sitting in the same classroom with you when I knew that you'd learned about *Sally Galloway.*"

Richard had lost all appetite for revenge. "Mr. Davidson," he said, "an hour ago I hated your guts. Now I don't. You're not worth it."

"You're right," said Oscar, and he stood and walked out of the room.

Richard never saw him again.

❇

On the third Saturday night in July, Richard got to the amphitheater at 7:30, a full half-hour before curtain time, because he didn't want to risk arriving after she did. Tonight was the last night for the three-week run of *A Midsummer Night's Dream,* and there would be a party for the cast, the crew, and selected guests in the Inn afterward. Very few members of the audience had taken their seats yet. The sun had not even set, but seemed to be poised at the distant mountains like a golden spotlight, turning the white concrete of the amphitheater into porcelain and brightening the greens of the grass and the boxwoods and the pines to maximum intensity. The air felt pleasantly cool. Overhead, the sky was a rich blue streaked with deep orange clouds. From out of the speakers behind him Richard could hear a Mozart divertimento. Richard felt good. His dislocated shoulder had come out of the sling two days ago, and the splints on his fingers would come off in another week. He had been able to sleep all through the night for ten consecutive days now. The doctors said he had absorbed the shock well.

A large party of ticket-holders clustered at the top of the aisle to admire the view before they found their seats. When they dispersed, Richard saw Moonie and her mother behind them. Anne Lindsey held on to Moonie's arm and walked with a cane, but she looked relaxed and happy. Both of them waved to Richard, who stood at the edge of the stage on the left-hand aisle. He waved back, whereupon they smiled and waved harder.

"They're waving to me, dork," said Tucker. He stood behind Richard on the grassy verge between seats and stage, in costume and makeup as Theseus. With the dark wig he looked a hell of a lot like their dad. When Milton Blackburn had been unable to perform, Patricia

Montgomery had simply returned to her original plan of doubling the roles of Theseus and Oberon. Tucker had done well, especially considering he'd had only one week to rehearse. That was how long Patricia Montgomery had allowed the opening to be delayed. The production had received good reviews and big audiences. Tonight's performance was a sellout.

"I still can't believe you were going to give Alex my car," said Tucker behind him. "My car. Richard, it was an automobile."

"Only if we didn't get a tape of Davidson confessing," said Richard. "Anyway, he would have abandoned it." He smiled and turned back to keep his eyes on the crowd. They'd had this conversation many times already. Alex would have left the car in a parking lot somewhere. And if it had turned out that he was the actual killer, Richard would have been able to give an easy description of his vehicle to the police.

"Is she here yet?" said Tucker.

"I haven't seen her. Aren't you supposed to be warming up or something?"

"In a minute, Casanova. Can't I speak to my studly little brother? With eye contact?" Richard turned. Tucker looked so noble, so handsome in his costume. "It's customary to exchange gifts at the end of a run," said Tucker.

"It's customary at the beginning," said Richard. "And you don't buy gifts for people not associated with the show. You're still dyslexic as hell."

"I didn't have a chance to get you this at opening night," said Tucker. "I got it now. So spare me your caustic tongue. Besides, you need to be congratulated on being reinstated at Montpelier."

"Now they're talking about offering me a scholarship," said Richard. "I think they're scared we're going to sue them."

Tucker said he'd heard from Moonie that the school had fired Oscar Davidson.

"He's moving to Richmond," said Richard. "Not far enough, but it's a start."

Tucker pulled a small box out from the folds of his costume. It was the size of a walnut and wrapped in white paper. Richard suspected a joke, but he opened it. It was a jewelry box, the kind that rings came in. Inside the box was a single wing nut.

"What is this?" said Richard. He held the nut up to the sunlight.

"It's what I put on the riding mower on the morning of my accident," said Tucker. "I found the loose wheel, Richard. I tried to fix it. But I put the wrong-sized nut on. You didn't cause the accident. I did."

Richard felt his eyes start to brim. "You're lying," he said.

"Maybe," said Tucker. "That accident was so long ago that I don't remember it very well."

"Yeah," said Richard. "I know about your horrible memory."

"It's very selective," said Tucker. "I don't remember the things that don't matter to me. And it doesn't matter, Richard. What matters is you."

"You're an asshole for making me cry in front of all these people," said Richard. "And I've got a date coming."

Tucker squeezed him hard on the back of the neck. "If it hadn't been for the accident," he said, "I don't think I'd be here right now. I'd be playing tennis somewhere." Then he pointed to the entrance to the amphitheater behind Richard. "There's Mom," he said. "And Dad."

Richard turned and saw his father on crutches walking behind his mother. They paused at the top of the center aisle to survey the scene. They looked very young, somehow, in the waning golden light.

Tucker said their mother seemed happy with her decision to stay in Rockbridge. "She'll like working at the Arts School," he said. "And she's already talking about what shows to direct at the Inn next winter." The Arts Council had released funds for the completion of the inside theater this summer.

"Get this," said Richard. "She told me she hoped we could work on a show together one day. That was pretty amazing. For her."

"She's trying," said Tucker.

Richard admitted that she was.

"I got to go," said Tucker. "Have you heard from Nancy Gale?"

"Yeah," said Richard. "She called this afternoon. She said she had two black eyes from the plastic surgery but that everything would look the way it did before, once she recovers. She's fine. She said to tell you she hadn't felt hungry since she'd been back in Atlanta."

"Hungry for what?" said Tucker. He took off for the backstage area behind the boxwoods. Richard walked up the aisle. He still had five minutes before she was supposed to be here. He would wait for her outside the theater. He wondered if maybe she was waiting outside for him, but no, even as he walked up the aisle, he saw her, Rebecca Taylor, dressed in cream and ruffles and looking fabulous. She saw him and smiled, and she started down the steps to meet him. It had turned out to be a pretty good summer after all. He would always remember it as the summer he discovered love. Richard had always heard that love was a kind of heat—a flame, a fire—and he supposed that it was possible to compare the physical kind of love to a blaze. But in his experience, it was anger, not love, which burned and destroyed.

"Where're we sitting?" said Rebecca Taylor.

"I thought we'd sit with my parents," said Richard. "I want you to meet my dad."

Love heals, love bridges, love works miracles, he told himself. *Love achieves what the flames of anger can never do. Love cools.*

"I thought you didn't like your dad," said Rebecca Taylor.

"That was somebody else," said Richard.